Praise for Mary Hughes's
Biting Me Softly

"I love, love, love Mary Hughes' writing style. It revs me up and keeps me going from the sheer excitement ...each time Ms Hughes delivers a new hero to her voracious fans they become hotter and sexier... Each time I think that I can love no other character as much as the previous one she gives birth to a new empyrean delight to torture and beguile the reader."
~ *Fallen Angel Reviews*

"Biting Me Softly is a sensational read that I could not put down! Mary Hughes brings it to the mat with this fantastic book...Logan, simply gives me chills with his electric sizzle and his "alpha" Vampire personae. He likes to be in charge, but when he meets up with Liese, let the battles begin. There is no way to say who will end up on top."
~ *Dark Diva Reviews*

"I absolutely love Mary's sense of humor which comes out in the richness of her characters...At times, it's laugh out loud funny and at others, well between all the action, danger, steamy hot hook ups, it's also a touching renewal of faith in falling in love."
~ *Sidhe Vicious Reviews*

"I love Liese. Her brain works at ninety miles per hour and I never knew what was going to come out of her mouth next. She has serious trust issues when it comes to men, but that doesn't stop her from being a little snarky, lighthearted, independent and stubborn. Then there's gorgeous and sexy Logan. This Alpha male vampire is everything you'd expect him to be: possessive, protective, loyal, dedicated and determined but able to bend when he comes to Liese."
~ *Literary Nymphs*

"There's trouble coming to Meiers Corners...This story had me smiling throughout; it was such a fun reading experience...Of course, this being a Mary Hughes story, it wouldn't be complete without hot, biting vampire sex. I recommend that this be read in front of the fan, on high, with plenty of cold drinks."

~ *Whipped Cream Erotic Romance Reviews*

"Mary Hughes proves that smart can be sexy in the wickedly delicious Biting Me Softly. Logan is to-die-for (no pun intended). He's mouth-wateringly gorgeous, highly intelligent, fiercely protective, and incredibly giving. In other words, he's the kind of hero that makes me want to write Ms. Hughes and ask if she can make him somehow appear on my doorstep (though admittedly, I've had this urge regarding every hero of Ms. Hughes's so far)... Ms. Hughes knows how to heat up the page... Love, laughter, and lust wound together in a wonderfully-written story makes for the ultimate reading experience."

~ *Joyfully Reviewed*

Look for these titles by *Mary Hughes*

Now Available:

Biting Me Softly
The Bite of Silence
Biting Nixie
Bite My Fire

Biting Me Softly

Mary Hughes

SAMHAIN
PUBLISHING

Samhain Publishing, Ltd.
577 Mulberry Street, Suite 1520
Macon, GA 31201
www.samhainpublishing.com

First Samhain Publishing, Ltd. electronic publication: April 2010
First Samhain Publishing, Ltd. print publication: February 2011

Dedication

To Dan, Bruce & Laura and Ed & Judy, who were there when the cosmic gas and debris that is Meiers Corners started to coalesce.

To Deborah Nemeth, my brilliant editor. Like the star Sirius, she is first magnitude.

To Natalie Winters, for bringing computer pixels to life as dream covers.

To Gregg, my Big Bang.

To you, Gentle Reader, for visiting with me in my slightly wacked-out Pluto-like orbit.

Chapter One

When I first clapped eyes on Logan, I thought, *Hot damn. Look what the Sex Fairy brung me!*

It was eight p.m. Sunday night, and I was at work. I do computers for the Meiers Corners Blood Center. The staff is me, the executive director and a part-time nurse named Battle. I was the only one who worked insane hours, but I was new and still trying to prove myself.

I don't know what made me look up. The cool March air, perhaps. Maybe the aroma wafting in, mystery and magic with overtones of raw sex.

Whatever it was, my eyes lifted and there he was, the most stunning male I'd ever seen. Smack-me-between-the-eyes gorgeous. Bright blond hair rippled to broad, muscular shoulders. Lean strength roped a long, lithe body. Laughter and intelligence sparked gold-flecked hazel eyes. Perfect lips curved in a smile so sensuous it made my innards go *bang.*

Then he opened his mouth and spoke. Talk about ruining perfection.

"Hello, gorgeous." His tone was deep and lazy. "I want to speak to the computer man in charge."

Right. Well that just spoiled everything, didn't it?

I crossed my arms under my breasts. "You're looking at *him.* I'm the head apple. Minus the stem, but those are overrated anyway."

My sarcasm didn't even faze the man. He tucked one spectacular ass cheek on my desk and leaned in, so close I could feel his warmth on my face. "You're L. Schmetterling? How...fruitful. And what, my Red Delicious, does the *L* stand for? Laurie? Lucy? Lovely?"

All that male beauty and a tight ass on top of it. I'd been burned once by a man with a flabby butt and no hair. This man would incinerate me.

I clutched the reminder of male perfidy on my ring finger and screwed up my most forbidding expression. "It stands for Leave. As in Me Alone."

"I live to do your bidding, princess," the man crooned, his lips inches from mine. He had perfect, chiseled lips—the kind designed by Michelangelo for kissing. "But if you're L. Schmetterling, I can't leave. I have business with you."

"Look, buddy." It came out all husky-voiced. I let go of the ring and tried to work back to reasonable. "Look, I don't know you, and it's late. Business hours are nine to five Monday through Friday. Come back tomorrow." I turned to my laptop and pretended I wasn't quivering to taste those chiseled lips. "You're just lucky I was here."

"Oh, I knew you'd be in." The man stood with lazy grace, the kind latent with power. I watched him from the corner of my eye. He was really quite big and though his body was lean, his shoulders were stunningly broad. He would be immensely strong. He leaned knuckles on my desk. "You work late every night. Most nights you're here until ten or eleven. *Alone.*" His tone held a touch of censure.

Strangely enough, I hadn't been afraid of him until then. My eyes jerked to his. Hard steel underlay his friendly expression.

I swallowed rising panic—though I was a black belt in Taekwondo, short and kicky was shit against strong and prowly. "What did you say your name was?"

"I didn't." He pulled a small leather case from his jeans pocket and tossed a business card on my desk with a careless snap of the wrist. The card should have skipped like a stone and sailed into my wastepaper basket. It landed right under my nose.

Gorgeous *and* talented. This guy would bear watching. *Aw, shucks*, my libido said. I ignored it. Eyes locked on him, I picked up the card. Dared a glance. *Logan Steel, CEO Steel Security.*

Smack me in the face with a Toshiba. Steel Security was the firm that installed a multimillion-dollar security system at Andersly-Dogget Distribution, my first job—one week before I was fired.

"Water under the bridge, Liese," my mother would say. "Put it behind you." Moms are always right, especially mine. But right doesn't equal easy.

I threw the card back. It hit the desk and rebounded into the trash, making my cheeks heat. "You can't be serious! Steel Security is the Ferrari of security firms. They do the biggest names in the world. Why would they be in little Meiers Corners?"

"*We* are here to install a system." Steel perched gracefully on my desk again. In his tight black T-shirt and open leather jacket he looked more like a well-muscled fashion model than a CEO.

"No way. Our Blood Center isn't Red Cross. Most people have never heard of the Hemoglobin Society. On the galactic scale of Steel Security, we're not even a comet."

Steel grinned at that, a smile so sharp and white that I was momentarily blinded. "Nice pun."

Wow. Mr. Fortune 500 (and Body 300) thought I was amusing?

Then reality kicked me in the teeth. I was a geek. When I talked, eyes glazed over. Amusing? Sure, and the Sex Fairy was real. "Why are you actually here?"

"Here's the work order, if you don't believe me." Mr. Logan Great-Ass pulled a paper out of his back pocket. Since his jeans were so tight they must have been painted on his incredible tush, I wondered how there could possibly have been room. He unfolded the paper and tossed it onto my desk with as much flair as the card. "You're wrong, Ms. Schmetterling. Gorgeous, but wrong."

Gorgeous? I shot to my feet. "Now I know you're lying. Fun time's over. There's the door."

Sleek eyebrows arched. "I assure you, everything's in order."

"You've forged those papers. Or...or maybe they're real, but the company's been typed over. I don't know what your game is, Mr. Steel, but this woman's not playing."

"No games, Ms. Schmetterling." Leaning across the desk, he hooked my chin with one long finger. "Though if you want games, I could be persuaded."

11

And he pressed his sculpted mouth to mine.

Steel's lips were smooth and warm and he knew how to use them. His kiss was the magical brush of angel wings. Heavenly golden heat spread through me, stunned me. My eyelids fluttered closed. Excitement hit me low in the belly, hot, shocking excitement that bubbled up as a soft moan of pleasure.

At the sound, Logan licked my lips open. Angel wings became angel fire. "You taste wonderful. All hot and wet. Mmm, can't get enough." His kiss deepened, his tongue started to plunge.

Heat flamed through me, spiraling quickly past my temperate zone. I was kissing a virtual stranger but it was so good, better than seven-layer chocolate sin cake. Logan nibbled at my lips, his teeth extraordinarily sharp. Instinctively I knew I was about two seconds from clamping my ankles around his superb ass, and damn the consequences.

So I jerked back and slapped him. "D-don't you...*ever*...do that again!"

He blinked, hazel eyes shading golden with surprise. His fingers hovered over his reddening cheek. I guessed with a face and body like his, Logan Steel wasn't refused very often. Of reaction A), B) or C), my slap had probably been D) none of the above.

I tensed against the inevitable anger or cold disdain.

"Hmm," he said. "Do you always overreact like that, princess?"

I gaped at him. "Overreact? That was sexual harassment, buddy. You're lucky I didn't pepper-spray you!"

"I'm here on legitimate business—"

"After hours, without an appointment. In jeans and a T-shirt better suited to a gigolo than a CEO."

His eyes turned hard. The gold shaded eerily toward red. "Please don't interrupt. Even if I was somewhat out of line—"

"You kissed me!"

"You liked it," he shot back.

"That's beside the point. You came in here, knowing I was alone, like a stalker—"

"I'm no stalker." He snatched his card out of the wastebasket and thumped it onto the desk in front of me. "I'm here to protect you from stalkers. I'm one of the good guys, Ms. Schmetterling."

"Is that how good guys behave? Forcing themselves on lone women?"

"Oh, for the love of..." Logan blew an exasperated breath. "I'm sorry, okay? I couldn't help myself. You're a beautiful woman and—"

"I am not beautiful!" I shouted at the top of my lungs.

My words fell into an astonished silence. Logan stared at me, a small frown creasing his brow. His eyes softened to a thoughtful hazel.

I started trembling. My heart was pounding, and I was breathing like a freight train. I wondered what the hell had just happened. I felt like I'd just fought for my life. Was Logan Steel right?

Was I overreacting?

Thankfully the phone rang, derailing my distressing thoughts. Taking a deep breath, I connected my Bluetooth headset. "Blood Center."

"Hey, sugar," a smooth alto greeted me. "It's Dolly Barton. I had a cancellation tomorrow. Want to move your appointment to six thirty?"

I winced. My appointment at the Curl Up and Dye was not for a haircut. "Sure. Yeah."

A pause. "You sound upset, sugar. Anything going on?"

"No." I sank into my chair. A gorgeous tush settled onto the desk next to me. Shizzle.

"It's not your ex-fiancé, is it?"

The last man to tell me I was beautiful. I glared at the mammoth stone on my right hand. "No."

"That Botcher. What a scumbag." Gum snapped. "Of course, office romances are thin ice anyway. You need to find someone new, sugar."

"No, I don't." Certainly not Edible Tush.

"Sure you do. A woman's got needs, if you know what I mean. It's been, what—a year?"

I flushed. "Sixteen months." Sixteen months since I had *needs*. Now all I had were issues.

Another crack of gum. "Well, not all men are like that, sugar. Some day you'll find the right one."

"And I'll know that, how?"

"Easy. He'll take you on a cruise to heaven."

As I hung up, I rolled my eyes. The only cruise my ex had taken me on was to the Isle of Itsucks.

A hand cupped my face. Warm lips pressed to mine, lips that circled gently, spreading heat and light. Before I could protest, they were gone.

"What the heck did you do that for?" I glowered into oh-so-innocent hazel eyes.

"You looked like you could use it." Logan picked up his work order, refolded it. "You are beautiful, you know. Hasn't anyone told you that?"

I had recovered sufficiently to snort. "Are we back to that nonsense? I may be small-town, but I'm not ignorant. I've seen world-class beauty, and I ain't it."

"Oh?" Eyes zeroed in on my mouth, Logan leaned toward me. I jerked just out of reach. He shrugged and smiled.

Sweet Stephen Hawking on a trampoline, that gorgeous flex of lips made me want to nibble him like tender cake. "Chicago has real beauties." My voice rasped, breath and every internal system I had going berserk at *lips*. "Long women with flowing hair and bodies so firm they could be eleven-inch dolls."

"Plastic? Ah, and manufactured. You're clever." Logan grinned like he was genuinely amused.

Pleasure warmed me, confused me. Distracted me long enough for him to palm my cheek. His big, hot hand could have melted plastic—it scorched my mere flesh. I jerked back again. The man was seriously dangerous. "They still look gorgeous."

"You *are* gorgeous, princess."

"Meiers Corners pretty, maybe." Blonde hair, blue eyes and generous curves from a diet of bratwurst and beer. The St. Pauli Girl-next-door. Compared to Chicago gorgeous, as exciting as a dumb terminal.

As if he read my mind, Logan said, "Beauty isn't simply physical, Ms. Schmetterling."

I made a rude noise. "Even pudgy, balding men go for butt and boobs."

"Perhaps I have different tastes." He leaned in until his tempting lips were a breath from mine.

I jerked back so hard my chair shot *bang* into the wall.

Logan grinned. "You're cute when you're flustered."

Cheeks flaming, other parts hot with a different fire, I scooted back into place. "It doesn't matter. If you have legitimate business, as you say, come back tomorrow during business hours."

"Sorry, can't. I have appointments all day. What does the *L* stand for?"

"Liese." I blinked, then swore. On top of gorgeous and talented, the man was sneaky. "Ms. Schmetterling to you."

Of course he ignored that. "Liese. Mmm." Even the prosaic Liese, purred in his luxurious voice, became incredibly sexy.

My insides clenched, parts that had lain dormant for nearly two years. Jingling jump drives, I did not want to be attracted to any male, certainly not one so casually, devastatingly sensual. "I prefer *Ms.* Schmett—"

"I prefer Liese. *Liese.*" Logan repeated my name slowly, as if he were tasting it. "So melodic. I'd say beautiful, but I don't want to get slapped again. Who hurt you so badly?"

I was already off-balance. That question, coming totally out of the blue, zapped me dumb. I stared at him, trying to reboot my brain into some semblance of an answer. Finally I spat, "Right. It can't be you making me angry. It has to be me. Some deep personal trauma from my past."

Logan cupped my chin with gentle fingers. "Anger often covers hurt—"

"What are you, a fricking psychoanalyst?" Shizzle. Logan Steel thought I was a kicked puppy. He thought I needed stroking and tenderness and care.

And damn me for an idiot, I *wanted* that. Wanted any man but especially this gorgeous, potent male to stroke me tenderly, to care. The wanting was so strong I actually leaned into his fingers...tilted my face toward his...closed my eyes...

The phone rang again. I jumped. Twisting out of Steel's fingers, I hit connect. "Blood Center."

A guy with a really bad Transylvanian accent said, "I vant to order carry-out, *bleh.*"

Carry-out from a blood center, right. Must be a Meiers Corners crazy. "Look, buddy. We aren't Der BurgerHimmel. Call them for your Mount Ararat o' Onions fix."

"I do not vant onions, I vant blood. And I am not Buddy. I

15

am Dracula. *Bleh.*"

"Yeah, well, *bleh* this, Drac. We don't do carryout. If you want blood, come in and sign up like the rest of the world."

"I cannot. I am in prison, *bleh.*"

Why was I not surprised? "Tough break. Tell you what—I'll send you the forms. Dracula, care of Castle Dracula, Transylvania?"

"Care of Meiers Corners Verk Camp."

I knew the place. Daycare for people who weren't quite in the same time zone as the rest of the Earth. "Fine." I tapped a few keys. "Papers are on their way." I hung up.

"That was nice of you," Logan said.

Another surge of warmth hit me. Immediately I quashed it. "Since when is rude and sarcastic nice?"

"You listened to him." He shrugged. "Not many people would take the time to talk with a psychotic."

"Yeah, I get the Nobel Nice Prize. What does that work order say, anyway?" I held out my hand. Business, the only solid ground in Swamp du Logan.

Logan's smile became slightly mocking, as if he knew I was running scared. But his long fingers dipped into the pocket over his superb butt (and why, oh why was I still noticing his ass?) and he pulled out the folded paper.

"It's for a full system." He passed it to me. "That's why I wanted to talk to you."

"Now I know you're lying. When you came in, you didn't even know who I was." I scanned the paper, several columns of densely packed numbers and technical terms. It was hard to read, except for the bottom line. That said *five hundred thousand* dollars.

"I knew I wanted L. Schmetterling." Logan's lazy shrug somehow emphasized the power in his shoulders. "I knew you worked nights. Since my appointments keep me busy all day, I was hoping you could pass a message to Schmetterling. How fortunate he turned out to be you."

"How fortunate," I echoed caustically, staring at the work order. It was hard to understand a half-million-dollar system at our Center. Not that upgrading our ancient alarm was a bad idea. Meiers Corners was as safe as Mayberry R.F.D., but occasionally I had noticed blood missing. Not a lot, but enough to start me wondering—and worrying. One of my jobs was to keep track of it. Would I get fired (again) over a few lost pints?

I needed this job, and not just for the income. "All this for a few thousand units a month? Are you sure you have the right place?"

"Call your executive director if you don't believe me."

"You think I won't?" My chin kicked up.

Logan's bright blond hair swayed as he shook his head, not in denial, but in gentle disbelief. "You really have some trust issues, don't you, princess?"

"I certainly do not." It came out too fast. I suppressed a grimace. "I just don't understand most of this order."

"Then let me explain." Logan took the paper from me, smoothed it on my desk and perched next to me. His body felt like a radiator, so hot that if I wore glasses, they'd have steamed up. As it was, Liese-Down-Under was starting to heat. He slid a bit closer, his gorgeous butt wiggling like delectable bait. My heart kicked from drive into race. That tight ass of his was begging to be grabbed. He shifted, muscles playing smoothly, and my hands clenched. Heat? Try steam. Poach. Shake and bake.

Logan's finger skimming the first couple lines of text thankfully distracted me from said butt cheek. Until I imagined me as that text. Pictured his finger skimming down my throat, around my breasts, over my belly...down to my...*whoo-ha*. Goosebumps woke from my neck down to my Xeon processor.

"This is the hardware we'll be installing," Logan said.

I blinked, forced myself to pay attention. He went on, finger still skimming paper. Lightly, like his angel-wing kisses. Kisses that would warm my neck, excite my nipples, my belly... Oh, bend me over and spank me with a netbook.

"Cameras, multi-sensors, the works. The equipment for a complete lock-down." Then he pointed to a few words that I did understand. "Here are the system requirements."

"An MMS?" I gasped. Taken from the gamer acronym MMO (Massively Multiplayer Online), MMS was a term coined by Steel Security for a blade-style supercomputer with a minimum of six multi-core CPUs, super-fast virtual switch and nanotube memory. I'd read about it in *Hot Processors Monthly* (a magazine I swear I did not buy for the centerfold). This system had *twenty* CPUs. "What the hell do you need all that power for? Can you

17

even harness twenty processors at once?"

"With our proprietary software, yes. That's itemized on lines thirty-seven through forty-two."

I reread those lines. Integrated intruder sensor, alarm program and safety lock-down routines. And—an automated warehousing program and distribution database.

My jobs.

I got cold. Was Black Saturday happening again? Was I about to lose my job? Second time in less than two years would not look good on the old resume. "We already have software to run the Blood Center," I croaked around the ice in my throat.

Logan caught my shift in tone. His eyes narrowed until they were twin scalpels that could cut the reason from my brain. The sensation of him digging in my head was so strong I mentally rattled off "Mary Had a Little Lamb" just in case.

"You'll need to convert your data to the new programs." He spoke slowly, stare drilling. "Standard formats, and I'll be available to answer questions."

Though I didn't say a word, something must have communicated itself because his gaze softened. "We're not here to put you out of a job, Liese."

Fershizzle. Sexy, smart and slightly scary. "Ms. Schmetterling," I corrected automatically. I didn't believe him. Who paid a half million dollars for an installation, only to turn it over to a small-town gal geek? "Ms. is more professional."

"I like Liese." His voice caressed my name.

No man should be better than chocolate. "Too bad. Ms."

Logan's bright head tilted and he gave my hair a quick tousle. "How 'bout Ms. Liese?"

"Stop that. I'm not a puppy."

"No, you're a woman. A beautiful but very prickly woman." He nudged me playfully. "Are you always so uptight?"

"*Uptight*?" Issues, maybe. But— "I'm not—"

"Ever party? Play naked on the beach?" Logan leaned his elbows on the desk, putting his face just inches from mine. He flashed me his wicked smile, all sharp white teeth. "Ever just fool around?"

My nipples tightened traitorously—and belly, thighs and pudendum. "No," I said, more to my libido than him. And to my sex, which was licking its lips and slurping a bit.

Logan's nostrils flared. He leaned closer, lips less than a breath from mine. His eyes shaded toward rose-gold. "I love how you smell. All musky and tempting."

I jumped to my feet. "I'm a geek. It's WD-40."

"It's you." He slid both glorious butt cheeks onto my desk and threw his legs gracefully over the other side. I backed up as he came to his feet, stalking lazily toward me. I backed until I hit wall. In the small office, it was all of three steps.

He kept coming until he pressed into me.

Logan's huge chest muscles, thrust seductively against his cotton tee, were level with my drooling mouth. I tore my gaze from those gorgeous pecs only to have it land on his face. His eyes were heated and intense—and, embarrassingly, on my slobbering trap.

"I want to kiss you," he rasped, his voice totally unlike the smooth insouciant tones I'd come to expect. "Are you going to slap me again?"

"Probably." I forced the word through suddenly tight vocal cords.

"Okay, then. It'll be worth it." His fingers threaded through my hair, and his head bent. But this time wasn't a soft brushing or gentle rubbing.

No. This time his mouth fastened hungrily on mine.

I gasped. He was quick to take advantage of my parted lips, stabbing into me with heat and deft skill. He tasted sweet and hot, like rich red cinnamon.

Logan kissed with amazing thoroughness. Not an inch went unplundered, his teeth, tongue and lips stroking, licking, biting, his fierce mouth demanding response.

My legs went limp, a rush of desire liquefying my very bones. I would have fallen if Logan hadn't yanked me tight against his hard body. Something grew between us. Something impressively long and thick.

My heart beat harder. Moisture dewed my skin. My breasts swelled, clamoring and throbbing for his touch, nipples distressingly stiff.

As if Logan heard my traitorous breasts, he palmed one, pinching the nipple slightly. Shockwaves ricocheted through me. The other breast tightened, shouting for equal attention. Logan heard again, took both my breasts in his big hands, his pinches becoming possessive.

His kiss became possessive too. His mouth slanted and he thrust his tongue down my throat.

Feminine systems long dormant came online with a bang. If I had an On button, Logan had punched it. My legs scissored around his muscular thigh. He pushed forward, grinding into my crotch. My eyes popped wide at the heavy flood of desire that hit me.

"Stop," I panted. "This is insane."

"I love insane." Logan's tongue ran down my jaw to my neck. "My favorite setting is insane." He nipped my throat, his teeth razor-sharp.

A hot, edgy need skated over my skin. "I don't even know you. How can I be reacting like this?" So fast, almost unnaturally so.

The word caught in my head. Unnatural—

"Do you want to slap me?" Logan's tongue soothed where his teeth had scored. His muscular leg started to beat a rhythm against my mons. My jeans were heavy denim and I shouldn't have been able to feel it. But somehow he rode the thick inseam so it yanked directly on my clit.

My thoughts disintegrated. I arched into him. "I'd slap you…if I could make my arms work."

Logan chuckled, pure male arrogance. "You smell so good. Mmm. So hot and ready."

"Like pizza."

"Like Liese." He pushed emphatically between my legs. "Like sweet, musky Liese. I've got to taste you." His tongue flicked the perspiration dotting my skin.

I wondered how that hot tongue would feel flicking something else wet. *Oooh.* My vulva clenched hard. My hips began moving in counterpoint to Logan's thigh.

"I want you, princess." Logan's eyes turned molten gold, almost red. "I want to make love to you." His cock expanded even bigger against my belly. Impressive became *OMG*. A thrill tore through me, ardor or terror. Movie-star gorgeous Logan Steel wanted to make love to me, to geeky Liese Schmetterling.

Probably terror. I was in way over my head. My total sexual experience was my ex-fiancé and my mini egg vibrator. Sex with Logan would be like playing baseball with the Cubs straight out of kindergarten. He'd easily slide into home, scary enough. As fast as I was reacting, he'd score off a single base hit.

But the baseball bat in his jeans? Terror. Definitely terror.

It reminded me forcefully that I didn't know Logan Steel at all. Seducing me, threatening my job—that was all too familiar. Old tapes whirred to angry, panicked life.

I slapped him.

"Kinky. Do you like handcuffs too?" Logan stepped back just enough to give me room to breathe. "Or do you prefer scarves?"

I pushed past him to my desk, tossed off my headset and grabbed purse and coat. I was leaving now, fleeing past or present, I didn't know and didn't care. I practically ran to the door.

A firm hand stopped me.

I hadn't heard a thing. I spun, eyes wide. "What the hell...?"

"You should turn off your laptop," Logan said. "Security, you know."

I jerked out of his grip, jabbed my computer off. I should have shut it down properly, but the way my body betrayed me scared me.

No. I wasn't scared, I was angry. A man I didn't know had touched me as intimately as my fiancé—who'd screwed me, screwed me over, and dumped me. Catching the glint of my two-carat "engagement" ring, which I still wore to remind myself never to trust any man, I wondered if being thrown away by a stranger was any less painful.

Not painful, aggravating. More angry than ever, and definitely not scared or hurt, I slammed out of the Blood Center.

Well, slammed isn't quite right. I had to arm the old model alarm, using the super-secret pass code one-one-one. That disarmed it too. Not very sophisticated, but Executive Director Dirkson wanted everything kept simple.

I punched in the numbers, threw open the door and dashed out, knowing it would shut and lock automatically. I should have waited for Logan, or at least told him about the alarm, which could shriek like a candy-deprived toddler. As I ran away...er, moved briskly down the street, I considered that maybe I had subconsciously tried to cage him, like a deadly lion. He certainly unnerved me enough.

"Where do you live?" a deep voice drawled pleasantly.

"Shizzle!" I spun.

The street lamp etched Logan's features into raw perfection, made his hair shimmer like silver silk. He glided closer, seductive, exquisitely male, sliding through the shadows like a big cat. My own pussycat started purring.

Just dropkick me. "Don't do that."

"Don't do what? This?" He bent and stole a quick openmouthed kiss.

I stared at him, flabbergasted. "Don't sneak up on me."

"Ah. Then I can do this." He gave me a longer, deeper kiss.

"No! Don't do that either." I scrubbed my mouth, trying to wipe away the hot, powerful taste of him. "For a businessman, you're not very businesslike." I walked away. Fast. Almost running.

Logan, damn him, kept pace easily. "So where do you live? No, wait. Eighth and Eisenhower, right?"

I spun again. "How did you know that?"

"Security research. L. Schmetterling, Eighth and Eisenhower." Logan tapped my nose gently. "That's half a mile from here. Where's your car?"

"Car?" I walked on, slower now. What was the point of running? With his long, strong legs, he'd just catch up. "For seven blocks? Even if it were seven miles, I'd walk. You get shot here for driving anything less."

"Ah, the joy of small towns. Wait. L. Schmetterling. I've heard that name before... Yes, at Andersly-Dogget Distribution. We did work there. Programmer, systems design and finally project lead. A brilliant computer specialist with an unheard-of ninety-eight percent solution completion rate. Always on time and under budget. Liese, that's you?" His eyes glowed gold.

"Maybe." I'd never been called brilliant. Somehow, I believed it more easily than *beautiful.*

"You were about to get a well-deserved promotion to head of IT. Hell, Liese, you could have run the whole company, according to the records. Maybe you should have. I heard they're not doing so well. Why did you leave?"

My happy hit a wall of reality and went splat. "Personal reasons."

Logan's smile faded. Perceptive as he was, he probably

figured out he'd stumbled onto a Touchy Subject. Hopefully he would drop my issue and turn to something less dangerous— like religion or politics. Hopefully—

"Is this connected with not believing you're beautiful?"

Logan Steel was incredibly perceptive, and, if he kept this up, incredibly dead. "You're still here, why?"

Unruffled, Logan said, "I'm walking you home. It's late, and I'd hate for anything to happen." As he glided along he passed through alternate bands of street light and moonlight. Both loved him, gently caressing his sculpted features. My fingers itched to do the same.

I jammed them deep in my coat pockets. "At the risk of sounding like an infinite loop, this is Meiers Corners. The worst crimes we have are part-time hookers and kids trying to steal bikes. Bicycles, not motorcycles."

"That was before Chicago gangs took an interest. You need to be more careful now." Logan's long fingers curled over my shoulder, stopping me with restrained strength.

I turned to him in surprise. He stared into the night, his nostrils flared, his eyes that heated gold. His expression was so far from his usual nonchalance that I almost didn't recognize him. He no longer looked like an urban playboy.

He looked like—a hunter.

Chapter Two

I blinked, but the image of Logan as hunter would not fade. "What do you mean, Chicago gangs? What's wrong?"

"Just a couple loose ends. Stay here, all right?"

"Yes, but—"

Logan was gone.

Not gone like receding quickly from sight, or swallowed by dark shadows. Gone like *poof.* Like "Beam me up, Scottie". Frankly, it was a little creepy. I stood there a moment, trying to decide if I was scared or not.

Ferocious snarling split the night air. And howling, echoey like ravenous wolves inside a cathedral. My stomach went cold, then hot and runny. Okay, that answered that. Scared. Definitely scared.

Didn't stop me from whipping out my pepper spray and galloping into the fray.

I was kind of weird that way. Maybe it was part of being a computer geek. See, even before Black Saturday, I was emotionally weak. My ex told me so, and why would he lie? Um, yeah. But I bawled at soap operas and weddings and Bambi's mom. So sue me.

Mentally, though, I was strong. My mind had all the stamina and courage my emotions lacked so I raced to the rescue. Trembling like a naked chicken, but hey—pepper spray's wide-angle. Trembling doesn't affect aim all that much.

The clamor came from the middle of the street where a manhole was suspiciously open and unguarded. Clutching my pepper spray I slid my legs gingerly into the darkened entry. My foot hit a ladder. More howling came, definitely from below, but fading as if it were moving deeper. With a deep breath, I started down.

Moonlight filtered in, rounds of silvery white that lit my way. The ruckus had almost died. I barely heard it over the spray can clanging against the rungs. Good, I could climb back up and go home... The hole opened onto a vast expanse of bare concrete floor. Information filtered into my brain from my seventh grade field trip to the sewage treatment plant. Meiers Corners had a combined system, which meant our sewers were connected to our storm drains. To avoid sewage spillover from heavy rains, we had several overflow areas. This overflow was thankfully dry, because being wet in March in Illinois is no joke.

Well, I was here. Might as well investigate. I took two steps and was struck blind.

No, the tunnel was just pitch black outside the shaft of moonlight. I needed a flashlight. Luckily I carried one in my purse.

Women keep a lot of stuff in their purses. Whole lives practically. I did a sociology experiment in college where I predicted a woman's occupation based solely on the contents of her purse. PDA, office heels, a book for the Loop "L"? Career woman. Pacifiers and ultra-versatile diaper wipes? Mom. Breath mints, extra undies? Date girl. Of course these roles overlapped.

I had the basics for makeup—tinted sunscreen and mascara (my eyelashes are so blonde, without mascara my lids look bald). My phone tripled as PDA, mood-timer and book-reader so I didn't need all the things normal women stuff in.

You'd have thought my purse would be practically empty then, wouldn't you? But pawing one-handed through its depths was about as effective as Googling the name Smith. I needed two hands so I shoved my pepper spray into my coat and tossed my practically-empty purse onto the moonlit concrete.

The *clang* of a dozen anvils rang like a dinner bell. Yeah. See, I kinda keep tools on hand.

I froze, hyper alert, listening as the Come-and-Get-It-Snarlythings echoes faded. Nothing sounded over my thudding heart and raspy breath so I dropped to my knees and started pulling junk out. Cordless screwdriver, snips of wire. Spare batteries, all dead. Mini soldering iron, electrical tape. *Shizzle, that's where that extra motherboard went.*

Finally I found my penlight. I shoveled garbage back (except for the drained batteries. I put those in, then pulled them out.

Then I put them back in—and pulled them out again. I did this three times before I finally tossed them. I'm congenitally unable to throw away batteries. Like if I kept them in my purse long enough, they'd magically regain their charges...sure, like you don't do that too, with paperclips or spoiled meat in the freezer or *something*). I slung my purse over my shoulder and twisted the light on.

A thin beam cut through the darkness. I headed into the tunnel, only slightly bent, the pipes being at least five feet in diameter. Apparently the Meiers River had a bigger flood zone than I knew.

I walked for two, three blocks. It was hard to tell underground. The deeper I got, the slower I went, and not just because I didn't want to stumble. After the howling and roaring, I'd heard nothing but dead silence. Emphasis on dead. Where was Logan? Was he connected to the ruckus? He'd certainly looked lethal up in the street. And it wasn't lost on me that several cubic tons of Meiers Corners perched over my head.

My flashlight swept over a dark smear on the curving wall.

I stopped, played the thin light over the spot. Dried liquid, paint maybe? Definitely dark, stark against the chalky concrete like blood on a corpse.

Like blood? Or *really* blood... Sure, right. Did this happen to everyone who worked at a blood center? I strode determinedly forward.

And tripped. The flashlight fell from my hand, bounced a few times, came to rest pointing away from me. Its beam dusted the sewer tube far into the distance. The tunnel was straight and long (the Meiers Corners way, even for poop). Except for the clatter and my hiss of breath, nothing sounded.

I put my hand out to push myself up. Instead of cold concrete my palm hit leather. I froze. Was this what tripped me? I brushed tentative fingers along the leather, identified a work boot attached to stiff fabric, like jeans. Moving farther I encountered what felt like a leatherette coat.

A man? If so, he wasn't moving, like...*a dead body*. I panicked, scrambled on hands and knees to find the neck, to find the pulse.

Where there should have been a neck, there was nothing.

A body, su-ure. Like the old story about five people feeling an elephant's parts, I was fingering trunk and thinking snake. I put my hand on the "leg" and levered myself up.

The leg twitched.

I shot to my feet. Dove for the flashlight. It popped out of my scrabbling hands and started rolling. Sewers are pitched ever so slightly. Normally I wouldn't have noticed but when my only source of light was zipping away from me at a zillion miles a second I noticed plenty.

It seemed like forever before I grabbed the light, but I actually caught it in two bounces. I took a few deep breaths then turned back to the headless "body" to find out what it really was.

As I turned, a scuffling came from behind me. I swung toward the noise instead, my light catching two shadows in the distance.

"You can't get us all, copper!" The voice was rough, male and belligerent.

"Still farming the corny dialog, Razor?" The second voice sounded suspiciously insouciant. "Cultivate new threats, please. Or at least rotate your 'croppy' clichés."

"Huh?"

"Bottom line, Razor, you won't get in, even with a new entrance. The security fence is three-sixty."

"So you got a bunch of numbers. We got the back way."

"Why you villains are always so literal-minded... Three-sixty means all around. Left, right, top—bottom."

A terrible roar greeted that information. Lumpy shadows grappled, with scuffles and whistling thunks like a knife biting meat. One shadow flew into the curved concrete wall and slid to a motionless heap at the bottom.

The second glided gracefully toward me. My beam caught a river of shimmering silk—which framed a contorted, feral mask with two glowing ruby eyes.

"Logan?" My hand shook. The quivering light blurred the form like it was disappearing in a cloud of mist.

Then it was right in front of me, grabbing me, crushing me to a hard chest. "What are you doing here, Liese? Damn it, you didn't see anything. You just got here and didn't see anything strange." Logan's voice, but hollow and dark. Alien. It echoed in my head.

First the howling, then the "body" and now the mad

Rasputin voice. This was seriously creeping me out. "It was too dark to see. But I heard wolves."

"You heard dogs," Logan said in that same dark voice.

"No. Definitely wild animals. And you were talking to someone named Razor and then you kind of fuzzed out. It was so weird."

"Shit." Logan dropped the hollow voice for annoyed. He gave a decidedly un-Logan grunt of disgust. "You're a perversely willful creature, aren't you?"

"What? No. Strong-minded, maybe."

"Strong-minded. Stars above." Logan's fingers threaded tight in my hair. I felt his lips touch the top of my head, a strange mixture of possessiveness and protectiveness. He expelled an exasperated breath and released me. "Liese, there's nothing to worry about."

"But why were you fighting that Razor? Is he okay?"

"Questions later. Right now, we'd better get out of here." He caught my arm and started toward the exit.

"But Razor might need help." I shook loose and trotted the other way.

"Liese...damn it, no." Logan grabbed me by the wrist and yanked me in.

I slammed into a wall of muscular male—rock-hard, powerful and hot. My breasts smashed into chest, my nipples tightened like nuts. My belly rasped against washboard abs. My mons hit zipper. Under it, the continental drift was piling up the Rocky Mountains. *Is that a cock or does Logan have Vesuvius in his jeans?*

Bolts of desire hit me like chain lightning. I sparked from top to bottom, inside and out. I lit so hard I must have glowed.

"Fuck." Logan's voice was rough. "You smell like all-night sex. Like desire glistening on sleek, hot skin." He spun me into the pipe wall, his hands landing next to my head with twin slaps. His body heat threatened to flash-fry me.

I jumped out from under him. "I smell like Ban roll-on." Heart thudding, I backed away, step by step. How did that happen? How did Logan Steel zap me from *Six Feet Under* to *Sex and the City: Monsoon Season*? Had the Sex Fairy smacked me upside the head with his wand?

"Gotta go help...help that Razor guy. Yup, that's it." I edged away, the wrong way but at that point I didn't care. "A friend in need is a friend indeed. That's Mom-wisdom. You have to follow Mom-wisdom."

"Come back here, Liese." Logan's voice reverberated with power laced with a dark desire that hit me square in the gut and froze me in my tracks. Slowly I raised my flashlight—and sucked in my breath.

He stalked me, big and muscular, a magnificent, dangerous male animal. Hunched because of the tunnel, but that only made him more intimidating.

"Come back?" I trembled, the deer caught in the hunter's sights. "Um...why?"

"Because I want you. I want to pound into you until you scream my name. Until you go dizzy with need. Until you explode like a volcano. And then I want to do it again."

Okay, I'm not always brave. I ran.

And went sailing over the lump of jeans and leatherette coat. The flashlight popped loose. I skidded a few inches, rolled to my hands and knees and tried to carry my momentum into a leap so I could continue running.

The not-a-body grabbed me.

I screamed. Scrabbled away, got *nowhere*. I shrieked again but fingers wrapped around my neck and it came out a choked whimper.

A curse exploded, quite near, sounding like Logan but rough and guttural. A couple hard smacks and the body let go. Trembling, I pressed myself against the curved wall, concentrated on getting my breathing under control. But I totally lost it again at the chunk and pop of meat being butchered. It was so real I expected to inhale the tang of blood but there was only musty sewer.

"Logan, what the hell is happening?" I shoved away from the wall, snatched up the flashlight and swung it wildly. The beam landed full on Logan and stuck.

His skin was hammered steel plates. His eyes glowed red. His teeth—shizzle. Either he had the worst overbite in history, or those were *fangs*.

My light shook. "What happened to your face?"

"Damn it, Liese, you are the most exasperating...infuriating..." He passed one hand over his forehead, as if he had the mother of all headaches. When he released it, he looked perfectly normal.

Except for his eyes. Two smoldering coals were locked on me, hungry, and not in any simple or normal way. No, his desire threatened to consume me. I pressed into the sewer wall. Eyes eating me up, Logan took a single step. I ran like a chicken.

Eating me...chicken. Okay, probably not the best of images right then.

Logan snared my wrist, hauled me back. The flashlight wedged between us, shining his eyes like a deep woods animal or a latter-day Svengali. "You didn't see my face." His voice reverberated, hollow and dark.

"Except I did," I squeaked.

His eyes narrowed. "My face looked normal."

"Um, don't mean to disagree." Especially with him going all science fiction on me. "But you looked like Kryten. Like you had a cubist mask."

"Damn." Logan stared down at me, his expression as close to frustrated as I'd ever seen it. "I thought so. You're immune."

"Immune? What are you talking about?"

His brow creased like his mental wheels were turning fast and hard—and this cerebral grist hurt. "And if you're immune, that means you're..." He looked at me like he'd never seen me before.

"Getting weird here, Logan. You, the howling wolves, the fights—"

Logan growled a single word before pulling me into a hard, soul-searing kiss.

The word sounded strangely like "Mine."

This was not lazy Logan, sprinkling butterfly kisses over my lips. This was not playful Logan, teasing a warm response.

This was virile, brilliant Logan, powerful and intense. I was instantly immersed in a flood of mouth and tongue, sucking lips and biting teeth. Awash in hands, fingers hot and abrasive. Blown and buffeted against the cliffs of a rock-hard body. Logan wasn't just kissing me—he was a force of nature, demolishing me.

My coat went sailing, my flashlight went clattering. Logan pushed me down onto the tunnel floor. Cool concrete hit my back, blazing hot male pressed all along my front. His hands ran over my body, undoing zippers and snaps. Flying buttons tinkled against concrete but I barely heard them over the roar of my blood. I went completely deaf when his skin burned naked against mine.

It all happened so fast. One minute I was running, the next my bare ass was on the floor. One minute I was clothed, the next Logan was rubbing his muscular chest against my naked tits. One minute I was worrying over Svengali eyes, the next I was straining into his heavy, hot body.

His nipples were sharp points caressing my breasts. A line of rough hair scraped my stomach. Something powerful pulsed like hot silk between my thighs.

Powerful and long. Ten inches and counting.

That huge something—a sleek, throbbing, incredibly thick torpedo—slid forward along its bay. Slick heat seared my skin. Urgent need bowed my body. My thighs parted eagerly.

A hot head nudged my labia. It felt as big and smooth as a five-pound sausage.

Holy episiotomy! I only had a one-pound casing. "What are you doing?" I scrabbled back. My pants, dusted by the light of the dropped flashlight, were hanging off one leg. My shirt and bra were completely gone. How the hell had he done that? I cut him a shocked look—

And wished I'd gone blind. Logan stalked me on hands and knees, and he was utterly, gloriously naked.

Clothed, Logan was gorgeous. Physical perfection, the magical gift of the Sex Fairy.

Nude, he was nothing so puny as gorgeous. Nothing so trivial as stunning.

Bare-ass naked, muscles pumped huge with desire, face etched with bold hunger, Logan Steel was overwhelmingly, fiercely male. Outrageously virile. I wanted to roll onto my back and flag him in for a landing with my feet.

But this was going way too fast. And I barely knew the man. What I did know didn't make sense. He was insouciant one minute, an intense hunter the next. He was deeply sensual, an experienced lover—and he was here to put me out of a job.

He was a man who told me I was beautiful, and seemed to mean it. And then there was all the weird red-eyes-and-

31

disappearing-mist shit.

I raised a shaking palm to him. "Don't. Touch. Me."

Something in my face must have told him I was serious, because he paused. Only paused, as if he were marking it unfinished business. But it would give me time to dress. To erect a fence of buttons and zippers between me and Mr. Golden Stallion over there.

Of course, stallions could jump fences.

In record time I got my jeans untwisted, up and zipped. Keeping one eye on Logan, I retrieved my flashlight and hunted up shirt and bra, leaving the shirt undone because the buttons were gone.

Through it all, Logan watched me, his eyes burning with a hunger that was not mere arousal. Deeper, starker, his intense stare shook me. I kept careful watch as I grabbed my purse.

Deedle-ee-ee. I nearly jumped out of my skin. Since my shirt was hanging open, that wouldn't have been hard.

It was my "Beer Barrel Polka" ring tone, free with the purchase of a quarter barrel from Nieman's Bar. I got it when I bought the whole city a Thank-God-I-Have-A-Job round on my first paycheck from the Blood Center. I fumbled for my phone. "*What.*"

"Liese? It's Elena." Intelligent, strong and beautiful, with a low and slightly husky voice, Elena O'Rourke Strongwell was Meiers Corners's top police detective. She also recommended me for the job at the Blood Center, earning my undying thanks.

"*Elena?*" I moderated my voice and tried again. "Elena?"

"You okay?"

Logan was tugging on his shirt, which would've been a relief if he'd put his pants on first. As it was, his thickly muscled thighs framed a jutting foot-long cock.

I gulped hard. "I'm fine."

"Fine, not counting that load of sand in your throat. Where are you?"

"Me? Well, I'm..." *Elena, I'm trapped in a sewer with a male so outrageously sexy I want to play doggy on his naked leg.* Um, no. "I'm at work. You know I work late sometimes."

"Working late, uh-huh. Except I'm here at the Center. So, you wanna try again?"

I glanced again at Logan. Still Mr. Huge Hat-rack. My

lolling tongue practically shorted out the phone. No, I definitely did not want to try again. It would only come out *ga-ga-ga* and Elena'd have to shoot me. Of course, that would put me out of my misery.

Finally Logan found his jeans and pulled them on—but he had trouble zipping up over the Incredible Hulk. I whimpered.

"Liese?" Elena sounded even more suspicious.

I covered my eyes. "Sorry, I was distracted. The truth is I was on my way home and I made a couple stops."

"What? Why?" Impossible as it seemed, she sounded even more suspicious. Then she floored me by adding, "There's not anything...*weird* going on, is there?"

Like wolves howling, headless bodies or late-night visits from Mr. Sexgod? I didn't say any of that out loud. If Elena thought I was mental she'd never recommend me for my next job.

Another glance showed Logan...gone. *Beam me up.* "No, nothing weird," I lied. Hell, I didn't want to end up in the "Verk Camp". "So why are you at the Blood Center?"

"Bo and I were patrolling and saw the lights on. We thought you were here and stopped to chat." Elena wasn't foot patrol but she and her husband were involved in a neighborhood watch. "Things have been tense since Chicago tried to annex us, the gangs and all. So I called to make sure you were okay."

"I'm fine." Something scuttled in the dark tunnel. I swept my flashlight but saw nothing. Big strong Logan would actually have been reassuring about then, but a tight three-sixty swish showed only empty sewer. I swept farther out.

Elena said, "So why'd you leave the light on?"

"I was in a rush." My flashlight brushed a misshapen bowling ball. Dark drips smeared something that could have been a forehead. A lump could have been a nose, and scraggly hairs under the lump, a mustache. But if it was a head, there wasn't any body.

"Why? Did something happen?"

"No, nothing." Nothing that wouldn't land me as "Dracula's" roommate.

Another rustle. I shifted my light, picking out a brownish, body-sized lump with boots, jeans, leatherette coat.

That moved.

I shoved my fist in my mouth. A head. And clothes that, as I watched, were *crawling toward it*. I backed away, my guts running acid and my brain wondering a mite insanely which was scarier, a decapitated head, a headless body—or clothes with free will.

Although wouldn't that make laundry easier?

"Liese, you okay?" Elena's suspicious bark was the only thing that kept me from screaming like a little girl.

As it was I gasped. I had to be seeing things. Bodies did not operate without heads. Even if they did, I couldn't tell show-me-the-facts Elena. "Um, something's come up." I clapped my phone shut and tried to force myself to think rationally—not easy with my scalp crawling and my insides turning to ice and my feet screaming run-run-run. Automatically I started toward the exit but my legs were shaky and the patch of outside moonlight seemed much too far away.

A rustle right behind me turned my trembling legs to blocks of cement. "Logan? Is that you?" I inched my head around.

Not Logan. Not by a long shot.

The leatherette coat was *sitting up*. The headless body wasn't headless anymore. Bald-and-bloody grinned—and jumped to its feet, grabbing for me.

I screamed and ran. Pepper spray and black-belt kicks were fine against normal thugs. But no chemicals would work here and nothing in Mr. Miyagi's martial arts curriculum had prepared me for ambulatory corpses. Maybe zombie-fighting was later, after we learned ninja invisibility.

"You can't outrun me, snack!" The voice behind me was gravel thrown on the tunnel walls.

Snack? This kicked into beyond weird. Weirdness overclocked, dual-core weirdness. Weirdness with Service Pack 3. I put on a burst of speed. Feet pounded behind me.

"Give up and die, snack." Closer. Harsher.

The ladder was in sight. I leaped for it. My foot landed on something round and rolly. I scrambled for balance. Stumbling, I hit another roller. It skidded out from under me. I tottered, arms windmilling wildly. I almost caught myself, hit another.

My legs flew up. My butt struck concrete. Round and rolly impediments spit like bullets. They skittered away, small, black and cylindrical.

My own damned batteries.

Boots pounded toward me. "Ha. Gotcha now—whoops!"

Shit-kickers went by, scrabbling like Yogi Bear off the edge of a cliff. Batteries scattered like hail. I covered my head to avoid their spray. Furious swearing was punctuated by batteries shooting everywhere. I heard a *smack* like something big hitting the wall. Then another smack like fist on bone, followed by—silence.

Slowly, I uncovered my head.

A dark form loomed over me, blocking the light.

I shrieked. Scrambled up. Would have run, but hands shot out of the shadows and grabbed me.

They shoved me toward the ladder. I struggled wildly. The owner of the hands didn't even notice, thrusting me inexorably forward.

"Stop! Who are you?" And because maybe I'd popped over a dimension or two, I added, "*What* are you?" I twisted to see, caught only shadows.

"What am I?" The shadows growled, pushing me up the ladder. "Pissed at you, that's what I am."

Chapter Three

I popped out of the manhole and sprang to my feet, prepared to kick the emerging monster...and saw waves of raw silk shimmering in moonlight. "*Logan?*"

"You're going home, Liese. And you're staying there." Logan rose from the hole, but not as I'd seen him yet. Not the lazy playboy, nor the unnaturally perceptive lover. Not even the fierce hunter.

His eyes were fiery gold with determination, his jaw was clenched. His shoulders were set, his posture uncompromising. His easy charm wasn't gone, exactly, but was hardened by a mantle of power and command.

This was Logan the mover and shaker, the Fortune-500 CEO. This was the Logan Steel who commanded a firm with national and international clients.

In the kingdom of business, *this* was Logan the Prince.

I was so astonished that I let him drag me three blocks before I dug in my heels. "Just what the hell happened back there? First you went all red-eyed and face-plated and pointy-toothed. Halloween's more than eight months away, buddy. And then—"

"Not so loud."

I fired an incredulous stare around me at the utterly empty streets. "Who's going to hear? And what was with that I'm 'immune' stuff? Immune to what sickness, you? Are you a fever and the only cure is more cowbell?"

"Liese, hush." Pulling me to him, Logan's hand clapped over my mouth. "I'd kiss you to shut you up, but I don't want to get slapped again."

Bodies and severed heads took a temporary back seat to

pique. The best kisser on the planet had done it just to *shut me up.* I should have known better. He hadn't kissed me because I was beautiful, or even because I reminded him of dinner. The lying fuck.

I was so angry I bit his hand.

"Kinky." Logan's breath warmed my ear. "But to break skin you have to bite harder. Liese, I didn't kiss you in the sewer to shut you up. I did it because I wanted you so badly I couldn't help myself."

He did? I let him drag me another block before I dug in my heels again. "And the red eyes and Batcave voice? What was all that? And where did you go? You were all—" *gorgeous naked stalking me on hands and knees,* "—Elena called, and when I looked, you were gone."

"You're persistent, aren't you? Probably what makes you such a good manager."

"Last I looked, manager implies underlings. I have two bosses. Three, if I count you. Why did you leave?"

He raised an eyebrow. "Did I leave?"

Enough was enough. I hit him. Roundhouse punch to the gut. I knew it wouldn't hurt him, given his iron abs, but I hoped it would leave a bruise.

Lightning-fast, he blocked me. Caught my fist—and *kissed* it. I snatched it away.

He gave me that knowing smirk of his. "The explanation's simple, Liese. There's a gang in Meiers Corners, and they've apparently made a base in the sewer. I surprised them vandalizing mannequins. I managed to drive them all off except for two, who I knocked unconscious."

"Dragging mannequins into the sewer to vandalize them, I see. Then you disappeared, why?"

He shrugged. "I thought I heard something outside. I went to make sure it wasn't more gang members. When I heard you yell I came back and saw one had moved. What did you do to him, anyway?"

"Um, tripped over him." I didn't mention the creepy illusion that Mr. Eat-Me-For-A-Snack was headless. "Has hallucinations" didn't look good on the ol' resume. "Razor?"

"No, Maim, one of the less pleasant members of Razor's gang. You need to stay away from him, Liese. From all of them."

"Less *pleasant*? What would a *more* pleasant gang guy be like?"

"Not joking, Liese." Logan dragged me onto my stoop. "Stay inside." Then almost reluctantly he added, "Please?"

We were home already. I should have been relieved but wasn't. I stuck my key in the lock. "I'll stay home if you do." It only occurred to me after it was out of my fat mouth that it sounded like I was inviting him to stay in the same home. Mine.

He pulled me into a tight embrace. Kissed the top of my head. "If I thought it'd help you be safe, I'd stay in a heartbeat." He kissed my forehead. "Who am I kidding? I'd stay just for me. Ah princess, what are we going to do?" It was apparently a rhetorical question because when I raised my face to answer, I got kissed soundly instead.

Logan's mouth circled gently, sweet and warm, nothing like the devouring he'd done earlier. This kiss was tender, his embrace sheltering. The silk of his hair brushed against my cheek, his body heat enveloped me. I felt warm and oddly safe in his arms. Instead of running in terror, I actually raised myself on tiptoes and skimmed my tongue over his luscious lower lip.

His arms tightened. One hand slid up, cupping the back of my head, holding me securely. A deep rumble came from his chest. "*Mmm.* Do that again." His interest stirred against my belly.

So I did. His interest raised its head. I did it again and interest grew long and thick. I licked his lips open and his hard, thick interest began to pulse. As I tasted the dark, rich cinnamon of his mouth I could feel the growing length of him throb against my belly.

His cock's progress bar was inching toward impossible again.

"Logan?"

"Mmm?" He nipped down my jaw line, nibbled to my earlobe.

Sweet jangles of need sang through me at the sharp feel of his teeth. "I was trying to...what happened in the sewer...oh, heavens above." The last was from a particularly sharp nip to the throat.

"I know, princess." Logan licked where he'd nipped, a hot swipe of lust. "Think later. Pleasure now."

"But—" But I'd left my porch light on. We were out in the open, lit like a theater stage. My ex-fiancé Botcher had insisted on under the covers with the lights out. This was raw, exposed. Frightening...and shamefully exciting.

"No buts." Logan's nimble fingers unzipped my coat. Without buttons my shirt was no protection against the cold air hitting my skin, but his hot mouth, biting lightly down my collarbone, shot me back to broil.

He nipped and kissed to the notch of my throat. There he lapped the soft, sensitive skin until I made a throttled sound, apparently his tongue's cue to slide boldly down my breastbone.

At the top of my sports bra he paused. He licked the edge then tried to worm his tongue under. The industrial-strength spandex didn't give a millimeter. *Stopped him.* I breathed a mixture of relief and disappointment.

He gave a cute little whimper, like a puppy wanting in.

My breasts poked their heads up. I could practically hear their nipply voices—"Here boy, here! Kiss here!" Breasts are so not picky.

Of course Logan heard them too. With a growl of satisfaction, his mouth closed over one tip and he began suckling. Through cloth, but the man's middle name was Hoover. At the deep tugging I nearly shot through the top of my head. I could only imagine what that hot mouth would do to a bare nipple. Licking, sucking naked pink skin, my breast swelling, tightening...steam began to blast out my ears.

"Logan...uhngh...we're outside...oh, damn." He had added teeth.

His hands clenched around my hips, yanked my pelvis in tight. OMG. Who made this man's zippers—Pyle Driver and Sons? I tried to wrench away but our skin had some sort of covalent bond going. Only a nuclear explosion could have pried us apart. I had to stop him before someone got caught in the fallout—like me.

"Logan," I said, only it came out "Uhhh." So then I tried to slap him, but someone had cooked my arm when I wasn't looking.

Logan, intent on suckling my breast, ignored all of this. He suckled until I wanted to scream—or maybe rip his face off and shove it down my bra where he could do some real good.

Instead I grabbed his head and pulled up. He popped off

my breast and I thought *yay* until his mouth landed on mine in a kiss so deep he excavated my tonsils. I groaned and thrust my tongue back in self-defense, swiping his lips and mouth and his sharp teeth. He tasted so good I licked everything I could reach, including the length of one—fang?

Like I'd punched *his* On switch, Logan growled and crushed me to him. "You drive me wild, princess. The way you smell. The way you touch me." His lips left mine to burrow into my neck. "I'm insane with wanting. Let me taste you."

Teeth nipped my neck until I shuddered. A warm tongue smoothed over the irritation. My pulse throbbed in my throat, thickening it. I couldn't say a word.

"Just a taste." He breathed in like he was scenting heaven. His nuzzling was punctuated by urgent nips. "Please, Liese. Just one taste."

He wasn't the only insane one. Caught in a sensual haze, I lifted my chin. He groaned, "Bless you, princess," and I barely noticed when something pressed into my skin, needle-sharp.

"Get away from her, you slime." A man's bellow cut through my daze.

Running feet neared. "I've got a bazooka," a second, feminine voice called. "And I know how to use it."

A low, warning growl slashed the air in response, a feral rumbling—vibrating against *me*. From Logan? Was Logan *growling*? I looked up. His eyes were shut tight, his jaw working. He took a deep breath, and another. Slowly the growl died. He opened his eyes and gave me a small smile, tucked my coat closed before turning.

"Hello, Viking, good to see you again. How are you and the esteemed Mrs. Viking?"

"Steel? What the fuck's going on?"

I angled around Logan to see a muscular mountain of Scandinavian incredulity, truck-sized fists on hips. Bo Strongwell.

Next to him his wife Elena was stowing a super-deluxe roll of Christmas paper, if Christmas paper came in gunmetal green. "Liese!" She hopped onto the stoop. "Why didn't you tell me Steel was with you?" An affectionate slap on the head was followed by a somewhat desperate hug. "Then I wouldn't have worried."

"You were worried? I wouldn't have guessed, with the phone call and you showing up on my doorstep."

Instead of zinging me back, she flicked a look at her husband. "The gang trouble's had me on edge."

"I met one of those gang guys. Pardon me if I don't think vandalizing mannequins is quite something to fret over." Although Maim had scared me at the time. *Give up and die, snack.*

"You met a gang member?" Elena said at the same time Bo said, "Vandalizing mannequins?"

Logan cleared his throat. "I surprised Razor in the sewers."

"*Razor?*" Elena's expression zoomed from worried to alarmed.

"Petty vandals, nothing to worry about." Logan flicked eyes to me. "Tearing heads off mannequins, that sort of stuff."

"Mannequins." Bo raised an eyebrow at Elena.

"Oh, right," she said after a moment's pause. "So Logan, did you take care of Razor and the, er, mannequins? Or is there cleanup Bo and I have to do?" She put a strange emphasis on cleanup.

"No, no, everything's taken care of."

"Except the Maim guy," I said. "And Razor. Logan knocked them unconscious, so we probably should call an ambulance."

Logan opened his mouth like he was going to contradict me, then smiled his brilliant smile. "Thanks for reminding me, Liese. I'll just go back and see to that while Bo and Elena escort you inside."

All three exchanged a glance I can only call conspiratorial. My key was already in the lock, so all Elena had to do was turn it. She latched onto my arm and Bo snagged the other. I now know what frog-marching is. Elena's five-nine and Bo's six-four made my little old five-six barely touch the ground. I hopped between them the best I could. "Stop! Or at least, slow down."

Elena released me to shut the door behind us. "Liese, with Razor's gang loose, you might want to take a few days off. Until the new security's online at the Blood Center."

If I didn't go back tomorrow, I might not get to return at all. "I can't."

"Then be careful, okay? If you're out after dark, you might want Logan with you."

"You trust him?" I stared at her. As a cop, Elena trusted even fewer people than I did.

"You don't?"

"Not any farther than I can throw him." Which, considering all his muscled height, might be no further than on top of me. Ooh.

Elena's phone rang. Flipping it open, she listened for a moment. "We're on our way." She turned back to me. "Liese, I'm just saying being with Logan might be safer."

I watched out the window as the Strongwells disappeared into the night. "Safer than what?" I asked, but no one heard me.

Nervy and irritable, I paced my apartment. *Not* because of Logan Steel—despite certain body parts voicing their opinion of letting him get away. What did they know? He was simply the first male to be interested in said body parts since Bernie Botcher. Although comparing Logan to the rat-bastard, well, there was no comparison. Logan was sex poured into a pair of yummy-tight jeans. Botcher was...the name said it all.

No, I was not nervy because Logan punched me *on* but never logged in. Ooh, logging *in*...and out...and in...shizzle. No, I was nervy because of the episode in the sewer. What had really happened down there? Was that a headless mannequin I'd seen? Maim had worn the same thing as the mannequin. Was that a coincidence?

Well, one way to find out.

I had my hand on the doorknob when my land line rang. I nearly didn't stop—it was after nine, and though the rest of the world was just popping its first Miller, Mr. and Mrs. Meiers Corners were rolling up the sidewalks and turning off the dog.

But caller ID was a Chicago number I recognized. I snatched up the handset. "Mom? Is something wrong? Are you okay? Did something happen at your radiation treatment?"

She laughed, a little weak. "Settle down, honey. The treatment went fine. I'm a touch tired, but we expected that."

"How tired? Shouldn't you be resting? Why are you calling if you should be lying down?" Despite the doctors explaining everything that would happen after the lumpectomy, including the radiation and its side effects, I was suddenly afraid. Her fatigue was how we'd figured out she was sick in the first place.

Fear, like an unwelcome houseguest, is bad no matter how long you've been expecting it. In fact sometimes the anticipation makes it worse.

"Liese. I'm fine. The medical staff is wonderful. And Cousin Rolf and his wife are taking good care of me. I'm calling to check in so you wouldn't worry." She laughed again, more her old self. "So don't worry."

"I just wish you were home where I could take care of you." Yes, guilt was another of my issues. Sometimes I felt like a mass of issues. But I loved my mother, would do anything for her.

"You *are* taking care of me, honey. I couldn't afford the Chicago doctors without your health insurance. Not many companies cover dependent parents, you know."

My wonderful health insurance, which I might not have much longer. "I would have driven you in for your treatments."

"It's your job to be at the Blood Center, honey. And I need you to keep your job." In a lighter tone she added, "Besides, this gives me time to win back my money. We play three-handed sheepshead every night and I'm down fifteen cents."

Attitude was half the battle. If she was joking, the least I could do was stop worrying—on the outside. "Don't tell me you let Cousin Rolf talk you into a nickel a point. Now I know you're not well."

She snorted. "Well enough to take him for a dollar fifty day before yesterday. And once I get past the nausea... Now, you're not to worry, Liese. I'll be winning Rolf's money again in no time."

"Yeah. No time," I echoed as Mom made goodbye noises and hung up.

After that I slung my purse over my shoulder, headed for dark sewers and moving mannequins and crazy men calling me *snack*...I paused, hand on the knob. I wanted to know what had happened. I wanted to see if Logan had called an ambulance for Razor and Maim. But what if the gang had come back? What if the explanation really was as Logan claimed? Bo and Elena seemed to accept it readily enough.

Though I'm a tiger when other people's safety is involved, when it's just me I'm not that brave. I decided sewers and mannequins could wait and went to bed.

43

Where I tossed and turned for hours. Again, *not* because Logan was so sexy he made my eyeballs boil. Because I got to wondering if the golden Adonis (Ewan McGregor of the Greeks) who showed up tonight was really *the* Logan Steel, CEO of Steel Security.

Sure, Elena had called him Logan Steel, but he might have tricked her too. And sure, Steel Security was legitimate. But how many men rose to such positions of power so young? Logan looked no older than twenty-nine—if a powerful, self-assured twenty-nine.

The problem was that Steel Security's CEO had never been photographed. With all the articles done on him, all the word-of-mouth he generated in the industry, no one had ever caught him on film. Some people said he was a mysterious hermit. Some said he was intensely private. Others said he wasn't photogenic (or, as Botcher put it, uglier than a five-drink lay). Whatever the reason, I couldn't use a picture to prove his identity.

Logan had suggested that I call the executive director to confirm his story. If that was a clever ruse to reassure me that he couldn't be lying, he didn't know how mistrustful I really was. I picked up the phone and punched in Dirkson's home number.

Three rings and a harsh voice barked, "What?"

Executive Director Dirkson looked like *Spider-Man*'s J. Jonah Jameson with a handlebar mustache tacked on. Gruff and abrupt, he sounded like Jameson too. He even chewed the cigar.

"Chief Dirkson? It's Liese Schmetterling."

"Schmetterling, do you know what time it is?"

I glanced at the clock. Oops. Two a.m. was late even for me. "Sorry to bother you, Chief, but I had a visitor tonight. He claimed to be Logan Steel. Said Steel Security's putting in a system at the Center. Like our tiny facility needs space-age technology." I laughed, willed Dirkson to do the same.

"You're calling about *that*? Yes, we contracted with Steel. About time we got some real security. Past time, what with the *trouble* we've had."

I sucked in a breath. "Trouble?"

"The blood trouble."

Cold lanced through me. *Dirkson knows about the missing blood.* Did he blame me? Had he brought in Steel because I wasn't cutting it?

I heard a scrabbling of papers. "Schmetterling. As long as I've got you on the line. There's a new board member, Ruth-something or other. Damn it, I know I wrote it down. Guy from Chicago, first name Lorne, or something. Ah, here it is. Got a pencil?"

Well, at least he wasn't firing me today. I palmed my PDA and forced myself to radiate ultra-efficiency. "Shoot."

"Lorne Ruthven." Dirkson recited contact information. "One of the high mucky-mucks at CIC Mutual Insurance. Too high, you ask me. Guy's snootier than old money."

"Maybe he's just spent too much time in the adminisphere. Lack of oxygen can damage the brain." Dirkson obviously didn't care for this Ruthven, which struck me as unfair. Everyone should get a break when they were new to a job, especially when it was only a few pints... I determined to try to like Ruthven. "I'll add him to the database."

"Do that. And Schmetterling." Dirkson's tone was abruptly severe.

Anxiety returned in a rush. "Yes?"

"Be nice to him even if he's a jerk. There's a center in Indiana that lost some blood and the board fired the whole lot, from the ExDir down to the third assistant peon. We don't want to end up like Indiana, do we?"

"No, sir." I expelled a breath and hung up.

Another bit of Mom-wisdom was work hard and don't worry over might-bes. So the next morning as I walked to the Center I pumped myself up to prove what a good and indispensable employee I was.

I scanned complete inventory in half the usual time. Pleased with my indispensable self, I sat down at my desk and plugged the scanner into my laptop. With a flourish I hit the switch that synced the scanner with my inventory program—and stared at the screen in disbelief.

We were missing a case of blood.

Chapter Four

A whole case, gone. I couldn't figure out how. I had checked inventory just yesterday. This morning the Blood Center door was locked. But sometime between eight last night and eight this morning, poof.

This was bad. A missing unit or two could be explained away as breakage or spillage. I'd half-convinced myself that was all they were. Now a case was gone, on my watch. How would I explain this to Dirkson? Would he give me a second chance, or would he just fire my ass—if hiring Logan Steel didn't mean that already?

In my numbness, I barely registered the roar of a large motor outside. A bus lumbered up the street, one of those big coaches with cushy seats and TV screens in the headrests. With a squeal of brakes it stopped in front of the Blood Center. The motor cut.

That broke through. Craning my neck, I saw Iowa plates. Out-of-towners, then, bound for Tourist Central one block south. Probably this was the only place they could find parking. I went back to brooding.

The bus's door *shooshed* open. A tanned, hard-bodied blonde bounded down the stairs. Talk about eleven-inch fashion dolls. Lush hair spilled around a heart-shaped face. Stylish capris showed off tanned, toned calves. A cropped tank bulged with unnaturally buoyant breasts and revealed a super-flat stomach, a diamond winking discreetly from the dent of a navel.

I stared. This was Illinois in March. Wasn't she freezing?

The blonde headed straight for my door and popped in with enough energy to fuel an Apollo booster. Her voice, when she killed me, was as smooth as honey. "I'm looking for Logan Steel."

Dammit, *this* was why I didn't trust men. They tell you you're beautiful, then Venus rides in on her clamshell and they dump you. Maybe I was leaping to conclusions, but past experience told me the only part we hadn't gotten to yet was the dumping.

I twisted my ring, kept for just this purpose. My constant reminder of the world of hurt I'd invite if I left my emotional flank open. "He's not here."

"When is he expected back?"

I shrugged, wishing she'd leave. No, actually I wished she'd burst into flames, but that seemed a little extreme.

"Maybe you can tell me where to find him?" She smiled, teeth Miley Cyrus bright.

Perky and dogged. I hated her. Flames was not extreme. "Sorry."

Cold air whooshed in. I craned my neck around the blonde—and cringed.

Not at the guy in bus driver uniform who had flathanded the door open. He was a heavyset duplicate of Ralph Kramden down to the dark hair curling around his blue cap and bouncing belly. No, what grabbed me in a chokehold was the blond boy who sauntered in past the driver. About twelve years old, inhumanly handsome, moving with lazy grace. Except for his blue eyes, the boy could have been Logan's twin. He stopped in front of Ms. Perky Buns. "Mom?"

Logan's twin—or his son.

My insides went Arctic. Logan's son...and Ms. Clamshell was his mother, meaning...I couldn't quite figure out what it meant except that I wanted to put my fist through her face and tear out all my hair while shrieking.

"Bud, what have I told you about interrupting?" The woman spoke with a fond exasperation. "Now come in so the driver can close the door."

Bud drew himself up. "I beg your pardon, Mother. Miss." He gave me a small bow. "Please excuse me."

Please? And a *bow*? Amazing manners for a thirty-year-old, much less a kid. Drilled into him by Sergeant Mom, no doubt. Not only a mom, but a Super Mom.

Great blue screens of death. Could things get any worse?

Of course we *all* know the answer to that one. The boy said, "I wouldn't have interrupted but Lilly needs to use the potty." He drew forward a golden-haired little girl.

No taller than my desk, the girl looked about three. Absolutely adorable, sweet as a honey-frosted sugar cube.

Yep. Things can always get worse.

I managed to force my voice past the snarled cable in my throat. "Sure. Bathroom. There." I pointed.

"Thank you." Bud gave me that little bow again.

"T'ank you," the girl piped, cuter than a kitten. I watched them disappear into the restroom. Such lovely, well-behaved children.

How different from their devilish, suave father.

Okay, I didn't have a shred of proof. But the resemblance was uncanny and I knew Logan would make beautiful children. Even if I were the mother they'd be beautiful and blond—but a helluva lot sassier.

Violently I shook that thought away. I wasn't jealous and I certainly wasn't *wistful*. I was mad. How could Logan come on to me when he had Suzy Supermom at home? This was worse than Botcher, who'd at least had the decency to wait until after he dumped me to take up with my replacement.

The bus driver slouched around the perimeter of the office, hands in his pockets. He didn't look at anything in particular and ended up outside the bathroom door so I assumed he had to go potty too.

"I don't understand." The woman was clicking away on a slim PDA. "I was told Mr. Steel would be here. Meiers Corners Blood Center, Fifth and Lincoln."

"Steel Security's putting in a system, but Logan's not here. Something about meetings all day."

From the bathroom, "Itsy Bitsy Spider" echoed in a clear little soprano.

I drew a cleansing breath. Kid couldn't help it that she was adorable. Supermom probably couldn't help it that she was perfect. I could at least be a little helpful. "He might show tonight. Maybe you could come back then."

"To*night*, of course!" Her eyes widened. They were disgustingly, brilliantly blue, framed by stupidly long black lashes. "How silly of me. The sun's still up."

Before I could comment on that odd phrase, she stuck out her slim hand. "Thank you, Ms....?"

"Schmetterling." My hand met a firm, warm clasp. I hated her even more. "Liese Schmetterling."

"I'm Zinnia," she said brightly. "Schmetterling? That means butterfly in German. What a beautiful name."

Super-clucking-terrific. Gorgeous, athletic and *smart*. I now loathed her. "It still sounds like a pile of poop."

"To the uninformed. It is some people's lot in life to be misunderstood." Zinnia took my hand in both hers. "We who are more fortunate must fight for the rights of those limited by racists or sexists or speciesists!"

"Species-ists?"

She released me. "Prejudice is prejudice, Ms. Schmetterling."

"But...because someone's a different *species*? Like—not human? Is speciesist even a word?"

But Zinnia was only getting started. She struck a pose, one finger pointed heavenward like she was lecturing God. "We must fight, sister! Take our righteous stand against the provincialism that would paint all breeds of humanity with one brush."

"Uh, humanity doesn't have breeds. We have races, and even that line is blurred—"

"Against the intolerance day walkers have for people of the night!"

"You mean second and third shift workers?"

"Mom! Ix-nay on the amps-vay." Bud had emerged from the bathroom, the door just shutting on the bus driver. Bud held his sister's hand and looked a bit shocked. Seeing me he gave a somewhat self-conscious bow. "Thank you, Miss, for the use of the facilities."

"You're welcome." Ix-nay was Pig Latin for nix. But amp-vay? Vamp—naw. "I'm surprised there isn't a toilet on the bus."

"It's broken."

Supermom Zinnia gathered up her two perfect children. "I'll come back tonight. It was nice meeting you, Ms. Schmetterling." With that she bounded with them out the door. It was unfair that she had that much energy, even more unfair that her butt was so tight I could probably bounce my state quarter collection off it.

As the bus driver emerged from the bathroom and left without a word, I slumped in my seat.

I set the mood-timer on my PDA for five minutes and sat back to indulge in a good feeling-sorry-for-myself (when you have issues you figure out ways to cope) but almost immediately the door whooshed open and several men and women bustled in. Their jackets were discreetly embroidered with the Steel Security logo. I punched the timer off, feeling cheated. The industrious eager-beavers proceeded to thread ceiling cable and snake filaments through the walls, busily installing all manner of high-tech equipment. An outside crew was even busier digging up the lawn.

Workers bolted a shiny new rack into the corner. They slotted two slim cases into the rack, then wrestled my sturdy Dell in between. My six-year-old eBay special looked like a minivan parked between a couple million-dollar sport coupes.

At three thirty the phone rang. I connected my headset, bracing for Dirkson or even "Dracula", but to my surprise it was Logan. He greeted me warmly.

I greeted him with, "You cheating fuck"—though I didn't actually say it out loud.

"Are my people there, Liese?" he asked. "Are they working hard?"

"Yes." I scowled at his eager-beaver, hard-working people. No, not beavers. Nothing so furry and loveable. Maybe bees, swarming and stinging...or ants, scurrying across a picnic, taking over *my* Blood Center, but I didn't say that either. "They left my server running. I thought you wanted me to convert my data to your programs."

"That's phase two, tomorrow. Today they're putting in the base security network. I had them rush it, after the sewer incident last night. I don't want you vulnerable, Liese."

Almost as if he cared. But I knew better. I hit him with, "Zinnia stopped by. Looking for you."

"Zinnia? The name sounds vaguely familiar. Did she say what she wanted?"

Probably to offload your kids on you. "Only that she'd be

back tonight." I couldn't stop myself from adding, "It seemed like she knew you."

"Huh. What'd she look like?"

Like your wife. "Blonde, blue eyes. Early thirties. Good figure. She came on a bus with Iowa plates.

"Iowa plates?" Logan groaned. "The interviewees."

Interviewees? I wanted to chew thumbtacks and spit computer chips. Not only was Blondie Bop here to warm Logan's bed, the whole bus was here to warm his little manager heart. If Logan was going to replace me, couldn't he have waited to interview until he was back in Iowa? Sure, his time was valuable, but so valuable he had to ship the whole busload here?

"Liese, I know this is short notice, but is there a place at the Center I could use to talk to people? Someplace private?"

"Why not just use your motel room?" I said.

"I'm putting up at Strongwell's."

"*What?*" Elena knew Logan well enough to host him, and she hadn't told me?

"Bo has a few extra rooms in his basement. He opens them to out-of-towners every so often." Sounding harassed, Logan didn't catch my reaction. And something caught at his tone, just at the edge. Something like—that wasn't pain, was it?

One of the discreetly embroidered busy-bees started buzzing under my desk, invading my personal space. Fine. I felt antsy anyway. Ha-fucking-ha. I got up and paced, twisting my ring. "Strongwells have a big parlor. Do your interviews there."

"I would, but the Viking's used to running things. Sometimes he sticks his nose into other people's business." He expelled a breath.

Like Logan sticking his nose into *my* Center. Although it would be *his* Center soon. Yet I found I didn't like the idea of Logan feeling harassed, much less being in pain. I released my ring reluctantly. Maybe he had some right to be asking for interview space. "You can use the office. I'll work in the back room." I tried not to sound too grudging. There was an outside chance he would let me interview too.

"I don't want to uproot you from your area. The back's good enough for me. I'll see you tonight, Liese, before seven." And then, to my utter consternation, he had the nerve to blow me a kiss before hanging up.

"You're married!" I yelled at the empty line. How could he be flirting with me when he had a wife? Especially when he knew she was here?

Although...he hadn't reacted to hearing her name. Maybe Supermom wasn't really married to Supersuave.

Or maybe Logan was simply a better actor than Botcher. That rat-bastard.

I wasn't sure if I meant Mr. Ex or Mr. Sex.

The phone rang again almost immediately. Popping on the Bluetooth, I resisted the urge to answer, "Grand Central Station".

"Hey, Liese. It's Nixie."

Nixie Emerson was a punk musician I went to school with. I'd known her all my life, but she rarely phoned me, and then usually texted. I wondered what was up. "How's the tour going?"

"Fan-fucking-tastic. It's been extended another two weeks."

"The tour" was the round-the-lakes circuit her band Guns and Polkas was doing in preparation for their big Milwaukee Summerfest gig in June. "Wow. That's great!"

"Yeah, really sweet. What, Julian?"

The last must have been to her husband. Julian Emerson was a high-powered Boston attorney (and, frankly, awesome studmuffin) who Nixie had married a few months ago.

"Oh, right. Sorry, Liese. Julian was just reminding me we have practice in five. So I'll get right down to business. Can I talk to Steel?"

"*You* know Logan too?" Punk rocker, international businessman—they didn't exactly travel in the same circles. And how would Nixie know Logan was *here*? Last night was the first I'd heard of Steel Security putting in a system at the Blood Center, and I worked here.

"We met at the Meiers Corners festival. I'd spew the deets, but we're due in five. So can you put Steel on?"

"He's not here. His people are. Want to talk with one of them?"

"No, it's gotta be Steel. What time is it, anyway?" A deep murmur in the background told me Julian was answering her.

"Huh. Feels later. Liese, can you steno a message? I tried Steel's phone but got caged in voicemail jail. Tell him he's gonna have to take the negotiations with Nosy, 'cause Julian's staying with me on tour. The meet's set for Friday night, six-thirty."

"What? What negotiations? And who's *Nosy*?"

"Steel'll know. Julian'd head back but we've got Nosy over the barrel, so this thing's a slam-dunk. Besides, Julian doesn't want to leave me 'cause I'm preggers. Hey, thanks, Liese. Well, gotta go."

"*Preggers*? Nixie what...?" I was talking to an empty line.

After that conversation, I felt a little like I'd been smacked by a solid-bodied guitar. Then again, Nixie affected most people that way.

The Steel Security people left around five. Logan said they were installing the "base security network", whatever that was. It wasn't the whole system, so I had a job for at least one more day. I decided I'd carry on like the good little trooper I was.

Besides, every day I worked was one less day of COBRA hell.

A little before six p.m. I was updating the shipment calendar when the door slammed open and a man dashed in.

He was tall and lanky with light brown hair cut in a mullet. A young Richard Dean Anderson except for the dissolute face, slouchy jeans and shapeless flannel shirt. MacGyver, yes, but melted a little.

Mullet-boy was flushed as if he'd run a marathon. He clapped hands to knees, breathing heavily.

First Logan and now this. I seriously needed to lock the door after hours. "Can I help you?"

He panted, "You Liese Schmearling?"

"Schmetterling. And you are?"

"Raz..." He blinked a couple times, like he'd forgotten who he was. "Uh, Race. My name is Race."

"Do you have a last name, Race? Maybe Bannon?"

Muck-Gyver pushed a hand through his mullet as if it would lighten the burden between his ears. "Uh...uh..." His eyes lit up. "It's Gillette."

I thought Jillette, and Showtime. "Bullshit! Where's Teller?" I beamed at him, waiting for him to get the joke.

His face was as blank as a hard drive in a magnet factory.

"Yes. Well." Obviously he only got basic cable, in more ways than one. "Welcome to the Blood Center, Mr. Race Gillette. If you're here to donate, our nurse is only available mornings." I brought up the shared calendar. "She's not here every morning, but if you'd like to make an appointment, she has an opening—"

"No!" Race Gillette waved hands like he was warding off an army of needles. "I'm not here to give blood."

Some of the biggest guys keeled over at the sight of a needle, seemingly contradictory, but there it was. I shrugged. "Is there some way I can help you, then?"

He shuffled a bit. Glanced at his arm. "I'm a friend of Nixie Emerson." He tipped his head like he was reading cribbed notes. "She said if I was in town I should look her up."

"Nixie's not in Meiers Corners right now. Guns and Polkas are on tour."

"'S'okay. She said I could talk to you." He looked up and saw me for the first time. Interest lit his eyes. "But she didn't tell me you were such a dollface."

I blinked. First, because *dollface* had dropped out of use in the last century. Second, though Nixie and I were friends, Elena was her best friend. "Me? Are you sure she didn't say Elena Strongwell?"

"Strongwell!" That panicked him more than the needle. "*No.* She said, 'Race, if I'm out of town, go see Liese, that cute little blonde at the Blood Center.'"

"That doesn't sound like her." Nixie was WYSIWYG to the bone (what you see is what you get). Her nickname for me was Cyberchick. She'd stab herself in the eye before calling anyone *cute.*

"I maybe didn't get all the words right." His fists hit hips. "But she said I should look you up."

"I thought you were supposed to look *her* up."

"I didn't...stop balling me up!"

Apparently Race had a bit of a fuse. "Sorry, Mr. Gillette."

"Whatever." He controlled himself with visible effort. "You done working? Let's go hit Nieman's Bar."

"You and me? I'm sorry, I have to—" stay here to let Logan in, to do his stupid interviews. Oh, yeah, it'd be nice to go drown my sorrows.

On the other hand, I might not have a job much longer. Maybe never again, considering my resume. I twisted my "diamond". "I'd like to, Mr. Gillette, but money's a little tight."

"Call me Race. My treat, dollface." He dug in his pocket, pulled out something round and red. "I'll let you push my Big Red Button." He waggled his eyebrows.

Language was just too dangerous to let some people use. "Um, no."

"C'mon, you can probably use the break. Things being tough now that Steel's shown up."

I jerked. "How did you know that?"

"I'm in the security biz too." Race smirked as he eased the BRB back into his pants. "I know all sorts of stuff. I know Steel's installing some big fancy system here. Using autoficial intelligence, so it's totally automatic."

"Autoficial...you mean *artificial* intelligence?"

"Whatever! It means no live humans needed." Race fired a malicious grin at me. "Whatever big words you use, *that* means you'll be out of a job. So I guess Nieman's sounds pretty good now, huh, dollface?"

Yeah, it did. I opened my mouth to agree—when he parked his butt on my desk. In a replay of Logan's arrival, Race leaned in so close I could feel his body heat on my face. I closed my eyes, imagining Logan's lazy drawl caressing me. *And what, my Red Delicious, does the L stand for?*

"So, dollface. Wanna go get a beer?"

My eyes flew open. Fleshy lips moved inches from mine. The breath that warmed me smelled of stale pennies. The ass that slid closer was bony, not buff.

I recoiled, sending my chair *bang* into the wall. Little bits of plaster poofed. "Love to, Race, but can't. I have to stay. Here. Right here. Work to finish up."

Race shot to his feet, posture stiff and distinctly threatening like he was about to turn nasty on me. He did have a temper.

But, grinding his teeth, he managed something that might have been a smile. "We'll hook up later." At the door, he turned. "I'll be at the bar if you change your mind."

After Race left I wavered between doing a lifetime's worth of work before Logan booted me out and doing absolutely fuckall for the man doing the booting. 'Cause Race had reminded me how this would play out. A case of blood was missing. I'd suffered enough politics at Andersly-Dogget to know the incoming genius had a six-month free pass to blame any and all problems on the previous fuckup (me). That the case really had gone missing on my watch only added to my misery.

I called Mom to vent but she was out shopping with Rolf's wife so I left a message and set my mood-timer. Five minutes later I put away my bad attitude but still had half an hour until Logan came so I pulled up Spider Solitaire, my latest addiction.

Sounds resonated around me as I played, normal blood center sounds. The hiss of my computer's fan. The drip of the old bathroom sink. The burr of the refrigeration units in back. The scrape of—scrape? That wasn't normal.

I got up to investigate.

The back room was a combination donation facility and storage area. Cheery wallpaper lined a nook with recliner on the north side. The south wall was filled with refrigerators. The scraping sound was coming from...below.

I got to my hands and knees to inspect the floor, carpet glued to bare concrete. Getting my nose right into the fuzzy threads, I could see where one corner had been peeled away. I tugged at it. It lifted easily.

Underneath was fresh concrete, still wet.

I sat back on my haunches, stunned. Had this been there all along? Well, obviously not, if it was still wet. But why?

Well, duh, Liese. To patch a hole.

Like between here and the sewer?

I followed that line of thought, didn't like where it led. Hole here. Gang guys below. Missing blood.

The connection was quite literal. There was a tunnel between.

And Logan—Logan had kept me from going farther into the sewer. Kept me from discovering the tunnel. He had gone to great lengths to do so, going even so far as to...seduce...me...hell.

He didn't want me so badly he couldn't help himself. It wasn't even to shut me up. Logan had slammed me into the male inferno of his muscular torso, had kissed the intelligence right out of me to *sidetrack* me.

Damn it, why did I have to figure it out? Why couldn't I be blissfully ignorant? Why couldn't I believe Logan wanted me because I smelled good or tasted good or even maybe because he really thought I was beautiful?

His attraction was nothing more than a sham. Another man seducing me for his own ends. I didn't know what those ends were but I knew the results. I'd lose my job—and gain more issues.

Logan had lied to me, big time. I quivered with anger, with justified rage. So when the donation room door opened and the man himself breezed in, all golden good-looks and muscular grace, I launched myself at him, nails scratching.

"How could you?" I screamed. Everything I knew about martial arts disappeared in a flood of despair—*anger.* In anger I pounded against the huge pads of his pecs. "How could you?"

"Liese, what's wrong?" His voice was warm with concern. "Sweetheart? Why are you crying?" He wrapped me in his hard, strong arms.

"I am not crying!" I shrieked, dashing at my wet cheeks. "I am tearing up with fury. With righteous indignation. Because you're a...a...a great big doody-head!"

"Of course, sweetheart," he crooned. "I'm the nastiest male there is. It's my fault, all of it. Shh, Liese, I've got you."

The last was because I was trembling and clutching him like he was a board floating from the Titanic. "How could you?" I was horrified when my voice broke piteously.

"How could I what, princess?" Logan held me tight, stroking my hair. And then his voice changed. "Oh."

He was staring at the upturned carpet. His hand continued to stroke me absently, but I could tell his brain was whirring. Thinking up a lie, no doubt. I trembled in his arms, waiting for him to lie to me.

"I was hoping you wouldn't see that." With a sigh, he released me. "Come sit down and I'll explain." He sauntered over to the donation bed and slid his perfect behind onto it. Patted the bed next to him.

I stared at him. He was being—reasonable?

"I won't bite."

"Are you sure?" My voice was rough.

"I won't bite right now," he said with a ghost of a smile.

The soft expression bemused me enough so that the gentle patting lured me to the recliner. Logan wrapped strong arms around me and pulled me onto his lap.

My butt fit him like we were interlocking puzzle pieces. I settled in almost automatically. His groin stirred. His eyes fired with sudden interest. I blinked in disbelief but my insides were already warming, melting—

"Mr. Steel! Are you here?" Zinnia Supermom, with impeccable timing. I groaned.

To my confusion, Logan groaned almost exactly the same way.

We exchanged a glance. My confusion grew. Logan was as dismayed by her as I was. Dismayed by his own wife?

And wouldn't a wife call him Logan? Unless Ms. Supermom was Ms. SuperProfessional as well. Wouldn't that just figure?

The door flew open. "Mr. Steel. There you are."

And here I was, doing a Plug-and-Play in her husband's lap. This would not end well.

Zinnia was digging in her purse and barely glanced at us. "I've organized the interviews for you, slotted in eight-minute increments with a two-minute break between." She whipped a sheaf of papers from an Elle purse the size of a cargo carrier. "Mr. Dodds is first. He's a little old, so you'll have to speak up, but I think he's worth considering. He's got at least ten good years left."

Instead of doing something sane like moving, Logan and I sat frozen in our embrace. I was depending on him for support. Strangely, I got the impression he was bracing himself against me just as hard.

Okay, maybe not wife but ex-wife, looking to get back into his life through the working relationship door. The Ghost of Wife Present or Past and hoping for Christmas Yet to Come. I couldn't believe the relationship was wholly innocent—after all, something had to explain those graceful, golden kids.

"In the second hour, Dr. Farah's the real find. A doctor in-house—oh, hello." Zinnia looked up from her papers. Her eyes landed on Logan's arms, tight around me. Wandered to my lips, puffy and red—from crying, but it probably looked like I'd been kissed real good.

I waited for the inevitable explosion.

Instead she shifted back to her papers. "Most are standard interviewees, except for two in upper management at their current companies. I can help you with those, given my executive secretarial background." She looked up and smiled.

Well, heck. If I wanted Logan and found another woman nestled in his lap—but he wasn't mine.

"This is your copy, Mr. Steel." Zinnia squared the papers and shoved them under his nose, or actually our noses. "Schedule times, names, some info on each person. Space for you to jot notes." I could see everything was clear and concise.

But when Zinnia pushed the papers toward Logan I heard that low warning growl.

Zinnia abruptly drew back. "Mr. Steel?"

I sighed. Just because she made me feel vulnerable didn't mean I had to act like a jerk. "Logan, take the papers." Reluctantly I added, "She did a good job organizing for you."

The growl stopped. He took a deep breath, slapped out a hand. "Fine."

Gingerly Zinnia shoved the papers into it. "Where are we holding the interviews?"

"Here," Logan snapped.

As Zinnia unstacked chairs a hesitant knock came from the connecting door. A gray head peeped through. "Excuse me. It's seven o'clock. I'm first, right?"

This must be the venerable Mr. Dodds, who had at least ten good years left. Time to extricate myself from Logan's embrace. At first he held on as if he didn't *want* to let me go. But he was going to have to, wasn't he? If only because it wouldn't look professional to the people he was hiring *to take my place.*

Issues on top of issues. They propelled me from the haven of his lap and I fled to the front office. I should have gone home but morbid curiosity drove me to see the kind of people he chose to interview. Yeah, that was it. Certainly I wasn't staying because Logan was in the next room and this might be my last chance to see him. Oh goody, another fricking issue.

Men and women trooped off the bus, their expressions a mixture of scared, hopeful and eager. Who could blame them?

In the current economy, even a bad job was better than no job, and Steel Security would be like winning the employment lottery. Heck, *I'd* want to work for Steel. I wondered, if I interviewed, whether Logan would hire me.

Assuming I could get on Zinnia's tight, well-organized schedule in the first place.

I tried to keep my hands busy. Some women knit. Some embroider. For me, it's a spool of cat-five and a crimper to make network cables, but tonight I couldn't seem to get it right. Either I cut the cable too short or too long, or I got a bad crimp and had to start over.

My cables got worse and worse as the interviewees got younger and lovelier, until they were *Girls of Spring Break* babes and I was trashing every other cable. Logan thought I was "beautiful", right. Compared to what, the women around when we first met? Even I could win Miss America against my old Dell.

I tossed another cable in the garbage. The tangled nest of failures reminded me of the state of my life and I wondered if things could get any worse.

Yeah, just strap me in black leather, put a ball gag on me and yell come-'n-get-it, Marquis de Sade.

A fairy in human skin glided in. She looked exactly like the character River Tam in *Firefly*, a slender brunette in the first blush of womanhood, an even bigger contrast to my well-fed curves than Zinnia. She made me feel like a cow.

Botcher would adore her. I wanted to puke.

"Is Mr. Steel here?" Her voice was soft, beguiling. *Arrgh*. It was so unfair. Couldn't she sound like a rusty gate, or have a tiny bit of cellulite?

I jerked my head toward the back which jerked my hand which twisted my crimp so bad the connectors looked like a second-grader's teeth. I flung the ruined cable into the garbage in total disgust. Two more cables hit the trash before the door reopened and sylph-girl glided back through.

From the back, Logan called, "Thank you for coming, Brianna. There are a limited number of spots open, but I'm sure we'll find you something."

Fairy-girl smiled. I punched the crimper so hard I broke the plastic.

Chapter Five

The phone rang. Oh, goody, another Meiers Corners crazy to distract me. "Blood Bank. Deposit or withdrawal?"

"Liese?" My mother, sounding doubtful. "Aren't you at work?"

Oops. Mom-wisdom #35 was on the importance of being sober and conscientious on the job. "It's not what you think. It's after hours and I was expecting Elena, and you know what a great kidder she is, ha-ha. Yeah. Why are you calling?"

"You left a message, sweetie."

"Oh. Well, you sound kind of tired, and we can talk tomorrow."

"I know that tone of voice, Liese. Something's wrong. Your job? Or a *man?*"

The greatest number of Mom-wisdoms had to do with men. Never date someone you wouldn't marry. Don't sell yourself cheap. No sex without a ring on your finger.

Until yesterday I had followed her advice. My fiancé was the first man to touch my breasts. Actually Botcher was the first man to even notice I had breasts, or any body parts other than a brain. And I'd loved him for it, idiot that I was. I blinked down at my huge worthless glass ring. "It's nothing."

As if she heard my thoughts, she said, "It's not that nasty Bernie Botcher, is it? I could kill that man for what he did to my little girl."

"Kill", to my mom, meant "lecture sternly". But it was a nice sentiment. "Thanks, Mom."

"He was the first man you loved, Liese. Naturally you were devastated. Say, I was shopping with Rolf's wife today and happened to read an article at the bookstore. Monogamy is a matter of genetics. Isn't that interesting? Physical intimacy equals love for some people. In fact, it's hardwired."

Wouldn't that explain an awful lot? I must have had a double helping of the M-gene because when I gave Botcher my virginity, I also gave him my heart. Even now he had a piece of it. A small, black, non-pumping piece, but he had it.

"When I read that I got angry at him all over again, leaving you standing at the altar." My mother's voice quivered.

Strictly speaking, the rat-bastard hadn't *left* me there. He never even bothered showing. See, I'd told him about my plan to save ADD a quarter million dollars. He stole my work and used it to gain his own promotion to head of IT. Then he fired me and married my replacement. And blacklisted me so I couldn't find another job.

But with all that, know what really ate at me? His little note, delivered at the church, telling me he hated having sex with me and could only get it up by doing double Viagras.

Yep, Black Saturday birthed several of my little issues.

"Don't worry, Mom. I know I can't trust men."

My mother only sighed.

"What's wrong? You *are* tired, aren't you?"

"A little. Cousin Rolf's wife can shop like a monster."

My problems were small beans compared to radiation. "I should let you rest. Good night, Mom. Love you."

"Love you too." With another sigh, she hung up.

I checked the clock. Still another couple hours of interviews. I tossed the crimper onto my desk, resolving to go. At that moment the back door opened and I heard Logan's deep murmur drift out. Oh, who was I kidding? I'd probably suffer through a marathon of odd-numbered Star Trek movies to see him one last time. What an ID-10-T I was.

A scruffy boy came in, the spitting image of an eight-year-old Opie Taylor, and started poking at the cables in the trash. "Whatcha doin'?"

I slumped into my chair. "Waiting for the interviews to be over."

"Me too. My dad's in there. He's a wrestler, stage name Thugs. What's your name?"

"Liese. Steel Security is hiring wrestlers?"

The boy snorted. "Nah. My dad's also a fixit man. I'm Billy Wilder. Are these wires for bombs?"

I smiled slightly. The boy was a potential scientist. We like blowing things up. "Cables for networking."

He eyed one critically. "You screwed up the crimps."

"Yeah." I swept the crimper into a drawer. As I did, Bud walked in, with Lilly and another little girl, a dark-skinned brunette maybe four years old, trotting behind. They were accompanied by a pretty black girl about Bud's age. Bud and the girl kept staring into each other's eyes like they were limpid pools and they wanted to dive in. Cute, at twelve or thirteen. It would be obnoxious at twenty-five.

"Ms. Schmetterling?" Bud addressed me but his dreamy attention was on his pretty friend. "May I take Angela and Lilly to use the potty?"

The girl gave him a sweet smile. "I'll take them." At my nod she steered both little girls into the small powder room.

I raised brows at Bud. "Girlfriend?"

Bud blushed. "Frieda and Angela are Mr. Dodd's grandnieces. As older sibs, Frieda and I have stuff in common."

"Itsy Bitsy Spider" echoed from the bathroom, a duet this time. I nodded. "Well, she's nice. I'm surprised so many interviewees brought their kids."

Bud touched his throat. "Steel Security is a family-oriented company."

"This is boring." Billy Wilder had dug a cable out of the trash and was stripping insulation with his teeth. "Are we gonna blow stuff up or not?"

Apparently I'd spent quite enough time being sorry for myself. Time to entertain the troops. "Mr. Steel might get a little peeved if we blow up his nice new computers. Let's see what else we can find." I dug a wire stripper and roll of electrical tape from my purse, handed the stripper to Billy and tossed the tape onto my desk.

The front door swung open. I braced myself for another beautiful girl but the one who entered was an eight-year-old going on forty. Her sparkly little pink backpack was decorated with the face of William Shakespeare. She planted herself in front of my desk with all the assurance of a born commander. "I have to urinate. Where's the bathroom?"

Bud hid a smile. "Ms. Schmetterling, this is Jane Austen Smith. Her mother's an English professor."

"Never would've guessed." Logan's interviewees were getting stranger by the minute. "The bathroom's over there, but it's in use right now."

"I'll wait." Jane plopped herself in a guest chair, pointed at the desk. "Is that non-conductive adhesive material?"

"Electrical tape, yes." Rooting in my bag past Carmex and key ring and a dozen drained batteries, I found my mini soldering iron. Well, that was always good for some fun. I set it and some solder next to the tape.

The door opened again. A thin, nervous-looking dishwater blonde skittered in, eyes on the floor. At least they weren't all Miss America contestants. She was holding a red-headed boy of about seven in front of her like a shield. She stopped at my desk. "Can Tad use the bathroom?" she whispered in my general direction. Still no eye contact.

"There's a line." I dug around, found more batteries, my sunscreen, two extra motherboards and a disposable camera. Now how the heck did that get in there?

She whispered, "A bucket, then? Tad had a little too much for dinner."

Tad's complexion did look a little green. "Um, I can look in a minute. Does he want to sit for now?" I indicated the other guest chair, nudging my wastebasket into position for quick speweous-interruptus.

"Yes, please." Tad slid gingerly into the chair. Before his mother could rabbit, Zinnia emerged from the back. "Mrs. Theodore, good. You're next." She latched onto Tad's mother and yanked her through the connecting door. Tad's mom may have whispered something about returning later.

Tad himself was looking distinctly green. I ransacked the stuff on my desk, decided I'd use the electrical tape on his mouth only in an emergency. That was when my eye lit on the camera.

I'd only seen it done on YouTube. But it might be interesting enough to take Billy Wilder's mind off blowing things up, take mine off the interviews, and maybe even take Tad's off barfing.

I picked out the camera and a couple six-inch lengths of wire. After pulling the battery, I disassembled the camera. While

64

I wrestled with the bulb, Bud's friend Frieda and the little girls emerged from the bathroom and wandered over to see what I was doing. I managed to remove the bulb without breaking the circuit board, then soldered the wires to the capacitor contacts. Gingerly I placed the battery in the circuit, then taped the hell out of everything (except the picture-taking button and the wires, obviously).

I held up the finished product. "Okay, guess what this is."

"A camera?" Tad's color was actually normal.

"Take my picture," Lilly chirped. Angela clapped her hands and bounced.

"It's not a camera anymore." I turned it so they could see that tape covered the aperture.

"A bomb?" Now Billy Wilder clapped his hands and bounced.

"It's a Taser."

All bouncing stopped. "Is not." Lilly pouted adorably. "It's a camera."

"Sweet," Frieda said. "Can I zap someone?"

Well. Another budding scientist. I was about to explain how the homemade Taser worked when the connecting door *whooshed* open and Zinnia bopped through. "Are you entertaining the children, Ms. Schmetterling? How nice. Something innocent and wholesome, of course."

"Of course." Blushing, I shoveled everything into my purse. "Interviews going well?"

"Wonderful, wonderful! But you children shouldn't take up Ms. Schmetterling's time. Back to the bus, now." As she shooed them out the next interviewee strode in. Zinnia fawned over the regal blonde, all Dr. Farah this and that. Farah was so beautiful and so obviously intelligent I wanted to puke.

Should have looked for that bucket. Or at least left out the electrical tape.

Five more cables, a totally unnecessary backup and ten games of Solitaire later all the interviewees had gone. I was thinking how beat I was even though I'd done nothing but crimp bad cables and play with kids when the connecting door *whooshed* open and Zinnia bopped through, fresh as a daisy. "You were absolutely amazing, Mr. Steel! What incredible interview technique. What patience!"

Logan glided out after her. Dark circles under his eyes spoke of something other than amazing for him. But even tired he was so disturbingly handsome he made me want to grab a blender between my thighs and push liquefy. Stupid female hormones.

He brightened when he saw me. "Liese. You stayed."

"It's only ten thirty. I like to give my employer good value."

"Mr. Steel?" The Zinnigizer Bunny flounced between us. "Why don't we go over the interview results? I have a preprinted table to list positives and negatives for each candidate. Then you can weigh the results—"

"Tomorrow, Zinnia." That firm tone was the CEO expecting instant compliance.

Apparently Zinnia's power meter wasn't as sensitive as mine. She plowed right on. "This list isn't going to get any fresher, Mr. Steel. Sooner started, sooner finished, as my Aunt Violet used to say. You only have until Monday to decide. 'Never put off until tomorrow what you can do today.' That was Grandpa Aster's motto."

Good grief. Zinnia, Bud and Lilly, and now Violet and Aster? Was there a whole garden of them?

"Zinnia. While normally I'd jump right on it—"

Even with all my worries, the image caught me. Two hundred pounds of muscular male, jumping right on it.

Zinnia caught it too. We both shuddered.

"—I have a previous engagement. With Ms. Schmetterling."

"But Mr. Steel—"

"Thank you for your help this evening, Zinnia. Good night." It was a clear dismissal.

"Oh." Zinnia got it this time. Her smile dimmed a few hundred watts and even her boobs seemed to sag. She trudged—*trudged*—to the door. There she turned. "Tomorrow, Mr. Steel?"

That's when Logan showed what made him an exceptional CEO. He demanded and received obedience, but he also knew how to solicit buy-in. "Tell you what, Zinnia. Why don't you start on the list yourself? Then give me a call."

I swear her breasts perked up. "After sunset, right?"

Such an odd way to phrase it. Logan, for some reason, flushed. "Er, right. Since I have meetings *all day*."

"Tomorrow night, then, Mr. Steel!" Zinnia bounded out the door.

It clanged shut. The sudden silence that followed made me aware I was now totally alone with Logan Steel.

Logan turned to me and I immediately saw we weren't going to talk about interviews or fresh concrete. His eyes had shot to flame-broil. I wheeled my chair backward out of habit. When my phone rang, I was grateful for the interruption. That's not contradictory. I wanted to see Logan one last time but I didn't want to actually deal with him. "I have to take this." I hit connect. "Blood Center."

"Hey, sugar," Dolly Barton greeted me. "I waited to call. Hate to break up a party."

As she spoke the bus roared away from the curb. "How do you know these things, Dolly?"

"Ways. But in this case it's because I'm next door and can see out the window. You missed your appointment, sugar. I hope you have a *good* reason."

"Shizzle." I forgot my appointment because it wasn't my usual trim but a free bikini waxing. Yeah, well, I'd won it in a sheepshead tournament and what self-respecting Meiers Corners resident turns down a freebie? Although being upset over Logan and the missing blood might have also contributed. Oh, and Zinnia, and the scraping, and the filled-in hole. And if I told Dolly even one of those things it would be MC Headlines at Ten. "It's just been so busy here."

"That's an excuse, not a reason. And not nearly good enough."

I cringed. "Er...what reason would be good enough?"

"Tall, blond and drop-dead handsome."

I stared in consternation at the phone, then scanned the room. Nope, Dolly hadn't installed surveillance, at least not that I could see. "Do you have a timeshare on a spy satellite?"

She laughed like I'd made a funny. I hadn't been joking. "Reschedule tomorrow at six?"

"Sure." I noted it in my calendar.

The instant I clicked off my headset Logan advanced purposefully on me. The gold flecks in his eyes were practically glowing now.

"Stop. This is way too dangerous." I jumped out of my chair, backed toward the wall. Botcher had burned sixteen months and all my savings. Movie-star gorgeous Logan would incinerate me. Sizzling hot, with his molten gold eyes and bright blond hair...maybe just a little taste of those luscious lips...maybe getting incinerated wouldn't hurt...much... *What am I thinking?*

I clutched my glass ring, erected an image of Botcher like a shield. "I said *stop.*" I thudded into the wall.

Logan arrested my ring-worrying with a gentle hand. "I thought you liked this." Snagging my chin with a forefinger, he raised my head for a Logan Special—soft kiss with a brush of heat. "And this." He kissed me again, lingering over it. "And this." He added a dollop of clever tongue.

Botcher shields dropped to forty percent. "*Arrgh!*" I tore away, ran to the other side of the room, all of two feet away. "What is it with you? Are you out to blast every brain cell I have?"

"Defensive fire, Liese. After all, you gun me down." He stalked me with that limber glide that made him look like a hunting cat. *Squeak.* "Your kiss is explosive, princess. TNT—tongue 'n torture. And only you detonate me. We're dynamite together."

I couldn't help it. I laughed. "How can you possibly be a brilliant Fortune-500 CEO? Those are the worst puns in the world."

"I know." He caught me, and soundly kissed my laughing mouth.

Have you ever been kissed while laughing? Happy endorphins bubble up like champagne. Lips are moist. Blood flows warm and fizzy. Wellbeing floods your system. Any shred of sanity flies instantly out the window.

Shields were gone, Captain.

The instant Logan touched me he knew. "Fuck, Liese. You're so ready—treasure for the taking. Prepare to be boarded, princess." One hand captured my face and he breached my pitiful defenses with a devouring kiss.

His tongue invaded me, stole my breath. His mouth overwhelmed me, his heat fierce and unyielding. Fingers slid into my hair to anchor my head for an even deeper kiss. When I moaned and tried to evade his plundering, his arm wrapped around me and yanked me tight into his muscular body. He seized my bottom, cupping and fondling. I arched helplessly into him, banging up against his pirate's prow, and it was a monster.

My brain overheated. My hips rocked of their own accord, my mons rubbing against his bulging fly. Logan growled, seized my butt in both hands and jacked me onto his hips. Whirling, he planted my back on my desk, fell on top of me. His weight was a mountain of force, pressing me into a lusty diamond. I writhed, trapped between hard wood and granite muscle.

He nuzzled me, his mouth hot on my neck. Sharp little nips sent shocks of delight zinging through me. A rumbling filled my ears, a deep purr that buzzed my belly and drummed against my chest like a vibrator.

Logan rolled his hips, pumping his ballooning fly against me. Hard denim rubbed my tender mound. Desire shot to a new level, liquid heat pooling in my pelvis. I arched into his heavy body. He ground into me, friction sparking. I was on the verge of igniting when his sharp teeth scraped over my throat, pressed into my pulse. I wriggled under him, at the very edge of something deliriously lovely.

He shifted just enough to unsnap and unzip my pants. "I want you so badly, princess. I've got to taste you. Say yes."

I've got to taste you. He'd used that strange phrase before, but what did I know of a lover's murmurs? Maybe it was a code phrase for oral sex. My own voice wouldn't work. I rocked my hips into him, the only way I could reply.

His tongue licked fire over my throat. "You've got to say it, Liese." He drove a hand into my pants.

Onto my clit.

I nearly shot through the roof. "Yes! Oh, Logan, yes." I caught his muscular shoulders, pumped against his hand. It wouldn't be long now. Another two, three minutes—

Logan bit me.

I arched so hard both my butt and head hit the desk. Lightning zapped me from throat to belly. Hot, jagged bolts tore into me, too fierce to be mere pleasure. No, I detonated. Every cell in my body combusted. I didn't climax, I exploded.

As pieces of reality gradually filtered into my buzzing brain I felt a rumble thumping against my chest and a tongue lapping my throat. A huge bulge pulsed against my vulva.

Logan was licking my neck. Botcher wanted to slam home at the first sign of moisture. What was Logan waiting for? The orgasm left me as wet as a monsoon. Was he trying for Noah's flood?

Although, with the size of Logan's submarine, flood might be good. Monsoon, flood, submarine. I closed my eyes, wondering if bad puns were a disease and I'd been infected by Typhoid Logan.

Or a very aroused Typh*oon* Logan, nuzzling me frenetically, not so much licking my neck as devouring it. "You taste even better than I dreamed, Liese. Like moonlight. Like soft summer breezes."

"Moonlight has taste?"

"Mmm."

Absently, I touched my neck, maybe to taste my skin and see what sex drug Logan was on. It would make a mint on the Internet.

My fingers came back red. I jacked up.

Logan fell back, his hand slapping over his mouth. His eyes were twin rubies.

We stared at each other. My fingers unconsciously wandered back toward my neck. Logan's red eyes followed them. I touched—wet. Sticky wet, like blood. On my neck. Like a vam...

In one step Logan was on top of me. He snared my wrist, used it to pull me against him. His head descended toward my throat.

"No!" I tugged, but it was useless. He grabbed my shoulders and immobilized me with a shockingly strong grip. Not simply male-strong but unstoppable-strong. *Inhumanly* strong. I struggled futilely as his head descended.

His tongue swiped across my throat, warm and gentle. Two swipes, three. He released me.

I wound up and slapped him good. The crack was loud enough to echo. "What the hell was that?" I yelled. "I don't know what Zinnia lets you get away with, but I'm not into kinky!"

His ruby eyes faded to a puzzled hazel. "Zinnia?"

I flushed. "You can't just waltz in here and try to seduce me and then start with that kinky stuff."

"Liese." His cheek was blossoming with a red hand-print. It

must have hurt like the dickens, but all he said was, "What does Zinnia have to do with it?"

"Nothing!" I laughed. It came out hysterical. I hopped off the desk, jerking at the feel of wet denim between my legs. "Absolutely nothin—what's that racket?"

Logan snared his cell out of his jeans pocket. The emerging ringtone sounded like the Chicago Symphony brass, so loud I covered my ears. He snapped it open and slapped it to his cheek. "What." A moment and his expression eased. "Good. I'll finish from here."

"Finish what?" I asked.

"That was my project leader." Logan snapped the phone shut. "The grid is connected, ready to go online."

I swallowed. "That was quick."

"Yes. I had them rush it."

"Oh." I tried not to feel threatened. Tried not to imagine the worst just because I felt vulnerable with Logan. He had them rush it. It didn't mean he had them rush it to get out of here and into Zinnia's slim, perfectly manicured clutches sooner.

"Because of the hole."

My eyes rose to his. The sexual heat in his gaze wasn't gone exactly, but had been gentled by sympathy. Vulnerable? Try completely defenseless. I crossed my arms, as if they could protect me from the warmth of his expression. "Yes, that hole. You were going to tell me about it?"

"Liese. I know you're hurting—although I'm not sure why."

My arms tightened automatically. Despite my Botcher shields, Logan had ravaged me to within an inch of screaming "Jump on bareback, cowboy, I'm a wild filly." Frankly that scared the silicon out of me but I wasn't going to admit it, especially since his quick brain had probably already figured it out. Bad enough he could make me helpless with sex. Logan smug would be overkill. "I'm *annoyed.* You knew about that hole. How?"

"I wish you'd tell me who injured you. You can trust me, sweetheart."

"Isn't that easy to say." My arms cinched so tight I cut off circulation to my hands. I let up slightly. "You want me to trust you, start by telling the truth about the hole in my Blood...in the Blood Center's floor."

"*Easy to say?*" Logan's eyes turned inward. "Yes, of course. You want me to *earn* your trust. Natural enough." He hit me with a smile so brilliant I nearly flash-fried. "I originally filled the hole in."

My mouth dropped open. He was actually telling me? No, it couldn't be this easy. "And when was this, exactly? You just arrived in town yesterday."

"I was here during the Festival. Razor's gang was causing trouble. We tried to keep it quiet because we didn't want to scare the tourists."

I dropped my arms. "Razor was trying to break into the Blood Center back in November?"

"And his gang."

"Oh, right. The Li'l Shavers."

Logan's smile quirked into a grin. He leaned against the wall, all negligent strength. "They weren't very sharp. It was easy to cut them down to size."

How did this powerful CEO morph so quickly into the mischievous boy? "So you personally *whiskered* in and *scraped* together the alarm system?"

Logan blushed slightly. "Er, no. I also head a...security force, I guess you'd call it."

His reaction confused me. "A division of Steel Security?"

"Civic sector, actually." Logan shrugged, a jerk rather than his usual smooth play of muscle. "Kind of a neighborhood watch."

I felt the start of a smile, first one in what felt like years. Logan Steel, corporate prince and indolent playboy, did charitable work. *And it embarrassed him.* Too cute.

And too good an opportunity to pass up. "That was *nice* of you."

"Not nice." He grumbled it.

Served him right. "Sure it was. And sweet. And cute. And—"

"All right, I'm sorry, okay? I'm sorry I ever called you nice. Now do you want to know about the hole or not?"

Actually, no. I wanted to tease him. It startled me. Logan Steel was going to take my job, deprive my mom of health insurance and leave me with a nuclear winter of doctor bills. And I wanted to tease him. Fit me with a paper gown for Nurse

Ratched, I'd gone insane. "Yeah, the hole. It was first dug in November?"

"Yes. I filled it in and patched the floor. I thought that was the end of it."

"But Razor dug it out again." And stole a case of blood. "He came in through the sewer, redug the hole and—you said it was mannequins. You *lied*."

Logan winced. "I'm sorry, princess, but I didn't want you to worry."

"Howling wolves was so much better?"

"Well, yes. Better than you worrying Razor had—past tense—direct access."

"But doesn't the timing concern you? Nothing since November, then wham, this Razor redigs the tunnel the week you put in new security?"

"Damn, you're sharp. Yes, that's another reason I rushed it. To make sure Razor stays out." Logan reached for me, stopped himself. Touched his red cheek and smiled a bit ruefully. "I was concerned for you."

Warmth suffused me. He'd fibbed, but then he'd come clean. I could almost trust him...except Botcher had lied and come clean too. This felt different, but I wasn't sure how. Maybe because Botcher had 'fessed up out of spite but Logan had done it out of lov—niceness. "That explains the scraping I heard earlier this evening. Apparently they didn't know you'd repatched—"

The first few bars of *Also Sprach Zarathustra* cut me off. Logan snapped out the cell just as the heavens opened and the brass and tympani exploded.

"Geez. Is that a phone or a home theater system?"

Logan grinned. "What can I say? I run a security shop. I have to keep up with technology."

"Or you have the latest toys to stay alpha geek."

"That too. Steel." Almost immediately Logan's tone moderated. "Yes, sir."

His tone was filled with respect, like he was speaking to an esteemed superior. But Logan was a prince of business. Nobody outranked him.

"Yes, Mr. Elias."

Ah, yes. I'd heard of Elias, president of Steel Security's

board of directors. Not so much a superior as a guiding light.

"A few new items on Project Shield, sir. The enemy is still unidentified but he's definitely a member of the coterie. And we've discovered that his target is a major Chicago landmark."

That didn't sound good. An enemy with a target sounded like grand theft. Maybe even terrorist, which made me think bomb which made me worry the major landmark might be the Sears Tower. Well, the Willis Tower now, but still a hundred and eight stories of vulnerable squishy people.

I would have asked what was going on but Logan took a sharp breath.

"You've set a deadline for Project Center? That explains your sending the bus of interviewees." His face paled. "Yes, Mr. Elias, I understand. Monday. One week to finish the job. No problem, sir."

The job. Called Project Center...taking over the Blood Center.

And eliminating me.

I might have doubted my conclusions but Logan was all business after that. Remote, almost cold. No more kisses, no more instant orgasms. I was glad of that. No, really.

He showed me how to arm the grid, which was monitored by the police 24/7. We'd had a perimeter system before, but this one also did ceiling, floor and twenty feet around the building. Motion detectors, pressure-sensitive plates, the whole thing ran on a computer no bigger than a trade paperback. The comparatively massive blade chassis parking in my Dell was the artificial intelligence.

Logan delivered the information like a lecture, automatic and impersonal. And without meeting my eyes once. "Tomorrow my people will configure the AI."

AI, the machine brains that would make my mere human one obsolete. After which, Logan need only replace my even-less-attractive body with Ms. Soccer-Mom or the nubile sylph Brianna. "Wonderful. By the way, Nixie called." My voice thankfully only sounded a tenth as frozen as I felt. "She had a message for you."

"A message." Instantly Logan stilled. He turned to me, not just his eyes but the entire focus of his being.

He knows something. Another secret. No surprise, but it

still hurt. Despite only having met him yesterday, despite knowing he wasn't mine, I had orgasmed with him. Apparently I thought that made us closer than we were. Damned monogamy gene. "Her tour's been extended another couple weeks. Julian's staying with her so you'll have to take some sort of negotiations. Friday, six-thirty—with Nosy, whoever that is."

Absolutely motionless now, Logan's attention was so fierce it hurt.

I cleared my throat, prompted, "Nosy. That's an odd name, isn't it?"

A dangerous, heavy silence underscored his stare. Just before I cracked and fled he eased his stance, deliberately, meticulously. "Oh, you know Nixie. Her crazy nicknames. Thanks for the message, Liese. Don't stay long."

Without further explanation, he left.

Chapter Six

I stood outside Nieman's Bar, shivering. The March night was cold, but my shakes weren't due to weather. Despite everything, I'd let Logan seduce me. If it hadn't been for my red fingers and imagining blood, followed by that phone call, I'd have spread my legs like a tablecloth and invited him to feast.

Apparently I had not learned my lesson with Botcher. It appalled me how easily Logan overcame my defenses. Like a stallion. A golden stallion, effortlessly jumping my de-fences. Ha-ha.

I groaned, covered my face with one hand. Not punny. Yet Logan's absurd sense of humor was part of his charm. Playful, innocent, almost childish. And it connected with me on that innocent, childish level.

I had to remember that Logan Steel was anything but a child. And what he did to my body was anything but innocent. Weird, kinky, yes (lapping at my neck—bloody or not—he definitely had some kind of vampire fetish going). Incredibly hot, but *so* not innocent.

And *so* like Botcher. Well, not the hot part. But the part where he seduced me, used me, and threw me away. Like sixteen months ago, but this time it wasn't only my bank balance on the line. This time my mother's life was at stake.

God, had it only been sixteen months? Mom had been living comfortably on her pension and my father's life insurance money. Then I'd crashed and she'd sold her house and moved to Chicago to support me. Her new mortgage was higher, her savings rapidly disappeared. We didn't worry, knowing I'd get a good job when I got back on my feet.

Botcher's blacklisting killed that hope. The cancer and

onslaught of medical bills wiped out the rest. It was only Elena's job recommendation that saved us.

Now I was the rock.

I had to remember this was a war. A nasty guerilla war, and I'd already taken devastating hits. Time to stop playing Ms. Nice SysOp.

Time to find allies.

Race Gillette was in the security industry and knew Logan. Race might have information I could use—like whether Logan had a flower fixation and had planted any zinnias in his bed. Garden analogies aside, Zinnia was still probably going to get my job.

I pushed inside the bar, saw Race sitting at a table with his arm slung around a scantily clad young woman. Her halter was two triangles designed by Edward Scissorhands, her leather skirt so short it looked like a belt. Six-inch platform shoes and a dumpster-load of bling completed an ensemble that said ten bucks a blow even to my untutored eye.

Well. Yet another male dumping me for someone sexier. Strangely, I felt relieved. I turned to go.

"Hey, dollface! C'mon." Race was waving at me.

WWMMD? Without even an inkling what Miss Manners would have done, I went over. Race swatted the woman's behind. "Go get us 'nother pitcher, honeypot." He let out a loud belch.

Her acid glare as she flounced off (displaying impressive balance on those skyscraper Fuck-Me pumps) told me "honeypot" didn't mean quite the same thing as "sweetheart" or even "princess". I hesitated. "I don't want to interrupt."

"The more the marrying." Race hiccupped.

"The more the...isn't it 'merrier'?"

"Whatever. C'mon, have a seat." He thumped the chair on his other side.

I nodded in the direction of Lady FMP. "Won't your girlfriend mind?"

"Nah. I'm a playa. She may get a little pissy, but she'll come back for my shweet...sweet lovin'." He tossed back his beer.

This guy, a playa? A stud with a lady in every port? Or two or three, like Logan? I gritted my teeth. I didn't care how many ports Logan sailed into. Or even how big his schooner was.

Honeypot returned, slapped the tray down and splashed out three beers. Yeah, Race would have to do some extra-sweet lovin' tonight. I was amazed he didn't pop holes from the barbs she was giving off—and she was shooting just as many at me.

Race took a deep draft of his refilled beer, set it down with a slosh. "So Liesh...Liese. How good do you know Sht...Steel?" The slop and slurs told me it wasn't his first beer of the night, or even his fifth.

"I only met him yesterday." Sunday. Was that all it had been?

"Not how *long*. How good."

In the Biblical sense, I knew him almost as well as my ex. And it had taken Botcher half a year to get as far as Logan had gotten in one day. "He's CEO of Steel Security, Fortune 500—"

Race slammed a fist into the table. "Everybody knowsh that."

I jumped and slewed a quick glance at Honeypot, but if Race was abusive, she wasn't worried. She was chugging her beer, drained it in four seconds flat. Impressive.

"Logan Sht...*Steel* is a crook." Race thumped a meaty finger on the table in front of me. "He says I owe him money. Says he won it fair and square, but he's a liar. And a *swaddler.*"

"You mean swindler?" Under his anger I heard a hint of fear.

"What*ever*!" Race gave an irritated poke at my glass. "Dirnk...drink your beer."

I took a sip. A pleasant warmth hit my stomach. "How did Steel win your money?"

"He didn't win it. He *stole* it." More table smacking, but this time I heard the fear clearly. Saw the helplessness lurking in his eyes. "Shome German card game. M'boss floated me half so now I gotta repay him too."

"Half? How much did you lose?"

Race's face reddened. "Drunk y'r brew. Frien's don't let frien's drunk alone."

"I don't think that's the way it goes—"

"*Drunk!*"

Well, that was rude. I would have said buh-bye and left him to his roar except for my hope that he might have more info on Logan. Shrugging, I drank. A pleasant feeling bubbled to my head. "So Steel stealed your money?" I laughed. "Steel, steal. Get it?"

Race stared at me. I guess he didn't get it.

"Baby, I'm bored." Honeypot draped herself over Race's shoulder. "Yeah? I got something you can play with."

When Honeypot slid off her chair to the floor, I jumped to my feet. "Did she just pass out?"

A smile spread slowly on Race's face. He didn't answer.

"She might be sick. We have to do something!" I fumbled for my phone, ready to dial nine-one-one, and stuck my head under the table.

And sprang back up, cheeks burning. Apparently there were other uses for a beer-chugging open throat.

"Peepshed pro'ly isn't even a real game."

I gaped at Race. He was speaking through that? When Logan just touched me I couldn't form coherent words. If he were to put his mouth between my legs, heat me with his breath, stimulate me with his clever tongue...I shuddered. Even the *thought* made me speechless.

"Why sh'ud I hafta pay? He's the golden boy. Has all the money, gets all the honeys. 'n now m'boss says get the cash or I lose my job. You gotta do somethin'."

The last was aimed at me. My gape became a gawp. "*I* do? Why me?"

"You wanna lose *your* job? No, you gotta hit Shteel before he—oh, yeah." Race's eyes crossed. "Yeah, baby, like that. Don't worry, dollface. We got your back."

"What? Who's *we*?"

"My boss. He's shmart. And rootless. Oh, yeah."

Ruthless, my mind supplied.

"And pow'rful. He can protect you from Steel. He's one of th' most pow'rful execrables in Chicago."

I guessed he meant *executives*. "But Race, what do you want *me* to do—"

"Hey, sugar daddy."

A young woman tottered toward Race on five-inch platform stilettos. She wore a short fur jacket and shorter skirt. From that and her mason-applied makeup, I guessed she was a hooker. From the Meiers Corners Fighting Dachshund tattoo on her cleavage, I guessed she was one of our homegrown part-timers.

"Hey, shweetie pie." Race's eyes were still crossed. I wondered how he recognized her.

"Who's this?" Seeing me, Shweetie Pie's expression turned distinctly hostile.

Not again. I gave her a huge smile, checking exit routes from the corner of my eye.

Fortunately Honeypot's head popped up over the table, kind of like a sock puppet. She frowned at Shweetie Pie. "Who are you?"

Shweetie Pie's glare swung to her. "Who the hell are *you*?"

"*I'm* his girlfriend." Honeypot shot to her feet.

"Yeah? Well, I'm his *new* girlfriend." Shweetie Pie seized Race's arm.

"I'm his *better* girlfriend." Honeypot grabbed his other arm.

"Girls!" Race laughed. "There's plenty Mac Daddy to go around. My shtubble...stable's got lots of room. You all my bitches."

Sudden silence.

Then Shweetie Pie slapped him so hard his head nearly did a Linda Blair. With a hair-toss, she stalked away. Honeypot and I watched her go.

Race touched his cheek. "The bizatch. At least my honeypot knows who's boss."

Smiling sweetly, Honeypot took the pitcher, topped off his beer. She lifted the glass to his lips. He puckered.

She dumped the beer over his head. While he sputtered, she slapped his other cheek. Beer droplets flew. She followed Shweetie Pie out, her stalk only slightly wobbly.

I finished my beer and rose. "Thanks for the chat, Race."

And because I needed to keep in practice for Logan, I slapped him too.

I tossed and turned that night. Race Gillette unfortunately had a point. Logan was a very dangerous man.

Although I wondered about the "man" part.

Race wanted me to do something about Logan. I couldn't just for myself, being barely able to raise a hand in my own defense. Yes, I run in where even stupid angels fear to fly, but only when someone else is in danger. Self-preservation? Wasn't in my command set, which was why Botcher had rolled all over me. Logan, with his muscular body, would steamroller me flat...with diamond-hard climaxes... *Focus.* Race's livelihood was threatened just like mine.

No one at ADD had stood up for me when Botcher had fired me. Race was an ass, yes. But when it came to one's livelihood, nobody should have to stand alone.

So. Race's livelihood and my mother's very life depended on me keeping this job. Not for me, but for them—I would get rid of Logan Steel.

But how? My options were limited. I'd sparred enough with Mr. Miyagi to know that in a frontal attack (ooh, Logan's powerful front—no, not going there) he'd beat me hands down (putting my hands down his front...*argh*). I'd have to strike first and hardest. Nasty and underhanded, but when fighting a much stronger opponent it was the only way.

An idea came through that long, sleepless night. I needed a concentrated charge. A quick, sharp offensive aimed at the three people powerful enough to eliminate the threat of a golden prince.

A knight. My boss Chief Dirkson, Executive Director of the Blood Center.

A queen. Dolly Barton, whose gossip network made the National Enquirer look like a grade school newsletter.

And a king. Mr. Elias, chairman of the Steel Security board of directors.

Tuesday morning I rose before the sun, showered and dressed with care for battle. My armor? My prettiest dress, silky pink with a billowy skirt and an empire waist. Softly clinging to my generous curves, it made me feel powerful, sexy. As I walked to the Blood Center, the skirt swirled deliciously around my legs. My courage ratcheted up a notch with every step I took. By the time I got to work, I was ready.

Cup of coffee in one hand, mouse in the other, I sat at my desk and waged all-out war. My ammunition? A picture. But not just any picture. The scene was the hottest I could find from FuckMeDungeon.com, two guys powering into a racked and handcuffed gal. Pretty torrid stuff. The guys were riding her like bronco busters.

One guy was decently toned. The other was pudgy with a

corset and bad toupee. He looked vaguely familiar, like every seedy porn star from the seventies. I spliced Logan's face (I blush to admit I'd snared one on my cell) onto the better-built of the two.

I have to say, the composite picture was good. The blend was seamless. You'd never have known it wasn't real unless you'd seen Logan's body. Then it was obvious, wasn't it? The Dungeon man was built, no doubt. A Porsche. But Logan was a Lamborghini.

Shizzle, even thinking about Logan made my engine rev. I *had* to get him out of my life, as quickly as possible, before I got idiot ideas about him and me, together. In Meiers Corners. In my bed.

Before I started seriously thinking of trying to make Logan stay.

I stared at the picture. Handcuffs would work for that.

No, no! I wanted Logan Steel out, out, *out*. And in. And out and in and...*grrr*. Clenching my jaw so tight I felt teeth break, I typed up the email. Attached the scandalous picture.

Paused with my pointer over "send". Could I really do this?

Logan would be removed from his position. Not fired. Nobody could fire a man—maybe a man—like Logan. But negative pressure would make him quit. He might never find another job, never hold his head up again. He'd be ruined, like I was before Elena rescued me. My hand slid away from the mouse. It was dirty and underhanded, and made me just a little sick.

But if I didn't do it, what would happen to my mother? To Race Gillette? I put my hand on the mouse and steeled myself to click "send".

And hesitated again.

Pop! A tiny woman appeared on my shoulder. Dressed in a slinky red gown, she looked suspiciously like devilish Elizabeth Hurley in *Bedazzled* (but with my face).

"Do it," she said. "It's a preemptive strike. Get that man before he can get you."

I frowned at her. "Who are you?"

She rolled her eyes. "Small imaginary creature? Like you, but with really great clothes? Guess."

"Um...Bad Liese?"

She clapped, sarcasm obvious. "You're not as dumb as you look. Destroy that man, Liese. While you still can."

"That man is named Logan," I said. "And I'm not quite sure he's a man—"

"Who the fuck cares? Look. If Botcher is an inch of dangerous, Steel is a couple hundred miles of death. If you don't take him out now, you won't get another chance."

"Nooo, it would be wrong." Another little Liese popped up on my other shoulder. She wore a pink ruffled pinafore over a blue-and-yellow gingham dress, no fashion sense whatever. "If you do this, you'll be no better than Botcher."

I blinked at her. "You're Good Liese?" I wondered if I was totally sane. "Why are you guys here? I've never hallucinated Mini-me twins before."

"Don't you know your imaginary creatures clause? Honestly." Good Liese tapped her tiny patent-leather shod foot. "In the event of a life-altering decision, the party of the first part—"

"That's you," Bad Liese said.

"Will be visited by the parties of the second part who shall, in turn, be either a bipartite personification of conscience or a tripartite phantom apparition—"

"That's kind of hard to understand," I said. "With all the parties and parts and such."

Good Liese heaved a put-upon sigh. "Please don't interrupt."

Bad Liese whacked me on the ear, much more direct. "For shit's sake. Look. It comes down to this. You get ghosts, or you get us. Scrooge got ghosts. You get us."

"Oh. Okay. All clear."

"Can we continue now?" At my nod, Good Liese cleared her throat. "Nooo, it would be wrong. If you do this, you will be no better than Botcher."

"But Logan *lied* to me," I said. "Just like that rat-bastard. Logan called the Blood Center *my* place. Why would he say that, if he weren't coming to stay?"

"He told you he isn't here to put you out of a job," Good Liese said.

"Obviously he lied about that too."

"Just like your ex." Bad Liese chortled from my shoulder.

"Botcher lied when he called you beautiful. He lied to get your position. And if that wasn't enough, he lied to get you blacklisted from any reputable firm in the entire Midwest."

I shuddered. "Thanks for reminding me, little Miss Exposition."

Good Liese shook a tiny finger at me. "Logan Steel is not cut from the same rotten cloth as Bernie Botcher. You must trust him."

"No, you have to eliminate him."

"No, you—"

I threw up my hands. "Look, this decision is hard enough. Your kibitzing isn't helping any."

They shot each other a look around my neck. But the bipartite personification of conscience, a.k.a. the gruesome twosome, took the hint and popped out.

Alone again, I took hold of the mouse. My pointer hovered over "send". My finger itched with indecision but I was leaning toward Bad Liese. Logan Steel was definitely dangerous. Yet…he called me beautiful and seemed to mean it. And he was so adorable with his puns. Did I have the right to ruin him?

"Do it," Bad Liese said. "Push send."

"*Nooo*, it would be wrong," Good Liese whined.

"I thought you guys were gone," I said.

"Don't do this," Good Liese said. "You'll never forgive yourself. You will remember it as the lowest point of your life. You know it's—"

"Wrong, yeah." The annoying thing was, she was correct. I always thought Black Saturday was the worst day of my life. But if I ruined Logan, I'd feel worse.

On the other hand, at least I'd still have a job. Mom would have her treatments. I could probably stomach a lot of guilt with a healthy mom and a regular paycheck.

My hand wavered between send and cancel.

"Penny for your thoughts," came a deep, masculine drawl.

I jumped, accidentally popping the "send" button.

Well. Decision made.

"Liese? What's wrong? You've gone white." Logan stood before me in all his muscular male glory. Just past him a limo sat at the curb, lit by the streetlamp. Though it seemed like hours, only minutes had passed. It was still dark out.

"Nothing's wrong. Nothing at all." Frantically, I minimized the telltale photoshopped picture. "I, um, thought you had appointments all day." I smiled, felt my upper lip tremble.

"Actually, that's why I'm here. Change in plans, I've got to go to Chicago. ADD's having some internal problems. Missing cash."

"Oh good, good."

He gave me a strange look before continuing. "They want to beef up their security. Bo's chauffeur is waiting for me but I have to explain a few things to you before I go."

Which meant Logan was going to be here for a bit. "Fine, fine." I pushed and held my laptop's power button. The system whined as it shut down. My hard disk was going to be so fragmented—matching my life about now. "What do you need to explain?"

"AI installation, remember?" Logan leaned on my desk, whispered in my ear, "Unless you have another installation you'd like me to tackle. I've got the latest hardware. You'd be very satisfied." His purring breath tickled my earlobe. "Mmm. You smell divine."

I swallowed a sudden influx of saliva, nearly choked. "You have to leave soon. Shouldn't we get busy? I mean to work? I mean..." I hopped to my feet. "AI?"

Logan's eyes did a pogo-stick scan of me, and a grin spread across his face.

Ah, yes, the sexy pink dress, donned to give me courage. In the reflection of Logan's hungry gaze it now felt like table linen at a Liese buffet. I shifted awkwardly in my sparkly pink sandals. The matching pink lace undies were dampening rapidly. His nostrils flared as if he could smell it, and his smile turned distinctly predatory.

This time I did choke. "Work." I coughed. "Right. We'd better get to it."

"Get to *it*?" Logan rounded my desk sinuously, winding like a cat. I was definitely feeling all dinner-ish. Only it was barely breakfast time. Maybe brunch-ish. Or brunchy. Whatever.

"Yes—I mean *no*." I backed away. "I mean, get to *work*." The feeling of being consumed wasn't helped by Logan licking his well-shaped lips. I backed away. "Work, you know. Just do it."

Logan's eyes flared instantly red-hot. "*Do* it?" He bared his teeth, white and sharp, his canines particularly pronounced. He stalked me into a set of flat filing cabinets.

I squeaked, trembling between cold hard steel and hot hard Steel. My lips parted on a gasp and in that instant Logan's mouth claimed mine.

His kiss was hungry, deep and driving, like he wanted to eat me to my toes. Fire swept my body, melting bones and muscles. I wrapped my arms around his neck to save myself from liquefying into a puddle of 10W-Liese at his feet. My breasts rasped against the thrust of his chest, my nipples cinched at the scorching heat. He grabbed my breasts two-handed, long fingers seizing the hard nubs and pinching them like vises. Lightning bolts of need streaked through me. My respiration shot into overdrive. I swallowed a cry and arched into his palms. His fingers clamped harder. I shrieked.

Strong hands cupped, pressed and rubbed. Need shuddered through me. Desire spiked hot in my belly. When I groaned, he pinched harder.

I whimpered. Still pinching me into oblivion, he started kissing his way down my throat. His kisses pooled on my cleavage, bared by the pink neckline. His tongue heated a trail of need along my exposed flesh.

My breath came faster. Last time my bra hadn't stopped him, but surely he couldn't suckle me through both bra and dress? Maybe he'd unzip the dress first but then he'd have to stop grinding me into the filing cabinet.

While I was distracted by logistics, Logan slipped his clever fingers under both bodice and bra and, with a single yank, stripped me naked to the waist.

My breasts tightened at the cool rush of air. My eyes snapped wide open. His flared bright red. "Gorgeous." With a purely male growl of satisfaction, he bent and latched onto one nipple. I threw back my head and moaned.

Logan suckled me until the hot tugging drove me insane. I writhed against him, pushed my breast into his mouth, mutely pleading for more. Then not so mutely. "Oh, Logan, please, I—"

"Und *vat* ist goink on here?"

I jerked, clanged into the file cabinet. The rough, accusing voice was an alto, if grizzlies had choirs.

Logan grabbed my arms in a steadying grip. "Breathe," he murmured. When I nodded he raised his hands and stepped back, fingers loose. Keeping his body a shield between me and the newcomer, he turned. Behind him I pulled up bra and bodice. When I was decent I peeped around his broad back.

Glaring at us was a Valkyrie crossed with a polar bear, her small beady eyes loaded with censure. I took a fortifying breath. "Hello, Nurse Battle."

Our part-time RN was two hundred fifty pounds of stone-crushing maternal warmth. A mother hen, if hens worked for the KGB. When I was learning names at the Center my mnemonic for her was Battleax. Someday I would slip and call her that out loud, no doubt making an amusing epitaph for my headstone.

She put hands on hips, three hatchet handles apart. "And what are you doing? I hope you are not—*making out?*" She said 'vat' and 'doink' and 'may-kink out'. Her accent was more German than a native's, thick and hard to understand.

Her expression was unfortunately quite clear.

"We weren't doink...I mean *doing* anything, Nurse Battlea—Battle." I smiled weakly.

"Liese got some dirt in her eye," Logan said, smoother than cream. "I was trying to get it out."

"Some dirt, so?" Battleax reached into an apron pocket. I think she shopped at the Mary Poppins Survivalist Store—the apron was white, frilly and stuffed with the instruments of Armageddon. She extracted a yards-long needle and aimed it at me. "Let me see."

"No! I mean...the dirt's out now. Logan...er, Mr. Steel got it out."

"*Ja?* This is so?" She turned the needle on Logan.

"Absolutely," Logan said without a flicker of fear. Damn, he was good.

A new gleam entered her beady eyes. "You are Mr. Logan Steel? Security consultant?" At Logan's shrug, she smiled a bear-trap of teeth. "*Gut.* The Executive Director told me you are coming here."

"Did he? Well I'm flattered—" Logan broke off when Nurse Battle grabbed his wrist with one ham hand.

"You will be getting employee physical," Battleax said with obvious relish. "Come." She tried to drag him toward the back room, leaning into it like an ox. She had at least twenty pounds

Mary Hughes

on him but he didn't move.

"I hate to point this out, dear lady, but I'm not an employee of the Blood Center."

"You are working here. There must be no contamination!" She released him to reach into one pocket and pull out a set of rubber gloves, which she snapped on like an executioner. "You *will* have full physical."

"Oh." Logan's voice was a little faint. "Well. If I must."

"We start with medical history." She grabbed him again and pulled him through the door. This time he went. "When was last digital rectal exam?"

88

Chapter Seven

Nurse Battle finished with Logan in fairly short order. She came wandering out five minutes later, alone, mumbling strangely about coffee.

She clutched my arm. "Red Eyes, Liese. It was Red Eyes!" She wouldn't let go until I promised to go get her a Red Eye from the Caffeine Café. On my way out, she thanked me. "Liese—fanks!"

But when I returned with her Red Eye, Battleax was nowhere to be found. Neither was Logan—on his way to Chicago, no doubt. Apparently the AI instructions could wait. I was both relieved and disappointed.

A squad of Steel Security jackets arrived at eight on the dot. They were armed with wafer-thin laptops, typed at two hundred m.p.h. and chattered rapid-fire about evolutionary algorithms and combinatorial explosions. Obviously the software division of the company, and even more obviously damned good at their jobs.

All that brilliant industry made me feel tired and outdated. I collapsed heavily in my chair. It was a nice chair. I would miss it.

Automatically I set my mood-timer for five minutes. It didn't help.

The instructions for the data extract were on my desk. I read them over. Black clouds obscured the lights, so it took me a while even though everything was spelled out, easier to follow than Lego instructions. The extract took me twenty minutes, half of which was spent coaxing my Dell to spit out the data. The black cloud darkened, enveloping me.

My job was now officially ended. The only thing left was the paperwork. I checked the time. Eleven a.m. Oh, boy. Seven hours before I could leave. Seven hours to comb online want ads. Monster.com, Geekfinder. I set my PDA's mood-timer for another five minutes and wallowed in my personal great depression. When it chirped I saw one of the super geeks handwaving holographic data around the room like Tom Cruise in *Minority Report*. I sighed and set the timer for another half-hour, wasted most of it looking at webcomics. This time when it went off I ignored it.

Sometime before lunch, the super geeks finished and left.

I'm not normally melancholic. Yeah, I have an electronics' closet of issues, but even without the timer, my black clouds don't last forever. And sure enough as I was popping my afternoon diet Dew a question occurred to me. Steel Software was good. But was it better than a small-town gal SysOp? Especially, was it was a half million dollars better?

Curiosity drew me out of my dark mood. Hey, would it hurt to look? Yeah, okay. But it was a puzzle—you know, like chocolate ice cream but without the calories.

The code was compiled *and* encrypted. I cracked my knuckles. I'd broken into a professor's program for my college hazing and I still had the routine. I used it to hack open one of the smaller programs.

Skimming the code, I realized the program controlled the external sensors and alarms. "Nice and tight," I admitted grudgingly. "Maybe not five hundred thousand dollars worth of tight, but...hey, that's kind of slick."

I found a couple nested if-thens that could run faster as case statements and changed them automatically. I also extracted a block of repeated code into a subroutine and massaged a few other sections. But otherwise I was impressed. Whoever had done this was good.

Oh, and I sort of put in a tattler subroutine.

Maybe I shouldn't have. But the program notified the police if the alarm was tripped. As long as I still had my job I wanted to know too. Dirkson hired me to have someone onsite during daytime hours (he'd actually said day*light*, but I'd translated that into eight to six). But what if I went out for lunch, or something? Not that I ever did go out to lunch but I might, right?

So I added a subroutine to text my cell phone with the

message *Help*. I stuck it into a dark corner of the code and named it temp1, a really lousy programming practice but great pretend-spy stuff.

I was recompiling the code just for fun when the front door clicked open. I clapped my laptop closed and leaped to my feet. Broad daylight, but the last twenty-four hours had been weird enough for Kiefer Sutherland.

A man strode in carrying a clipboard and wearing a Hemoglobin Society badge. "Johansson. I've got a thousand units from Michigan."

Only a delivery. I scanned the boxes in with my portable barcode reader and saw the blood safely refrigerated. As I signed for the shipment, Johansson said, "That bar coding's cool. Did you get that donated locally, or are all the Hemoglobins getting one?"

"I bought it. Why?"

He took the pen and stowed it under the clip before tucking the board away. "You haven't heard? Units have gone missing. Not from my truck, thank goodness. But from clinics, and even some distribution centers."

I tried not to look too interested. "Someone's stealing blood?"

"Most folks use the word 'missing'. A few units here, a few there—except for Valparaiso and Lansing. Valparaiso's an interesting situation."

"Oh?" Cool, nonchalant...and my ears were vibrating.

"Couple months ago they were taken over by a group of businessmen. Next day most of the employees were fired. They started losing a case of blood a week. The workers that were left—" Johansson shrugged. "They stumble around muttering things that don't make sense. It's like they've been mesmerized or something. I get in and out as fast as I can. It's...uncomfortable."

Svengali eyes. Rasputin voice. I swallowed hard. "Does this group of businessmen have a name?"

"Dunno, but they've done it before, apparently. They look for smaller private blood centers. The ones in financial trouble, mostly. Vulnerable to takeover. Can I see that barcode thing?"

I handed him the scanner. What he said scared me. Our Center was small and private. We were vulnerable.

"Lansing's even more interesting." Johansson turned the barcode reader over in his hands. "They had a fancy-schmancy security system put in a week before a whole shipment was stolen. I don't know about you, but I don't trust technology. Give me real intelligence, not the artificial stuff."

He handed the small gun back to me. "Anyway, I think this is pretty neat. I can understand it, know what I mean? If you come across a spare couple hundred dollars, maybe you could send some to the other centers."

With a touch of paranoia, I personally locked the door after Johansson left. When I opened my laptop to enter the shipment's details, the Steel Software program was still up, and some strange parameters (numbers to normal people) caught my eye. They were limits to tell the alarm program the difference between a burglar and a rabbit.

Maximum weight was three hundred fifty pounds. Seemed heavy. Top height was eight feet. A clown on stilts?

Top approach speed was forty miles an hour. *Forty.* And not like forty on a moped. The alarm was set to go off if someone was going forty m.p.h. *on foot.*

Frowning, I paged down.

Max heart rate was faster than a hummingbird having fits. But my brain did a double-clutch and puke when I saw a special alarm for *no heart rate at all.*

These weren't parameters for people. These were parameters for superhumans.

Or monsters.

Unnerved, I closed up the code. Then, for good measure, I deleted the hacked file. It wasn't my Blood Center anymore. Not my problem. Strictly speaking, the monster parameters were Logan Steel's headache, not mine.

Which made me worry all the more.

At four thirty a loud knock made me jump. "Is Mr. Steel in?" chirped a bright voice.

Oh, jolly jingling joy. Not a monster, but all that pep was unnatural. I opened the door. "Hello, Zinnia."

Today she wore pinstriped hipster trousers and a matching jacket opened to reveal a frilly cotton blouse. Very corporate, except for the stud winking discreetly at her navel. "Is Mr. Steel here? He and I need to go over the interview results."

And naturally the first words out of her mouth were about Mr. Corporate Navel-raider. I dropped into my chair. "Logan's in Chicago. Security upgrade."

"Oh. When do you expect him back?"

"Tonight." Now I should invite her to come back in a couple hours and shoo her out. But there was a reason they called it "morbid" curiosity. It was making me sick—was Zinnia his SO or not? "So, um, do you have a last name?"

"Jones." Before I could even think about spelling relief she added, "I hope to make it Steel, soon."

I just bet she did. Not his Mrs. then, or even ex. But To-be. "Logan's quite a catch."

"Isn't he, though?" She practically vibrated. "Such *marvelous* training."

Logan had trained to be a guru of sex? What, he had a Ph.D. in Positions, his dissertation on the Kama Sutra? And what university would that be from? The Massachusetts Institute of Titology? Nooky Dame? Studford?

Fortunately Zinnia wasn't expecting a response from me. "I have no doubts Mr. Steel will be marvelous. The Ancient One is very thorough."

"You mean Mr. Elias?" Old yes, but ancient? And how had he trained Logan to be marvelous? Kissing, licking, rubbing...ew. Just the thought of a wrinkled geezer tutoring gorgeous Logan Steel in any of the above was definitely barfy.

"Mr....oh, yes. I see." Zinnia made a big show of looking around, then winked at me. "Yes, Mr. Elias has groomed Mr. Steel very carefully for his important *business* role."

Curiouser and curiouser. That was no more than the truth. Elias was a prime mover and shaker in the international business scene. Logan, besides being very successful on his own, was Elias's right-hand man.

So why was Zinnia doing the wink-wink nudge-nudge routine?

She dug into her Godzilla-skin bag. "It isn't that long until sunset. I might as well wait." To my consternation she sat down in one of the guest chairs and pulled out her list.

I pretended to work, but really I was playing solitaire while watching Ms. I-Hope-To-Make-It-Steel-Soon. Industrious Zinnia perused her list, made a little tick mark. Perused, ticked. Perused, ticked. I wondered what the ticks were for.

I wondered, if my name were on the list, whether I'd get any ticks. Echoes of my gray mood returned. I hit the mood-timer, gave myself two minutes before sucking it up and getting back to work.

I was going over my patch list when the front door opened and little Lilly trotted in, followed by big brother Bud. "May Lilly use the bathroom, Ms. Schmetterling?"

"Still broken?" I approved a couple security updates. "Sure." Several strains of "Itsy Bitsy Spider" later the golden children came out. As Bud headed for the door, Lilly headed for Mom. "I'm bored, Mommy."

Without looking up, Zinnia said, "Mommy's working, honey. Bud will read to you."

"We read all my books, Mommy. I want to watch cartoons."

"There aren't any cartoons here, Lilly. Now go with Bud."

I perked up. I could help Lilly. But I'd have to admit a deep, dark secret. A big black tick mark in my negative column—if I were ever lucky enough to make it to Zinnia's list.

Have I mentioned that I'm idiotically brave when it comes to other people? "I have cartoons." I opened up my bottom right-hand drawer, where I kept forbidden items like games, magazines and cheesy curls. "*Animaniacs* was a favorite of mine as a kid. I have the DVDs. We can play them on my laptop."

Lilly clapped her little hands in delight. "Oh, thank you, Ms. Sme'lling. Cartoons!" She bounced in glee, so adorable I wanted to shoot myself.

Zinnia held up a hand. "Now, Lilly, it's very nice of Ms. Schmetterling, but we don't want to interrupt her work."

"I'll be leaving for the day soon, anyway." I opened up Volume Two, picked a disk, and stuck it in.

"Ms. Schmetterling?" Bud came over. "If you don't mind, I'll stay too. To, um, watch Lilly." His eyes were not on Lilly. They were on the computer screen where the Warner Brothers and the Warner Sister had just appeared. Yakko, Wakko and Dot hovered near the list of selections. Bud grinned suddenly. "Hey—the Halloween show."

"You like that one? Me too." I cued it. Scooting up my chair for Lilly, I pulled the remaining guest seat behind the desk for

Bud.

Both kids' eyes were immediately glued to the antics of the Warners. It was the episode in Dracula's castle, "Draculee, Draculaa". I leaned against the wall behind them to watch.

The count came on-screen. Pale green face, red eyes, yellow fangs. Very vampy. He poofed into a bat in best vampire fashion.

Zinnia rustled her paper. She ticked, but her pen was less decisive.

Wakko Warner joined Dracula in the air. "I'm a bat!" Wakko crowed. Zinnia gave up ticking and joined us.

"You are not a bat," Dracula said.

"Oh, you're right. But this is." Pulling out a baseball bat, Wakko clocked Dracula.

"I'm not well," the slightly crinkled vampire said.

Zinnia's mouth dropped open. Her face suffused with color. "This...this is horrible!"

I straightened from the wall. "It's not *Sesame Street* but it's clever and funny and—"

"How can they torture that poor vampire so?"

My surprise turned to astonishment. "You're upset because they're baiting an evil creature of the night?"

Zinnia drew herself up. "Vampires avoid the sun so the narrow-minded see them as evil. But they are no more evil than you or I, Ms. Schmetterling. Surely you of all people understand that."

"I do?"

"Of course you do. I recognized that right away. You're a sister in the fight. Freedom from oppression!" She struck a pose, fist to breastbone. "Seven score years ago a great American, in whose symbolic shadow we stand today, signed the Emancipation Proclamation. It was a beacon of hope to millions—"

"Um, Zinnia? Isn't that Dr. Martin Luther King's 'I Have a Dream'?"

"I may have heard it before. But it applies to vampires too."

"If vampires existed. Nice metaphor, though. Vampires, meaning displaced people."

Zinnia gave me a funny look. "What's a meta for?"

"Ha-ha," I said, but she wasn't joking.

"Draculee, Draculaa" segued into an episode of Rita and Runt. Zinnia sat back down. "It's not good to teach the children intolerance. I'm going to start a letter-writing campaign." She made a note. "Of course, it'll have to be after this moving thing is settled."

"Moving thing?"

She smiled brilliantly at me. "Our move here, of course." And she went back to her happy ticking.

That night I left on time, partly because of the Supermom particle accelerator, partly because I was a little Over the Rainbow and hunting for my creepy umbrella.

But mostly I left on time because my waxing was scheduled for tonight at six.

The new AI-run system locked at six and armed automatically with the last person leaving the building. So after telling Bud how to shut down my computer, I headed out. A blast of cold air met me.

"Hey, dollface." Cold air—and Race Gillette, hands in his pants pockets.

"Hi, Race. What are you doing here?"

"I'm gonna walk you home. Since you been hungry for me, like all the honeys."

"I'm not going home."

"Sure you are. Where else can you can have a big bite of my delicious hotdog with the works, if you know what I mean." He pushed his pocketed hands forward, making his pants bulge.

Oh, sheesh. And I thought the Big Red Button was tasteless. "That's nice of you, Race, but I have an appointment." I jerked a thumb at Dolly's.

His grin faded, confusion taking its place. "You don't wanna go home with me?"

Not even if Norman Bates was stalking me and Race had the last locked bathroom on Earth. But I didn't want to hurt his feelings, so I pasted on a disappointed look. "Can't. I already missed one appointment."

"But I need to talk to you. Now's as good a time as any." He grabbed my upper arm. "So, did you do Steel?"

"*Do* him?" Like kissing and rubbing and licking, and climbing Mount Zipper? My cheeks flushed hot. "Not exactly."

"What d'ya mean? Did you ax Steel, or didn't you?"

"Oh! Ax him. Do him, as in, er, *do* him." I thought of the dungeon picture. "Yes." Unfortunately.

"How?" Race's hand tightened. "Come on, tell me everything. We're co-constipators, you and me."

Con*spir*ators, my mind supplied. "Race, I can't. We're in public. Anyone might overhear, like—" The street was eerily empty. I improvised. "Electronic surveillance. Or, um, someone with really good hearing."

To my surprise, he released me with a nod. "Good point. Steel's got supernaturally good hearing, another reason he's gotta be taken out. Bein' that he's a vampire."

"Uh huh. A vampire. Logan Steel, a bloodsucking monster." Never mind that I'd thought the same thing myself. How could I doubt it, hearing it from such reliable people as the Energizinnia and Bertie the Brain-dead Baboon?

"He is." Race looked offended. "You ever seen him during the day?"

"Yes."

"Yeah, but outside? And has he ever gone kinky on you? Had a real neck fetish?"

That stopped me.

Pop! Bad Liese appeared on my shoulder. "Told you so," she crowed. "Logan Steel is a wicked, mythical being from legends."

"Look who's talking," I muttered.

Bad Liese pouted. "I'm just saying."

"Dollface? Who you talkin' to?"

"Nobody." I brushed my shoulder. Bad Liese danced around my fingers before giving me a raspberry and popping out of existence. "So you think Logan Steel is a vampire. Literally."

"I dunno about throwin' trash on the streets."

Throwing trash...oh. Literally, littering.

"But he's a vampire, sure as I am...sure as I am Race Gillette! And you need to be real careful, or he'll suck you dry. He's evil incarnal."

"Incarnal." That was one too many. I couldn't help myself, my day had just gone past surreal to comic. "I do not think that word means what you think it means." I waited, but he didn't get the *Princess Bride* reference. "Race, the man heads a multi-billion dollar company. He wouldn't jeopardize that by biting random people."

"He can make them believe they weren't bit. Using his Vampire Compulsion." Race wagged his eyebrows at me like a mad—Rasputin.

OMG. The Rasputin voice. That hollow ringing tone Logan used in the sewer when he was trying to make me believe I hadn't seen him. It hadn't worked because I was a *perversely willful creature.*

Logan Steel, one of the undead—although with his sex appeal, he'd be one of the Grateful Undead...yeah. But if Logan was a vampire, what was his true interest in me? Business, sex, or food?

Pop! "Told you so, told you so!"

"Shut *up.*"

"Told you so, told you—*ack.*"

I popped Bad Liese with a two-finger serve that could have pinged a steelie into space. She went flying face-first into a street post. Her arms and legs stuck straight out like one of those Halloween witch decorations. All she needed was a little broomstick up her ass.

"Look, Race. Whatever Logan Steel is, corporate bloodsucker or just plain bloodsucker, I took care of him, okay? Now I have to go or I'll be late." Two steps took me to Dolly Barton's Curl Up and Dye. The door's bell tinkled, announcing my arrival.

Dolly was the town gossip like Steve Ballmer was reasonably well-off. Dolly knew *every*thing that went on, sometimes before it happened. Some people said Fox News got their best items from Dolly through a mysterious contact called Deep Comb-over.

Dolly herself was a seventy-year-old platinum-blonde dynamo. She was four-foot-eight, 42-D and looked exactly like the country singer except older and shorter. She wore a pink fifties-diner-style uniform and chewed a wad of gum as big as your head.

"Hey, sugar." Dolly called everyone sugar. "Nice dress."

I flushed. I had forgotten about my pink battle armor. "Uh, thanks."

The bell tinkled again, underlined by a growl. Race stalked into the salon behind me. "You ain't escapading from me that easy, dollface."

Before I could even think of *escapading*, Dolly trotted up. "Oh, no, sugar. No, no, no." She thrust her hands through Race's mullet. "This has got to go."

"What...stop that, lady!" Race batted at Dolly, uselessly. Decades of unruly hair had given her hands like steel grapples.

"Good healthy scalp." She was feeling Race up so intimately he blushed. "Yes, I think we can save you."

"Save me?" Race squawked. "What are you talking about? Save me from what?"

"Certain horrible disaster." Dolly bustled over to her appointment book (I'd tried to computerize her when I came back to town but she firmly resisted, probably because she wrote half her gossip in the margins). "I can squeeze you in Friday morning. Haircut, blow and style." She sized him up. "And a shave. You have a good jaw."

Race backed up, all thoughts of molesting me apparently forgotten. "I...I, um, don't do mornings."

"Sun shy, hmm? All righty, sugar, I'll come in early, say five a.m.?"

But Race was already out the door. As the bell tinkled she yelled, "Do you need a card?"

We watched his retreating back. That boy could move.

With a shrug, Dolly went back to her current customer, Mrs. Mayor Meier, teasing her hair with something that looked like a rake. The mayor's wife had reached that age when hair soaks up just a little too much blue rinse. When Dolly was done, Mrs. Meier could have posed for Separated at Birth: the Unknown Twin of Marge Simpson. Marge—I mean Mrs. Meier tipped Dolly a dollar and ducked going out the door.

"I'm ready for you now, sugar." Dolly led me back to a private room. "So, what are we doing today? The full Brazilian?"

"*What?*" Complete deforestation of my nether hair? "Why would you think I'd want *that*?"

"For your new boyfriend." Dolly pulled out the wax kit. "Nice bod, but I gotta be honest with you. From that pic, he seems a little kinky. Mind you, I like a good chain and shackle myself sometimes. Blows out the old carburetor, if you know what I mean."

"Uh, Dolly..." I really didn't want to think about Dolly's

carburetor getting blown. And then— "My boyfriend?" I had sent the dungeon picture anonymously. *Unsigned.* How could she have connected it to me?

"The gorgeous blond doing the doggie trot," she clarified, popping gum. "What Robert Pattinson wants to look like when he grows up. Lay on the table and pull up your dress. I'm glad you found someone, sugar. You know, after that scumbag Botcher. Sixteen months? Time to put it behind you. Now pull down the panties. Nice pink lace."

I removed my underwear, wondering just how involved a bikini wax was. I'd never had one before. "They just came up in the rotation. That they match my dress is totally coincidental. Honest. Dolly, how did you know the picture was from me?"

Dolly's crack of gum told me she didn't believe me about the panties. "My mailing daemon. Close your eyes, sugar. I'm throwing in a free eye compress. Cucumber and cream, great for those dark circles."

Circles which were getting even darker from her revelations. A daemon in this case was not an underworld imp, nor even the luscious Warlord Prince of Anne Bishop's *Black Jewels* books. It was a small computer program that ran in the background on any multitasking operating system but most often in Unix. Windows used Services. "Dolly, how did you get a mailing daemon?"

She clicked scissors, started trimming. "You know Marge Meier, just left? She knows Josephine Schrimpf, who eats at the Eincastle Country Club with Donna Marter, who knows head chef La Pastralli, that Italian genius who sometimes cooks for the Seattle branch of Rusterman's restaurant where Bill Gates sometimes eats."

"*Bill Gates* wrote your daemon?" That was like Barack Obama campaigning for your Student Council bid.

"He didn't want to at first, something about not coding in eunuchs."

"Unix," I said faintly. A warm, slightly sticky fluid brushed onto my crotch. It felt a little too close to center field, if you know what I mean, but again I was new at this.

"Whatever, sugar. But nobody can say no to La Pastralli. So I got me a mailing daemon." Scissors clicked again, sounding like she was trimming cloth.

"And it told you I sent the email."

"I already guessed, though." Dolly patted cloth onto me. "Now, this won't hurt a bit."

Right. It already hurt. Because if Dolly knew I'd sent the picture, then who else knew? Elias? *My* boss? *Logan himself?* "Did you tell anyone?"

"Of course not." Dolly sounded affronted. "I'm no blabbermouth."

Coming from the town gossip, this was not reassuring. I heard a rip. I wondered what had caused it. "Did you hear—?"

Bees, thousands of them, jabbed me viciously in the crotch. "Fuck!" My hand dove down automatically to cover my vulva. Trying to protect it, too late. My fingers encountered only naked, puffy skin. I threw off the compresses and glared at Dolly. "What'd you do that for?"

"Just trying to be discreet." Dolly looked slightly miffed. "If you want me to tell people that you sent the picture, I will."

Chapter Eight

Once I convinced Dolly I didn't really want her to tell anyone about my little—heh-heh—joke on Logan (tipping her a couple Hamiltons), I stuffed my pink undies into my purse, took my poor denuded crotch (yes, I let her finish the job. What part of *free* is unclear?) and slunk out into the crisp evening. I headed east on Jefferson toward Der Lebensmittelgeschaft (MC grocery store), to pick up a few things. Despite my squawking genitals I still had to eat.

"You shouldn't be alone at night," a deep voice drawled.

Nerves scraped thin by the morning from hell, the unexpected blood delivery, the eerie alarm code params and the double-shock of Dolly buckled. I leaped out of my skin like a pole-vaulter, only to be caught by two strong hands.

"Jumping quad cores!" I glared up into the sparkling eyes of Logan Steel. "Don't do that appearing-out-of-nowhere stuff. At least do the smoky thing first."

He went still. Not surprised still. *Weird* still, as if time itself had stopped. No breath, no movement, not even a twitch. Alien still. "What do you mean?"

"The smoke-and-mirrors stuff you security experts do. The super-spy thing."

"Oh." He relaxed into a more normal stillness. "Super-spy smoke. Of course. Where are you headed?"

"Grocer's. I'm out of cheesy curls and diet Dew."

"Ah, the staples." He held out his hand, indicating I should go first, and fell in next to me.

I gave his saunter a sidelong glance. Damn, the man even walked like sex. "I can get there by myself, okay? You don't have to come."

"But I'd like to. *Come*, that is." He gave me a saucy wink.

I rolled my eyes. "Is everything a big sex game to you?"

His sparkling leer said it all.

"Come," I repeated with a snort. "What a stupid word for orgasm. Who thought that up, anyway? I mean, who connected the word for *enter* with sexual climax? A guy poking a door open with his erection? 'Darling, I'm coming?' Only what if the door slammed shut?"

Logan winced, then stared at me like he was seeing me for the first time—and what he saw unsettled him.

Well, that was a nice change. Suave Logan Steel, unsettled. "And *blow job*. How ridiculous is that? *Blow*, implying pushing out, when it's all about sucking in, isn't it?"

"Um, yeah." Logan adjusted his jeans like they were suddenly uncomfortable.

"And what about all the idiotic words for genitals? Prick, like it's a teeny-weeny poker. Pussy, like it's furry with sharp little teeth. What's with that?"

Logan covered his face like he wanted to either laugh or cry. "You can use the Latin terms. Penis and vulva."

"Peee-nis." I tested it on my tongue. The word, not the thing. Although I wondered what Logan's—*not going there*. "Too much like wiener. And vulva sounds like a car."

Logan uncovered his face. "A car."

I adopted a deep announcer's voice. "Fellatio. An Italian Sports Car for Real Men."

"You mean for guys who read slick magazines with articles like 'Make Her Shriek in Bed'."

"Exactly! And cunnilingus. Doesn't that sound like a disease carried by mosquitoes?"

"You know, you've put me off oral sex for the rest of my life."

"Somehow I doubt that."

"You're probably right."

We walked in silence for a few blocks. When I wasn't arguing with—or running from—him, Logan was surprisingly easy to walk with. He had a long, loose stride that he matched to mine and a pleasant habit of looking around as if interested in every bunny and building he saw.

We were strolling across the river and I was beginning to

enjoy myself when he said, "All the security programs are installed and tested."

"Oh." Why did he have to keep opening his mouth? It just spoiled everything.

"I saw you did the data extracts so I did the imports. Hope you don't mind."

Mind that my job was now gone? "No. Great. I'll just turn off my programs, then."

"Already done," Logan said cheerfully.

"How helpful."

"Should we go over there?" He pointed at Settler's Square, Meiers Corners' main park. "That band shell looks interesting."

"Sure." Might as well stake out a bench for when I was out of a job.

"Anyway, I'll train you on the new programs tomorrow. My guys fought over who gets to do it. But I put my foot down."

Logan's words didn't make sense. I was getting trained on the new stuff? I gave him a sidelong glance.

He flashed his brilliant white smile as he mounted the steps of the picturesque Oom-pa-pa Bandshell. "Being the boss has some perks."

Boss. I groaned as I followed. Logan wouldn't be a boss much longer. Not once Dirkson and Elias horsewhipped him over the photoshopped picture. And if Logan figured out who'd sent it, I'd be lucky to *only* get fired.

Logan Steel, for all his insouciance, did not strike me as a man to cross lightly.

Hitting the stage, he cocked his head at me. "You're not as excited as I hoped."

The shell amplified the deep concern in his voice. Concern for me. I winced. "Training is good. It's just that...well..."

"It's *him*, isn't it." Logan actually snarled. "The man who hurt you. The one who made you so mistrustful. The one who gave you that fucking fake ring that you use like a shield." His anger reverberated off the giant cone around us. "I'll kill him. I'll tear out his throat—with my teeth. I'll rip his cock off and stuff it in his lying, cheating mouth."

"How do you know he lied and cheated?"

"Oh, Liese, it's obvious." Logan took me by the arms. "You're like the sun, honest and bright. Only someone the

104

complete antithesis of that could steal your sunshine."

Ouch. "Logan, I'm not as honest as you think."

"Sunshine," he repeated. He kissed me, then kissed me again. "You're made for joy, princess. For lovemaking. I want to make the sweetest love to you. In fact, I think I'm falling in—" He raised his head suddenly, nostrils flaring. "Hell. Not now, damn it."

At the far edge of the Square, something moved. Several somethings.

I was glad for the interruption. Because for just one moment, I'd forgotten the misery I'd made of my life. For one moment I'd actually wanted Logan to make love to me, wanted the joy and sunshine he could bring. Logan Steel was a sorcerer, making me believe the impossible. I was glad for the oath that broke the enchantment.

I was glad, dammit.

Logan pushed me behind him. "It won't do any good, Shiv." His voice carried, magnified by the band shell. "The complete security's installed. We've *cut off* Razor's avenue of crime. *Shaved* his options. Don't come any closer, unless your gang can handle a *sharp Steel blade.*"

Shiv? Another of Razor's gang? Footsteps rang on the Bandshell stairs. I craned my neck around Logan, glimpsed a scary guy before Logan palmed me back. Rail-thin, skull-headed, with blazing red eyes, like Gollum grown up.

"So?" Shiv had a contemptuous, whiny voice. "She'll know the codes to shut your fancy security down."

Instantly Logan's insouciance was gone, his graceful teasing not even a memory. "You will leave her out of it."

"Hey, don't blame me. You're the one who brought her into it."

She? Zinnia or Brianna? I was surprised how much that hurt, way more than Botcher. But anything that turned Logan serious was a real threat. Again I tried to see, caught lithe forms emerging from behind playground equipment before Logan grabbed my wrists and yanked me flush against his back.

"If you *dare* touch her... Did Razor put you up to this?" Logan wrapped my arms over his taut belly and held me pinned with one hand, my face plastered to his jacket.

"Naw. He's trying to be subtle." Shiv cawed laughter. "I like the more direct approach. Four of us, one of you. Once you're out of the way she's unprotected."

"She doesn't know anything." Logan's growl burred against me where I pressed to his back. "And the system is automatic. There are no override codes."

Several snarls greeted that information. But Shiv gave a wicked snort. "You can lie better than that, Steel. You wouldn't risk one of your precious donors getting electrocuted."

"Get it through your thick skull, Shiv. *She's not my donor.*"

Logan had a personal donor? Whoever this "she" was, he cared enough to be deadly serious when it came to her. Oh, to be that lucky *she.*

Or to be loose to kick some ass. I'd take that, too.

"Come on, Steel. Why have a chew toy if you're not going to—chew?" Another laugh, a real villain's cackle. Whoever this Shiv was, I didn't like him at all. I expected him to break into a creepy chorus of *my precioussss* at any moment.

"Believe what you will. But believe this. You even *touch* her and I will not rest until you are in *pieces.*"

"Yeah, yeah," Shiv sneered. "What you gonna do? Sic your Ancient One on me? *Ooh, I'm scared*—ack."

Logan's free arm jerked like he was drawing a weapon, sketched a couple quick slashes. I couldn't see what he was doing—but I saw the result. Red liquid sprayed onto the concrete platform, splatting like oily rain. I didn't think it was raspberry jam.

Acid hit my stomach. I wrenched back but Logan held me in an unbreakable grip. Beyond him I heard angry snarls, the rest of Razor's gang. "Logan, let me go." I struggled in his grasp. Didn't he realize I could help? "Logan, let go!"

He spun, grabbed me in a brief hug. "Sorry, but I don't want you seeing this." He tackled my lips with a quick kiss—and pulled my dress up over my head.

"What the hell?"

"Blame Julian Emerson. It's his idea."

A few quick tugs and the dress was tied off. I was trapped in a bag of coat and silk skirt. If Logan's objective was to blind me it worked. I was grudgingly impressed—I wasn't the only one good at using materials at hand. But what in Pascal's name was so awful he had to trap me?

A chill wind blew over my exposed hips—and I realized I had bigger problems. With my undies in my purse, I was literally butt-naked.

From beyond my cocoon of coat and dress, I heard an indrawn breath. A rattle, like someone choking. A wheeze, someone else having a heart attack. And an absolute storm of coughing.

"Good Lord, Liese." Logan's voice was hoarse. "Are you trying to kill me?"

"Um...no." I couldn't cover myself, with the silken straightjacket. "Let me out?"

"I can't even move, sweetheart. Damn. That pretty little pink slit..." He groaned.

"Steel," a new voice shouted from beyond my prison, unisex gravel, the Lucille Ball from hell. "You're gonna pay for what you did to Shiv. We're gonna slash you, Steel. We're gonna pull out your heart and...and...what the hell is that?"

"Nothing *you* should be seeing."

I heard a whistling, like knives slicing through the air.

"Ow! My eyes. Hell, I'm half-blind. Skiver, Scythe—get Steel."

Shiv, Skiver and Scythe? What, and their kid brother Weed Whacker? Couldn't they be a bit more imaginative with the names?

Two voices answered. "Hang on, Maim!"

Nope.

"The female snack's mine," the gravelly voice of Maim shouted.

Uh-oh. That didn't sound good. Without hands I couldn't pepper spray. In these high-heels, I couldn't kick. Hell, I was in danger of falling on my naked keister if a stiff breeze came up.

But sounds of furious three-to-one fighting booming in the band shell meant I had to do something. Even if Logan had almost blinded Maim, even if he'd done something bloody-splat to Shiv, there were still Scythe and Skiver trying to split his leather. I needed to do something, *anything* to even the score.

I turned my butt toward the ruckus and bent over.

Someone stumbled. Someone else swore. A roar of confusion was followed by the sound of bodies blundering over each other and hitting the concrete stage.

"Stuff your fat drooling tongue inside your head and get out of my way," shouted the Lucille Ball-deep voice of Maim.

Hey, Lucy had done a film version of Auntie Mame. This guy really was a Mame. I smiled in my cocoon.

A hand fastened onto my bottom. "You're mine now, blood-bitch."

I clamped my teeth against a shriek of frustration. TSTL, just toss me into the too-stupid-to-live pile. While I was distracted by my idiot pun, he'd caught me.

But this close, I could land a kick. A back-kick, square in the breadbasket, would take out even the strongest goon. Tricky, though, with no hands and in heels. I had to get it exactly right. If only I knew where his solar plexus was.

He groped my bottom, his heavy breathing rasping in my ears. Besides *yuck*, I couldn't tell if he was in front or behind me, turned or straight on.

Maybe I could pull his orientation from his voice—if I could get him talking. I blocked out horny hands and stale breath. "So, Maimie. Do you really take the blues right out of the horn?" No answer. Either he wasn't a musical buff or he'd heard it before. I tried again. "'Life's a banquet,' hey, Maimie? 'And most poor sons-of-bitches are starving to death'."

He hissed a laugh. "Very funny, blood-cunt."

Yay! But the shell's reverberation meant I'd need more to pinpoint. "So, Maimie—"

"*Silence*, snack." His hand slid down, fingers creeping toward my slit. "Mmm. I'm gonna enjoy this." A finger brushed my labia.

Planning, aim, *any* rational thought flew out of my brain. I spun a hook kick through the jerk's head. Maim bellowed in pain.

I tried to land but missed my footing and went down. Tucking into a roll absorbed some of the impact but the dress bag made me awkward. Concrete scraped butt and thigh. Blood welled hot on my haunches. I curled up, thin streaks of pain slicing my hip. Maim swore, fell *right on top of me*.

He recovered first. His hands dug into my thighs, wrenched them apart. His anger beat into my skin, his fingers tight enough to bruise. He yanked me hard against his hips and I knew I was one zip away from outrage.

A terrible roar shook the shell, a beast beyond fury. Maim's weight was suddenly gone. Knives whistled. Another roar was accompanied by a terrifying splat.

Then, ominously, absolutely nothing.

I lay on the stage, pain subsiding to nasty throbs. I finally realized nothing was broken, so I rolled up to my knees, tense and waiting. No one grabbed me. No one spoke. There was only silence. I had no idea who had beaten whom.

But I got the horrible feeling people had lost their heads, literally. I could only hope one wasn't Logan. Tentatively, I called his name.

"Liese." His voice was so rough I barely recognized it. "Are you okay?"

I scrambled to my feet. "I am now. What's going on?" I pushed at my cocoon. "Let me out?"

"In a minute. I have to...recover some. Damn. Why do you have to smell so good?"

"I just want to clean up." I turned my scraped and bloodied haunches toward where I thought he was. "See?"

Logan released a groan so deep I thought it was coming from his very soul. The next thing I knew his hands were wrapped around my hips and his breath was hot on my naked flank.

A warm, wet tongue touched me. Licked me gently. Began to lap, washing me, hot and slick.

"Logan, don't." The scrapes stopped hurting, but he was licking *blood*. "Stop that...what are you doing...*oh*."

His mouth worked down my buttocks, kissing now as well as licking. His lips pressed intimately into the crease of my thighs. His breath warmed flesh chilled by the early spring night. My ex-fiancé had never kissed me like this. Never put his mouth down—*there*.

Logan tilted my hips back and took a long lick of my exposed sex. I quivered at the touch. He did it again and deep muscles clenched. He lapped a third time and I felt myself open to him like a rose.

"Oh, Liese," he breathed against my bare labia. "You smell so good. You taste even better."

There was such sincerity in his voice I had to believe him. "Logan, I'm...I'm..."

"Yes?" He lapped ardently at me, his tongue sinking into my blooming pussy. "What is it, princess?"

Goosebumps ran up and down my thighs. "I'm cold."

"Dear heart. I should have thought." Logan gathered me into his arms, held me close. "I don't feel the chill like you do." He made short work of the tie that bound me, picked me up and glided off.

His smooth stride was deceptively fast. I dug out of my cocoon barely in time to see the rapidly disappearing scene behind us. No broken heads. No bleeding and battered bodies.

But I knew I'd heard something horrible. "Logan, put me down. We need to call the police."

"Later. Now, I'm taking you home." Logan's voice was rough with emotion. The hand he used to shield my face was trembling.

"But those men—"

"I'm taking you home," he repeated. "We'll sort all that out later."

"But—"

"I've got your taste in my mouth, sweetheart. I'm afraid I can't wait."

"Logan." I wriggled until he was forced to pay attention to me. "Being attacked by four men is not something we can sort out later. Especially if they were the gang trying to break into the Blood Center. Logan, stop."

"I'll handle it, princess."

"You're not the police. At the very least I need to tell Elena."

He finally set me down. We were already ten blocks away. How...? *Forty miles an hour*, I remembered. *On foot.* "Fine." His tone, rough, said it was anything but fine. "Give Elena a call. Maybe once you've unburdened yourself, you'll feel free to go home with me." He crossed his arms, pumping muscles in both arms and chest. Even after all that had happened my tongue wanted a long, hot lick of that.

And then... Go *home* with him? I swallowed hard. "To play *World of Warcraft?*"

His eyes darkened. "To make love."

"Oh. Um...yeah." Burning in Logan's heated gaze, I nearly forgot roars and splats. Only sheer determination got the phone out. Good thing Elena was on redial.

The line flipped open. "H...hello?" She sounded breathless, like she'd been exercising heavily. Running, or skipping rope, or—

Oh, snap. "It's Liese. Am I calling at a bad time?"

"No, of course not." She said it too quickly. A deep murmur and her answering yip made me clap my phone shut.

"She's busy." I was fire-engine red. "I'll just call the police station instead." I opened my phone, punched 9-1—

"*No.*" Logan snatched the phone from me so fast I punched the last 1 in the air before I knew it was gone.

"What are you doing? Give that back." I reached for it.

Logan grabbed my wrist and yanked me in. As my breasts smashed against the Cliffs of Dover, I screeched. "Not again— *mphf.*" He ambushed my lips with a masterful kiss and proceeded to eat me alive.

Fire swirled in my brain. "Stop it, Logan." It came out *Mush mush momush,* so I guess I don't blame him for not understanding.

Oh, that man could kiss. The drugging bliss of his mouth on mine, his hard body rubbing hotly against me nearly made me succumb. But this was important. With the last of my willpower I clapped a hand on my phone and pulled. Logan hung on. I faked a tug down. When his resistance kicked in I yanked up with all my strength.

I ripped the phone away, but the backlash sent my arm spinning up hard enough to clock him.

He fell back, one hand to his cheek, his eyes wide. "That wasn't just a slap. Why?"

I felt bad, but it had stopped him. He was so charming, could so easily walk all over me. "It was an accident. But you were kissing me to shut me up, don't try to deny it." As he'd kissed me to shut me up all the other times. Because he couldn't help himself, my geeky patootie.

I didn't say the last out loud, but his eyes narrowed on me in that Amazing Kreskin way I was coming to know. "I have easier ways to shut you up, Liese. Tonight—*and all the other times*—I kissed you because I wanted to. Because I want *you.* I told you that." He reached for me.

I edged back. "Liar." Wanting it (even desperately wanting it) didn't make it true. "You kissed me because there's something weird going on. You kissed me to distract me from figuring it out."

"There's nothing weird—"

"The more you deny it, the more I know I'm right. Mannequins, disappearing bodies—"

"I'm not lying about this, Liese. *I want you.* And I'm going to prove it." He picked me up again and strode down the street.

Exasperated, I said, "Just tell me the truth. You could have tons of gorgeous women. I know you have no real interest in me. Admit it."

He set me down with exquisite care, then grabbed me by both arms. "You are driving me *nuts.* Well-groomed, symmetrical little automatons aren't beautiful, not to me. You're gorgeous. I love your curvy breasts, your sweetly rounded buttocks. Your glistening little slit—" His eyes squeezed shut and his voice trailed off into something almost like an animal's growl.

"Oh, come on. All women are the same in the dark."

Logan's eyes snapped open, that eerie red-gold. "No. They're not." He grabbed my hand and took off.

I tripped after him. "Just admit it, Logan. Please. I know I'm not beautiful. I promise not to yell, or throw a fit. And if you really want sex I won't object."

He spun me toward him. His eyes were wide, appalled. "For heaven's sake, Liese. This isn't about me getting laid. I'm not the kind of male who lies just to get laid."

My face must have said I wasn't convinced.

"No? Fine. If you want to be cynical." He released me to tear open his jacket and shirt. Grabbing the neck of his T-shirt, he ripped it in two.

My eyes popped out of my skull at the mountains of sleek muscle revealed. His skin glowed like golden silk in the lamplight.

With a wave of his hand, Logan indicated his ripped torso. "Maybe you'll believe I'm not the kind of male who has to lie just to get laid."

Okay. True. Yeah. Tongue-lolling *bladah-bladah* true.

"Now, princess." He grabbed my hand, extracted my key from my purse, dragged me to my door and unlocked it. "You don't believe me when I say you're beautiful. That I want you for *you.*" He scooped me up and swept into my apartment. "So I'm going to show you, very physically. That can't be faked."

I watched my couch and stereo go by as if they were a stranger's. Things looked very different six feet off the ground. "Logan, I know physical things *can* be faked. Little blue pills—"

He screeched to a halt just outside my bedroom. His easy charm dropped away and he was actually angry. "Liese. I am not taking any medications."

"But you could be."

"*He* did, didn't he?" Logan stalked through the doorway and tossed me onto my bed. "I swear, killing's not good enough. I'll feed his own dick to him—and make a bib with his testicles."

"Logan! That's crude." But, thinking of my ex, kind of funny. I pictured Botcher's sac stretched like a lobster bib under his chin and laughed.

"That's my Liese." Logan knelt at my feet. "I'll make you forget all about that miserable excuse for a man. I'll make you happy, sweetheart. Lean back."

It took Logan one second to make me forget Botcher. He spread my thighs and French-kissed my sex.

I gasped. Logan's tongue speared into me. Hot breath beat against me. I bucked. His hands opened on my thighs, holding me steady for the muscular thrusts. His tongue rasped over my slit, spreading it. He sucked one lip into his mouth and I bit back a shriek. He scoured my hole with his tongue and the shriek emerged.

He took one long lick, and another. And then he fell to.

He devoured me, nipping and lapping and sucking like I was a whole dessert tray. Heavens above, that man could love with his mouth. If he'd been practicing for centuries he couldn't have been better. Insistent and hot, his licks were delivered over and over with increasing force until I had a small shuddering climax.

Then he added fingers.

Two long, clever digits thrust into my heat. I arched back, gasped at the delicious pressure crowding my bottom. He pulled out slightly, the small sucking sound caressing my ears, and thrust again. His fingers slid deeper.

His mouth opened on my mons, his breath warming the smooth skin. His tongue slid hot into the slit, holding my clitoral sheath steady while his thrusting fingers jounced me. I was tossed between tongue and fingers, pushed higher and higher, until I trembled violently with desire.

Suddenly he stopped. Wracked with need, I nearly shrieked my frustration but the bed shifted and then he was drawing my dress over my head. My vision cleared to the sight of naked, pumped golden male. Whoa. When'd that happen?

And *how*? 'Cause clothes-melting might just revolutionize the porn industry.

Logan's eyes burned. "I want you, Liese. Like I've never wanted anyone else." His taut, packed belly undulated rapidly with his panting breaths. "Let me love you, sweetheart. *Completely.* Say yes."

I licked my lips. Logan might have faked the sincere tone. He might have viagra'd the enormous erection jutting from his hips.

But he couldn't fake the sex rash mottling his chest or the fierce desire in his eyes.

Or the huge, straining fangs glistening between his lips.

"What the hell?" I knifed up. *Fangs*? I had to be seeing things. Okay, I'd thought the v-word, but that wasn't reality smacking me in the face. I reached trembling fingers toward his mouth.

Logan pushed me flat. Straddled me with muscular thighs. "You're gorgeous, princess. Looks, smell, feel. *Taste.*" He leaned over me and pressed wet kisses to my neck, my collarbone. His hot lips were segmented by something smooth and long.

Two somethings. With very sharp points. I tried to squirm away but he held me trapped. He palmed a breast and I could only gasp.

"Believe me when I say you're beautiful, Liese. All of you, but especially these." Logan shifted to suckle me. The fangs rode on either side of my nipple like electric prods.

I arched, unable to stop myself, pressing into his warm mouth. The sleek length of his canines felt like living marble on my skin. The fangs freaked me, but my body liked their throbbing press so much that my nipples were tight snaps and my breasts strained for more.

Logan groaned to the pit of his belly. He closed his eyes. Took a deep shuddering breath through fiercely flared nostrils.

"Lord, Liese, you smell wonderful. I'm dying to penetrate you. Please, sweetheart. Say yes." His tongue swirled around my nipple.

I couldn't speak, caught by the unreality of it all. Logan was making love to me—mind-banging enough—with fangs.

Like something that started with a *v* and ended with an -*ampire*. Yet it would explain so many things. The Rasputin voice, the red eyes. The superhuman speed, the nocturnal hours, licking my blood off my skin, Zinnia's caterwauling on species rights, the 40 mph (on foot) alarm parameters...yeah. All so plain in hindsight but even Superman tricked Lois Lane with only a pair of glasses and a bad haircut.

If Logan were a vampire, my own sexual response to him could be safely labeled Erotic Power of the Undead. And it was power—electric bolts sheered through me from his deep suckling. Violent need shook me. I grabbed his head, wanting to push him away but only clutching harder and mewling in passion's terror.

Logan's mouth immediately gentled. His hands caressed me, warm and sweet. Comforting, like he knew I was freaked and wanted to reassure me I was safe with him.

Like he cared about me.

That actually scared me worse than the fangs. If Logan were a vampire, I should be his snack. Yet he was touching me like a lover.

Say yes. Here was the real reason I couldn't say it. Not his fangs or even the power of my reaction to him but the sense that this was about more than sex. That, even if it started out as response to the dark appetites of the vampire, something had changed for me. Something significant. I was no longer responding with my wet, needy sex.

Logan might be making love to my body, but I was responding with my heart.

Shocking enough. But when Logan said, "Only you, princess. Only you make me feel like this. I want you so badly," as if he were echoing my thoughts, as if his heart were involved too, an avalanche of fear hit me. He couldn't really mean it.

He moved to suckle the other nipple. The sharp points of his fangs scraped my cleavage along the way. "Say yes."

My throat was too thick. He pressed the canines into my aching flesh and I whimpered.

"Say it." He suckled my nipple until I wanted to scream. Until I no longer cared about hearts or fangs or fears, only about slick writhing bodies. Something had to give.

I couldn't say it. So I grabbed his ears and rammed my breast into his face.

Prongs of fire drove into my flesh, his needle-sharp canines. Lightning struck, twin bolts of pleasure. A shivering, out-of-the-blue orgasm rolled over me like thunder.

His tongue immediately pressed against the throbbing pricks. "Damn, Liese. I'm sorry I slipped but—aw, hell. No, I'm not sorry. You taste *incredible*. Beyond moonlight and soft summer breezes. More, sweetheart. Let me give you more. Let me love you fully. Completely. *Say yes.*"

His lips roved over my breast, sucking gently. My blood leaped to attention. *Ached*. His hand slid between my thighs, hot. "More, sweet Liese." He began to stroke.

It would have been insanity to say yes. But Logan boldly stroked my clit until I shrieked. Until I cursed. His hand rode me as if he were inside my head, fulfilling my desires before I even had them. As if he'd been born knowing how to drive me insane.

And the wetter I got, the more he pleaded.

"*Please*, Liese. Let me take you to heaven."

Rich, powerful Logan Steel. Begging to give me pleasure. His mouth blazed fire down my cleavage, his hand worked slickly between my legs. His monster erection seared a throbbing beat against my thigh. It would be heaven inside me. Heaven, all for the price of a single word.

I gasped his name, wanting to say *yes*, wanting to scream it. *Yes, Logan. Make love to me. Impale me on your thick cock. Fill me with your flesh. Love me, completely*—bite *me*. But would that make me his love slave, or worse? Sex with a vampire might kill me.

"Liese. Please." Logan nuzzled my throat, fangs whispering against my skin. Powerful, deadly fangs. But he wouldn't use them unless I agreed.

Strangely, that released me from my fear. Logan had given me a choice. What kind of evil creature gives you a choice? Botcher never had.

Botcher also had never taken me to heaven. Even if Logan

killed me, he could take me there at least once before I died.

So, live enslaved to the painful past, scared of the future—or grab a chance at heaven?

That was a no-brainer.

I arched under Logan's muscular body. Threw back my head, exposing my throat. "Love me, Logan. Love me completely."

Logan *snarled*. He sprang over me, covered me like a huge male beast. His golden hair tumbled forward over his broad shoulders. His biceps stood rigid, his belly taut. His chest was flushed and pumped. My thighs fell open at the sight.

He thrust himself between. His erection kissed my nude pussy, the head nestling into my swollen lips like a homecoming. Threading his long fingers through my hair, Logan turned my head, anchored it, exposing my throat. Nostrils flared, he lowered his mouth.

Which was when my land line rang.

Chapter Nine

Logan swore viciously. I sucked in a shriek of frustration.

"This is Liese," I heard my own voice say. "Leave a message."

Don't leave a message, I thought. *Let me have this moment of fantasy, uninterrupted.*

Beep. "Hey, Liese. Long time no see, heh-heh."

I nearly screamed. It was a voice I'd hoped never to hear again. *Why now?*

"Babe, I could really use a favor," said that scheming rat-bastard of an ex-fiancé. Bernie Botcher, my personal hell. "Heard Steel Security is doing some work for you. Seems they installed digital cameras here and one sort of caught me with my pants down, heh-heh. I know you'll help me out. You're a peach, Liese. Thanks." *Click.*

Listening to Bernie, Logan's eyes had narrowed until they were slits. "Who was that?"

"Head of IT at Andersly-Dogget."

Logan stared at me, saw something in my expression that made him hiss. "It's him, isn't it? He's the man who hurt you."

He was so damned perceptive. I closed my eyes, too ashamed to deny it. "It was ages ago. Sixteen months."

"What did he do to you? What did that man do that was so horrible you're hurting over a year later?"

I blinked. Logan was furious. So angry, on my behalf. It was, well, sweet. Tenderly, I brushed a strand of long blond hair from his face. "Do we have to talk about it now?"

"He's the one between us, Liese. He's the reason you don't believe me when I say you're beautiful. The reason you don't trust me."

"Then take me somewhere I can forget him. Take me to heaven." I seized Logan's beyond-gorgeous face in both my hands and kissed him.

After a moment's hesitation, Logan responded fiercely. His mouth ground into mine, his sleek canines lengthened against my lips. He kissed down my jaw to my exposed throat. My pulse leaped under his mouth.

His erection filled and thickened. The head pulsed between my labia with searing heat. Anticipation flared through me. I trembled under him, knowing I was about to feel him inside. If anything could drive away the memory of Botcher, it was Logan's big, beautifully shaped cock.

He pressed forward, unbearably slow. Inch by inch, his erection spread me, filled me. I panted as he licked down my collarbone, kissed the notch of my throat. He kept pushing, sheathing himself, throbbing inside me. I trembled. Penetration was burning me up—what would loving me completely be like?

And once Logan was fully inside, he *stopped*. As if he had all the time in the world, he kissed my neck. Licked my skin. Nuzzled me.

"Logan!" My pussy spasmed helplessly around his thick rod. I grabbed the muscles of his sleek ass and tugged. His tight butt fit my palms perfectly, feeling even better than it looked. I dug my fingers into that taut ass, pulled for all I was worth. Urged him without words to *impale* me.

He didn't move an inch.

Hell, did he need more incentive? I kicked my head back, baring my throat. *Please please please*, my thumping pulse roared.

Logan latched onto my breast instead. He suckled me with his hot mouth, hard tugging that made me a squirming mass of sheer screaming want, nailed to the mattress by his enormous erection. He suckled my breast until I was shouting. Until I streamed liquid desire.

I pumped against him, trying to ease the heavy, hot, almost unbearable pressure.

"You still didn't say the word," he growled, his voice more beast than man. "Say it, Liese. Say yes."

Swollen with need, about to rupture, I couldn't think much

less form words. Slowly Logan withdrew. I whimpered, clung. *Please,* my clutching hands said. Penetrate me. Deep, hard. I wasn't sure if I meant cock or fangs.

And he was withdrawing! My pussy sucked at him, trying to pull him back. If *I* was desperate, *it* was frantic.

It unlocked my tongue. "*Yes,*" I shrieked. "Yes, yes, do it!"

Roaring my name, he drove into me with single fierce thrust. I gasped. His cock mushroomed inside me, powerful and heavy. I never knew a penetration so potent.

Until his fangs sank deep into my breast.

Intense sweet fire burned through me, so bright it hurt. I trembled on the cusp of detonation. Logan's deeply thrust cock, his electric bite, were erotic invasions of my flesh that threatened to tear me apart with ecstasy.

And finally he began to move. Not languidly, not casually at all. Logan, any pretense of laziness vanished, fucked me like a jackhammer. His fangs came out of my breast to be replaced by his tongue lapping at me like a frenzied dog.

His huge cock rode my delicate sheath so hard I thought I'd ignite from the friction. I panted, rubbing my belly into his rough line of hair. His tongue rasped my tender flesh like sandpaper.

His mouth left my breast to assault my neck, kissing and licking. When he nipped sharply, I throttled back a scream. My blood was boiling, hot with need. It jumped at the touch of his fangs, longing to escape, like a teakettle screaming for release. No, forget the teakettle. Like a volcano, filled with lava and about to explode.

I arched my neck. Logan's tongue rasped over my pulse, his mouth open wide. The sharp tips of his fangs scored my skin, fiery lines of need that branded my throat, making me writhe. I squirmed under him until, with a low, guttural sound, he pressed his fangs to my neck just enough to pin me, an animal's possession. I felt my blood well up around the tips, hot pearls of dark desire.

He stopped. Poised on the brink, a moment of intense promise pounded between us. More than sex. More than lust. Soul-searing pleasure, yes.

But no turning back. Not for either of us.

Logan groaned to the bottom of his heart, just before he bit deep.

Liquid heat burst against my neck, his hot mouth and my pierced desire. I could feel my blood spurting. It should have scared me. I should have been appalled, repelled.

But as he bit, Logan thrust his cock so deep he hit my eyeballs. He erupted and I did too, climaxing so hard the top of my head blew off. He shouted, I screamed. He lapped at my neck and shuddered and filled me. I gasped and clutched him and wrenched my back as I arched in extreme orgasm.

And for the first time in my life, I went to heaven.

I floated down on angel wings. Logan gave my neck a final lick before gazing at me, his eyes a soft, golden hazel. "Liese, sweetheart. You had a wonderful time."

"It was perfect." I sighed.

"Blotting out the man who hurt you."

I smiled. How right he was.

Logan whispered directly into my ear. "You didn't see fangs."

Slapping both hands to his chest, I shoved him back. "The hell I didn't." I knifed up to glare at him. "You have some serious explaining to do. I definitely saw fangs."

"Damn. I forgot." Logan grimaced, still managed to look gorgeous. "You're so bloody strong-minded."

I crossed my arms over my breasts. "That's better than perversely willful."

The corner of his mouth lifted. "I can explain about the teeth. I had some dental work done as a kid, and the dentist was a charlatan and a crook—"

"You're a vampire."

Logan stared at me, actually speechless.

Even now some part of me wanted him to deny it. Hoped he would say no, of course not. But then he'd be lying and I'd hate him for that. *Enough with issues. Deal with it, Liese.* "Either you're a vampire or you're going to upchuck all over my bedspread in about five minutes. Because I know you drank my blood. As thirsty as I am, you drank a goodly amount of my blood. And blood is an emetic."

"In humans." Logan's voice was faint.

"Right. So are you upchucking?"

He shook his head.

"Ergo, not human."

He blinked a few times, like he was searching for words. "That doesn't mean I'm a vampire."

"Oh, come on. Why do I never see you outside during the day? Why don't you want me to be alone at night? And I'm pretty darned sure you sliced heads off gang guys. If they were humans you're a serial killer, but if they were vampires..." I let it hang.

"Damned if I do, damned if I don't." Logan blew a frustrated breath. "All right. Let's say you're correct. What then?"

He'd as good as *admitted* he was a vampire. But I wasn't afraid. While we'd made love...had sex...that was because of an emotional reason, a sense of Logan being a good guy. Well, and plain desperation. Now I also realized he'd had plenty of opportunities to jump me and drink all my blood, and he hadn't. In fact, he'd actually protected me from being a Liese shake of the month. "Then I have a question for you."

"Just one?" A brief half-smile touched his lips.

Not afraid of him, but definitely scared of the way my heart leaped at that charming smile. "Is the security system at the Blood Center to take control? Or are you really trying to protect it?"

Logan relaxed, his mouth curving fully. "That's two questions." He sounded a bit more like himself.

"That's zero answers." And he was right, I had plenty more questions. "What will you do to me now that I know? And what have you *done* to me? Am I going to turn fangy?" Although if it'd help lose those last five pounds...what was I thinking?

"Ah, princess." Logan pressed a brief kiss to my forehead. "Liese, you're not going to turn from a few love bites. Only the dead turn, and then only rarely."

As I released a relieved breath he lay back on the bed. Folding his hands behind his head made his biceps really stand out. Yummy. He caught my hungry look and grinned. "And we're really trying to protect the Center."

"Why? Wouldn't it be like a smorgasbord to you guys?" I wiped away all desire for yummy biceps. Said yumminess was on a self-admitted deadly creature of the night, and besides, I'd just gotten the lay of my life. How could I be lusting after biceps so quickly?

"We're not all the same, Liese. Like humans, some are good and some are bad. Some are just desperate. The good guys protect blood—and humans—from the rest."

"Like Maim and the Corny Names Gang?"

Another grin. "And other rogues."

"For the right to drink Blood Center blood?"

"Of course not." Logan managed to look offended. "That's strictly for transfusions. To save human lives."

"No good-guy vampire would touch it?"

"I'm not saying one of us wouldn't buy some, if pressed. But we have other ways of supplying our needs."

"Donors." I remembered Maim's accusation.

"Yes. And other ways. Liese, I'm sorry I didn't tell you, but it's not just my secret. The existence of every vampire on the planet is at stake. Um, so to speak."

I smiled. "You'd pun in your sleep." Abruptly I sobered. "But now that I know, what are you going to do to me?"

Logan caught me with one hand around my head, hauled me to him. I sucked in a breath. He looked at me with eyes darkening to old gold. "I thought I'd try again to make you forget the fangs."

"That didn't work." My breath started to come faster.

"Maybe I didn't try hard enough," he murmured, and kissed me.

I didn't forget the fangs, although Logan worked like a tiger through the night. But after twenty incredible orgasms I did forget that rat-bastard what's-his-name completely.

At dawn, as Logan was dressing, a brief spike of fear returned. I'd had night-long bloody sex with a *vampire*. And I now knew a secret which could threaten them all. "So you never answered me. What are you going to do now that I know?"

Logan paused buttoning his shirt. "Actually, your knowing we exist will simplify some things in the future."

Which implied there would be a future for me to be alive in. Relief made me incautious. "Like the alien alarm parameters."

"Alarm param...you hacked our code."

I started twisting my ring and he immediately covered my hand to stop me. He was too damned smart. Part of his attraction, though, as sexy in its own way as his stun-me smile and cute puns and of course he was such an amazing lover...good lord, I was gaga over a vampire. Store me in *Warehouse 13*. "I wondered why the respiration and speeds were so weird."

"If it wasn't that, it would have been something. You're too smart not to have figured it out eventually. Makes me proud of you." He grinned as he finished dressing.

"But other people have figured things out, right? What do you do to them?"

"Hypnosis if we can. Householding if we can't."

"I thought hypnosis had to be voluntary."

"It does. You'd be surprised how many people want to forget seeing a vampire."

I made a noise of disbelief. "No woman who's had sex with you would want to forget."

He kissed me hard and fast. "That's sweet. But I don't have blood sex with human women."

"Blood sex?"

He chomped his teeth. "The bitey kind."

"Oh." My whole body heated. "And householding? What's that?"

Slowly he sat next to me on the bed, ran gentle fingers through my hair. "That's when a master vampire accepts you into his home. Takes responsibility for supporting you and protecting you in return for the gift of life."

I swallowed hard. "Sounds like a serious commitment."

A shadow crossed Logan's face, so fast I almost didn't see it. "It is." He rose. "I have to go. The sun's coming up and I didn't get any sleep yesterday. Will I see you tonight?"

"At sunset? Where?"

"The Blood Center first, to show you how to run the security system. And then—would you like to go on a date?"

A date? With Logan Steel, supernaturally gifted bed partner and all-around droolable guy? Whoo-ha! Fan me with a jet engine.

Then I pulled mental reins. He still might be leading me on for some reason. And even if he wasn't, it wouldn't do to seem too eager. Women probably fell for him like rain. I wanted to be different. To stand out. To be *special*.

"Sure," I exclaimed, and could have smacked myself.

Like the Cheshire Cat, Logan simply grinned and misted out.

I had barely fallen asleep when the "Beer Barrel Polka" blasted me awake.

"Wha...what?"

"Is this Liese Schmearling?"

The Schmearling cued my fuzzy brain that this was Race Gillette. "Yes." I yawned. Stretched. Realized I had some very sore muscles. I guess I got my money's worth when I ordered the full Logan workout.

"Nice job on the picture."

I froze mid-stretch. "What picture?"

"You know. Dungeons of Steel." Race laughed. "That'll do the trick. Elias is a note-odorous tight-ass."

I face-palmed, as if covering my eyes could blind me to my sins—or at least black out Race's wonky vocabulary. "Um, you mean notorious?"

"And your own Executioner Director," Race said over me. "Dirkson. Isn't he Chief of Police? Nobody more civic-minded than that."

He knew an awful lot. And since he normally was sharp as a hamster ball... "How did you find out?"

"I've got my sources." His rasp dropped to a whisper. "Secret security stuff. Hush-hush."

"Dolly Barton told you."

"Well, yeah." His whisper turned sulky. "But I still have my sources."

"Super secret, I'm sure. Sub rosa. Honeypot under the table, as it were."

"Huh?"

"Never mind." I pushed out of bed. Logan's scent wafted after me. "Why are you calling?" I padded to the kitchen to start coffee.

"To congratulate you on the quick work. My boss is real pleased." His voice returned to its normal volume. "And to reward you."

That stuck in my craw. "My thirty pieces of silver?"

"Don't got no silver."

I sighed. "I don't want any reward."

"But you deserve one for bringing down Golden-boy Steel. I'll buy a round tonight at Nieman's Bar. Six p.m."

"Race, I can't. I have a date." I pulled coffee beans and mug from the cabinet.

"Break it." His abruptness surprised me.

"I can't—"

"You want *everyone* to know what you did?"

My throat dropped into my belly. When I found my voice, I said, "Race, apparently everyone already knows. At least everyone with a T-one into Dolly Central."

"Sure. Then you don't care if I tell Steel."

The bag and mug dropped from my hands. They hit with a crash and splatter of beans and ceramic shards. "You wouldn't."

"You owe me, dollface. I'm the one who made you see that Steel is dangerous."

"Logan was only doing his job."

"Don't tell me he suckered you too. Naw, you're too smart. You must know his Prince Charming is all an act."

My cheeks heated.

"And if it's charm you want, give me a try, dollface. Tonight. I can be just as good. And as an added insensitive"—he meant incentive, I supposed—"I won't tell Elias or Steel who 'shopped that X-rated pic."

I shuddered. "I'll think about it."

"Think all you want, dollface. Then be at Nieman's, six p.m. sharp." He hung up.

Mechanically I stooped to clean up the mess on the floor. If only a dishrag would fix the mess of my life.

I was awake so I showered, then dressed skin-out in worn-soft jeans and a T-shirt from the bottom of my closet (no clean bras, and after the Brazilian waxing and repeated pounding, it felt better to wear air panties) and trudged in to work. Blackmail first thing in the morning could really KO a gal. I wondered how in Carl Sagan's wide universe I was going to get out of my date, either one. If my life were a reality show, at this point I would have voted *myself* off the island.

And why the heck was Race so insistent about meeting with me? I didn't want any thanks. In fact I wished I hadn't done it, even though my pocketbook and my mother's radiation bills would be happier.

Outside the Blood Center, I pawed one-handed through my purse for keys, the other covering my yawns. I dug past a motherboard, a pill bottle of screws, and six batteries (heaven help me, they were reproducing in there) before finally landing on my Pinky and the Brain key ring. Covering yet another yawn, I raised key to lock.

There was no keyhole.

I stared, wondering if my personal memory chip had shorted out. The lock was gone. In fact—my eyes rose. In fact, the whole door was gone.

In its place was a state-of-the-art security door. Polycarbonate with titanium mesh, if I remembered the specs right. On the brick wall next to it was a pad, no numbers, just touch screen. I brushed fingers over the wall, wondering how to get in.

Unless that was the point—I wasn't supposed to get in. My job was gone, over, kaput, and this was how Logan decided to tell me. No severance package or job planning. No pink slip or even a Post-it note on the polycarbonate.

I just got a locked door.

"The pad is keyed to your fingerprints. Go ahead, try it."

"Logan?" I swiveled my head to find the disembodied voice. If there was a grill I didn't see it. "Where are you? How are you talking to me?"

"I'm inside, princess. Speaking through the miracle of technology. Digital intercom. Try the fingerpad."

I pressed my index finger to the pad, a little unnerved when the lock clicked open and the door immediately *shooshed* wide.

Logan, bent over my desk, grinned and waved me in.

I felt awkward, and not just because we'd had deal-breaker sex last night. My Blood Center was now foreign territory. "I thought you were going to take a nap."

"I was. But I got a phone call." His grin morphed into a grimace. Not a welcome call, then. Hopefully not Race Gillette.

As I rounded the corner of my desk I saw my bottom drawer was open. Sweet Turing test, my cartoons and cheesy curls were exposed to an international CEO. "What are you doing?"

"Looking for your install discs." Logan's grin returned. "I

saw Visual Studio on your laptop. Figured it ran on your ancient hardware like a squirrel in lead boots. So I brought you some new hardware."

He gestured to a slim, sexy notebook sitting next to my old laptop.

It was a seventeen-inch Falcon Northwest. Warmth suffused me, driving away the chill. "Is that a FragBook?"

"Yep." Logan looked awfully pleased with himself. "*Two* nVidia GeForce 9800 GTX, so your games will scream. Speaking of games, where are your DVDs? I want to try out *Fallout 3*."

Logan was loading my software on his hardware. Ooh, and didn't that just smack of sexual overtones? Then I realized— "You hacked my laptop?"

"You hacked our code." He shrugged, perfectly balanced strength. The smooth play of hard muscles under his tight T-shirt—I choked on my own spit.

Discreetly wiping at my mouth, I said, "Someone else's bad behavior is no excuse for yours. Besides, my install DVDs are at home."

"Oh well. I enjoyed looking in your drawers." He wagged his golden brows, his eyes particularly bright.

"You keep your hands out of my drawers, buddy. And that goes double for any other tools you happen to have with you."

"But Liese. You so enjoyed my big tool last night."

I blushed. "Do you have to hammer it home?"

"Good one, princess. You really nailed that pun." He flashed his white grin.

Ye gods, that smile burned out my retinas and zapped my brain synapses. "So help me, if you mention your humongous screwdriver I'll nail your ball bearings to my desk."

His grin brightened like a supernova. "Do you really think my screwdriver is humongous?"

I was now legally blind. "Close your mouth. Now! Just close it." I peeked. His grin had subsided to a smirk, but at least it wasn't twinkling me out of existence. "It was a nice idea, Logan. But next time, ask first, okay?"

He slid my drawer shut and sauntered over. "Ask what first?" He ambled right up to my toes, stared down at me with that particular heavy-lidded look.

I fell back a step. "Um...ask before you load my software on your hardware."

He grabbed my coat and reeled me in. Murmured millimeters from my lips, "And what about loading my hardware *in* your software?"

Sirens whooped. Red alert, Mr. Spock. Every cell was instantly wide awake. I was in imminent physical danger. My eyes were so wide I poked mascara into my brows—

Only to have them flutter shut when Logan sealed my mouth with his.

Have I mentioned that the man—er, vampire—could kiss? All sense of self-preservation drained from me, ran right down my legs and out my toes, leaving me limp. I was instantly as needy as if last night was only foreplay. A whole night of plunging, driving, steamy-hot foreplay. And only a sampler because his creativity had apparently been stifled by not being able to openly fang up.

He wasn't hampered anymore. Logan, kisser extraordinary, proceeded to teach me a whole new set of exercises. He rubbed the elegant lengths of his canines against my greedy lips, flicking the seam of my mouth with his tongue. My lips parted and he dived in, so deep he tongued my epiglottis.

My hands found his broad shoulders, clutched. His caught my hips, pulled me into jeans stretched tight by a jackhammer erection. Talk about tools.

One kiss and I was already in a frenzy. My fingers dug into his hard muscles, pulling in tight to lick his mouth and suck on his lip. He tasted like elegant wine and smoky sex. I drank him in, my heart pounding wildly, teasing, tasting. When my tongue curled over the ivory-smooth length of one fang he groaned. So I did it again.

Logan jerked. His hips jacked into my belly, the Grand Teton gouging me. I gasped—and sucked his fang harder. He howled, urgently rubbed his enormous erection against me. He licked frantically at my lips, tonguing every square millimeter of skin he could reach.

I drew deeper on his fang, suckling rhythmically, swirling my tongue over the smooth enamel. He howled again. His fangs grew longer and his hips rocked frantically.

And I was the one doing it to him. It was so lovely I expected at any second to be interrupted by a phone call or Nurse Battleax or Zinnia and her little sprouts.

Logan backed me into the wall where he began to beat his swollen zipper against my pubic bone so hard my butt thwacked drywall. I sucked his fang the whole way, sliding my lips up and down like it was his lovely thick erection.

And maybe they were connected, because his fangs shot out full length as his zipper strained to the point of bursting.

His breath rasped. His rhythm changed to bang and grind. Bang, so hard my eyes popped open. Grind, the erotic pressure unbearable. Bang and grind, driving himself against me with the finesse of a sledgehammer, albeit an elegant, lithe sledgehammer.

My pelvis throbbed. He was so strong, thrust so hard, I was going to be bruised. And I wanted more. More pounding, more grinding. I wanted him to smash me into bits against the wall, grind me into dust. I sucked both fangs into my mouth.

He threw his head back and *roared*. His bellow was so loud and harsh I thought he'd bring down the ceiling. Tendons stood out in his neck, muscles pumped like balloons. And his pants—he was so huge I thought he'd explode from his clothes.

He tore open his zipper. The Loch Logan Monster sprang from the depths, fully formed. I fumbled with my top snap.

Logan pushed my hands away, undid and yanked my jeans to the floor, pulled them off over my shoes. I had no panties, but neither of us cared. As he rose he hooked my knees, lifted me off my feet. My legs folded as he slid me up the wall. My knees pressed into my breasts and my butt hung down under me, hips tilted in just the right position.

He drove into me with one hard thrust.

I screamed in ecstasy. Logan began to ride me with fast waves of his hips, bouncing me shatteringly into the wall. Bolts of pleasure hit me from clit to coccyx. Need sparked my whole pelvis. My heart hammered. My vulva quivered and spasmed. I was climbing to the peak of desire, ready to take the plunge.

"Hello?" Someone started hammering at the door. "Anybody home?"

"No," I shrieked. "Nobody here. Go 'way."

"Nice try, lady. My school marching band is raising money to go to Washington D.C. Wanna buy some cookies?"

"*No*," I bellowed as Logan sank his fangs into my trapezius.

"How about concert tickets?"

I hit the edge and shot over. But this time I didn't drown in the huge waves of pleasure.

"What about band candy?"

No, the maddening band kid distracted me just enough so that I rode that orgasm like a surfer. Skimmed the top of a climax so big and powerful it pushed me far out to sea.

"C'mon, lady. Nobody can say 'no' to band candy. It's chocolate."

The orgasm washed me oceans away. It went on and on, the endless lapping of waves finally setting me down gently on the warm, sandy shores of heaven.

Or maybe that was Logan settling me gently on my feet.

"Hey, lady—how about candles? We're selling wreaths too. Never too early to think about Christmas gifts."

Logan slipped my jeans over my shoes and up. I let him, having only enough energy to stare dazedly at his exposed hips. His giant redwood had apparently yelled "Timber," too. It looked as pleasantly exhausted as I felt.

"We're also selling gourmet popcorn. If, you know, you're on a diet."

"You okay?" Logan propped me up with one hand and used the other to deftly tug up and close his jeans. No underwear on him either. I should have guessed—or been surprised the jeans weren't painted on, after all.

"Yeah, just...just give me a sec." My syllables were mush covered with drool.

"Three kinds, lady. Caramel, butter and white cheddar."

I could barely stand. It was Logan who sauntered to the door. When he closed it a moment later, he had arms full of candy, cookies, candles and for all I knew concert tickets for the whole season.

"Now." He dropped the loot behind my desk. "Where were we?"

Chapter Ten

"You can think after tha'?"

Logan smiled, teeth normal now except for the supernaturally white sparkle (think Tony Curtis in *The Great Race*) gouging my eyes. Ow, ow, ow. "Are you kidding, Liese? I feel terrific after that. Like I could do a triathlon, climb Everest and spec an alarm system for the Crown Jewels."

Figured. He got chatty after sex. I just wanted to roll over and go to sleep. If we weren't the most backward of couples—

Couples? Where had *that* thought come from? I stammered the first thing that came to mind. "What are you doing here, anyway?"

"Like I said, I got a phone call. And since I couldn't sleep, I decided to come train you. On the new systems, remember?"

The systems I would never get to use, because of that damned incriminating picture. For a moment I couldn't remember why I'd sent the stupid thing. It seemed like such a good idea at the time. I forced myself to keep to the conversation. "But it's daytime. How did you get here?"

His smile faded. He'd heard something in my tone, no doubt. The man—vampire—was so perceptive he was scary. "Bo's limo is shielded. That's how I traveled to Chicago yesterday. He's got a shielded Maybach sedan too." He paused. "What's wrong, Liese?"

I closed my eyes. "Please. Only one conversation at a time. My brain is still pudding."

"Then tell me what's the matter." His warm hands engulfed my upper arms.

"Wrong conversation." I opened my eyes, saw the concern on his face. Genuine concern. He would listen to me if I wanted.

He would listen patiently while I spewed my problems, then cuddle me and stroke me like he had before.

And I wanted that, with a deep gaping need that scared me. The urge to unburden myself was so strong I actually laid my head against his rock-hard chest. His heart beat steady and strong. I drank in the illusion of trust and safety. Just for a moment.

Have you ever wanted something so heart-aching bad you didn't recognize fact from fiction? Didn't know what was real and what you only wanted to be real? It was why I'd kept the glass ring, to remember I was so easily fooled.

I stepped away. I was my own rock. My own safety. Me, and my mother. I could trust her. Everyone else was suspect, especially Mr. Broncobuster here. Only, what a fast, hard ride...shizzle. "If you have a shielded car, then why all the after-dark subterfuge? Why wait until night to show yourself the first time?"

"Traveling by day is not as safe as it sounds." Logan shrugged, a sort of flip of one muscled shoulder. His shrugs, I was coming to see, meant different things. This one spoke of deadly perils faced, of grace under pressure. "Sun damages us, no matter what time of day. Even reflected sun."

"All vampires? Even the new ones?"

"Actually, young ones are more susceptible. Fledglings need full dark, regardless of shielding. An older vampire can withstand short periods of daylight, especially early in the morning or late in the evening."

"And you're out this morning. You're older, then?"

"Yes. Dawn and dusk, as long as the exposure's brief."

"And if you stay out longer? What happens then?"

"I'd rather not go into the gory details." He ran long fingers through his golden mane, disheveling it. My fingers longed to do the same.

I clenched them hard. Intimacy with this man—vampire— was a drug, addictive. The more I had, the more I wanted. "Please. I know so little about you."

He lowered his hand, slowly. "Would it help you to trust me?"

"Yes," I said, though I didn't really think it would.

"Well, sun damage is like sunburn, at first. Red skin,

133

blisters. But internally, our body temperature rises. The longer we're exposed to even small amounts of sunlight, the hotter we get. Too long, and we burn, literally.

The implications were horrific. "You mean—you go up in flames? And that's just sunrise or sunset? What if you're out at high noon?"

"Depends on the age of the vampire. I'd fall unconscious in about a minute and fire up soon after. Strongwell could stand three or four min—"

"Strongwell? *Bo* Strongwell's a vampire?"

"Yes. You started this conversation, Liese. Please don't interrupt. Strongwell could stand three or four minutes. But when he flamed he'd go like a bonfire. *Foosh.*" Logan made an exploding gesture with his elegant hands. "Now will you tell me what's wrong?"

He was intelligent, perceptive and possessing a terrific and stupidly persistent memory. "No. Why would Bo last longer?"

Logan's slight roll of the shoulder was almost a sigh. "Strongwell's older than me. A bit over a thousand. Emerson is older than that."

"Julian *Emerson's* a vam—" I caught Logan's pointed look. "Okay. Bo's a thousand? A thousand what?"

"Years," Logan said, matter-of-fact, as if he hadn't just rocked my entire conception of age.

"O-kay." I swallowed my incredulity. "And you are...?"

"Just shy of four hundred."

"So Bo outranks you? He's your master?"

At that, Logan threw back his head and laughed, ripples convulsing his strong throat. "Hardly. Bo's older, and so I respect him, of course. But my training easily puts me on equal footing with him. Liese, if you're not going to tell me what's bothering you, I'd like to get cracking on the new systems. We can discuss the vagaries of vampire age and relative strength over dinner tonight. By the way—I've got something for you. A gift."

"Um, yeah. About dinner—"

"I thought I'd take you to that supper club on the edge of town. The Alpine Retreat and Bar. I hear they have good food."

That sidetracked me. "You eat?"

"You know I eat." Logan slanted an evil leer at me. With his blond good looks, it was less creepy and more...seductive.

I imagined that leer rising up from between my spread thighs, all sparkling eyes and lush lips—and mentally whacked myself with my Microsoft Action Pack. "I meant food."

He grinned. "Not food. But you do eat, and I can pretend. What kind of date would it be, if I didn't buy you a fancy dinner?"

If it weren't for Race... "That's awfully nice, Logan, but you don't have to go to all that trouble. In fact, since I may have to work late, um, learning the new systems, well, in town might be better." I pretended to get a bright idea. "Like Nieman's Bar."

Logan's smile faded. He'd caught my panic, but hopefully not the reason. "Liese, what is it? You can tell me." He stared intently into my eyes as if he could *will* me to tell.

How I wanted to trust him, to unburden. But it was insanity. I couldn't let my stupid need to be loved overrule my common sense. After all, a primo hunk of man—damn it, vampire—like Logan Steel would never get involved with a dumpy, nerdy woman like me. At least, not on the permanent double-M monogamy-gene basis that I needed.

Logan's stare had sharpened to x-ray. I started babbling. "I like fish, see. And Nieman's has Friday Fish Fry. And Wednesdays during Lent too, which I guess would be Wednesday Fish Fry. Or maybe Wednesday Lent Fry...I mean Lent Fish Fry." The more I babbled, the pointier his stare. "So, anyway, um...how about it? Nieman's, say eight?"

Logan took a step toward me, his eyes set on awl. "I don't want you staying here alone that late. Six."

"No! I need time, time to, um, get ready. You know, changing, grooming, uh."

The last was because Logan had again backed me into the wall, doing his ultra-alpha vampire thing again. His hazel eyes lit almost pure gold, boring into my head like halogen high beams. "Liese. What's going on?"

I grabbed my two-carat glass reminder of bad trust and twisted.

"What's wrong, princess?" He pried my fingers from the ring, gently. Gathered me to his chest, rocked me. "Please tell me."

Sex, I could have handled. Interrogation, I could have

handled. Even boring into my head like a latter-day Svengali I could have handled.

But his warm concern finally undid me. "Oh, Logan. It's—"

The intercom clicked open. A bright voice chirped, "Mr. Steel? Zinnia Jones here. Let me in, please. It's already Wednesday so we have to go over this list right away if we're to get everything finished before Monday. I know you're in there. Mr. Steel?"

I jerked straight. Logan stiffened like a board.

We exchanged a look. Shared a moment of perfect understanding.

He grabbed my hand and we hightailed it for the back room.

"Let me in, Mr. Steel—before I have to call the Ancient One."

Logan screeched to a halt like lightning had hit him. His fangs shot out, his eyes fired bright red. All his muscles bunched, so tight he quivered. Even his long hair floated out and crackled.

Well, stab me with a fish fork. This was the third time I'd heard that phrase. Who or what was the Ancient One, and why did TAO unsettle the CEO so much? My hand was turning to pulp from his squeezing it. "What is it, Logan? What's wrong?"

He blinked at me, his red eyes cooling slightly. "It's...complicated."

"I have my phone out, Mr. Steel. I'm dialing..."

Logan swore, his voice so loud and harsh that even outside Zinnia's petal ears must have burned. Creatively too. I don't think he repeated a single word as he rampaged back into the office, although half his cussing sounded French so I wasn't a hundred-percent sure.

He hit the handicapped door switch on the wall, hard. I was surprised it didn't shatter. Zinnia popped through, took one look at his face, expression set to *annihilate*, and cringed.

But to her credit she straightened and said, "Thank you, sir. I've gone through the list and made recommendations. You need to review my suggestions and make a final decision." She held a manila folder out to him.

He didn't take it. She waggled the file in front of him. "Mr. Steel, or should I say, Master Logan. Do not make this harder on both of us. You know what will happen if you put this off for too long."

This time Logan was the one who winced. "Believe me. I know better than you ever could." He looked like a cornered beast.

Powerful, golden Logan Steel, cornered. The Ancient One must be some powerful guru if the mere mention of he/she/it could make Logan almost desperate.

Of course, a desperate Logan would be twice as dangerous.

Exasperated myself now, I snatched the file from Zinnia. "For goodness sake, Logan. You're head of a major security company. You must have hired employees before. What's in this little folder that could possibly alarm you so?" I opened it for a look.

No monster jumped out at me, not even a pink slip. Inside were three pages of spreadsheet with names neatly typed in the first column. Handwritten positive comments were in the second column, negative comments in the third. Zinnia's personal notes were scribbled in the far margin.

The comments were strange. Instead of stock phrases like "completes work on time" and "shows initiative", one person "came from five generations of donors" and another "requires consideration because of severe personal trauma". Zinnia's note on the last was "attacked by three rogues".

Rogues. Logan had used that term for bad-guy vampires. But what could it mean, on an interview list for Steel Security?

The intercom clicked open. "Ms. Schmetterling? It's Bud. Lilly has to use the restroom. May we come in?"

A new set of controls was on my desk. One was helpfully labeled *Intercom*. As I punched open the line, I absently noted a light labeled *Phone Messages"* was blinking. "Be right there, Bud."

I handed the folder back to Zinnia so I could use the door button on the wall. There was probably a control on the desk, but it wasn't labeled.

Bud sauntered in, little Lilly in tow. One chorus of "Itsy-Bitsy Spider" later they were on their way out, but Bud paused. "Ms. Schmetterling? Could, um, Lilly watch cartoons?"

Since Logan had already been in my drawers and knew the worst, I said, "Sure. Come sit down."

Zinnia sniffed disapproval. "Not that awful bigoted cartoon again. Isn't there enough misunderstanding in the world?"

"Mother." Bud flashed her a warning look.

Logan watched me take *Animaniacs* from my drawer. "Bigoted? You obviously never saw cartoons in the forties."

"Having a history doesn't make it right, Master Logan. You of all people know that. How long have the Children of the Night struggled against prejudice? Against intolerance that labels them evil when they're simply dentally challenged?"

"*Mother.*" Bud started flailing like a berserk traffic cop.

But I was starting to enjoy myself. Zinnia's rants were making sense at last. "Dentally challenged? Isn't that taking political correctness a little too far?"

Zinnia, just winding up, leaped to her feet. "We all must fight for the less fortunate, for the blood poor, the hemoglobin disadvantaged. Equality is for all people, regardless of race, creed, or dietary restrictions!"

"*Mom.* Ix-nay on the dead-unay." Bud shot a look at Logan, shifted his eyes significantly to me.

Logan understood instantly. "It's all right. Liese knows."

"A sister in the fight," Zinnia agreed. Since Bud didn't appear convinced, I nodded. Zinnia said, "Ms. Schmetterling is with us. A defender of optional respiration."

I nodded some more.

"And Master Logan's sex thrall."

I nodded—"*What?*"

Logan coughed. "Zinnia, could I have a word? Back room." He ushered her out before I could do anything. Good thing, or I might have made *her* respiration optional. Sex thrall my ass.

Setting the kids up with their cartoons cooled me off. That, and the graphics quality of the FragBook really blew me away. With Zinnia's sprouts occupied, I checked voicemail.

The first message started. The voice was as deep and black as an underground cavern. Filled with the self-assurance of a man totally in command of himself and everyone else around him, that dark voice chilled me to the bone. Logan might be a prince, but this was a king.

The man's voice scared me, but his words made me want to pee. "Ms. Schmetterling. This is Mr. Elias of the Steel Security Board of Directors. I received an email from you yesterday that we need to discuss. I will be out of town tonight and tomorrow, but I will expect a call from you Friday after six p.m."

He rattled off his number, which took me three hearings to copy down because my hand was shaking so badly.

I was doomed. How had Elias figured out that picture was from me? Then I slapped my head. Dolly Barton had a mail daemon. What made me think the chairman of a huge security firm would be any less well-informed?

I wasn't doomed. I was dead. Even if Logan didn't bite me and drink all my blood because of this, I would lose my job for sure. On top of the fiasco at ADD, I would never get another. And no job, no medical insurance. Theoretically COBRA would extend coverage, but without a job how would I pay the premiums? No, I would never hold another job. Unless—

Unless I could convince Bernie Botcher to stop blacklisting me.

He'd phoned last night wanting something from me, so I had leverage. Something to do with Steel Security.

Maybe I could talk Logan into helping Botcher. Then Botcher would stop blacklisting me, and when Logan fired me for ruining him, I could find a job.

I'm ashamed to admit I considered it. Use Logan, then abuse him, like Botcher had done to me. But I had issues, not a total meltdown of conscience. I couldn't do that to a mosquito, much less a man I loved...er, loved having sex with.

But if not that, then what? Because no job, no eat. And no radiation. And while I was kind of fond of eating, I knew I couldn't do without Mom.

The second message started. It was the only thing that could have scared me worse than Elias.

"Hi, honey. It's Mom. I'm calling with good news, Liese."

Excellent. Because if one more thing went wrong I was going to cut off my right hand, bronze it, and use it for a paperweight.

"I've enjoyed staying with Cousin Rolf. And they're glad to have me bunk with them." For which I was grateful. "But apparently my being here interferes with Rolf's performance. And it ain't his singing."

Oh, crap. Did she mean what I thought she meant? My mother? My holy sainted virginal mother? Okay, I knew she'd had sex at some point in her life, where else had I come from? But that didn't mean I wanted to *think* about it.

"Cousin Rolf has been reduced to visiting Rosy Palm and her five lovely daughters."

Oh for the love of bite me!

"But naturally he wants to get some with his wife instead. So I'm coming home for a few days between treatments. See you tonight, honey."

I hung up, numb. If one more thing went wrong—why, oh why did I think that? Meet Race Gillette at six, or he'd rat me out. Somehow get rid of him before Logan arrived, or be exposed. Deal with the fallout of that damning picture. Dolly knew I had sent it. Elias knew. Even Race, with his M.A. in Stupid, knew.

As if all that weren't enough, my mother was coming home.

Bronze my right hand and use it as a paperweight? Just call me Lefty. Goodbye, sex life. No more late night visits from golden vampires. No more supernaturally gifted lovers in my bed, taking me to heaven.

That, I realized, was the worst of all. No Logan in my bed.

Although he was pretty good against the office wall too.

"Liese? What's wrong?"

I looked up to see Logan returning from the back room, his face filled with concern for me. If only I could believe it was real. If only I could sink into his arms and tell him about the picture. Trust him not to cream me, then can me. Hmm, time for breakfast.

I pushed away from the phone. "Nothing. Or, not much. My mom's coming home for a few days."

"Oh." Then, "*Oh.* Well, there's always the file cabinet."

I goggled. Great minds really did think alike.

Zinnia followed Logan out. "Ms. Schmetterling? Master Logan explained everything. About how you're not his thrall, but his girlfriend." She smiled brightly.

"Glad we got that straightened—girlfriend?" If sex thrall smacked me in the face, that punched me in the gut.

"Does that mean Ms. Smelling is coming to live with us?" little Lilly piped up.

Out of the mouths of babes. I pictured Logan and me living together. In bed together. Waking up together, having coffee together. Having morning sex together...that was shattering enough, but when I pictured *all* of us together, an ocean-sized bed with me and Logan and Zinnia and her whole flower garden *and* the busload of interviewees...that was just disturbing.

Zinnia patted Lilly's guinea-gold curls. "Of course, sweetheart. She's Master Logan's girlfriend, after all."

It hit me a second time. *Girlfriend.* Oh, the bruises. I ignored them. "What's with the 'master' stuff, anyway?"

"Master of the new Iowa Alliance household, of course." Zinnia picked up the manila folder from the desk where she'd dropped it and bustled over to Logan.

I stared at him. "You're starting a household? As in, serious commitment and responsibility?"

Logan grimaced as he finally accepted the folder. "Yes."

Zinnia looked over his arm as he opened it. "The list is totally objective, Mr. Steel. You can see all the interviewees' positives and negatives. It's just up to you to pick."

"Wait." I scooted to Logan's other side. Stared at the list of names. "Are you saying these people were interviewing for positions in your vampire household?" Not Steel Security positions? *Not my job.*

If anything, Logan's expression got grimmer. "Yes."

"They're all candidates—"

"Yes."

"—for lovers?"

"Yes—no! Good heavens, Liese. Householding's not about, um, carnal desires."

"It isn't? But last night, after se—"

"Shh. Little laptops have big webcams." He gave a significant glance at Bud and Lilly. The children were no longer watching the cartoons but staring attentively at us.

So I said, "Then what is it about, if not ess-ee-ex?"

Bud rolled his eyes. "I can spell, Ms. Schmetterling."

"Me too," Lilly said. "What's essy-ex?"

"Householding's about tradition," Zinnia said. "About protection."

I scanned the list. There were a preponderance of young women, true. But also older women, and men. Unless Logan was even more adventurous than I thought, these couldn't *all* be potential lovers. "Protection from what?"

Zinnia's blue eyes flared with anger. "From the real evil creatures, Ms. Schmetterling. Rogues. They gang up on humans and drink them dry, or open a vein and let the human bleed out."

"But why Meiers Corners? We don't have a rogue problem." I'd never seen vampires in town before. Except for Bo Strongwell, but I hadn't known he was one.

Logan closed the folder. "Remember Razor and his gang?"

"Yes, but they're out-of-towners, right? From Chicago?"

"They're *in* town now."

Zinnia said, "The household won't actually be in Meiers Corners, since there are two here already."

"*What?* Meiers Corners has two houses full of vampires—and nobody knows?"

Bud shook his head. "Not full of vampires, Ms. Schmetterling. Full of people. Each household has about two dozen donors, as well as several children and elderly."

I stared at Bud. "You don't even live here. How can you know how many people our households have?"

"It's simple math." He paused the cartoon and assumed an earnest, scholarly expression. "Vampires need blood. Regular transfusions, about three times a month."

"So they only eat three times a month, so what?"

"It's not food, Ms. Schmetterling. Vampires are like people who can't make their own blood, so they take donations." He sounded like he was reciting a school lesson. "People can safely donate about five times a year. That equals six to eight humans per vampire. Assuming three vampire protectors per household, that's eighteen to twenty-four people."

A school lesson in the economics of blood. Weird. "And the humans? Why would they agree to being—what word did you use? Donors?"

"Humans need to be protected from wild vampires. Even fledglings are stronger and faster than the strongest human. Many centuries ago the first households were formed, a symbiotic relationship between vampires and humans. That tradition carries on today."

Another school lesson, vampire history. Please, hit me over the head with a laserjet to balance the pain. "Are there that many wild vampires?"

"Turnings have skyrocketed," Zinnia said. "Just in the last twenty years."

Bud nodded. "There have been surges in the past, during things like the Black Plague and the reign of Vlad the Impaler. But nothing like now, although no one knows why."

Apparently the vampire science class wasn't as advanced as economics and history. I looked from Bud to Zinnia to Logan to little Lilly, who'd unpaused the cartoon and was ignoring us all. "But...with all these vampires...hasn't anybody stumbled onto the fact that they're real?"

"Bud has a theory about that," Zinnia said proudly. "Go on, honey. Tell Ms. Schmetterling your theory."

Bud shrugged, a graceful gesture reminiscent of Logan. "Subconsciously, I think people know. There's been a spike in vampire literature, movies and even television shows. More traffic in chat rooms and more groups on the Internet. I did a paper on it."

He did a paper on it. Feed me through the laserjet and print *Alice in Wonderland* on my naked skin, 'cause it sure felt like I was falling down the white rabbit's hole. "For school? Isn't that a bit risky?"

Zinnia answered. "Bud is home-schooled, Ms. Schmetterling."

Of course he was. I turned to Logan. "And you're choosing to start one of these households. Be its master."

"Yes." His hands tightened convulsively. The folder crumpled in them.

I stared at the warped folder. "You don't want to?"

"Of course Mr. Steel wants to." Zinnia pried the folder out of his hands. Smoothed it on my desk. "He's CEO of a major business, on the board of several more. How hard can running a little household be?"

"It's not so little." Logan's jaw worked, and I caught the glint of pointy teeth just behind his lips. "Four vampire protectors. Thirty human donors, a dozen children and old ones. Not so little."

"Come now, Mr. Steel." Zinnia spoke briskly, as to a recalcitrant child. "You've trained for this. Longer than any of the Ancient One's lieutenants, from what I've heard. You'll be fine. Now, the list?"

"No. Not yet. Maybe tomorrow."

"I see." She tapped her nails against her arm. "And do you want to explain to the Ancient One why you haven't met his timeline, or shall I?"

"When you put it that way...fine." Logan slapped the folder open. Zinnia had pushed exactly the right button to get him to cooperate.

The right button. Logic gates opened in my head. As Zinnia peered over Logan's arm and pointed, I began to see my way clear to meeting Race without tipping off Logan.

All I had to do was get Logan to agree to meet me at Nieman's at seven, one hour after I was to meet Race. An hour, knowing Race's button, would be plenty of time.

Chapter Eleven

Zinnia and Logan retired to the back room while the sprouts and I OD'd on cartoons. The Ralph Kramden bus driver ploughed in to use the restroom, taking a turn around the office afterward to stretch his legs. He paused at the server rack, earning my grudging respect. I thought the razor-slim cases and flashing lights were pretty awesome too.

Somewhere around two the phone rang. "Blood Center."

"Liese, where've you been?" The whiny note identified him immediately. Bernie Botcher, the rat-bastard.

"Hello, Bernie. And goodbye."

"Now, Liese, don't hang up. You've gotta help me. You've got to save my job. I need my job."

So had I. "Bernie, I don't have time for this. Good—"

"Honeypot, just listen."

I grit my teeth. Now I was the honeypot. "What."

"The wife and I just bought this bigger house, see. And I need a new car 'cause I got into a little accident with the Audi. Look, I just made a little mistake at ADD."

"Really." My tone would have sucked the water out of desert sand.

"Honest! It's such a small favor. One little favor and I'll be forever grateful, honest."

Honest and Bernie Botcher did not strike me as being in the same gravitational sink, much less on speaking terms. "I see."

"Help me and maybe I'll see my way clear to giving you a job reference."

And there it was, of course. The Golden Carrot.

"It isn't fair, babe. My entire life wiped out, because of a tiny mistake."

For the first time I realized the man I had loved, given my research to, given my *life* to, was a giant pain in the ass. "Bernie, just spit it out."

"It's easy, Liese. Get rid of Steel for me."

I laughed, no humor in it. "Bernie, for your information I've already done something about him. And I'm not proud of it."

"You've done it? Oh, happy days. Then I'm safe. You're the best, Liese." Botcher only heard what he wanted. Why hadn't I noticed that before, either?

"It backfired, Bernie."

"I'm not safe?" Fear choked his voice.

"He may still go down. But I'll go with him."

"Then you've got to finish it, Liese. Finish it right away, before it's too late. Do it for us, Liese. For our love. I do love you."

And there they were—the Golden Words. I sighed. "Even if that's true, Bernie, you love yourself more."

"Babe, don't you remember I called you beautiful?"

"I remember. I also remember you didn't mean it."

"Of course I meant it. I said it, didn't I?"

"Your actions and your words tell me two different things, Bernie. And they can't both be true."

"Come on, honey." Desperation tinged his tone. "You know you still love me."

Unfortunately, I did. But it was tiny, withered and nearly dead, and I might just love Logan Steel more. Oh well, one mistake at a time. "Good-bye, Bernie."

"The job recommendation, then." Botcher's rapid breaths rasped over the phone. "You've got to finish Steel for me. Liese, don't—Liese—*I'll never forgive you for this!*"

Despite my vulnerability, despite Mom's radiation, I hung up.

I pushed into Nieman's Bar, then paused for a deep centering breath. I had a plan to get rid of Race Gillette, but if it didn't work, Logan was going to meet him. And since the fourth law of thermodynamics (according to the great physicist Murphy) was "if anything can go wrong, it will", that meant

Race would blab about my blackmail. I took another cleansing breath and made my way to the bar and ordered a couple pitchers of beer. I had to believe my plan would work.

Buddy loaded pitchers and glasses on a tray. I added bowls of salty bar peanuts and made my way to where Race sat with yet another female. She was rubbing herself against him, her neck curved in a way that made me think of Logan's orgasmic bite.

Huh. Either that was suspicious, or I was starting to see everything in Fang-o-vision.

Race caught sight of me. "Hey, dollface. Come join me and my babe, here." His babe, right. Like his Honeypot and his Shweetie Pie.

But his come-hither wave was unsteady. Empty glasses littered the table. I allowed myself to hope. My cunning plan to get rid of Race (a plan so cunning its Bond villain name was Dr. I-No) was already started, without me doing a thing.

Race eyed the pitchers appreciatively. Babe eyed me much less tenderly. I grinned and stuck out my hand to her. "Hi. I'm Liese, a business associate of Race's."

She looked at me like I was bellybutton lint. "What kind of *business*?"

"Wha...oh, no. *Security* business." Not hooker business. No way I'd do that, unless Logan was my exclusive customer...hmm.

She eased up enough to give me a smile. One of her front teeth overlapped the other, giving her a girlish, wistful look. "I'm Babe." She shook my hand.

Huh. She really was his Babe. Well, in Meiers Corners coincidence was so normal it was Meal Deal #3, so I just topped off both their beers. Race gulped his down, wiped foam off his lip, belched, then set the empty in front of me with a thump. I filled it again. "So, Race. Why am I here?"

"To get drunk." He took an empty glass off the tray and slapped it down in front of me. "Keep up this time, dollface. I'm watchin'."

I poured, stopped when a thought hit me. And yes, it hurt. Botcher got me drunk when he wanted to get laid. Race couldn't want *that*, could he? "Why?"

"Drunk's trust. I don't trust nobody who stays sober while I drink."

I started pouring again. "That's a relief. I thought you might want to take advantage of me."

"Hey, good idea."

Me and my big mouth. "What about Babe?" And Honeypot and any other female who thought sleaze equaled sex appeal because both started with *S*.

"There's plenty of this studmuffin to go around, dollface." Race fumbled with his belt. "Lemme show you."

"No!" I clapped a hand over his. "Trust is a good enough reason. I'll try to keep up." Actually, having been raised in Meiers Corners, where beer was cheaper than water, I could probably drink him under the table. But no reason to show off, right? "And just to prove to you I'm on the level." I took the glass, opened my throat and tossed the beer down in eight seconds. Not as good as Honeypot, but I was out of practice.

"Pass one down here, Razey-poo."

I jumped at the voice from under the table. I snuck a peek then shot back up, red-faced. So that's where Honeypot was tonight. I peeked again. She was going at Race with relish. Had he dipped it in chocolate?

But now instead of just Race, I had to consider Babe and Honeypot too. Did this change my plan? Pouring a glass for Honeypot, I considered my options. A couple of pitchers was enough for a small party. I decided my plan could still work, as long as I stayed soberest of the bunch. I passed Honeypot's glass to her.

That was when the first beer hit, making me really warm. But not fuzzy, right? *Right*? Panic hit me. *How would I know*? Granted, in college I could drink like a whale but since Botcher the most I'd had was a glass or so. What if I'd lost the ability to guzzle?

A test. I needed a test to prove I was still sober. I picked a couple peanuts out of a bowl, leaned under the table. Honeypot was still going at it. I aimed at the dark spot in her low-rider jeans, sank one peanut, then another. Two for two.

Yep. Still sober. I headed back up. My cunning plan to hit Race's button, his temper, and hit it hard, could still work. Just a little push and he'd get belligerent.

What's so cunning about that, you may ask? Nothing,

actually. The brilliance was getting him drunk. See, Buddy the Bartender also was Buddy the Bouncer. Belligerent Race was just weeknight entertainment but drunk belligerent Race—well, Buddy would launch his ass through the door so fast I was hoping Race'd achieve planetary orbit.

With Race gone I could meet Logan safely. We'd have our talk. Another reason to keep as clear-headed as possible. Logan and I were going to talk about some sensitive issues. Which meant sipping my beer, very carefully—

"Drink!" Race shoved the bottom of my glass forehead-high.

I gulped beer, half of it pouring down my cheeks and chin. Sputtering, I grabbed a paper napkin off the tray, swiped my jaw.

I scrubbed nose instead. Darn, was I getting drunk? I leaned over and shot another peanut at Honeypot's plumber's crack. It hit her left heel. Shizzle. I groped around for a few more peanuts, fired off half a dozen, put four in the hole. Okay, not so bad. I surfaced. "You know, it's a fallacy that drunk people tell the truth."

"What's blow jobs got to do with it?"

Fallacy, fellatio. So close—yet so not. "I mean I can lie even after a few beers."

"You're havin' more than a few. Drink." He gave my refilled glass an irritated poke.

I didn't want to wipe beer off half my body, so I drank. Filled our glasses again.

Honeypot surfaced. She and Babe were still working on their beers so it was just me racing with Race. Get it? Racing Race? I giggled. Oops. Time for a soberness test, but my personal Stanford-Binet was standing now, so no more chucking peanuts into her jeans. What to do, what to do? I tossed up a couple peanuts and tried to catch them in my mouth. They bounced off my chin and landed in Babe's cleavage.

Okay, that worked. Hey, I sunk 'em, didn't I? Another couple beers would get rid of Race. Half an hour, tops. Just enough time left to sober up before Logan came. I wouldn't be completely clearheaded, but close enough. I sipped my beer, very carefully—

"Hey, Liese. What's up?" A husky alto, *right* behind me.

I choked down half my beer. Came up coughing.

Elena and Bo stood bracketing me. Bo pounded me helpfully on the back. I gave a weak smile through my coughing. "Hi, guys—" cough, cough, "—what're you—" cough, cough, "—doing here?"

"Bo's taking me to fish fry," Elena said. He gave her a look and she amended, "*We're* going to fish fry. Both of us are eating fish fry."

"It's okay. I know about v—"

"What's *he* doing here?" Bo's eyes flared sudden hot violet, glaring at Race. "Go back to Chi-town, Ra—"

"*Race* Gillette, glad to meet you." Race leaped to his feet, teetered, slapped one hand to his head which apparently steadied him enough to thrust the other toward Bo.

Bo shut his mouth with a snap. A rather loud snap, like an angry dog.

"Well, *Race Gillette*, I imagine you were just leaving." Elena patted a bulge in her jacket, right where a gun would be.

Race withdrew his ignored hand. "Like that little peashooter could hurt me? Come back when you've got your big gun." He wagged his eyebrows suggestively.

Yuck. Logan's eyebrow wags were cute but not Race's— although some of the yuck might have been the crotch-rubbing he did with the eyebrow-wagging.

Elena reached into her jacket. "I do have my big gun."

I stiffened. Bo grinned, fang tips just showing. Race fell back a step. Even Honeypot and Babe froze.

And Elena pulled out—a pack of cards. I relaxed. Race, to the contrary, started stuttering. "No. Anything but Shpees...Shpits...cards. It's unnatural, is what."

"You, me, Bo and Liese." Elena pulled up a chair and shuffled. "Afraid to take on a couple of women and a Viking, *Race*?" She riffed cards with a practiced flourish.

"Go get 'em, Razey-poo," Honeypot said.

Razey-poo turned bright red. "Um...we can't. There's only four. We can't play with only four."

"We could use a fifth." Bo looked at Babe and Honeypot. "Which one of you—"

"Ooh, a fifth! Good idea." Babe raced off to the bar.

"I guess that decides it." Elena dealt Honeypot in.

We played for a quarter a point. Elena tended to play by the book, which meant she usually broke even. Bo was pretty good and so was I.

Either Race was better than us all, or he had Lady Luck firmly on his side because he won almost every hand. 'Course maybe Lady Luck had help from the fifth of tequila Babe brought back. Race insisted on *everyone* doing shots.

I was still half-sober though, at least by the Babe-cleavage meter. I sank one out of every two peanuts. Although that might have been because she started chasing them down, her hands on her boobs like they were catchers' mitts.

But Elena lost. Bo lost. And I lost, *big* time. And not just money.

"Fish fry?" a familiar croon came. "I think it's more like *you're* fried, princess."

I jumped. Heart pounding, I twisted. "Logan? Is that you?"

Which was actually pretty silly. Who else called me princess in that deep, seductive voice? But before I could utter any other immortal phrases suitable for chiseling on my frickin' headstone, Race croaked, "Lord Logan?"

Or maybe it was "Lord! Logan?" Yeah. That was it.

Bo jumped in. "Logan, this is *Race*. Race Gillette."

"Race. I see." Logan acknowledged Race with a faintly mocking smile. "Hello, *Race*. Don't you owe me money?"

Race coughed. "Um, I don't carry cash."

"That pile of quarters in front of you looks like quite a bit of cash." Logan pulled up a chair next to Race, reversed and straddled it. Stirring a long forefinger through Race's winnings he cocked his head. "Sounds like...sixty-two dollars. And fifty cents."

I blinked. "You can tell from the sound?"

Logan slung me a smile edged in smug. "Money and I have a certain affinity."

"Handy for a CEO," Bo said. "I just raid for mine."

Elena punched him on the arm. "You do not."

Race, eyes wild and glued on the exit, pushed quarters haphazardly at Logan. "Take it all. I gotta go!" He jumped to his feet and ran.

Before he got two steps Logan snared his wrist. Race spun, hit the table and rebounded to crash into his chair. Immediately he leaped to his feet, tried to jerk away. He even did it correctly, pulling at the thumb-forefinger gap, but Logan moved with him and kept hold.

"Sit down, *Race*." Logan pitched Race onto his chair. This time Race stayed.

"W...why? I'll get more cash, promise. But this is the only money I have now. Really."

"Let's think this through logically, shall we?" Logan bared gleaming teeth at him, not anywhere near a smile. This expression was savage. A hunter, stalking his prey, bringing it down. Eviscerating it. "You owe me money. You have no cash. Therefore I'll just have to give you a chance to win it."

Race whimpered.

Logan picked up the cards and shuffled with a professional flourish. Race started blubbering.

"Logan—" I put a cautionary hand on his arm. Race had been winning easily. Race hated Logan. Race would take Logan to the cleaners.

Logan's predatory smile softened. "Are you worried, princess? That's sweet."

"Don't you understand? He beat us. Elena, Bo, me—we're all experienced players. But Race took almost everything we had."

Logan leaned close, his murmur heating my ear. "I'm *experienced* too."

"I don't mean sexually!"

Eyes widened around me. Blushing, I hissed, "Elena and I have been playing sheepshead all our lives. Since school, during lunch."

"I'm sure it was fun in high school—"

"First grade."

"I'll try not to embarrass you too much." Logan began dealing. "Shall we play for a dollar a point?"

What followed next was almost too gruesome to describe. Within an hour Bo lost fifty dollars and Elena lost a hundred. Babe and Honeypot teamed up, but even together they lost over two hundred.

Which might seem odd since they only started out with fifty. But when the HoneyBabe team was down to a couple bucks, Babe disappeared for five minutes. She came back minus the peanuts and plus twenty. Then Honeypot disappeared. She returned three minutes later with forty bucks—and a satisfied look. Of course, she was the one with the open throat...no. I did not want to know how they were getting their money.

I played a good, solid game which should have kept me even. Tonight it only kept me from losing my life's savings.

And Lady Luck's favorite, Race? His pile of quarters dwindled to nothing. He began writing I.O.U.s with an ever-whitening face.

Shockingly, the big winner was *Logan*. He played sheepshead as if he were born with ten queens. His skill was breathtaking and his daring had me cringing in my chair.

Neat stacks of quarters grew in front of him like little houses. Then little hotels. Then little skyscrapers. In no time at all he'd amassed a whole city, Race's I.O.U.s filling the streets like deep snow.

By the second hour, Race was breathing heavily. He shot a desperate look at Bo. "You're almost out of quarters. Don't you have to go patrol or something?"

Elena shrugged. "Dispatch will call if something comes up."

"And I still have cash." Bo pulled out his wallet, withdrew a fifty and gave it to Honeypot. "Get three rolls from Buddy, and another couple of pitchers of beer. Keep the change."

"Tequila?" Babe held out her hand too.

Bo rolled his eyes. Elena plucked a twenty from the wallet and put it in Babe's palm. "Boilermakers for everyone."

By the third hour Race was hyperventilating. "Are we done? Babe? Honeypot?" He tried to high-sign his honeys. But Honeypot had just earned...er, got from somewhere...er, she had another fifty and they were flush.

Logan leaned over. "You're playing well, Liese."

"When this is all I have left?" I indicated my single stack of quarters.

"Race is down five hundred dollars. Bo's lost a hundred, Elena almost three. You've lost less than fifty."

"I still lost."

"But you play very well. You could even beat me, if you'd let go and trust yourself. Take a few more chances."

Take more chances? Yeah, right. I'd taken a chance with

Botcher and look where that got me.

Pop! "That's getting old, Liese Schmetterling. I expect better of you." Prissy little Good Liese stood on one shoulder, shaking her tiny unmanicured finger at me. Apparently, after a couple boilermakers, I was starting to hallucinate.

"Planning hasn't gotten you very far, either." Bad Liese popped up on my other shoulder, with much better nails. Oh, and a cute little pedicure too. "You planned to get rid of Logan but he's still here. Worse, Elias is lying in wait for you instead."

"You planned to get Race drunk and out the door," Goodie Locks said. "The only thing planning's gotten you is locked in a game with a sheepshead *monster*."

Hey, they were ganging up on me. Wasn't that illegal? Against the imaginary-creature code of conduct or something? I was pretty sure it was in a rule book somewhere. "The Sex Fairy is *so* going to squash you guys with his wand." Which made me think of Logan's wand, which—

"Liese? Is something wrong?" Logan was eyeing me strangely.

"No, no. Just, um, getting more beer. Want some?" I didn't wait for an answer, plucking up tray and empties and hurrying back to the bar. Counting heads I ordered three pitchers and nine glasses.

"Nine?" Logan stared at me like I'd started programming in Korean.

"I miscounted." I poured beer in all nine glasses. B-Liese popped onto the rim of hers, sipped up foam. Waited a moment then belched, "Bernie Botcher's mother has a mustache." The funny thing was, she did.

G-Liese, apparently not to be outdone, popped onto the rim of her glass. And promptly fell in.

I laughed.

"Are you sure you're okay, princess?" Logan put his warm hand on my back. Rubbed between my shoulders.

"I'm fine," I said, and burst out crying.

He gathered me in, hid my face against his chest and stroked my hair. I caught the expressions around the table, flushed, embarrassed. Awkward.

I tugged from Logan's embrace, sat up, wiping my eyes. Logan handed me a paper napkin, so sweet. I blotted the worst of the damage. "I'm fine," I repeated emphatically.

"Maybe we should go." Race's tone was uncomfortable.

Hell. A weepy geek was harder for him to handle than losing hundreds of dollars. Come to think of it, Botcher never knew what to do with me crying, either.

Logan did. He kissed my forehead. "He's right. We need to go home." He leaned closer and whispered into my ear, "I have something for you. A surprise."

I perked up immediately. Home, where a golden stallion could gallop—and I could ride. No, fly. Fly to heaven. Have him *bite* me—

"Liese, honey. Here you are, and with so many new friends. Are you going to introduce me?"

I whirled. And nearly tossed my cookies.

A woman stood there, one hand on her tiny waist, the other holding a cocktail. A black spandex miniskirt outlined her rounded hips and exposed incredibly long legs. Generous breasts overflowed a pink leather bustier. Her hair was professionally dyed champagne blonde with pure white highlights. Her face had a classic, ageless sort of beauty. Her body was that of a high-priced courtesan.

I'd never known that about her.

The woman made a gesture at my friends. "Introduce us, Liese."

"Yeah." Race was panting a little. "Introduce us, dollface."

Oh, I so did not want to. But... "Race Gillette. Logan Steel. Um, and Honeypot and Babe." Elena and Bo already knew her, unfortunately, which meant I couldn't just run away. I took a deep breath.

"Meet Hattie—my mother."

Chapter Twelve

As soon as I could pry my mother from Race's roving hands, I dragged her to the women's restroom. There I grabbed her by both arms. I think I wanted to shake her, like I could rattle some sense into her. Or at least shake some sense into my life.

"Where the hell did you get these clothes?" I yelled. My rock, my anchor was now a bombshell slut. Whose German mother was this?

Mom tut-tutted. "Language, Liese. I brought you up better than that."

"You brought me up better than *this*." I released her, threw a disconcerted hand at her...well, they weren't really clothes, were they?

"Cousin Rolf's wife helped me pick them out." Her tone was stiff. "I think they're very nice."

"Nice? What happened to classic A-lines and sensible shoes? To spending more for something you could wear forever if you took good care of it?" *What happened to the only person I could trust?*

"I just wanted something fun." She blinked. "Something cute to take my mind off...you know."

Oh, shizzle. My mother was going to cry. I felt like a heel. "It is cute," I lied. "Fun."

"Isn't it?" Mom perked right up. "Cousin Rolf's wife is so good for me. Makes me feel young again. She introduced me to fun makeup and cute shoes and vibrators and—"

"Vibrators?" I shrieked. My sainted mother, talking about *vibrators*? What kind of friends was she hanging out with, anyway?

"And you'd never believe what you can do with a good, big cucumber."

I clamped my jaw and shuddered. Please, I thought. Do not let my mother mean what I think she means.

"Of course Cousin Rolf's wife has a Stryker. That's a dildo molded from porn star Jeff Stryker's goodies. I wanted to try it but—"

"Okay! Right. Glad we had this discussion. Let's go home."

"But sweetheart. You were playing sheepshead. And losing. You never lose." An odd gleam entered her eye. "Of course, you were losing to that nice-looking young man. The blond. Although the other one was very nice looking too. He reminds me of someone I once knew well. But I'm sure your young man felt good about winning. Very masculine and capable. Is the other one single?"

"Oh, for the love of... Mom, I didn't lose to Logan on purpose. He's just that good."

That only piqued her interest more. "He's a *schafkopf* player? And a good one? That takes brains, you know. And nerves of steel."

"Yeah, Logan's got both." And buns of steel. I thought of cupping Logan's amazing glutes with my hands—

"You know, sweetie, you look exactly like I did when I tried out the Stryker."

"Enough." I grabbed her wrist and dragged her out of there, before she came up with something worse. Like what exactly she could do with a good, big cucumber. Or like—

"Let's play strip sheepshead!"

My jaw dropped, hit the floor, and bounced around my toenails. I picked it up—just as my mother slid onto Race's lap.

"Mother!" I yanked her off, got her a chair and plunked her down. Resisted the urge to sit on her—or put her on a time out. "You don't want to encourage him."

"Why not?" she asked, all Mrs. Innocence.

"Oh, for the love of Steve Jobs. Because Race is a bad-boy. He has a stable of honeys, and I don't mean bees!"

"So?"

"*So?* That's all you can say? Mother—he's not the marrying kind of guy."

"Sweetie, at my age, my first interest isn't marriage."

Logan leaned over. "Your mother has a point."

"You keep out of this."

"But if she's occupied elsewhere—"

I growled at him. How could he think about sex when my mother's chastity was on the line?

"Liese, honey, if you don't have a better reason—" Mom began to slide back onto Race's lap.

"Mother—shizzle. You'll do it *because I said so.*" I yanked her back onto her chair.

"Well, if you insist, I won't get fresh with this cute young man. Not right now, at any rate." To my absolute disgust, she winked at Race. *Winked* at him.

He winked back. "So Hattie, let's play strip peepshed."

"You got it." My mother picked up the deck.

"Mother, no," I screeched. "You have all of three pieces of cloth covering your body." She shuffled. I was hyperventilating. "Don't you dare do this, young lady!"

She dealt. Picked, went it alone, and won.

With a broad grin, Race stripped off his belt and laid it on an empty table next to us. Bo did too. Bo's was longer. Elena, who was sharing a hand with Bo, took off a shoe. Feeling cornered, so did I.

Logan shrugged and removed his shirt. Great galloping gamma rays. The only thing saving me from complete meltdown was the fact that he was wearing an undershirt.

Honeypot and Babe weren't playing, but they took off their tops too.

They weren't wearing bras. After two guys at the next table fainted dead away I suggested we move our game to the large back hallway where only the drunks staggering to the bathroom would see us. Logan and Bo moved the table, Honeypot and Babe tottering after with belts, shoes and iron-on nipple patches (or were they tops?), which they dumped on a small stand in the back corner.

The next hand, Logan picked. For those who've never played sheepshead, there are thirty-two cards in the deck. We played five-handed, which meant six cards for each player and two left over, placed face down on the table and called the blind. Logan's taking the blind meant he thought he had enough points to win. He called ace of hearts for a partner. It turned out to be my mother. They walked right over us.

Three hands later a pile of socks and shoes were on the stand. Mom hadn't lost a hand. Logan lost one more, a belt. Race was barefoot and so was Bo.

The more clothes that came off, the more beer went in. Or vicey-versey. Vysa-ver—whatever, my lips buzzed and the next thing to go would be major. Elena was already there, unsteadily peeling off her top. She looked all hot in her lavender lace pushup bra. I thought hubby Bo's eyes were going to pop out of his skull.

I had the deal. After distributing somewhat unsteadily, I eyed my cards. Three jacks, a queen and the ace of diamonds, along with two fail.

Couldn't I have dealt myself some big guns? I never picked with less than two queens. Of course Elena never picked with less than five. Since there are only four queens in the deck, she rarely picked.

I passed, hoping the big guns were distributed evenly. They weren't. After some tense play, my mother won that hand too, partnering Race.

"Damn, I wanted us to lose," my sainted mother said. "I wanted to see me some beefcake." She ogled Race's chest. "Guess I'll have to settle for getting another pitcher."

"I'll help you." Babe rose unsteadily to her feet. Honeypot was off somewhere "finding" money.

As Mom and Babe tottered toward the bar, Logan untied and threw off a shoe. Bo pulled off his T-shirt. His bare chest was nicely muscled but not as honed as Logan's.

"I've faced killers, but this is going to take some real courage." Elena drained a full glass of beer. Then with a grimace, she shimmied out of her jeans. Her lace panties matched the bra.

Race watched avidly. When Elena turned to put the jeans on the stand (and we all saw it wasn't panties, but a lavender *thong*), Race said "Woo—"

The "hoo" was cut off by Bo's hand, clamped around his throat. "That is my wife." As Bo forced the words around tight lips, I caught glints from two extremely long canines. "You will keep not only your hands off her, you will keep your eyes off."

Race, gaze now glued to Bo's ruby red one, nodded. Bo

released him. Race glanced at the stand where Elena's jeans lay and smirked.

Fangs erupting, Bo seized Race by the throat again. "You will not only keep your eyes off her, you will keep your mind off her. You will not say, do, or *think* anything that even remotely connects my wife with sex. Understand?"

"Um, Bo?" Elena gestured toward her mouth. "Your, er, slip is showing."

"Understand?" Bo growled, ignoring her.

"Un'sta," Race croaked.

Bo released him.

All eyes were on their little drama. I used the opportunity to pull off my T-shirt.

Logan choked.

"What?" I covered my chest.

"Don't you ever wear underwear?"

Race grinned. "Woo—"

Too fast to follow, Logan smashed him to the wall by the throat. Race's neck was certainly going to be bruised. "Don't—"

"Sh's no' yr wife. I cn loo'."

"You want to test that theory?" Logan's blood-red eyes belied his pleasant voice.

"Uh...no."

"Smart boy." Logan released him to grab my shirt and toss it to me. "Come on, Liese. We're going home."

As I drew it on, my mother returned. "Home, already? Oh well. We can buy a six pack to go, put in a frozen pizza and play Uno."

We played Uno until midnight, when Logan announced he had work to do and left. I had stopped drinking and fought off sleep until then, hoping my mother would go to bed and Logan and I could, um, cuddle in my room. I might not trust him, but I didn't need trust to get the comfort of rubbing body parts.

"You lie as badly to yourself as you do to other people."

I had gone to bed alone (unfortunately), so that meant...I blinked at my shoulder. It was empty.

"Yoo-hoo. Over here. Ow."

Bad Liese sat on my nightstand, propped up against a glass of water. She was pressing her forehead to the glass like she had a really bad headache.

"Hangover?" I rooted around in the nightstand drawer, found a bottle of aspirin and popped it with my thumb. "Take this."

The white tablet was half as big as her face. She nibbled it delicately. Grimaced. "Don't you have any sugar for this?"

"Not here. What did you mean by that, me lying badly to myself?"

"Ain't it obvious?" She took another tentative nibble on the aspirin. Her tongue pushed out repeatedly. "Maybe other people don't need trust to have sex. But you do."

"Do not."

"Too. Otherwise why has your only lover since Botcher been your hand?"

"Don't be crude. It's because nobody's been interested until now."

"Not."

"Too."

"N—"

An authoritative clap of hands cut us off. "Girls, girls." Good Liese, at the foot of the bed, was disgustingly chipper. "Don't fight."

Bad Liese held her head on with both hands. "Ow. Do you have to be so loud?"

I closed my eyes. "Or so bright?"

G-Liese smirked. "She's right, Liese. You're not going to make love unless you actually love."

"I don't love Logan Steel."

"Su-ure you don't."

"Because obviously *saying* it makes it true," B-Liese said.

"I don't." My voice rose. "And let me tell you—"

There was a knock on the wall. "Everything okay, Liese?"

The three of us exchanged looks of panic. Three forefingers slapped to lips. "*Shhh.*"

"Liese, answer me. Do you need me in there?"

G-Liese pressed her tiny ear to the wall. "She's getting up. Do something!"

"Why me?"

B-Liese rolled her eyes. "Who's the real person, here? Say

something."

"I'm fine, Mom." I put every ounce of sincerity I could into my voice.

Bad Liese snorted. "I'm fine," she warbled in imitation. "Could you sound any more like a sick cow? *Moooo.* I'm a cow." Good Liese shook with laughter, tiny hands holding her stomach.

I flicked G-Liese off the end of the bed. She landed on the floor with a tiny poof. Putting my face up to B-Liese I yelled, "Just getting an aspirin, Mom." B-Liese clapped hands to her head and tottered off the nightstand.

I popped the nibbled aspirin in my mouth and washed it down with the cold water, then turned my back on the disgusting duo. "I am not in love with Logan."

G-Liese grunted from the floor. "Not completely."

"Not yet, at any rate," B-Liese said right into my ear.

I flinched. Glared at her. "Why don't you guys just go away and let me sleep?"

G-Liese popped onto the same shoulder. "Imaginary creatures clause, remember?"

"I already made the life-altering decision, remember?"

"And now you have another."

"Oh, goodie. Let me guess. I have to decide whether or not to love Logan."

"That's not a decision." Good Liese *tsked.* "That's a feeling. Didn't you study psychology?"

"Computer science majors only have to take Communications for Engineers."

Bad Liese snorted. "Now there's an oxy*moron.*"

"Hey!"

"The point is," G-Liese said, "feelings just *are.* You can't hold a gun to your head and say, 'Feel happy.' The decision's not whether to fall in love with Logan, because you already are. The decision is what to do about it."

I stared at them both, incredulous. "You're saying I'm already in love with Logan. And that the *only* choice I have is how to deal with that?"

"Yep." G-Liese's smile was smug.

I shook my head. "That's easy, then. I push him away."

"What?" Smug gave way to shock. "What about True Love?"

"What about getting laid?" B-Liese screeched. "What about heavenly orgasms and the best sex of our life? You're going to just *push that away*?" She gave G-Liese a wild-eyed look. "She's insane, you know that? This is your fault."

"My fault? How is this my fault?"

"You're the one who told her feelings just 'are'. Couldn't you have lied a little? Told her it was already too late?"

"Excuse me—" I began.

"No! You're the liar, remember?"

"Not even just this once? When the outcome is so desperately important?"

"Pardon me, ladies—"

"She would have figured it out. If the decision was already made, why would we be here?"

"We could have lied about that too."

"Shut up!" I glared at them both.

A thud on the wall. "Liese, are you *sure* you're okay?"

"I'm fine, Mom." *Not.* If these two were personifications of me, I was going to have a brainectomy. "Ladies, the decision's made. Your contract's complete. Now poof out."

"But—" Good Liese poofed.

"You can't—" Bad Liese started. But I could, and she went poof too.

Unfortunately, they were right about one thing. I was dangerously close to falling in love with Logan, a man—dammit, *vampire*—who I didn't, *couldn't* trust.

Which meant one thing. I had to get rid of him. Not physically, this time. No, this time I had to figure out how to cut Logan Steel from my heart.

When it was just about sex, it was scary enough. But my little imaginary selves had driven it home—this was about *love*. Damned monogamy gene.

I had loved Botcher with my young unformed heart, and his betrayal had practically destroyed me. Logan was not a man—vampire—sexy male—for half-measures. I would love him irrevocably, with my whole heart. His betrayal would annihilate me.

I couldn't take the chance. So how to drive in that wedge?

Heh. Wedge in the heart. Logan, in that insane way of his,

would point out that the metaphor was stake in the heart, and then make a slew of puns on stake. I smiled. He was so cute.

Cute? I covered my face. How was I ever to get him out of my heart when he was constantly on my mind? He was gorgeous and strong and fun on top of it.

My hand slid slowly off. Logan was fun and gorgeous and powerful. Who wouldn't love such perfection? But if I could find a place he wasn't perfect...yes, that might do it. All I had to do was find a flaw in Logan Steel's incredible character.

Oh, right. A cinch. Find a flaw in the male who was not only an industry leader but a terrific fighter and a sexual partner to die for. A male who was bright as a supernova with a sense of humor, to boot. The only time I'd seen him less than his best was with Zinnia—I sat up. Not Zinnia, but what she represented.

His own household.

And suddenly I knew exactly the stake I would use to cleave my heart. Logan's Achilles heel, householding. If I found out why he was so disturbed by it, it was sure to cast him in a bad light. But how, when Logan obviously did not want to talk about it?

I could ask Zinnia. Sure, if I wanted an hour sermon on the misunderstood undead. Who else knew about vampires? Nixie, apparently, if Julian was one. But she was out of town. The only other person I knew who was in on the secret was Elena Strongwell.

A glance at the clock told me Elena would be at work for another couple hours. She worked third shift (and didn't that just make sense now that I knew her hubby was literally a creature of the night). But every Thursday morning she had breakfast with her sister Gretchen at the Caffeine Café. As soon as the sun came up, I headed there.

The two sisters sat at a small table in the back of the café. They were half-sisters, actually, but you'd never guess they were even related from their looks. Tall, slender Elena had glossy dark curls falling past her shoulders. She leaned her chair against the wall, the casual pose a cover for her constantly roving dark cop eyes. A plate of bacon, eggs and hashed browns sat in front of her.

Gretchen looked like a petite cheerleader, only nice. Her

short, sassy blonde hair shook as she dug into a scone. Her blue eyes closed in pleasure as she ate.

Except cheerleader-slim Gretchen wasn't so slim anymore. In fact, she looked distinctly pregnant.

Elena saw me first. "Liese. Glad you're here. About last night—"

"You don't have to explain. May I?" I pulled over an empty chair.

Gretchen moved her scone and herbal tea to make room for me. "Do you mind me not waiting? I'm eating for two."

"Congratulations." As I hung my coat over the back of the chair I raised eyebrows at Elena. "I can't believe no one told me."

Elena grimaced. "Things have been kind of busy. But about last night—"

Gretchen laughed. "I heard about how Elena got drunk and stripped again."

"Again?" My legs went out from under me. Thank goodness for the chair. I grabbed the back and managed to maneuver myself into the seat.

Elena jerked her hand toward a barista, an irritated signal. "The first time was in the line of duty."

As if supercop Elena stripping at a bar wasn't shock enough, the owner of the café came running over at Elena's wave. Diana Prince rarely waited on customers, and never served them personally. Now the elegant proprietor smiled at us. *Smiled.* "Can I get you something more, Elena?"

"Whatever Liese wants," Elena said.

Diana turned to me. "Large coffee, ranger cookie?"

"Y...yes." I never knew Diana herself noticed me, much less remembered my usual. As she hurried away I turned to Elena. "What was that all about?"

Her cheeks reddened. "She feels indebted to Bo. He saved her life once."

"A couple times," Gretchen corrected, digging into her scone. The scent of raspberry cream filled the air. "So what did you mean, Elena didn't have to explain about last night?"

"Well..." Gretchen was Bo Strongwell's sister-in-law but it didn't mean she knew his secrets. On the other hand, this might be my only chance to talk with Elena. "I just meant I already knew about Bo's, um, dental issues. And his problem with...pink eye."

"Pink eye." Gretchen nearly snorted tea. "Like Strongwell's a cute white bunny. Not normally what you'd compare a master v-guy to."

"You know about vam—"

"Shh. We don't use the v-word in public." Gretchen twitched her head at nearby tables.

Elena was watching me with an expression close to horror. "Who told you?"

Diana Prince hurried over with my coffee and cookie. She slid plate and mug onto the table then sashayed away.

She'd *warmed* the cookie. I stared at it, wondering if someone was filming this for YouTube. "No one told me, exactly. Logan said a few things, and did a few things, and I figured it out."

"Logan Steel?" Elena's chair clopped down. "What'd he say?"

"And what'd he do?" Gretchen wagged her brows.

I cleared my throat. "Well...he bit me."

Two clunks greeted that, Elena and Gretchen dropping mugs.

I looked from one sister to the other. "What's wrong?"

"He bit you? As in *bit*—" Elena clacked teeth, "—you? Is he out of his mind?"

"That's not allowed," Gretchen said.

"V-guys don't bite?" I asked.

"Only rogues drink from uninitiated humans." Gretchen spat the word. "Civilized v-guys have donors. Donors know what to expect."

I remembered Professor Bud's lecture. Good guy vamps protected humans, who voluntarily gave them blood in return, like a co-op.

"Logan is the Ancient One's lieutenant. His first lieutenant." Elena shook her head, curls swishing vehemently, as if she could shake loose the alien idea of Logan biting me. "The Ancient One is going to kill him over this. Disembowel him."

That didn't sound good. Though I wanted to get rid of Logan, I didn't want him disemboweled. "Um...it might have been an accident."

"No way. Biting...drinking...it's no accident."

"Well...it happened during—" I cleared my throat again, "—sex."

Both of them gaped at me. Elena said, "Sex? As in, him having sex with *you*?"

The incredulity in her voice made me burn red. "Yes. Granted, I'm not the greatest catch—"

"Vampires never have casual blood sex with humans."

"—but he'd probably screw anything with tits and working lungs...huh?"

"Elena," Gretchen cautioned. "Don't use the v-word."

She waved a hand. "Fuck super-secret spy codes. Liese, just to be crystal clear. You're telling me Logan had sex with you? And during sex he bit you? Not little love-nips, but actual fangs-in-skin drinking?"

"He, um, asked permission first." I hoped that helped with the evisceration thing.

"Stars above. He asked permission." Elena's gaze rolled toward the ceiling, as if the instructions for patience were painted there.

Gretchen shook her head. "Liese, what's going on with you two?"

"Well...I was hoping you could tell me." I had come on a mission, and that hadn't changed. But their reactions had shaken me. "Logan's been paying me kind of a lot of attention. But he's such a playboy, I know he couldn't be interested in me. Not really."

"Liese, if Logan's having blood sex with you, *interested* doesn't begin to describe his feelings. Fascinated, maybe," Gretchen said. "Or bewitched."

"That's impossible." Perfect tens weren't fascinated by five-and-a-halfs.

Elena snorted. "You're having sex with a mythical monster. I think you went past the bus stop for impossible a few streets ago."

Gretchen laughed. "Haven't we all?"

My cheeks heated. "But I don't trust him. I *can't* trust him. He's lied to me, about a hole at the Blood Center, and about mannequins, and even about what he is. How can I trust him?"

"Oh, Liese." Elena reached across the table to clasp my

hands. "Lying is just the way vampires are built. You've got to understand—they're powerful but vulnerable. To sun, but more, to the sheer mass of humanity. They've been underground for centuries, pretending to be human. Secrecy is their watchword. It's what keeps them alive."

"It's ingrained." Gretchen took a delicate bite of scone. "V-guys have so many secrets, starting with their very existence. As the Ancient One's first lieutenant, Logan probably has more than most. But he's probably not lying about his feelings."

"If lying is ingrained, how can I know that? How can I know how Logan feels about me, really?" Mission disintegrated. I had a sick feeling it was my heart asking the questions now.

Gretchen said, "Sometimes you have to beat the truth out of them."

Elena laughed. "I remember when I first met Bo. He tried every way he could to keep me from discovering the truth. He even kissed me to distract me."

I flushed red. Logan's kisses to shut me up weren't even original.

"But it's not personal. Love is rare for them."

Love. "How can kissing you to shut you up...I mean to distract you from discovering the truth..." I was getting all balled up, so I moved to the punch line. "What does that have to do with *love*?"

Elena patted my hands and released them. "Just that love requires trust."

Love and trust. Maybe they weren't linked for everyone. But for me, yes. And for Logan too? I picked up my cookie, broke off a bit. "I got the impression Logan knows quite a bit about making love."

"Sex, sure. V-guys are highly sensual creatures with great endurance."

The cookie crumbled in my fingers. "So Logan's had a lot of practice. You don't have to rub it in."

"He's had practice *making* love, yes. Being *in* love, probably not so much."

I tossed the crumbs onto my plate in disgust. "Then how do you know it's not just sex and lies?"

Gretchen said, "*You* can't. It's more recognizable on their side."

Elena nodded. "They find they can't control your mind, which makes sense, if you think about it. V-guys can't bond with someone they totally dominate."

I thought so. You're immune.

"Then they find your smell and taste irresistible." Gretchen popped the last of her scone in her mouth and washed it down with herbal tea.

I thought of Logan, licking me and purring. "And you know this because you're Bo's sister-in-law?"

"No. My husband's one."

"*Steve?* But then...how..." I waved helplessly at her heavily distended stomach. A horrible thought hit me. "Or *what...?*"

"Bo assures us the baby's entirely human," Elena said. "But it's apparently another sign of a match. V-guys can have sex all night long without consequences. But if they even look cross-eyed at the right one, *bang.*" She made a round gesture across her belly.

"But you and Bo—you've been married over four months." She made it sound like instant mommy. Surely if anyone were a vampire's mate, it was Elena.

She laughed. "I'm just carrying low."

"You're *pregnant?*"

"Doesn't show, does it? I'm five months along but I've been keeping in shape." She said it with some satisfaction.

"Whereas I look like I swallowed a watermelon." Gretchen forked some egg off Elena's plate. "But it's not anything to do with working out. It just shows more on my petite frame."

"You keep telling yourself that, baby sister." Elena slid her plate away from Gretchen and finally began eating.

"Wait," I said. "You're five months gone and you haven't told anyone?"

Elena chewed efficiently. "It took the first month for me to wrap my head around the idea. I told Nixie and Gretch but thought I'd better wait before telling anyone else. You know, make sure it's a baby human."

"Shizzle," I said. "I feel like I've been sucked into an alternate dimension. Like someone made a *Farscape* plot out of me."

"You get used to it," Gretchen said. She tried to sneak some of Elena's potatoes, got her fork firmly stapled to the table by

Elena's.

"So v-guys can really form, um, emotional attachments to humans?" I asked. "They don't consider us livestock?"

"The good-guy ones don't." Gretchen tried to wiggle her fork free before raising her hands in mock-surrender.

"But the only humans they usually form bonds with are their donors, because of the secrecy thing." Elena pulled her fork loose and stared at it with disgust, maybe wishing it was her gun. She signaled Diana before continuing. "And for masters, with the members of their household."

I thought of Zinnia. "And humans they have sex with."

"No." Elena pointed her deadly fork at me. "They have sex with anybody and everybody but they only *bite* humans they have feelings for."

"Like donors." Sensuous, beautiful donors.

"For shit's sake, would you listen? V-guys *never* confuse donation with blood sex." Elena underscored the *never* by stabbing the table next to my fingers with her fork. The tines stuck deep in the thick amber varnish.

I slid my hand away. "But...if they bite and drink during sex...what's the difference?"

"Do you confuse my offer of a bed for the night with an offer of sex?"

"Oh. No." The lights suddenly seemed brighter and my appetite returned. I squooshed cookie crumbs with my fingers and slipped them into my mouth. Gooey chocolate and crisp sugar burst on my tongue. I licked my fingers clean.

Diana Prince brought Elena a new set of cutlery and Gretchen another scone. The sisters settled back in companionable silence and I drank hot coffee.

With the infusion of sugar and caffeine, my brain started to work. Logan had rescued me several times. He'd had blood sex with me. He couldn't control me with his Rasputin voice. And he seemed to go nuts over my smell and taste.

Maybe he *wasn't* lying. Maybe he really did think I was beautiful. It was so tempting to believe I put down my fork and imagined it. Pictured golden vampire Logan Steel really loving me. It was a dream come true.

Which was exactly what made it so dangerous. I grabbed the Ring-of-False-Promises, tightening my hold until the prongs dented my fingers. Enough. I had to find the wedge, get the info to harden my stupid heart against Logan once and for all. "Speaking of householding, do you know what exactly bothers Logan about it?"

"You know, I wish you'd get rid of that thing." Elena nodded at the ring. "I think you'd be happier. And clutching it while asking about Logan...why?"

Whoops. Darned cop's hair-trigger suspicion. "No connection." I released the ring. "I'm just pretty good at running projects. I thought maybe I could help Logan out running his new household."

And hey, that made sense. In fact, it was a pretty good idea. I'd been up for head of ADD's IT department. And if I could run a blood distribution center, surely a household was no big?

I slid my fork off the table and stabbed myself in the leg. Because obviously I was dreaming again and had better come back from drool-land. Since I was wearing jeans I didn't actually break skin, but I did wince.

"Liese?" Elena's eyes narrowed to slits.

"Yes, um, Logan, household, problem? Something I can overcome?"

Elena's eyes were narrow on me for just a second longer. Then she leaned back and shrugged. "Bo said Logan had a household once but something went wrong. He didn't say what. Why don't you ask Logan?"

"Oh, sure. Of course. Should have thought of that in the first place. So, how 'bout them White Sox?" I stuffed cookie in my mouth and smiled.

Chapter Thirteen

After that illuminating chat I knew what I needed to do. I called Logan and asked him to come to my apartment at seven. Then I girded my loins with research (at the Center, but the AI had reduced my job to less than an hour of actual work. I had to at least look busy, right?) and a shopping trip over lunch.

It was six p.m. when I got to my apartment. I had just put my key in the door when it flew open and my mother skipped out in low-rider jeans, a shortie top and a jacket that would have looked skimpy on Zinnia. My eyes flashed down. Nope, no navel-winking stud. But...was that a rose tattoo?

She gave me a quick kiss. "I'm going out."

I almost said, "Dressed like that, young lady?" but caught myself in time. "Do you need the car keys?"

"No, a friend is picking me up."

"*Friend*? Who?"

"If you must know, Race Gillette. We're going to Oakbrook. He says he knows where I can find a good vibrator."

"Mother—"

"Don't start with me, Liese. He makes me feel young."

I stood in front of her, hands on hips. "That's because he *is* young."

"And just what do you mean by that? You think I'm not attractive enough to have any man I want?" She turned up her nose. "Well, stick your ageism, missy. For your information Race and I went to school together. I knew him as Ray Zorinbach." Her lips curved slightly. "He was a bit of a bad boy."

"Mother, he can't be the same guy. He'd be fifty years old."

She sniffed. "Forty-seven."

"No way. Race is lying to have his way with you. Or he's Ray's son...or they look alike and he's taking advantage of a hazy memory."

"No, it's Ray. I know it's him. He has this sexy birthmark on his left testicle—" She covered her mouth.

"*Mother.* How do you know that?" Oh, duh. "You were intimate with him!"

Her chin went up. "So what if I was?"

"So *what?*" I barely kept from screeching it. "*You* were the one forever harping on not selling myself cheap. Avoid bad boys, Liese. Only go out with men worth marrying, Liese. Nice guys, good boys...sweet Centrinos, Mother, you hammered that into me until I felt like a nail."

Her face paled and she sat abruptly on the stoop, crumpling like all the air had gone out of her. In her thin little jeans, that concrete must've frozen her ass off.

But now I felt like a heel. Again. I folded myself beside her and put an arm around her shoulders. With the surgery and radiation, her bones were hollow reeds under my arm. "Mom, I'm just worried. This is so unlike you."

"No, Liese." Her voice had dropped in pitch and become almost steely. "This is who I was all along. I made my mistakes and paid for them. I just didn't want you to make the same mistakes I did." She took a belly-deep breath. "Liese, I had a child out of wedlock."

I blinked, not trusting myself to make the right reaction. "Okay," I said, trying to buy time, trying to remember Communications for Engineers, or at least enough not to screw this up. "Um...tell me more?"

She gave a dark laugh. "Such an old-fashioned term. Out of wedlock. He was a bad boy. I was sixteen and thought I loved him. It was so exciting being with him. Until I told him we'd made a baby, and he left."

A baby. My mother, not much more than a baby herself. And her bad-boy boyfriend...*Race?* "Wait. Are you saying Race...and you...Mom, what happened to you? To the baby?" Did I have a baby half-brother or sister? Not a baby anymore, I realized with shock. Actually older than me.

Her eyes got sad, and at that moment she looked every one of her forty-seven years. "I kept Kat for nine months. Nine months of heaven—and hell. I couldn't do it. I thought I could

173

but the responsibility...alone, it was too much. I gave her up for adoption."

I rubbed her shoulders. "You did the right thing."

"Did I?" She looked at me and her eyes glimmered wetly. "Did I really?"

Even I knew the correct response was not "How the hell should I know?" but that was how I felt. Her tear-stained gaze was pleading for something from me, maybe understanding, maybe just acceptance. No matter how many times I might have considered it in the abstract, seeing Mom's face, her anguish, I knew I'd never be able to make that kind of decision until it came right down to it.

So I just said, "Yes. You made the only decision you could. You're a different person now, Mom. You raised me just fine."

"I did, didn't I?" Her thin arm crept around my waist and she gave me a hug.

Thank God. I'd said the right thing. "Did you ever try to find Kat?"

"No, I...I was too afraid." Mom didn't say afraid of what, but that I could guess. Afraid of rejection, maybe afraid she'd see she'd done the wrong thing after all.

"So that's why you always warned me off bad boys. Because of Race." I hugged her, then put her at arms' length with a frown. "Then why are you going out with him now?"

"You said it, Liese. I'm not the same girl I was. I'm a woman now, and I know what I want. What I need." A mechanical roar came from down the street. She slid from my hands and stood. "And I need some excitement in my life."

I opened my mouth to object when she added, "Something to *live* for."

"Mom—you have me."

"And I'm grateful." She pulled me to my feet, wiry strength surprising me in her light, cancer-wasted frame. "But some day you'll find the right man and you won't need me anymore. Maybe a nice blond man who plays a killer game of sheepshead."

"Logan's not exactly nice, Mom." Not exactly a man, either.

"Well, maybe that's exactly what you need."

A motorcycle pulled up. I was grudgingly thankful to see a full-sized Harley. "At least he's not taking you out on a crotch rocket."

Race dismounted with a grin, held out a helmet to Mom. "Coming, Sugar Cakes?"

Honeypot, Shweetie Pie, Babe and now Sugar Cakes. "Watch out for that one, Mom. He's got a sweet tooth. And he already has a bunch of other honeys."

Mom cocked an eyebrow at me. "I'll just have to steal his insulin, then, won't I?"

I snipped the tags off my new scarlet bra and thong. As I laid them on my brand new white silk bed sheets, I forced the conversation with my mother out of my head. Right now I had work to do, and it wouldn't be easy.

Scented candles stood unlit at key points, arranged to cast a soft golden glow over the bed. Wine was positioned strategically nearby on my nightstand. Already open, one glass down. Well, I had to try some, didn't I? To make sure it was good enough?

Mother was out of town for at least two hours, shopping for a new vibrator with Race...no, not thinking about that until later. I had to have all my wits for a black ops more hazardous than breaking into Steel Software code.

I was about to try the fine art of seduction.

I needed to pump Logan for the reason he didn't want a household. And when did Logan get chatty?

Yep. After sex.

Seduction comes naturally for most women. Maybe because I'm a geek, I don't have the social cues for the grocery checkout line, much less for being spontaneously sexy.

Yet here I was, pitting myself against a powerful, virile male with centuries of experience. So I had mapped my battle very, very carefully. First I'd gone on the Internet and read about Mata Hari and Madame de Pompadour and other great courtesans and mistresses of the ages. Then I'd taken an extended lunch and driven over to Woodfield Mall to explore lingerie.

According to the books, seduction was as much mental as physical. Half the battle was *thinking* sexy. My only hope was that the books were right.

'Cause reality was I probably didn't stand a chance.

I took the same care with my body that I had with my room. I washed and conditioned my hair until it shone. Bath oils softened and scented my skin. I ran a hand over my thanks-to-Dolly naked labia, but there wasn't even stubble yet.

Just in case, I rubbed some lotion in. I pictured Logan, his bright hair tumbling over his broad, muscular shoulders. Saw his gorgeous face tightened in ecstasy. His hard pecs and taut belly, flushed with desire. His huge erection, straining for me.

Suddenly I was silky wet and hot.

Fershizzle. The idea was for Logan to get carried away, not me. I drained the tub, applied war paint (mascara, etc.) and hustled into the bedroom. Six forty-five. Fifteen minutes.

I shimmied into the lacy red thong and demi bra. Lit all the candles. Poured two glasses of wine. Arranged myself artfully on the clean sheets. Checked the time.

Six forty-seven. Ack. Any other woman in the world, that woulda taken half an hour. Stupid geeky efficiency. I changed position, leaning back on my elbows. Glanced down to judge the body appeal. Stomach mostly flat, but not enough cleavage. I sat back up.

More cleavage, but now my rounded tummy was plain. Hmm. I needed a position halfway between. I plumped up some pillows, leaned against them, and stretched out my legs. More cleavage, less tummy.

And *really* uncomfortable. I shifted again, plumped some more, leaned against the headboard, tried scooting down—and scooted my thong into pussy floss. One lip and half an inner lip stuck out. It looked like my vulva was giving me a raspberry. I shoved both lips back under.

"Liese," Logan's croon came from the front room. "I'm here. Are you ready?"

I jumped. A bolt of sheer desire sang through me. *Showtime.*

"Hang on a sec," I yelled, and winced. So not seductive. Mental attitude, I scolded myself. Sexy was in the mind. I pitched my voice low and added a little throat. "I mean, just a mo-ment."

Fumbling with my underwear, I arranged it best I could. A quick body check told me I wasn't going to do a photo shoot for

Maxim any time soon. Just pray mental attitude could make up for it. "I'm not quite ready," I called huskily.

"I'll wait," he called back. "Our dinner reservation isn't until seven thirty."

"Right." That was how I got him here. Asking him on a date. Apparently he'd thought that meant dinner. "I'm almost ready. Um, why don't you take off your jacket and come in here to wait?"

"Okay. I've got a surprise for you. I was trying to give it to you yesterday, but—"

I registered Logan like a downloading webpage. His outline sketched in first, filling the doorway. Shimmering blond hair, broad shoulders and incredibly lean waist developed. His form sharpened—chiseled jaw, jutting chest, rock-hard biceps, washboard abs. The details locked in last, blazing gold-flecked eyes, flared nostrils, sculpted lips.

And protruding fangs, lolling tongue...he choked. "Fuck me with a jackhammer, Liese! Are you trying to give me a heart attack?" His eyes roved over my nearly naked body like I was an all-you-can-eat dessert bar. The crotch of his jeans suddenly poked out.

Okay, this was better than I hoped. I remembered my plan to be the seductress and recited my personal mantra, stolen from Susan Ivanova of *Babylon 5*. *Boom-shacka-lacka-lacka.* "Have some wine." As I reached for the glass, I stretched along the bed with lazy grace. Or at least what I could remember of how Logan moved.

"Oh. Fuck. Yeah." He came like a puppy, sat down on the bed next to me. Stared.

His burning gaze made me feel like supper. Vampire supper—how close I'd been to the truth all along. Well, not exactly, since they drank blood for their veins, not their stomachs. But it felt as if Logan wanted to eat me. And that was bad, right?

Bad? Not! my breasts said. *Eat me,* my pussy joined in. I shook a mental finger at them. *Seductress,* I scolded myself. *Boom-shacka-lacka-lacka.*

I half-sat to hand Logan a glass, making sure to press my arm against my breast as I did so. A mound of breast plumped up.

Logan's tongue fell out.

Wow. Maybe I could do this seduction stuff after all. I gave him a sultry smile as I offered the glass. It was a good sultry smile too. I'd practiced with my webcam.

But his eyes were riveted to Mt. Cleavage. Fine. Going with what was already working, I pressed harder—and my breast popped out.

Fershizzle, this was awkward. And too soon. I'd planned to strip for at least half an hour, or however long it took to get the first bottle of wine down him. I stuffed my tit back in.

In my haste I spilled half the glass down my chest.

Well, heck. Couldn't I do anything right? Wine all over my breasts, so *not* sexy...I heard a soul-deep groan.

Logan grabbed me with both long-fingered hands. The glass dropped and rolled unnoticed across the carpeted floor. His head plunged to my chest.

One broad lick took half the wine off my breasts. A second took the rest. Logan kept going for a fevered third lick, and a fourth. He licked so eagerly, my breasts quaked under his mouth like mounds of gelatin.

I fell back under the assault. He crawled over me, still licking, his mouth scorching hot. He latched onto one lace-covered nipple and suckled hard. My thighs clenched, bright need bolting through me.

Seduction, I panicked. This fast, we'd be done before we started. I thrust my thumb into the corner of his mouth, managed to pop him loose. Slithering from under the muscular cage of his body, I rolled off the bed and took in the damage.

Logan crouched on the mattress, red eyes on mine, fangs fully extended. And what sleek fellows they were. I had to squelch the desire to jump him and suck them raw.

No. *I* was the seductress. *Boom-shacka-lacka.* I cocked out one hip. "Mmm. Nice. But let me do the work this time, huh, big fella?" I sauntered to where the empty glass lay, bent to pick it up. Flashed my red-thonged ass, also practiced via webcam. I gave him another sultry smile over my shoulder as I refilled the glass.

His glowing eyes followed my every move. The sizzling promise in his gaze nearly incinerated me. Maybe I'd better speed things up a little, before we both hit flashpoint. Time to move into position.

I'd researched a bunch of them on the Internet. Missionary, sixty-nine, doggie (Botcher's favorite). Since I was the seductress I'd decided on the Cowgirl. But that wasn't possible right now, not with him in the Hunting Lion position. Somehow, I'd have to get him to lie down on his back. I took a fortifying sip of wine, nerved myself to poke a finger into the velvet-covered boulder he called a shoulder. Pushed.

To my amazement, he collapsed obligingly back on the bed.

Well fry my circuit boards. I'd felled ultra-powerful Logan Steel with one finger. Confidence returning, I straddled his flat, muscular belly. His washboard abs rippled against my crotch. I stifled a moan. His hands opened on my thighs and I stifled another. His fingers caressed my flesh firmly and I nearly swallowed my throat stifling.

I had to get control back. Sliding the glass to his lips, I purred, "Drink," as seductively as I could.

He opened his mouth. I tipped the glass.

Sadly, I'd never done this sort of thing before. All the mental attitude in the world didn't make up for basic clumsiness. I spilled half the wine down Logan's cheeks.

I was mortified. He'd laugh his ass off at the chubby geekette trying to play siren. I'd have had better luck making a supercomputer from bailing wire and earwax than a seductress out of *me*. Cheeks burning, I watched the stupid wine run down his jaw, soak into the collar of his shirt. It pooled in that interesting notch at the base of his strong throat. Well, at least I could start on cleanup. I bent to lick.

He bucked at the first touch of my tongue. I sat back, startled. His eyes were squeezed shut. His nostrils were flared, his mouth open.

He was *panting*.

Tentatively, I touched tongue to liquid again. His fingers tightened on my thighs. A low groan rolled his abdomen against my crotch. "Liese." He gasped my name. "You're slaying me, princess."

I blinked rapidly. Incredible. It was working. I had no natural sexuality, couldn't turn a man on if I duct-taped cans of cold beer to my naked body. Botcher had to use chemicals, for pity's sake.

But now, tonight, I had it. I was turning a male on—or rather, turning Logan on. Maybe I only had *it* for him. I clamped down on that thought, quick.

The first few buttons of Logan's crisp shirt were already open. I worked the next couple loose, noting how the pale yellow cotton picked up the white-gold strands in his hair. And no undershirt, boy-oh-boy. I dipped my fingers in the spilled wine and smeared it down the swell of his muscular chest.

Then, ever so slowly, I licked off the smear.

He jacked up with a roar. Tore—and I mean ripped like a violent tornado—his shirt off. Threw me under him and plunged into an open-mouthed kiss. The wineglass went flying.

I flattened my palms against his hard pecs and pushed. He didn't move an inch, continued to plunder my mouth with smacks and licks and driving tongue. Slipping out from under him was impossible. He imprisoned my body simply by crushing me with his weight. But I tried. He trapped my wrists and pressed them into the bed next to my head, completely immobilizing me.

And all the while he kissed me, that open-mouthed, hot thrusting of a dominant male, the hungry assault of a sexual beast staking its claim. Burning, virile kisses that softened me like liquefying butter.

My legs fell open. Logan was quick to claim the gap. He started thrusting, his jeans-covered erection driving rhythmically and hard against my sex. The insistent pounding sent shocks cascading through me. My eyes flew wide.

In about two seconds he would tear open his jeans and possess me, fully, deeply. I couldn't let that happen. I had a mission. *Boom-shacka-lacka.*

I wrapped my legs around Logan's hips and clenched tight. He continued to rock into me, restrained by the cage of my hips and thighs. He groaned, his strokes lengthening and softening. He reached for his zipper.

I could not let him get to it, dammit. I gripped with all my strength, welding myself to his hips. He shoved his hand between us but I was using my thighs, some of the strongest muscles in my body. He couldn't move them without hurting me.

With another, deeper groan, he rolled to his back, bringing me up on top of him, one hand still wrapped around a wrist.

"Behave," I panted. My palms planted on his luscious bare pectorals.

180

"Princess—"

"I said behave." I found his nipple with thumb and forefinger and pinched. He shot up off the bed.

"Liese...please..." A low, guttural groan came from his deepest pit.

"Let go of me." I underlined the command with another vicious pinch.

He snarled, but his eyes burned with arousal and his hand dropped from my wrist. I felt for the second wineglass.

"Now drink your wine." I grabbed him by his gorgeous long hair and yanked his head up. Masses of silk ran over my skin, teasing, caressing. I leaned closer, rubbing my belly against him. When I poured alcohol down his throat, it went in.

I set the empty glass aside. His lips were glistening from the wine and I couldn't resist a quick taste. I pulled his head in with both hands.

His arms braced on the bed behind him. His jaw kicked up, lips parted. His eyes closed, lashes long and golden against his cheeks.

I tasted his mouth slowly. Licked the delectable corners. Nibbled his luscious lower lip, warm and wet.

It was heady, and it was frightening. Heady because he tasted oh-so-spicy, male. Frightening, because as I nibbled I realized just how much bigger his mouth was, how much bigger *he* was. How immensely powerful. Where he could take my whole lip in one bite, it took me a couple nips to catch all his.

But he didn't move a single muscle as I tasted him. Didn't try to stop me or take control again. All that size, all that power, thrumming under me, yielding to me.

I got more daring. Bit his lip. Raked teeth over his earlobe. Nipped along his jaw. His neck. His chest.

He hissed with my sharp bites. Stiffened just a little more with each, until his hips actually raised from the bed. His eyes flared open, golden with lust. His cock tented his jeans like Liberty's torch.

Feeling for the glass, I found and filled it again. I did it slowly, allowing time for some of the tension in his body to ease. But not all. *Seductress.* By no means all.

When his hips touched down I dipped a fingerful of wine and painted it across the tops of my breasts. His eyes, so very hot on me, made being sexy and tempting come more naturally. "Now if you promise to behave, I'll let you lick this off." I didn't have to work so much at the purr either. Not with my throat tingling and body buzzing.

Tentatively, Logan reached out with his tongue. It was sweet, how the masterful male was acting almost shy. Slightly drunk by now, his natural imperative to dominate softened, maybe he had lost full control of himself. *He's enjoying this*, I realized in a flash of insight.

Or maybe he let me take over simply because he trusted me. That was a scary thought.

His tongue touched my breast, flicked lightly across the wet skin. Tiny supple licks, oh so light. I painted myself again.

He licked more boldly, broader swipes, leaving great swathes glistening along my breasts. His lids lowered until his eyes were golden, gleaming slits. A rumbling purr started from his chest.

I painted myself a third time. He sat up fully, his hands finding my thighs, strong fingers wrapping around me and holding me in place.

I set the wine aside, cupped his golden head and pressed him into my bosom.

His easy grace faltered. He began licking me urgently, became almost raw in his need. His tongue was rough, like a cat. His fangs scraped harshly against my skin. I decided I loved Logan uncontrolled. His mouth worshiped me, devoured me. He began to take little nips, suck little love marks.

But when his fang tips pressed intimately into my breast, I put one hand under his glorious hair, lifted it away. Bent and whispered directly into his ear. "Behave, Logan."

His mouth paused. His breath heated my skin as I waited. His eyes closed and his nostrils flared. I could just see the beat of a vein in his temple as he fought to restrain himself.

He lost the battle. With a soft moan, he bit down.

So did I.

Logan's lobe was tender between my teeth, and I bit hard. He gasped, bucked, but didn't withdraw. Didn't try to stop me when I bit again.

And his rumbling purr got so loud it filled the room.

The heady smell of arousal mixed with the scent of warm

candle wax. I cupped both hands around Logan's granite jaw and pushed. His fangs popped out of my breast. Blood trickled hot down the curve.

Logan jerked under my hand, his nostrils flared wide, his eyes burning. Even I could smell the coppery tang. The scent must have been driving *him* insane.

Just the way I wanted it.

I slowly reached for the wineglass. "Drink."

"But I need—"

"*Drink.*" He opened his mouth and I made him drink off every last drop before I let him lick the hot threads on my breast.

When I finally released him he fell to, lapped and lapped at my bosom, his tongue like fiery toweling. He was so lost in the act that he never registered me opening the snap and zipper on his jeans.

I pushed him flat with a single, hard shove. I never thought I'd be grateful for tenth grade gym, but a quick squat thrust laid me out along his legs. My face over his hips, I was in perfect position to suck his cock down my throat. I opened my mouth and pushed my head down on his prodigious length. Then I half-swallowed, torturing the sensitive glans with rippling cartilage.

Logan arched hard. His hips drove forward, thrusting his massive erection past my larynx. I gagged, pulled back, coughing.

"Oh, fuck, Liese, I'm so sorry." Logan knifed up, caught me with concerned hands. "I didn't mean...I should have controlled..."

Swinging a knee over his hips, I shut him up simply by hooking the crotch of my thong aside and ramming my wet sex onto his erection.

He shouted, unintelligible words, but the sentiment was *hot damn fuck.* I knew because I felt the same as lightning jags skewered me from the crown of my head to the soles of my feet.

With Logan's powerful body pinned under me, his enormous erection throbbing deep inside me, I went just a little crazy. I lost track of seduction, I lost track of slow. Hooking my ankles over his thighs, denim crisp against my insteps, I held him in place for the pummeling of his just-shy-of-four-hundred-year-old life.

I rode him like an animal. I had no thought beyond my own pleasure, no need but my own orgasm, building beyond hot to explosive. My thighs rubbed raw against his jeans. My nails bit into the rocks of his pectorals. My pubic bone slammed into his with such force it almost cracked. My breath wheezed, fire in my lungs.

I couldn't stop. My climax was coming, bigger and sweeter than anything I'd ever known. Logan arched back, his eyes closed and his fangs straining. His hands gripped my upper arms. "Fuck, Liese." His voice cracked. "You're an oven. I can't...I'm trying to hold back but...fuck me, I'm coming!"

"Not without me, you're not." I snarled it, riding him so hard I was nearly weeping.

Instantly he seized my hair. With incredible, negligent strength, he pulled me down. My arms buckled, my stroking hips faltered.

His hand splayed over the base of my spine, pressing me flat to him. For that instant I lay motionless, his skin silky and slick against mine, his heart beating hard, his purr rumbling my bones.

"Lord, Liese. I love you." His murmur was hot against my neck, just before he bit me.

Fangs sank into my flesh, unleashing a thunderstorm. Orgasm hit me like lightning, blew through me like a typhoon.

Holding my hips captive, Logan pistoned up into me, driving me higher into the storm. He rolled and pumped with a muscular male strength that overwhelmed me. I burst again. My legs quivered and collapsed. He purred and rode and licked with as much power and dominance as if he'd been on top. And bit my neck again.

I climaxed a third time, a bright blast of pleasure that leveled me. My whole being exploded. The orgasm ripped through me so hard I could feel my vagina spasm around his thrusting cock, clasping it, milking it.

Logan roared and drove in to the hilt. He ruptured, hot pleasure pouring into me. His hand fisted in my hair, his fingers dug into my butt. He wasn't so much licking my neck as devouring it. And groaning between licks, "I love you. Oh, Liese, I love you."

Afterward I lay boneless on his muscled torso. My mind

was a comfortable blank.

That way I wouldn't have to deal with those terrible three words.

I was scared shitless, of course. Afraid the words really didn't mean anything. Botcher had said them all the time and they'd turned out to be worthless.

Strangely, I was even more afraid Logan meant every one.

Tonight was supposed to be about driving a wedge between us, not bonding us closer. I clenched my jaw. Didn't matter if Logan meant the words or not. I had to dig him out of my heart then cauterize the wound. I had to finish this.

My plan was to bring down Logan Steel's powerful personal barriers with sex. To discover his deepest, darkest secret. Now I just had to find out if it had worked.

I hesitated. Did I really want to know? Did I deserve to know?

Probably not. But it had to be done.

Just get on with it. "So," I said as casually as I could. The fact that I was still limp as a cat in a sunbeam helped. "Do you want your own household?"

"Mmm?"

"Because you're a perfect choice."

"What?" he murmured.

Wasn't he supposed to be the chatty one after sex? "You're perfect to head a household. You can make things happen. You're a problem solver, organized."

"Mmm."

He was falling asleep. I prodded him. "Zinnia says you've even trained for it."

One eye opened sluggishly. "I hate that woman."

That made me smile. "No, you don't. What you hate is that she's right. She represents something you don't want to do, but know you have to. What I can't figure out is why."

"She's a sadist," he mumbled.

"Not why she's doing it, silly. Why you're avoiding it."

"Oh. 'Cuz." His hand rubbed drowsily over my spine. But I got the feeling he wasn't as sleepy as before.

I rolled off him. "Because why?"

He drew in a breath, let it out slowly. Drew another. Let it out on a grunt. "So doggedly stubborn." He gathered me in his arms, taking the sting out of his words. "Can't we just cuddle a little?"

I snuggled into his side. "Elena said you had a household before this. Was your past experience that bad?"

A silence. Definitely awake now. "Define bad."

"Um...Zinnia badgering you to march down Pennsylvania Avenue for vampire rights?" When that failed to get even a small laugh I winced. This was not going to be pretty.

Finally he said, "It's rather...painful."

"All the more reason to tell me." I laid my hand on his chest. His heartbeat had accelerated. "You'll feel better sharing it. Please?"

"Liese, if I'd tell anyone, I'd tell you. But it happened centuries ago. Over, *fini*. No one remembers it, not even me."

I peeked up. His eyes, topaz pain, said otherwise. "Not even the Ancient One?"

That drew a grunt. "He remembers. But only because he remembers everything. Liese, I really don't want to talk about it."

"But it's important." I raised myself on my arms and took his gorgeous face between my palms. Sure, I needed to know his secret to drive a wedge into my heart. But now there was more to it than that.

This secret was *hurting* Logan. Like Botcher had hurt me. Strong Logan Steel was troubled over householding because something bad had happened. And not just bad enough to smart sixteen months. Bad enough that the pain was vivid *centuries* later.

Soul-scarring bad.

"Logan, you need to talk. Trust me to handle the truth."

He blew a vexed breath. "Doggedly stubborn? I should have said pigheaded. Liese, I had a household and decided it was too much work. End of story." He tried to glare.

But I met his eyes, letting the warm compassion I felt speak for me.

His gaze softened, puzzled, hesitant. "It's not very nice."

"I know. I'm sorry." I kissed him gently.

"Well...if you must know... I had a household but it didn't make enough money. You know I'm a businessman, and money—"

"Logan, you don't have to lie. I want you to tell me, but I'll wait until you're ready."

A silence descended. This was no longer about my need, but his. Whatever he had to tell me, I'd listen.

Chapter Fourteen

Expressions crossed Logan's face. Puzzlement, annoyance, and finally a glimmer of raw pain. "You shouldn't know. That I'm lying, I mean. I should be able to make up a story to satisfy you. I've had centuries of experience. I should be able to lie to you and make you believe it." He clenched his eyes shut. "But I don't want to."

When his eyes opened again, they were a shimmering gold. "I don't want to lie to you anymore, Liese. If anyone deserves the truth, you do."

Again he closed his eyes, perhaps searching for strength. Powerful, implacable Logan Steel, searching for strength. It must really be bad. My heart ached for him.

"Well. My first and only experience householding. I had just turned one hundred. That's when the ability to mist manifests."

He was doing it. Logan was actually telling me his deepest, darkest secret. This was big, huge. A flash of intuition told me to keep my reactions low-key.

Yes, I had a flash of intuition. If I weren't concentrating so hard on not screwing up I would have been amazed. "You have to be able to mist to be master of a household?"

"You have to be able to defend your household. The ability to mist is a huge advantage in doing that. Misting's iffy the first few years, but not for me." A self-mocking smile twisted his lips. "I was especially good at it. I thought I was ready."

"That's why you formed the household?"

"No. I formed it because Adelaide insisted."

Jealousy curled in my stomach. I sat up, drawing my knees to my chin. "Your wife."

He rubbed a hand along my spine. "Not wife, and not mine. Adelaide was my brother Luke's fiancée, a human. Like most human females of the time, she wanted to marry. Luke was besotted, would have done anything to please her. I founded a household so they could settle down."

Logan had a brother who was a vampire? Did that explain Zinnia's golden children? "Why didn't Luke form the household? Or live just with her?"

"Luke wasn't able to mist yet. At least, not reliably. He asked me to help."

"The three of you." An Adelaide sandwich. By himself Logan burned me to cinders. With two of them, she probably had to change her name to Char.

"Householding was the only way Luke could safely settle down. This was before blood banks, when we still had to drink directly from humans. As nomads, Luke and I could move on if anyone got suspicious. Staying in one place risked people discovering what we were."

I wrapped my arms around my shins. "So settling down was dangerous."

"Yes. Oh, we could hypnotize people into not remembering. But the human mind is tricky. Someone might recall something at any time, or put together repeated episodes of dizziness. I thought a household would decrease that risk."

"Because the donors are in on the secret?"

"Yes, and because it's voluntary, and they have a vested interest in it. I thought it all out very carefully, rationally. We were so young in those days." Logan fell silent. Remorse sat starkly on his gorgeous features.

"What happened?" I reached out to brush a strand of hair from his face.

He captured my fingers, kissed them one by one. "With a household, the risk is decreased for the vampires. But if the master isn't seasoned enough, it increases the risk for the humans. They're sitting ducks, you see."

"Aren't all humans sitting ducks?"

"Well, yes, but in those days...there's a feudal mindset that's hard to explain. The closest is the parent-child relation. The child expects the parent to make it all better, no matter what. It's beyond trust, it's a belief."

"Your humans believed you could keep them safe."

"Yes. And, cocky imbecile that I was, I believed it too. Until the rogues struck." Logan passed a hand through his golden hair. "I can still see it, skewed, like a nightmare. Five of them, two of us. We were strong, fast. Two of the attackers were fledglings, easily dispatched. I was enjoying myself—*enjoying* it." He blew out his disgust. "We'd beheaded two of them. Luke was fighting the third. I was grappling with the fourth, an older one. Bigger, heavily muscled, but slow. Not yet a hundred. I tasted victory.

"But the fifth rogue was older than any of us. He waited until I had my opponent in a headlock, then slashed my ribs so hard it felt like a bolt of lightning. While I finished my opponent off, the fifth rogue misted to penetrate the house." Logan sat up abruptly, like guilt had knifed him in the belly. His head bent and he fell silent.

"But you said you could mist too. Didn't you go after him?"

"Certainly I went after him." Logan's voice was low, self-mocking. "I dropped into mist—except it didn't work. I tried again, stayed disturbingly solid. I tried a third time and found I wasn't as proficient as I thought. At least, not under stress."

"Couldn't you get inside another way? A door or something?"

"That's what I finally had to do. I ran like the wind. But mist...mist is almost instantaneous. I was too late. The rogue had opened Adelaide's carotid. Drunk her dry."

He dashed away a wetness in his eyes. He managed to make the gesture look powerful and masculine. "I can still see it. The rest of the household cowered in the corner of the room, men, women and children. I'd taught them that, you see. When rogues attack, come to the dining room and stay together. I was so fucking smart.

"I engaged the rogue, but he was old. Much stronger and faster than any vampire I'd ever met. And he used mist to fight. Disappeared, reappeared behind me. Slashed me open before misting out again. I knew if I lost, my humans were easy pickings. My humans knew that too." Logan groaned, a sound of deep misery. "I can still see their faces, the despair. The knowledge that they were going to die."

"So they all...all of them? Even the children?"

"No. Not because of my brilliance and strength, though."

Logan gave a scornful laugh. "By the grace of whatever agency, an Ancient was in the area and heard the fighting. The instant he misted in, the rogue misted out."

"And it was over."

His jaw clenched. "It was just starting. Luke's wife was dead. Luke was devastated. The humans of my household were so traumatized I didn't know what to do. Hell, I was just as shocked. I don't know what I would have done, if the Ancient One hadn't taken us all into his care."

"But Logan...you were young then. You're trained now. It couldn't happen again."

He raised his head, and his eyes were bleak. "Couldn't it?"

I didn't have an answer for that. "Didn't any of them fight back? The humans?"

"How?" he spat. "Vampires are faster, stronger. How would they fight back?"

"I get the impression Elena holds her own."

He blinked at me. "I do love you, you know. That was exactly the right thing to say."

My face heated. "Just lucky."

"No." He kissed me gently, his lips soft and warm. "You're perceptive. And kind."

"Don't forget nice," I muttered.

"Sweet. Very—" kiss, "—sweet. Liese." His eyes glittered red-gold. "What would you say to leaving your job?"

I reared up. "No! I mean, I like my job." *I* need *my job.*

He flinched. To my surprise, slashes of red flagged his cheeks. "No, of course not. How stupid of me." He ground fists into his eyes. "Well, look at the time. I know we had a date but...I've got some work to finish. Vital. I'd better run." He set me aside with easy strength, whirled his shirt on like a cape and was out the door before I'd had time to register he was gone.

I should have pulled off his jeans. It would have taken him at least another two seconds to dress.

I stared at the empty doorway, feeling decidedly odd. I'd been a successful siren. The sex had been cataclysmic. Logan had said "I love you" a gazillion times. He'd told me his darkest secret.

Then he ran away. That hurt, but I ached more for him, for

his pain.

He still hurt deeply for those frightened people, hundreds of years later. Questioned himself, agonized over the mistakes he'd made.

I now had the information that was supposed to cut Logan from my heart, but it only embedded him deeper.

With nothing else to do, I finished off the bottle of wine. Then I lay down and tried to get some sleep.

Every time I dropped off I'd hear whispers. "He's so sexy." Giggles. "I love it when he kisses us." More giggles. "Makes me stand right up."

Like a damned slumber party. And I couldn't even blame G-Liese and B-Liese. No, these pseudo-teens were my breasts. Never knew breasts could giggle.

Or maybe they were titters. Get it? Tit-ters?

Yeah, I was fork-in-socket insane.

I woke seemingly minutes later at the buzz of my alarm. I slapped it off, showered, ran a dry toothbrush over my teeth, and slogged into work. I felt sluggish and irritable. My head hurt. My stomach turned at the thought of food. The early morning sunlight was too bright.

As I stumbled into the Caffeine Café for my morning fix-o'-joe-to-go I wondered if I was turning into a vampire. Probably too much wine and lack of sleep, but it made me wonder how v-guys were made. Had to be dead first, according to Logan. I wondered if dead-on-my-feet counted.

At the Center, I dug in my purse for a couple minutes before I remembered the fingerprint reader. Touching it popped the lock. That was pretty chill.

My desk and the new laptop were where I'd left them. So I still had a job—for a few more minutes, anyway. Whine, whine. I sat down and started my morning routine.

At nine the lock clicked open automatically. I got up to check the door, just in case. Clouds were gathering outside, sullen as a preteen gamer without Internet. I stood in the doorway, disgusted. We were about to be treated to a spring rain.

Spring rain. Gentle, warm showers, dropping like soft glitter on flower petals, right?

Not in northern Illinois. Here, chances were fifty-fifty the "rain" would be little white pellets punching holes through your skull. Even if it was liquid, the drops would freeze your eyelashes shut and turn you into an ice sculpture. Not to mention frigid winds often accompanied said rain—or rather, drove it like needles into every inch of your exposed flesh.

The gathering clouds made it closer to night than day so I went to turn on the lights—and jumped when they flicked on automatically. Apparently the AI did more than run the perimeter and check for monsters. If it weren't going to cost me my job, I'd be impressed.

In the middle of this daylight dark, the door *whooshed* open. Cold wind and rain swept in with a narrow, older man carrying a black umbrella and wearing an overcoat and a scowl. He looked like a cross between Mr. Banks and Lurch.

"May I help you?"

"You are Liese Schmetterling."

Logan, Race, and now FrankenBanker. My job was not normally customer contact. Yet for the third time in days, someone was asking for me personally. Truly bizarre. "What do you want?"

"I am Lord Ruthven, Liese Schmetterling. You are expecting me."

"Not that I know of." The name hit memory. "Oh, *Lorne* Ruthven. Sorry, I misheard. You're the new board member, right?" I remembered Dirkson not liking him and my determination to be friendly to compensate, so I smiled.

To my surprise, his lips drew back in a snarl, exposing extra-pointy eyeteeth. Or maybe I was just fangtasizing. Ha.

"I am he, Liese Schmetterling. And you will bend to my will." Ruthven's voice was hollow, but not hollow-rich like Logan doing his Rasputin thing. Hollow-tinny, like a transistor radio.

"Bend to your will. Sure, sure." From working in Chicago I knew people in fast-paced international business sometimes got a little pushy. They didn't mean anything by it. *Be friendly, Liese.* "And what is your will, Lorne?"

"*Lord* Ruthven. My first command is that you call me by my proper name, Liese Schmetterling."

I certainly wished he'd stop calling me by mine. It was getting annoying. "You're a British lord, huh? I should have clued in from the umbrella." Although his accent was more like rip-off Lugosi. "Our Center's certainly rising up in the world."

"Yes. The Blood Center." Ruthven made it sound disconcertingly like bluuhd. "As to that, Liese Schmetterling, my second command is for you to procure me a sample." He pulled off his glove finger by finger, dusted a guest chair with great disdain before settling in. He saw me still standing there, snarled, "Well? What are you waiting for?"

"Um, sure. Right away. But...a sample of what?"

"Are you a simpleton? Of blood, of course."

I blinked. I wanted to like him but he was making it hard. "Are you nuts? We don't give samples—"

"How dare you!" He blasted to his feet. His eyes turned red as rubies.

Oh duh. Red eyes and sharp eyeteeth and he wanted a sample of bluuhd. Sometimes I was as slow as a 286. Lack of sleep or too much sex? Wouldn't that be a kicker—my IQ lowered ten points per orgasm. At Logan's rate, I'd be brainless before breakfast.

But sure as my name was Liese Du-uh, Ruthven was a vampire.

"My apologies, Lord Ruthven." The question was, was he a good-guy or a rogue? Logan or Zinnia would know. Or Nurse Battleax. She wouldn't actually know—but she could sit on him until I figured it out.

No one came conveniently to my rescue. Delay Ruthven then, while I tried to think what to do. And keep my pepper spray handy, just in case.

"I'll get that sample for you. It'll just take a minute." I slid open my drawer, fished the spray out of my purse, and slipped it into my pocket.

In back I grabbed a unit from one of the new refrigerators. A little *ding* announced the inventory counter automatically decrementing. Efficient, annoying AI. "Tattletale," I hissed at it.

Ruthven was bent over the server rack in the corner when I returned. He straightened abruptly. "Finally. I was beginning to wonder if I would have to fire you for laziness."

"I had a few more hoops to jump through than usual. New security, you know." As I offered the bag to Ruthven I glanced at the servers. Looked okay from the front, but I'd recheck the programs later. I was remembering Johansson's visit and connecting the dots. Here was a businessman in our small, vulnerable distribution center. Coincidence, maybe. But something had made that system fail in Lansing. And if their system was Steel Security, I doubted it was anything less than sabotage. Besides, I was paid to be suspicious.

Ruthven turned up his nose at the bag. "I hope you do not expect me to consume it like this, Liese Schmetterling."

How could one vampire make my name sound like sex and another like a hammer? Temper fraying, I slapped the blood onto the desk. "How do you want it, then *Lorne*? Over the rocks? Shaken, not stirred?"

He gave me *such* a look. Fangs extending he lisped, "I am a civilized man, Liese Schmetterling. I will have a glass."

I barely suppressed another sarcastic comment. After all, he was a vampire. Extra-fast, extra-strong. "All I have is this." I held up my empty paper coffee cup.

His face twisted with even greater disgust. He took the cup gingerly. "What is this, Liese Schmetterling?"

"It *was* a dark Italian roast." I got scissors from my desk. "Want me to pour?" And because I couldn't resist (okay, I could have, but apparently stress brought out the snark in me), I added, "Lorne."

He handed me the cup with obvious reluctance. "Barbaric."

"Don't you mean 'Barbaric, Liese Schmetterling'?"

His eyes went blood red. "Do not trifle with me, Liese Schmetterling. I am Lord Ruthven, Ruler of the Night."

"Good. So for the mailings, how did you want your name?" I cut open the bag (I didn't want to futz with the ports) and glugged some into the coffee cup. Yuck. To keep the rest from spilling I closed it with a binder clip and stuck the bag clipped-end-up into my top desk drawer. "Mr. Ruler O.T. Night? Lorne Ruthven? Lornie? Or just Lor?"

He slammed a fist into the desk. *"You will not mock me."* His hollow voice slammed into my head.

I froze. Boy, and I thought Race Gillette had a temper.

Ruthven surged up, Svengali eyes stabbing into mine. I expected to see his irises turn into little pinwheels. This guy lived up to all the vamp stereotypes. I should have been scared but somehow, all the vampiness just made Ruthven look cheesy.

Until he said, "You are fired."

"*What?* You can't...oh, God." He could. I slumped in my chair, because even the cheesiest vampire on the planet was scary when he was in charge.

The front door slid open behind Ruthven. *What now?* I thought just as Logan glided in. "Hey, Liese. The automatic counter registered—*you*." He slammed to a halt. His glare was so enraged, Ruthven should have shot up in flames.

Ruthven leaped to his feet and sidled around my desk, crab-like, unnaturally fast. "This is not over, Liese Schmetterling."

He dissolved into mist and disappeared.

Actually, he didn't disappear, *poof*. Before my flabbergasted eyes the mist collapsed to the floor and began flowing like a ghostly snake, arrowed for the back door.

It sounds slow when I describe it, but the whole process took less than a second.

"Damn it." Logan bolted past me, plowed into the back room. I darted after but by the time I burst in Logan was already at the rear door. The emergency exit was wide open, the alarm jangling.

Hitting the reset, Logan swore again. "What the hell was he doing here?"

I made my way to the donation bed where I sat, breathing deeply to get my heart rate under control. "He's one of the Blood Center's directors. His name is Ruthven." I didn't mention Ruthven'd fired me. Maybe in the flurry of rabbiting he'd forget. "Did you recognize him?"

"Oh yes. Ruthven's second in charge of the Lestats."

"The who?"

"Razor's gang." Logan shut the exit. "Their leader is Nosferatu."

"Whoa, wait. I thought Razor was the leader of Razor's gang."

"It's complicated." Logan stalked across the room toward me, not his hungry stalk but one of total disgust. "Damn it, if I'd known they were sending him, I'd never have agreed to sit in on the bargaining." He slammed a palm against the wall.

"Stop, stop. Let's have a 'Previously on *Stargate SG1*', shall we?"

He gave me a small, reluctant smile. "A recap?"

"If you don't mind."

"It may take a bit. Let's go back to the office where we can be more comfortable." He helped me up, rubbing my shoulders as we made our way to the front where he deposited me in my desk chair with soft kiss on the cheek.

Logan touched me a lot, as though he liked it. Maybe Elena and Gretchen were right. Maybe he *did* want me. "What are you doing here, anyway? I thought you'd be sleeping."

Logan slung himself with muscular grace into one of the guest chairs. "A unit of blood was taken from storage. It triggered an alert. It seemed odd and since I knew you were here I decided to handle it personally." He picked up the paper cup of blood. Sniffed delicately. "This it?"

"Yes. Um, since it's already poured, do you want to drink it?"

He set it down. "Of course not. This blood's for transfusion."

"With a dash of caffeine? Zesty, but I don't think so."

A small smile curved his mouth. "Intravenous caffeine. Might be a big seller."

But something he said caught at me. "You knew I was here? As in, more than figuring it was my working hours?"

"Yes. I, ah, know where all my donors are."

I sucked air. "I'm your donor? Don't I have to agree first? Sign papers or something?"

"Sorry, that's a euphemism. A polite term meaning I've tasted you. I can locate anyone whose blood I've tasted within about a mile, if I concentrate. It's in the olfactory memory."

"I see. So who is that Ruthven guy? And what does he have to do with Razor? I know you said it's complicated, but give me the Wiley's version."

"The Coterie for Dummies?" Logan smiled. "All right. Picture a pyramid. At the top is Nosferatu. He's got three underlings, Ruthven, Camille, and Giuseppe Marrone."

"Giuseppe...you mean Joe Brown?"

Logan laughed. "Yes. Each of those directs six top-level vampires. Together, these executives are known as the Coterie."

"Coterie, huh. Sounds like a breed of lapdog." I pulled up

zDictionary.com on my new laptop. It had exceptional response time. I felt a zing of pleasure. "A small, exclusive group with a common purpose."

"In this case the purpose is to obtain power." Logan's smile faded. "In our world, that means blood. The Coterie is trying every way possible to get control of the nation's blood centers. We managed to convince the federal government that the Red Cross is a strategic national resource. They're protected, but that leaves smaller, private centers vulnerable." He stared at the cup, twisting it in his fingers.

"You really shouldn't let that go to waste."

He blinked, released the cup. "Later, maybe."

"I remember your using that term, Coterie, before. In connection with something called Project Shield."

"Ah, you have a good memory. The problem is there's a turf war heating up inside the Coterie. The challenger's threatening terrorist-like attacks to discredit and disorganize Nosferatu, trying to make the Coterie ripe for takeover. Which wouldn't be a problem if the challenger was only terrorizing vampires. But our agents report that he—or she—is planning to take out a Chicago landmark. We don't know how and we don't know who, though. So the Alliance is forming a ring of key households around Chicago, to act as a sort of first-alert and shield. My household will be at the core." He grimaced. "I'm one of the few who has the intensity of training needed to live right in the middle of enemy territory." He started playing with the cup again.

"Drink it, Logan. You don't have to worry about grossing me out."

A slight smile returned. "Are you a mind-reader?"

"I wondered the same thing about you."

The smile widened, became gut-splatting. I gasped. *Someone please get the heart paddles.* "Drink, please." If only to hide his Death-by-Chocolate smile, at least for a bit. "What about the Lestats? How do they figure in?"

"The Lestats are the Coterie's muscle. The bullies that keep other vampires in line." Logan picked up the paper cup and sipped, watching me carefully. When I didn't flinch he took another sip, then made a face. "I can taste the coffee."

"Yummy, isn't it? All these vampires, Coterie and Lestats. They're all Chicago?"

"No. The Coterie's based in the Windy City. But there are branches of Lestats all over, just like urban gangs."

"So what's Ruthven doing in Meiers Corners?"

"The Coterie's been trying to gain control of this Blood Center for a while now. I told you about the attempt at the festival in November. I think they realized with the new security that they had no chance of a direct takeover."

"So Ruthven was reduced to bargaining."

"Nosferatu, actually." Logan sipped more blood. "The head honcho was supposed to be here himself. But he probably felt it was beneath his dignity to bargain with us youngsters and sent Ruthven in his place."

"Nixie's phone call," I remembered. "The message for you that Julian couldn't meet with Nosy. Nosy is Nosferatu?"

"Yes. And she calls Ruthven 'Ruthie'. If anyone was less like a Ruthie..." Logan snorted. "Emerson would normally be the mediator. Since he's out of town, I was deputized to sit in with Bo." He sipped blood again. "You know, this grows on you. It may be a future drink for the Caffeine Café."

"What would they call it? Mocha *Rouge*?" I smiled at him.

"Café *au Sang*, perhaps? Or maybe Transylvanian Espresso." He smiled back, eyes warmed to a golden brown.

Our eyes met and held. Smiles faded.

That was the instant I fell fully, irrevocably in love with Logan Steel.

I blinked, tried to cover by babbling. "Ruthven...why do you hate him so much? I mean, more than Nosferatu? I mean what...I mean where..."

"Ah, Liese." Logan's bright head tilted. "You're cute when you're running scared."

I shook my head in denial and his eyes sparkled knowingly, gold flecks bright in the rich hazel irises. Sweet vector equations, the male was gorgeous. If faces were phaser settings, Logan's would be incinerate. I cleared my throat. "Glad I amuse you. Look, could you just answer the question?"

Logan's smile faded. "Remember my first attempt at householding?"

"You were attacked by rogues. One of them was older than the rest, and—oh, no. Not Ruthven?"

"The same."

"*That* was the monster who killed your sister-in-law?"

"And terrified my household. Yes." Logan's jaw worked like he was fighting to control his fangs.

And suddenly it wasn't a terrible tragedy from centuries ago but a clear threat *now*. Ruthven, who'd terrorized Logan in the past, was here. Worse, Logan was scarred from that past encounter—how much would that insecurity have grown over the years?

How much stronger was Ruthven really? How much deadlier? Would even all Logan's training be enough?

And if not, what would happen? There were implications beyond Logan losing another fight to Ruthven. Logan was important to the Iowa Alliance. What would his loss mean to them? To *us*, the humans? Because if I'd gleaned anything, it was that the Alliance stood between humans and rogues, who'd treat us like blood on the hoof.

"But Logan—why hasn't anything been done before this? Didn't you know he was practically next door?"

"Oh, I knew. But by then he was part of the Coterie. Any move against him would have caused trouble for the Alliance." A low growl underlay his words. "Damned politics. I think I liked it better in the old days. Kill or be killed. Nice, simple. No need for messy arbitrations and stupid negotiations."

"You mean...you can't fight Ruthven, Logan." *What if he killed you?* But I didn't say that out loud. "Not if it means trouble for the Alliance, right? I mean, what if you killed him?"

"Then I would be a very happy vampire." Any trace of softness in Logan's eyes was gone, leaving only the hard, relentless hunter. Ruthless. Could I hope that would be the result, if Ruthie and Logan met now? That we'd be Ruthieless?

Oh, great. I'd gone beyond sarcasm when stressed and was starting to pun—thanks to Logan, of course. The more time I spent with him, the more of his traits I picked up, like an old married couple...aw, phooey. "But if you and Ruthven fight, what would happen to the Blood Center? He's one of twenty-two leaders, you said. Wouldn't there be a backlash from the other twenty-one?"

Logan snorted his disgust. "Yes. That's why I haven't destroyed him until now." He looked at me and his eyes fired ruby-red. "But if he laid one hand on you—"

"No, Logan. He was high-handed and chauvinistic. But he

didn't touch me." *Only fired me.* I'd have to find some way to fight that.

"I don't even like that he was here alone with you." He drummed fingers on my desk. They went *tick-tick-tick.* Like he had extra-long nails or—I stared. Logan was tapping real live inch-long talons of death on my desk. "If he even threatened you I'll—"

"Logan, no." This was escalating too fast. I didn't want Logan to fight Ruthven but even I knew I couldn't say so directly. "Ruthven's only here to negotiate, so you play nice." I adopted my best mother-voice. "And put away your claws, young man."

He stopped tapping. Stared at his hand and frowned. The talons dissolved, leaving his long, beautiful fingers. But his glorious mouth was turned down, for all the world like he was pouting. It was absolutely adorable.

I must have had rocks in my head. "But I think it's sweet that you care."

One corner of his mouth, reluctantly, turned up. "Can I at least put a skunk in his coffin?"

"You may not. Do you guys sleep in coffins?"

Logan laughed. "No. Except for Ruthven. If there's a corny cliché, Ruthven's got it nailed." He sobered. "Thanks, Liese. You coaxed my brain back online. Excuse me a moment. I have to report this." He pulled out his cell phone, hit a speed dial. "It's me, sir. There's been a slight hitch." His tone was that warm respect that meant he was talking to Mr. Elias. "No, sir. Negotiations are still on for tonight, here at the Blood Center. But Nosferatu sent Ruthven to handle them."

The only thing that stunned me more than finding out negotiations were happening *here* was Logan was talking to Mr. Elias about a vampire.

"But I think this will surprise you. He's joined the Blood Center board of directors, the opening gambit for a takeover."

I wondered how Elias would react. Zinnia had said he was old. Given Elias's exalted position in the business community and the respect Logan paid him, I believed it. But how old? I hoped Logan's surprise wouldn't shock the poor, frail old man into a grave.

Although, remembering his voice, there was nothing poor or frail about Elias.

Logan's face took on a look of sheer incredulity. "How did you know that?"

Apparently there was nothing slow about Elias, either. Huh. Competition for Dolly Barton. I wondered if Elias looked like Dolly. I pictured him small, blond, and stacked...okay, maybe not.

"One more thing. Ruthven cornered Liese Schmetterling alone in her office today. Do you have any recommendations?"

I imagined old Elias counseling tact. And patience. And—

"That extreme? ...oh, I see. Yes, sir. Of course, Mr. Elias. Thank you." Logan shut his phone and slipped it away.

I had to be wrong. Elias was a guiding light of rationality. "What did he say?"

Logan shrugged. "I'm to destroy Ruthven."

Well. That was pretty clear. And what it meant...oh, no. I was going nuts. Totally bonkers, *Lost,* season *N*-plus-one. Elias was counseling destruction of a vampire... Truth burst on me. Elias was a vampire too. And not any vampire but the Ancient One, a super-duper übervamp.

Although it did explain that *voice.* "Now? Not after the negotiations?"

"Elias leaves those decisions to me."

I breathed a sigh of relief. "So you'll wait?"

"It depends." Logan leaned forward. The desk was between us but he pumped up so big and strong that mere wood was no defense. "I'll do whatever I have to in order to protect you, the Blood Center and Meiers Corners." He tapped a single claw on the desk to underline each point. "In that order."

I smiled weakly. Logan wasn't wearing his CEO face, or even his hunter face. The Logan I saw at that moment was an executioner.

Saner heads needed to be present. Headsmen, heads. Ha. I'd have let Logan in on the joke but something told me he wasn't in humor receiving mode right now.

All the more reason for me to be at the negotiations tonight.

Chapter Fifteen

Logan left after that to prepare for his encounter with Ruthven. I didn't like the gleam in his eye, which looked way too martial.

But that wasn't my only worry. Logan's call to Elias reminded me that this was Friday. Elias was back in his office and expecting my call.

Oh yeah. I was doomed. I didn't even bother setting my mood-timer. When doomed, despair is a perfectly proper and rational response.

Time passes slowly when you're mired in your own misery. I had years to ponder what was left of my future. Elias knew I had sent that picture, betraying Logan, his trusted right-hand man. Vampire. Yeah. Elias would chop me into little bits.

Oh, snap. Elias was the one who'd told Logan to destroy Ruthven. Doomed? I was dead. I almost longed for the days when the worst life threw at me was bankruptcy and blacklisting by Botcher. Compared to execution by a golden prince and a chasm-voiced king, a yipping rat-bastard was almost funny.

At lunchtime the door *shooshed* open. Now what? Logan, Zinnia or Ruthven, it was bound to be more bad news. I pretended I hadn't heard the door. Maybe whoever it was would go away.

A picture slapped onto my desk. "Have you seen this?"

I jumped. Looming over me was the red face of John Dirkson, Executive Director and my boss.

Note to self: when bad news comes through the door, do not stick head in sand. Running is more effective.

Dirkson was big and burly like an 1800s circus strongman,

his handlebar mustache and woolly sideburns straight out of the same century. Like his appearance, the chief was ultra-traditional, not likely to take the dungeon scene well.

He thumped the paper. "It came in Tuesday's email but I didn't open it until today. Well? Have you seen it?" He chomped his thick cigar like he wanted to chew it to death.

"Uh...no." I glanced down, hoping against hope. But it was the dreaded photoshopped pic, printed out on an old color inkjet. Hmm, the registration needed adjustment. But talk about a career-limiting move. My eyes unhappily scanned the male bodies, so much punier than Logan's, then returned to the Chief. "Um, why?"

"You might recognize one of those men."

I swallowed. I couldn't believe I had angled for just this moment. Had planned to crow, "I recognize him! The supposed security man. Security, ha."

But now, I couldn't do it. Not only was Logan an astonishing lover, not only was he kind and funny, but he was protecting people. *And I loved him.* I didn't want to guess what all that might mean, but one thing was certain—I had to come clean. Admit I'd doctored the photo. That I'd sent it, and why.

I'd lose my job. And without a recommendation, blacklisted by Botcher, I'd never find another. But I'd have my pride. And I'd have protected Logan. Food and shelter were overrated anyway. Maybe my mother could live at Cousin Rolf's and his insurance would cover deranged dependent aunts.

"It's not what you think, Chief."

"Yes, it is," Dirkson thundered. "Look at that!" He stabbed the photo with the gnawed end of his cigar.

"It only looks like him. It's not—" I broke off, seeing who the cigar pointed to for the first time.

Not Logan's face. But the *other* man in the picture.

"That slime." Dirkson stabbed again. "Do you believe this?"

"Shizzle." Take away the corset and the wig—

It was Botcher. Bernie Botcher, the man who'd ruined my life.

"That's your ex-fiancé. I knew he was scum, but this proves it."

I couldn't believe it. Bernie Botcher, a *porn star*?

"Dolly Barton told me everything that bit of walking

pestilence did to you at my weekly moustache waxing...*grrr*." Dirkson stuck the cigar back in his mouth.

The phone started ringing. I was still trying to wrap my mind around Botcher as a porn star. What would his stage name be? Ballher U. Betcher? The Viagra Kid?

"Somebody ought to call this fuck's boss." Dirkson waited a moment. "Aren't you going to answer the phone?"

"Uh, yeah." Dazed, I hit connect.

"Liese, good news." Logan, but so excited I almost didn't recognize him.

"Logan?" I croaked.

For once he didn't catch the strain in my voice. "I had a little time on my hands before tonight. You remember that call you got from your ex? Well, it was highly suggestive, to say the least. So I did a little digging. The ADD security feeds reveal Botcher's had his hand in the till. He embezzled thousands of dollars, and it's all recorded. I'm alerting the company as soon as I get off the phone with you. Told you I'd eviscerate him, princess. That man will never hurt you again."

"You're so good to me," I whispered. As I hung up I choked on a huge sob.

"There, there." Dirkson patted my shoulder with one big paw. "I know you must be very happy."

"Yes, very...happy." I sniffled. And when he handed me his big red hankie, I covered my face and wished the world would go away.

After Dirkson left I phoned Mr. Elias. I wanted to admit my guilt, then commit suicide by ice cream or something. I'd never see Logan again. Five days of heavenly orgasms were going to have to hold me for the rest of my life.

Heavenly? That's how Dolly said I'd know the right man... Logan Steel was the Right One. Aw, shizzle. Maybe I'd kill myself on double-chocolate fudge.

Mr. Elias's secretary was polite, efficient and firm. "Unless this is an emergency, Mr. Elias is not to be disturbed before six."

"It *is* an emergency," I tried to tell her.

"That means immediate physical danger," she said.

In most companies a missing paperclip constituted an

emergency. Her reply was refreshing, but unhelpful. "Please," I said again. "My name is Liese Schmetterling. I'm with the Blood Center in Meiers Corners."

That got a reaction. "Meiers Corners? Mr. Steel's run into trouble?"

"You might say that," I muttered. "It's avoidable trouble. If I can speak with Mr. Elias before six. I know he's in. Logan talked with him this morning."

"Mr. Steel has Mr. Elias's private number. But..." The iron secretary was weakening. I scrunched my eyes and wished really hard on the Sex Fairy. She said, "I'll see what I can do, Ms. Schmetterling. If Mr. Elias becomes available, I'll tell him you called."

"Thank you." I hung up and waited.

And waited. My work was done, thanks to the efficient Steel Security programs. I chewed off my fingernails. I cleaned my desk. I reorganized my pencil cup. I sorted my cable ties by color. I chewed off my cuticles. The phone was silent.

So I trundled over to the AllRighty-AllNighty to pick up some plastic cups and paper napkins. After all, if Logan went through with the negotiations, we'd need to serve refreshments.

That took half an hour.

I came back and waited some more. They say a watched pot never boils. Physics ensures that it eventually does, but I swear Stephen Hawking was laughing his ass off over the laws of Liese. I felt like Schrödinger substituted me for his cat.

At four thirty the door swooshed open, making me jump. The guy who came in with clipboard and uniform looked a twin for that loud redheaded comedian—flaming curly hair, a delicate, almost pretty face, and muscles like Jiffy Pop. Carrothead, Jr. He tossed me the clipboard. "Delivery."

"Where's Johansson?" I signed.

"Out sick. It's a small load anyway. My van's out back. Open the rear door?"

"Sure. Flu?" At least this would occupy me for a time.

Carrothead followed me back. "What?"

"Johansson. Did he get the flu again?" I coded off the alarm and opened the back door to see an appalling cherry-red van in the alley.

"Oh. Yeah, if flu comes in a Jim Beam bottle."

"Really?" Didn't sound like Johansson, but how many of us really know our fellow workers? Logan, for example. How many employees knew why Steel Security had the extra-deluxe dental plan?

It took six minutes to unload the van. Normally checking the stock in would take another fifteen but thanks to you-know-who's software, I was at my desk two minutes later, brooding again.

At five to six, the phone finally rang. The jangling sounded deeper somehow, like a cloister bell. The Ring of Death. I hit connect. "Hello?"

"Ms. Schmetterling." The canyon-deep voice was unmistakable, permeated with effortless power. Like Michael Dorn (think Worf on *Star Trek: TNG*), drenched in testosterone.

"Hello, Mr. Elias," I said miserably. "About the picture—"

"Yes, good quality work. Usually there's a change in coloration where the image has been photoshopped. I couldn't see it on your picture, and my eyes are quite good."

"You...you know it's fake?"

"Certainly. I've known Logan Steel for a long time now, Ms. Schmetterling. He would not indulge in a *ménage à trois*." The phrase rolled off Elias's tongue like silk. "It's not his style."

Were we talking about the same man? Logan Steel, a male so sexy hot he made galaxies ignite? An almost omniscient lover who'd cracked my Botcher shell easier than hacking email? "Logan probably has women all over the country, Mr. Elias. The world! I'm sure he does ménage à three all the time—ménage à four or five too."

"No, that's his twin. Logan's the conservative one. Luke's a bit of a lady-killer."

"He's *more* of a playboy?"

"He has a few issues to work through. As does Logan, but you've already discovered that, I believe. Now, as to that picture."

I had to make this right. "I faked the picture, Mr. Elias. You can't punish Logan for it."

"I won't, Ms. Schmetterling."

I slumped in relief. "And me?"

"Ah. Well, that's up to Logan, isn't it? Good night, Ms. Schmetterling."

Up to Logan. I grabbed for Dirkson's red hankie.

I didn't get to make things right with Logan before Bo and Elena showed up at six ten for the negotiations. The meeting wasn't until six thirty, but maybe they were on Meiers Corners time (twenty minutes early for everything).

Or maybe they were preparing for battle too. I buzzed them in and they cased the office like it was a warzone.

"Logan's not here yet?" Elena carried a yard-long green wedge with topside sight and cockpit controls underneath. She saw me eyeing it and grinned. "New grenade launcher. XM25. Does air bursts. I'm trying it out."

"Um, isn't that a bit overkill? Can't you grab a stake, stab and—poof?"

Bo rolled his eyes. Elena said, "Nah. You have to punch out the heart to stop a vamp. Bones are in the way, so unless you're superstrong, a bazooka's the only way to go."

"What about pepper spray?"

"You'd have to get it directly in the eyes, and most vamps move too fast. Besides, pepper spray doesn't work at all on mist."

"Oh. Great." Apparently I was helpless.

Bo prowled the perimeter of the small office, as grim as I'd ever seen him, reinforcing my anxiety. So when he said, "You'd better go now, Liese," I nearly did.

But Elias had told Logan to destroy Ruthven. While I wasn't against that per se, there was the small matter of the last time they fought—when Logan lost, not just physically but emotionally. He'd trained since then, but it was obvious he still felt hurt and betrayed. That was a huge potential weakness.

I'd thought about it a lot (in between wondering just how low I'd have to grovel to Logan to make up for the photoshopped picture. My knees, maybe. With my mouth just at his hip level. Hmm. Maybe groveling would be kind of fun).

I decided I had to stop Logan from fighting Ruthven, any way I could. Physical intervention, if necessary. Of course if I got between them, I'd probably be ripped to shreds. Painful, but worth it if it slowed them enough for cooler heads to prevail. Or at least for Elena to bring her Wedge-o'-Death into play.

So though I wanted to skedaddle home to hide, I parked my

butt behind my desk. "I'll stay."

"Nothing to stay for, Liese," Bo said. "Nothing involving you."

"Bo, I know about the negotiations. And the Blood Center involves me very much."

That stopped him in his tracks, his eyes narrow and red. "Things might get violent." He grabbed for me.

I leaped up out of the way. "Last I heard, negotiations involve crossing words, not swords." *Brave front, Liese.* "Besides, somebody has to see to chairs and drinks." I ducked around Bo and headed for the back room.

I knew better than to consider the matter over. Bo was super-fast, super-strong. If he wanted me gone, I'd be gone. But hopefully as a good-guy vamp he'd avoid drastic action, at least until it was too late to throw me out. I gathered chairs and dragged them into the office.

Bo and Elena continued to argue with me. I made agreeable noises and escaped to fetch sodas from a fridge in the back (I waited for the meter to decrement but nothing happened. Damn, that AI was good). For the toothy guys I still had the open bag of blood. Even without the temperature button I knew it wasn't good for donation anymore.

While I worked, Bo and Elena paced the office like a set of caged tigers, arguing with me, wielding similar reasons in almost the same tone of voice. Talk about couples becoming alike. I nodded placatingly while pouring cups of blood.

At six thirty my new laptop chimed. Well, whadya know? The meeting was in Outlook already. Vampire turf wars made almost civilized. I popped up a view of the camera covering the front door. Sure enough, Lord Procure-Me-A-Sample hovered outside along with Race Gillette, of all people.

I barely recognized Race. His mullet was gone, exchanged for a tousled, slightly spiky cut that brought out strands of red and gold. Gone too were the jeans and flannel, exchanged for smart khakis and Oxford shirt. A small ruby glinted in one ear. He looked—dapper.

I buzzed them in. Bo and Elena ground to a halt at the sight of Ruthven. If looks could kill, Ruthie should have flopped like a fish and had little *x*'s for his eyes. He edged into the room, hand just inside his coat. Seeing no Logan he straightened and cocked an arrogant head at the cups of blood. "You have learned your place, Liese Schmetterling." He picked up a cup and I felt a wash of relief that he'd apparently forgotten about firing me—until he drank. His Adam's apple bobbed as he swallowed.

Ruthven was gulping blood. I could tolerate it when Logan sipped, but yuck. I ran into the bathroom, pretending it was to comb my hair, but really it was just so I didn't puke in public. Still hadn't found that bucket.

The click of the outer door alerted me to Logan's arrival. I braced myself for a peek. The Logan entering the office was not one I'd seen before, not playful Logan nor Logan the CEO. This wasn't even the hungry predator or executioner.

No, the dangerous male who shimmered with inhuman speed through the door had fangs like knives, muscles of steel cable and eyes that burned hotter than rivers of blood.

This was Logan the dark vampire prince. And he was one scary mutha. I cowered just a little behind the bathroom door.

Ruthven whirled. The empty cup crushed in his hand. "I claim right of pax!" He didn't exactly squeal it but his voice was high and strained. "I come to parley, Steel."

"Really?" Logan glided, eerily smooth, into the room. His glittering eyes were hard on Ruthven. "I come to fight."

Ruthven backed into my desk. "You can't! Not without horrible consequences."

Logan glided closer until he was toe-to-toe with Ruthven. "The Ancient One considers the consequences well worth shouldering, to rid the world of *you*."

Ruthven swallowed hard. With the desk in the way, he couldn't retreat further. His hand stole toward his open coat.

Before I could even squeak a warning, Logan backed off. "However. Both the Ancient One and I have no wish to cause trouble for the master of this city."

"*I* don't mind." Bo's voice was rough, practically a growl.

Elena unshouldered her XM25.

Time for cooler heads to intervene. "*I* mind." I emerged cautiously from the bathroom. "A turf war is never nice to the *turf.* If you're going to fight, boys, take it outside."

Logan must have been concentrating on Ruthven to the exclusion of all else because my appearance surprised him. He whirled on Bo. "Damn it, Strongwell. You were supposed to get her out of here."

The corner of Bo's mouth turned up. "I don't know if you noticed, but your female's kind of stubborn."

Your female? As in Logan's female? As in I was Logan's—shizzle. First sex thrall, then girlfriend, now this. Was everyone delusional?

"I know," Logan said. "That's why *you* were supposed to persuade her to leave. She won't listen to me."

"*She* is right here," I pointed out. "You can complain about *her* to her face."

Logan heaved a huge breath, turned to me. "Liese, this is vampire business. No humans should be here." His eyes' angry fire cooled as his gaze rested on me, but the fangs remained out. It occurred to me to wonder how he managed to speak around them without lisping.

"No humans? What about Elena? What about Race?"

"Elena's part of our world—"

"Race?" Ruthven frowned. "Who is Race?" His eyes bounced from me to Logan and finally to Race. And then he just cackled. "Oh, *Race*. And she believed it. That is rich."

"Liese, allow me to introduce Ruthven's second for these negotiations." Logan waved a hand toward Race. "Razor."

My face heated. Yeah, I should have known. But it floored me.

And after a moment I decided it really pissed me off. Logan hadn't told me. And this lie didn't affect only me. My mother was dating a rogue. Okay, she knew she was dating a rogue, but not that he wasn't the normal human kind. Race was a v-rogue, much more dangerous. Bo and Elena had known too, but it was Logan's deception that hurt. Like our intimacy hadn't meant a thing, like I wasn't worth telling the truth. Like the only way I'd get it was if he was drunk. Great, drunk truth. Brainless Race was right. I felt slightly dirty.

Race...*Razor* gave me a salacious grin. "Now you get why I coulda done you good, dollface?"

"You all knew," I choked out. "At Nieman's the other night. You knew he was a vampire and didn't say anything." Though I spoke to all of them, my eyes were cutting Logan a new one.

"Liese." Now Logan's fangs did recede. "I—"

"I don't have all night, Steel," Ruthven cut in harshly. He

snatched up another cup of blood. "Are we negotiating, or aren't we? Because if we aren't, I have things to do."

Flashing me a final, frustrated look, Logan drew back his leather jacket. "We are. I declare my peaceful intent by offering my weapon." With supple strength he drew a gleaming three-foot saber and placed it on my desk. My jaw dropped.

"I offer my weapon." Ruthven withdrew a slim stiletto and laid it next to the saber. It was insignificant compared to the sword, except for the heavy crust of rubies and sapphires on the hilt. Well, and the evil green poison-like tinge on the wicked point. A poisoned dagger, just inside his coat...I shuddered.

Bo stepped forward, reached over his shoulder and drew a huge blade, so quickly and smoothly I knew it wasn't the first time. He laid it on my desk where it lopped over the edge. I wondered how I'd missed seeing such a giant thing. "I declare pax on this gathering and offer my weapon as proof."

"Yeah, likewise." Race...*Razor* pulled a foot-long black rod out of his jacket. I was still wondering how Bo had hidden that huge sword. Must have been in a scabbard under his jacket, but how did I miss the hilt? Wrapped in leather, yellow crisscrossed with ecru, almost a foot long—oh. Blended with his hair.

Razor dropped his rod onto the table. At first I thought it was a cudgel of some sort, harmless compared to the sharp blades. Logan caught my unimpressed glance. "Don't be lulled. That's a switchblade. And he has been known to carry a meat cleaver."

I shivered. A fricking foot-long, deadly switchblade.

"What about her?" Razor nodded at Elena, who was leaning on her XM25.

Ruthven shrugged. "She is human. She does not count."

Didn't that just figure. At least it wasn't just me. Apparently *all* humans weren't worthy in his vampire eyes.

Logan grabbed one of the guest chairs, set it in front of him. "I stand as representative of the Iowa Alliance. Who stands as my second?"

Bo grabbed another chair, set it opposite Logan's and stood behind it. "I do."

"The Iowa Alliance is fully represented. Who stands for the Chicago Coterie?"

Ruthven nodded sharply at Razor, who jumped to set a chair between Logan's and Bo's. Ruthven stepped behind it. "I represent the Coterie. This one is my second." He waved at Razor, who was dragging the last chair across from Ruthven to make a square.

"The requirements are satisfied," Logan said. "One principal and one second from each faction. Weapons set aside. The territory under dispute is the Meiers Corners Blood Center. Let us sit."

When they weren't trying to blend, vampires in motion were *weird*. One moment the four were standing behind their chairs. Then they—well, flickered is the only word I can think of—and a moment later they stood *in front* of the chairs. When they sat it was with a fluid strength that went beyond words like *power* and *grace* and came uncomfortably close to *ooze*.

As I said, weird. If I hadn't been so mad, I'd have been impressed.

But I was mad. That negligent show of alien strength and dexterity only made me madder. Whose Blood Center was this, anyway?

If the blood was for human transfusions, why were vampires fighting over it? Fighting like dogs over a bone. Well, maybe negotiating, not fighting, but still. Why were no humans included? Did they think we weren't worthwhile?

For all their grand words, did even the good-guy vamps really think of us as blood sheep, with no will of our own, or at least none worth worrying about?

I've mentioned how I couldn't defend myself from a mosquito but when other people's welfare was at risk, look out? Well, this wasn't just other people we were talking about. This was humanity. And I was getting right royally pissed.

"We are agreeable to letting you keep the Blood Center," Ruthven said in his opening salvo. "If you concede rights to the distributions."

"Keep the building, but lose the blood? How generous." Logan leaned forward, face intent. His eyes were that sharp, glittering gold. He was so damned gorgeous. I had to work to remember it was all just part of his vampire's bag of predator's advantages. "Let me make a counter-offer. You leave the Blood Center alone, promise never to interrupt its shipments, and the Alliance will leave you alone."

"We get nothing?" Ruthven *hmphed*. "That is not a serious offer."

"You get immunity." Logan's eyes flicked to his saber, then back to Ruthven. "You should remember that my master gave me leave to destroy you."

"The vaunted Ancient One? And why would you be so generous as to spare me if Elias wants my head?"

Logan's grin turned deadly. "Let's just say I have a vested interest in keeping the waters smooth in Meiers Corners."

"Why us, anyway?" Bo spoke for the first time since giving up his mammoth sword. "We're small potatoes, even distributing for the Midwest. Why aren't you raiding distributors in Chicago, or one of the rich suburbs? Or even Milwaukee or Rockford?"

Race poked his hand up. "Ooh, I know that one. Master Nosferatu won't let us. He says it'll expose us to too much pubicity." He sat back, a delighted grin on his face.

Ruthven grimaced. "Pu*bli*city, you imbecile."

Logan's eyes turned thoughtful. "The very fact that Meiers Corners is small is an attraction to him. Fewer people to catch on. Elias suggested something of the sort."

Bo glared at Ruthven. "You're saying you've been hounding us because we have the most blood for the least *risk*?"

"*I* didn't say it." With a black glare at Razor, Ruthven added in a mutter, "Nosferatu is a coward."

"You're making my life hell because *nobody will notice*?" Bo's fangs extended. "Fuck that."

Elena gripped her XM25. "I say we cap them here and now, and damn the consequences."

Razor shot to his feet. Bo's eyes turned blood red.

"We are under pax," Ruthven snarled.

"My city is not a toy." Bo sliced one hand through the air. His fingers were tipped with wicked-looking talons.

"Lieutenant." Ruthven went sheet-white but his voice was imperious. "Defend me."

Razor made a dive for his switchblade. Bo leaped to his feet, brandishing claws and fangs. His chair toppled with a crash.

It would be all-out war.

Chapter Sixteen

But a while back I'd read the escalating situation and eased to my feet, pepper spray ready.

Oh, and I'd swiped Razor's switchblade from the table.

Even with his supernatural advantage, Raze-man couldn't go back in time. As he dove for the now-empty spot on the desk I flicked the knife open with a snap of the wrist. It made a very satisfying ka-*click*.

Razor skidded to a halt mere millimeters from impalement.

"Sit." I pointed the blade at his chair. He looked like he wanted to argue, so I raised my other hand, which held—a battery. Damn, it'd felt like pepper spray. I really was going to have to clean my purse. I dropped the battery, grabbed the knife with both hands and jabbed at him. "Sit, before I have to hurt you. *Sit*."

Razor eyed the knife warily. "I could take that away from you in a second."

"You'd better do as she says." Logan's tone was laconic. Unlike the other four, he lounged in his chair. "She doesn't need a knife to cut you. She can slice and dice you with her wit."

Hearing that, Razor subsided into his chair. It might also have been because Elena pointed her XM25 between his eyebrows.

"Good. Now." I waved the knife at the four vampires. "I listened to you all argue and make arrogant remarks and beat your chests like barbarians."

"We weren't—" Razor half-rose.

"*Enough*."

He sat. Logan smirked, damn him. He was enjoying this.

"This is how it's going down. This is a human blood center, providing human blood—for humans. Since you vampires apparently don't understand property rights, we're going to have to do this the hard way. A fight."

Logan's eyes swung to me, speculation gleaming from their golden depths.

Elena's hand tightened on her grenade launcher. "Liese, no. You can't fight vampires. They're stronger, faster—"

"In a battle of sheepshead, ladies and gentlevamps." I pointed at Logan and Bo. "You two will represent the Meiers Corners vampires. You two—" Ruthven and Razor, "—the Coterie. One hand, winner take all."

Bo growled. "The loser gives up all claim? I don't think—"

"No, you *don't* think. Human blood, remember? Ours? Or was that just Alliance propaganda bullshit?"

"Hey, that's right," Elena said. "It's our blood. Why are you guys negotiating?"

"Elena—" Bo glanced at her. She unleashed a really nasty combo of the Cop Glare and The Look on him and he shut his mouth.

"So." I gave them each a penetrating stare. "Agreed?"

Ruthven's eyes had gone from blood red to a sly, glittering black. "Sheepshead, hmm? It has been a while since I have played. Still...agreed."

"Damn me, she's right." Bo slapped his leg. "Agreed."

"Not me. Not if he plays." Razor pointed a claw at Logan. "He's a sheepshead monster. Anyway, he's not from Meiers Corners. He can't play for their team."

"I'm Julian Emerson's designated agent." Logan smiled, lavish lengths of fang showing. "For the purposes of these negotiations, I'm a Meiers Corners vampire."

"Bah," Ruthven said. "You argue semantics, but I care not. I will defeat you and the Blood Center will be mine, without a single Lestat falling. Then Nosferatu cannot fail to award me the lion's share of the spoils. Very well, Steel and Strongwell against me and my lieutenant. Four-handed sheepshead. Let us begin."

"But boss—" Razor began.

"We'll cream you," Bo said.

"Bo, remember," Elena said. "You can't trust them."

Ruthven cackled.

"Not four-handed." I stabbed the knife into my desk with a *thunk*. There was instant silence. "Five-handed."

Ruthven glared at me. "Meiers Corners vampires against Coterie vampires. There are but four."

"You highhanded pigs forget who owns this place. *Humans.* *I'm* playing for us. And I'll whip you all. Let's take this gig over to Nieman's. Oh, and leave the weapons here."

They started objecting. I swept past them all to the door. "*Enough.* Are you vampires or, um, vermin? Let's go." I punched the door open.

With a certain amount of grumbling, the Coterie contingent moved out. Bo and Elena followed, Elena casting worried glances back at me.

"Liese," Logan began.

I silenced him by flicking a glare at Race Gillette, a.k.a. Razor to everyone but me.

Smart as Logan was, I didn't have to say a word. He heard "You lied to me" loud and clear. With a wince, he followed everyone out.

I got a fresh deck from Buddy the bartender and brought it to the table Bo'd set up in the back corridor, the only place empty enough in case things got fangy. The occasional drunk wove through to use the restrooms, but they wouldn't notice anything.

I shuffled the cards and passed them to Ruthven, watching him cut. His hands flickered briefly and he slid the cards back with a smug smile. Cheat.

I'd expected that, though. I passed the cards to Elena for her to cut a second time. "Double cut, and Bo deals."

Ruthven's smug deflated.

I passed the cards to Bo, wiped my palms discreetly on my pants. A single hand of sheepshead. I'd wagered not only the Center's future but that of the entire city on one hand of cards. What had I done?

What I had to do. My body was nervous but I sure as hell was not. This was the only way I could fight back, and I was determined to battle with everything I had. This total disregard of the humans shot me well beyond hot anger to a cold, frigid, *how dare you.*

I swiped up my cards. Ace, eight and seven of hearts, nine and seven of diamonds and ace of clubs. I carefully schooled my face against disappointment. It was not a winning hand. Some decent points though, enough to throw in with Logan, nudge his team for the win.

"Pass." Razor snickered. Probably all trump. Damn *mauerer* (German for slimy suckbag sleazeball).

Bo threw a dark look at Razor. He'd caught the snicker too.

"I pass," Ruthven said, tapping one finger against the table. He looked cool, untouchable. Like he had half a dozen queens up his sleeve. Probably did, the cheat.

I wiped my palm again. Damn it, I wanted to beat Ruthven just because he was such a cheat and jerk. He and his Loser-stats didn't deserve our Blood Center.

But if Ruthven didn't deserve the Blood Center, neither did Logan, who'd wanted me to trust him but lied about Razor. I looked at my hand again. Only two trump, both low. But with the aces, not good for a leaster, either.

Ham it to Dell, not a winning hand either way. But if I didn't even try for a win, humans would get shut out, voiceless.

I picked up the blind. Maybe there'd be eight queens.

Logan looked at me like I'd gone nuts. Which meant he had as many power cards as Razor. Which meant...the blind was the ten of hearts and the king of diamonds.

A partner could save me. If it turned out to be Race or Logan, who apparently held the strong cards, I could ride along for the win.

The problem with sheepshead is you can't actually pick your partner. I could only call an ace. If I called an ace that Logan held, humanity would have beneficent masters. Oh joy. If Razor held it, humanity would share the Blood Center with a group not known for playing nicely with others.

Still, either was better than Bo or Ruthven, the two weaker hands. Then I'd lose. Humanity would lose.

But what else could I do? Logan had said I could win if I'd take more chances. Time to see what truth there was to his words. Take a chance. Call an ace and hope...no, *pray* the right vampire held it.

I took another look at my cards.

Fuck it. If humans were going down, we were going down as humans only.

I slapped the ace and ten of hearts face down on the table. "I call no-ace." No partner.

Elena grabbed my shoulder from behind, fingers biting though her face was cop-blank. I shook my head, once. She let go.

If the big guns were evenly distributed, I could still win. If not, even Superman couldn't save me. With Razor's snicker and Logan's incredulous look, I rather thought I was staring green Kryptonite in the face.

I had no hope. I had only skill. And a shitload of defiance.

Razor led the seven of spades. And the game was on.

In sheepshead you have to follow the suit led. Well, unless you cheated, but that was dangerous because you lost a whole lotta points if you got caught. So we all had to play a spade if we had one.

Bo laid down the ten. Ruthven played the ace.

Stars in the freaking sky. This trick was already worth twenty-one points and *I didn't have any spades*. I tossed down my seven of diamonds and held my breath. The trick was mine—until Logan beat it. Given the look he'd slewed my way, he probably had eight zillion trump led by the Queen of Death.

Logan's lips twitched. "One for you, princess." He tossed on the king of spades.

I clamped my mouth shut to keep my jaw from falling off. It was my trick. I pulled in twenty-five seriously lovely points. But the game was far from over. One trick out of six, and I still had the weakest hand. "You are the weakest link," Anne Robinson sneered in my head. I gave her a mental backhand.

"You lead," Bo prompted.

"Right." In normal play I should have come back with my strongest trump. But I didn't *have* any strong trump. Recklessly, I tossed out my strongest card, the ace of clubs.

Behind me, Elena sucked in a breath. It would never walk, I knew that. Every single person at that table would have to have a club. The chances against that were—well, hell, I'd only gotten a B in probability and statistics, but it seemed like they must be astronomical.

Logan tossed on a nine, Razor the ten. Bo failed off with the seven.

Ruthven smiled and drew a card. Elena tapped him on the shoulders. With a hiss, Ruthven threw down another card instead—the eight of clubs.

The trick had walked. It had frickin' walked, with twenty-one more points.

I gathered in the cards, trying to think. I had to be wrong. Twenty-one points buried, twenty-five on the last trick, twenty-one on this.

Nope, not wrong. I had just won the game.

Logan cut me a glance. I kept the triumph off my face but somehow he knew. He gave me a wink.

We played it out. I did what I should have done last trick, which was play my king of diamonds. Logan slapped on his queen of clubs, and sure enough punched the next two tricks with two more queens. Bo took the last trick with the king of clubs. But it was already too late.

We counted points and it was official. I'd won.

Ruthven shot to his feet. "This is outrageous! You cheated."

Logan rose, lazy but with a lethal edge to his stance. "No, Ruthven, *you* cheated. You false cut the cards. You stalled on the first trick, you reneged in the fourth, and in the fifth you actually used a palmed card."

"You couldn't have seen...I mean...never mind!"

"Just admit it." I grinned. "I won fair and square, Ruthie."

Ruthven's thin hand dove into his coat, extracted something long and sharp. "If you think I'll let a simple human defeat me—"

A metallic *chick-chick* cut him off. Elena's grenade launcher was aimed straight at Ruthven's chest.

Ruthven snarled. "You won't get away with this, Steel. I'll *destroy* you—and your pet human too." He whirled out. Razor chased after.

Bo put both arms around Elena, disregarding the XM25. "You did great, Detective." He kissed her. "Partner."

"Partner. Come on. Let's go to the Center to clean up and get your sword."

The sappy look they gave each other made me want to puke. Or burst out crying. I'd never have that with Logan. Without a word I pushed out the back door.

Logan emerged into Nieman's lot after me, walked me home in silence. It gave me way too much time to realize exactly what I'd done. I'd won for humanity, yes. But by challenging him. By beating him, the prince of business, a man not challenged lightly.

The last time I'd spoken to Botcher on the phone, he'd yelled *I'll never forgive you for this*! If Botcher'd never forgive me, how much worse would Logan's reaction be? Guts strewn, no doubt. Mine, and in small, bloody pieces.

We got to my townhouse. The car was gone. Mom wasn't there to protect me, or even mop up the pieces. I blindly opened the door, wondering when Logan would eviscerate me.

Eviscerate. The last time I'd thought about evisceration was in connection with the photoshopped picture. Aw, hell. I hadn't even come clean about that.

I nearly jumped when his warm hand touched my shoulder. "Liese? Aren't you happy you won?"

"Ecstatic." I shut the door behind us. It made a hard, nail-in-the-coffin sort of sound.

"Because I'm proud of you, princess."

"I know. You hate—you're what?" My eyes flew up to his.

Golden flecks glowed. "Proud of you. You believed in something so much you fought for it."

I think my jaw knocked the floor louder than the sound of the door. "I could have lost everything."

"I'd have won if you lost. But I knew you'd win. I said so, remember? All you had to do was let go and trust yourself."

I frowned. Trust myself. Trust myself to win at sheepshead? Or more? Trust myself to handle any situation...trust myself to be smart. To be attractive. To be employable. To take care of Mom. To handle getting dumped. To handle being vulnerable.

Good lord. Could it be so simple? Could all my issues be simply a matter of trusting myself?

Maybe. And maybe it wouldn't always work. But when it did... I'd won the Blood Center by trusting myself. What more could I win?

"Yes, but...Logan, aren't you mad? I beat you. I wrested the Blood Center from the v-guys. All of them, even the good guys."

"How can I be mad? You're brave and beautiful and you fought for your beliefs." He kissed my hair, warm angel wings. "I couldn't have done better myself. And we never wanted control of the Center, Liese. We just want to protect it."

He wanted to protect, not control. Unlike the bad-guy vamps. Unlike Botcher who wanted to control but never to protect me. "I can't believe you're not angry."

"This is about the rat-bastard, isn't it? He's got a lot to answer for. I can't make up to you for what he did. But I can try to offset it. Here." Logan held out a small box, exactly the size and shape of a jeweler's ring box.

Not only wasn't he angry, but he had a present for me? Had he really eviscerated me and this was my dying hallucination? I took the box gingerly.

"Open it." He smiled, not his zap-me expression but a small boy's eager grin.

I snapped it open and nearly dropped it. Inside was a huge sparkling ring.

"What...what is this?" My tone was kind of gaspy.

"A diamond. A real one, two carats, flawless. Platinum band, for what it's worth."

Which would make it worth thousands of dollars. Ten or twenty at least...Logan had spent that much on *me*? I glanced at Botcher's two carats of glass. No. No way any male would spend that much on me, much less Mr. Prince of Hawtness.

This was one of the rare times Logan misinterpreted my reaction. "No pressure. It's not an engagement ring, or anything. Just a gift."

And no male would spend that much without expecting anything out of it. I tried the ring on my right hand. It was too small but it fit perfectly on the left-hand ring finger. "This doesn't make me trust you. You can't coerce trust, you know, or buy it. Feelings just are." I had to stop from face-palming myself, spouting philosophy learned from imaginary creatures.

"I know, princess. Doesn't matter." Logan kissed my forehead. "Trusting yourself is the first step in healing. And that's enough for me."

I groaned. "Fricking psychoanalyst."

"No, just a security man with a few years' experience under his belt." He gathered me in his arms, hugged me close. "Come on. Let's cuddle on the couch."

"My mom might come home."

"Which is why we're only going to cuddle. Want to watch *Animaniacs?*"

And because I was all done, wrung out from fears and hopes and ups and downs, I did. Tomorrow I'd fight again. But for now it was nice just to burrow into his strong arms and laugh at truly clever cartoons.

About two my mom wandered in, looking too damned sated for my taste. But I kept my mouth shut and she went to bed. I was so comfortable snuggling against Logan on the couch that I just waved her goodnight.

We watched cartoons until four in the morning. I was drowsing against Logan's broad chest, his fingers running gently through my hair, when my purse exploded, "Beer Barrel Polka" like an alarm going off. Logan's long reach snagged the purse to my side. I dug inside, had to paw through half a Radio Shack store before laying my hands on the cell. "Hello?"

No one answered. "Hello?" I croaked a few more times before staring at the readout. Text message.

I pulled up the menu and stared. It was from the Blood Center. It said simply, "Help."

The message I'd programmed into the Steel Software alarm program. But I'd deleted the hacked code—oh hell. I'd deleted it, but not before I compiled it. My altered code was running on the Blood Center's server. And my code had called for help.

An intruder was at the Center.

"Help? Who's that from?" Logan asked.

I clapped my phone shut and jumped to my feet. Damned preternatural sight. "Nobody."

"I see. Then where are you going?"

"Nowhere." I shrugged on my coat. The original routine was also supposed to alert the police. "Um, you should check your phone. Maybe Elena's called."

"Elena? Why would you think...Liese, what's going on?" Logan followed me out.

"Um, nothing. Much. I think." I dug for my key ring while I headed for my car, popping the locks the instant I found Pinky.

"You're driving? For seven blocks? Liese, has hell gotten central air?" Logan slid into the passenger seat. He watched me put my seatbelt on and arched one blond brow. "That was a joke."

"Ha. Yeah. Did you check your phone?"

He took it out, tapped some keys. "No missed calls or messages. Should I have gotten one? And why would you think Elena, not Bo, would—oh, no. Liese, you didn't. Looking at code is one thing but altering it is another."

I winced. Damned lightning-sharp brain. "I just added a subroutine. I didn't change any existing code."

"No? Then I should have heard something." He tapped more keys.

"The police should have, certainly."

"I had the software division set me up with direct notification too. I wanted to make sure you were safe."

I pulled to the curb in front of the Center, parking behind a red van. "Wow. When I get a chance I'll be—" What? Impressed? Annoyed? Hope it meant more than it did but be doomed to disappointment? I pushed the car door open, left the statement and my feelings hanging. "Damn, that door's ajar."

"Liese, wait." Logan exited the car behind me, came round the hood with purpose. Fast, in dark vampire mode.

I squeaked and ran for the Center door.

He caught me just outside. "Liese. If the alarm didn't go off—" His voice was baby-soft. "Something's very wrong. Let me handle this."

A noise came from inside, a scuff of shoe that signaled someone emerging. An instant later the door opened and a muscled body barreled out.

I got face-butted. Falling back I stared at the substitute blood delivery man, Carrothead Jr. I rubbed my poor nose, the absurd thought hitting me that Johansson would never have been so gauche as to deliver before dawn. But of course Carrothead wasn't really a Hemoglobin Society driver, a truth made obvious when a tin-can whine came from behind him.

"What is the problem, minion?" Ruthven.

Logan gave a growl of disgust, grabbed Mr. Minion and threw him aside like a trash bag. As I stumbled into the Center behind Logan I saw his back pump up like King Kong. I could barely see Ruthven's face beyond that flared back, but I did catch black eyes widening, slowmo. Or maybe that was just my own shock slowing things down.

Time snapped. Ruthven spun and ran. He bowled over a

couple goons carrying boxes in his haste. I recognized Razor's not-so-sharpened gang, including the Gollum-like Shiv. Razor himself was missing.

As if the impact shook Ruthven's molecules loose, he shivered into mist and shot under the back door.

Flinging aside Razorettes, Logan ran after. This was the second time I'd seen Ruthven escape by mist and Logan just chase him. It was as if seeing Ruthven made Logan forget how to dissolve. "Mist, Logan," I called to him. "You need to mist too!"

But Logan only ran to my desk. Damn it, couldn't he mist? Was he was too excited or did Ruthven intimidate him? Or— Logan hit something on my control console. He shouted, "Ruthven! I don't know how you overrode security but override *this*."

The front door slammed shut behind me. A hum snapped around us. The whole room seemed to vibrate with it.

Or maybe that was the growls coming from Maim and the Weed Whackers. They ringed us and were closing in like a constricting snake. I backed into my desk.

Logan only rolled his eyes and pulled something from his jacket. A touch released a deadly sharp blade, the *tzing* barely audible but the gleam blinding. Then, with negligent grace and a stunning ruthlessness Logan proceeded to separate heads from Lestat bodies.

Maim and company fought back but they were awkward. They ran straight into Logan's sure punches and kicks, almost offered their necks to his dancing dagger. I grabbed my desk and shut my eyes to the carnage.

Finally there was only the low hum. "Logan, what's happening? What's that sound?"

"Just a minute, princess. Keep your eyes shut." He picked me up and carted me in the direction of the back room. "The hum is current. There's an electrical layer just behind the drywall."

I heard a door open and shut. "Is it dangerous?"

"No. It's only thirty milliamps. But it's enough to keep vamps out—or *in*."

Sure enough, when I opened my eyes we were in the donation room and Ruthven was there. He was leaning against the back door, holding his hand to his skull like he had a doozy of a headache.

"Ran into the electric field, hmm?" Logan's tone oozed false sympathy. "Aspirin? Ibuprofen?"

Ruthven's eyes slit open on him, lancing pure hate. "My lieutenants outnumber you badly, Steel. They will destroy you."

Logan's pleasant manner dropped abruptly. "Even if I hadn't already unseated your four Horsemen of the *Ass*-pocalypse, you think that would matter?" He stalked, loose-limbed, until he was nose to nose with Ruthven. "Every agonizing exercise Elias threw at me, I thought of you. During every murderous drill, every unbeatable test, I'd grit my teeth and work through it, thinking of you, of the day we'd meet again. Of facing you. Of killing you."

Ruthven backed until his spine pressed flat against the door. "I can still take you, Steel. But I'd rather have my lieutenants get the practice." He raised his voice. "Maim. Shiv, Skiver, Scythe. Attack." Ruthven waved an imperious arm at Logan.

Nothing happened.

"Maim, I call you. I *command* you."

Long seconds ticked before the door from the office opened. "Yeah, about that."

The hulk that entered wasn't Maim but blond Viking Bo Strongwell. He smiled, his lurking dimples coming out to play for just a second. "Maim and company are kind of tied up at present. Hey Liese, thanks for sorting those cable ties. Really made it easy to match color to villain. Sorting heads wasn't so easy, but I think we got them matched to their bodies okay. Shiv's the bony one, right?" Bo strode in until he stood a step behind Logan. "Got your text message. Elena and I came as soon as we could."

"How'd you get in?" I asked. "Doesn't the electricity affect you?"

He held up one big hand. "Fingerprint recognition. Really sweet."

"You tied up the trash?" Logan's gaze stayed riveted on Ruthven.

"Yeah, bound 'em hand and foot. Since they're not old enough to mist, that'll hold them until Emerson's lieutenants come collect them. Now for Ruthven."

Ruthven's calculating eyes darted between Bo and Logan. "Strongwell. I can make it worth your while if you offer me safe passage. I have a great deal of money...and blood."

"Excuse me." I crossed my arms and tapped one foot. "This is my Center—I won it, remember? I get to decide what happens to you."

Logan's flinty gaze switched from Ruthven for the first time, leveled at me, hitting me like a punch to the gut. "Strongwell's territory. Strongwell decides."

"My territory—" I began.

"My vampire," Elena called from the office. She'd propped the door open with one foot and was listening in. Through the crack I could see her gun trained steadily at the unseen gang. "Bo knows the politics, Liese, human and vampire. Let him make the call."

"Yeah but—"

"My city," Bo said in a tone that said he was done discussing and anyone who thought otherwise would lose teeth. Since I had medical insurance but no dental, I shut up. "Here's what's going to happen. At dawn Ruthven gets into my shielded limo with me and we head to Chicago. Elena and my first lieutenant Thorvald will follow in the Maybach. Between the sun and Thor, Ruthven will be trapped."

"Chicago?" Ruthven sneered. "How long do you think to hold me in my own stronghold?"

Bo simply smiled. "It's Nosferatu's stronghold, remember? He's not going to be too pleased with what you've done here."

Ruthven's sneer collapsed. "And Steel?" Real fear entered his voice for the first time.

Logan shrugged. "Oh, I'll abide by whatever deal Bo and Nosferatu work out. I'll play by the rules." He put one finger on Ruthven's chest and pinned him with a disemboweling glare. "As long as you do."

Ruthven shuddered.

Julian's lieutenants came and mopped up the Lestat vampires. Just after dawn a limo purred to the curb, an elegant sedan sliding smoothly behind. As Bo and Logan hustled Ruthven into the limo, the human Carrothead Jr. jumped out, maybe to try to spring Ruthven loose.

Elena whipped out her service revolver and warned him off. Red backed up, reluctantly. The limo took off. Elena shoved into the driver's seat of the sedan and followed the limo. Carroty Jr. waved a select finger at them, then took off in the opposite direction. I started after.

"Let him go."

Logan stood in the Blood Center doorway, face very flushed. Remembering what sun did to vampires, my priorities shifted abruptly. I put both hands on his chest and shoved, not moving him an inch, of course. "Get inside."

"Yes, ma'am." He backed up with a slight smile on his face. "Going to punish me ma'am?"

"You wish," I muttered. A sudden vision of me in a black leather bustier and him writhing under me made me break into a hot sweat. I decided now would be a really good time to make a belated check on the server rack. Logan followed me into the office.

Sure enough, a small flat piece of plastic was slotted into the back panel. I pulled it out, held it up. "I bet this is why the alarm didn't go off."

Logan's eyes narrowed. "A USB key? Ah. Containing a virus to infiltrate the perimeter defense code."

"Or a root kit. But Ruthven would have to know your software to create it."

"You hacked our code," he pointed out.

"I had it in my hands and unraveled it—the key being I had access to it first."

"Unfortunately someone does have access, an Eastern European Steel Software wannabe. We found out New Year's Eve. That's actually why you were hired, Liese. Bo and Elena patrol at night but we needed someone onsite during the day, to discourage human minions. Apparently Ruthven is working with them."

"So this hacked in?" I joggled the thumb drive at him.

"And injected code to stop the external alarm. But the programmer couldn't have known about my first and *best* line of defense." Logan beamed at me with pure pride. "An even better hacker."

I blushed. But it was a happy blush.

And since Logan was trapped here until the sun went

down... I was starting to consider the possibilities of walls, file cabinets and desks when the theme from *CSI* sang out, complete with vocal.

"Wow, that really is a home stereo system," I said as Logan pulled out his cell.

He frowned at the small phone. "Unknown number... That's impossible."

"Caller ID isn't perfect. I get unknown numbers all the time."

He shook his head. "You don't understand. Steel Security is tapped into the world's phone service suppliers. We have even hidden registration information."

"Isn't that illegal?"

"If people knew vampires were real, I suspect our *existence* would be illegal. This may be a touch illicit, but it's only done out of self-preservation." He flipped the phone open. "Steel. I see. No. Yes. All right. Where and when? Yes. I'll be there." He clipped the phone shut and slid it away.

"What was that all about?"

Logan's face was grim. "Apparently Ruthven had already started laying plans for revenge after last night's card game."

"That was one of your Iowa Alliance guys?"

"No. An anonymous informant. He says he has more to tell me if I meet him in Chicago tonight.

"You're not going, are you?"

"Normally I wouldn't. But this man, he says Ruthven's not just after me. He's after my—" Logan's jaw clenched, "—household."

"Well then," I said. "I'll just have to go along."

Chapter Seventeen

That evening we drove up Lake Shore Drive, headed for the vast concrete warren of Chicago's underground parking. I sprawled in the luxurious seat of Logan's Porsche, enjoying his masterly handling of the powerful vehicle. Logan had tried to keep me from coming but I'd just pointed out I could drive myself and follow, and he'd been forced to acknowledge I'd probably be safer with him. "We're going to hear the Chicago Symphony because that's where the guy who called wants to meet?"

"Yes. He has information on Ruthven's plans. Since Ruthven laid those plans before Bo dragged him off to Nosferatu's judgment, they may no longer have any teeth. But I don't want to take chances."

The theme from *Jaws* erupted from the dash. Not a CD. Logan had stuck his cell phone to some sort of ultramodern polymer pad.

He raised an eyebrow at me, not asking permission but being polite. I nodded. He hit connect, followed by speaker. "Steel."

"Hello, darling," a throaty alto purred. "Congratulations on defeating Ruthven."

"Camille." Another of Nosferatu's seconds, like Ruthven. "What do you want?" The tips of Logan's fangs peeked from between his lips.

"Just to thank you, darling. You got rid of a very thorny obstacle for me. But really, darling, couldn't you have made it just a bit more permanent?"

"I'm in no mood for games, Camille. Goodbye." Logan reached for the *end call* button.

"Oh, pooh. You never were any fun. But maybe this will interest you—because of that dreary hick Strongwell, Ruthven's been banished to Springfield. They're driving him down tonight for the Hundred Years. Superbly boring, but the end results are more pie for me and Giuseppe."

"You know I'm not going to take your word for this, Camille."

"Confirm away, darling. But Nosferatu chucked him in one of your charming little electrified cages and carted him away just an hour ago. I wish Nosferatu had exposed the bastard, but official exile will have to do."

Logan's jaw clenched. "Springfield is the state capital. Ruthven could get up to his old political tricks."

"Unfortunately. That's why I wish you'd destroyed him. But stamped Outcast is almost as good. Well, just wanted to call to gloat. I mean, to *thank* you. Ta-ta."

Logan punched *end*, jaw working.

I said, "She's a real sweetheart."

He flashed me an amused, grateful look, his fangs receding. "Isn't she?"

"What's that Hundred Years thing? Ruthven gets buried in a cage for a century?"

"The cage is just for transport. But Hundred Years' Exile is pretty harsh. There's a nasty stripping ceremony that culminates in the outcast being buried in foreign soil. He has to stay within ten leagues of his grave for a century and a day. Vampire society is big on tradition and rite. I think it's because we live so long."

"But if Ruthven'll be free tomorrow night, couldn't he just come back?"

"Only a fool would buck official exile." Logan punched a speed dial.

"Steel." Bo's voice came after one ring.

"Viking," Logan said. "Just heard from the Spider Woman. She says Ruthven's been cast out. Is that true?"

Bo confirmed the details then added, "Nosferatu invited me to tag along for the ceremonies when they chuck Ruthven's ass in the ground. Elena and I have to get back to Meiers Corners, but I'm sending Thorvald. He'll call me when the deed's done. You want notification too?"

"If you don't mind. It'd be one thing off my mind."

"Will do."

As Logan disconnected I said, "So do you know who tonight's informant is? Or why he wants to meet during the symphony concert?" My head turned as we passed the famous Buckingham Fountain. Even though the water wasn't on, it was still beautiful.

"I didn't recognize the voice. Apparently he wants to stay anonymous. Given Ruthven's preference for nasty, back-stabbing revenge, I can't say I blame him."

"Couldn't he have given you the information over the phone? Being an international security guru, you've got a secure phone line, right?"

Logan shrugged. "Apparently he wasn't as confident about his end. Thus the need for this somewhat dramatic meeting. But he has a point. With all the Lestats and minions in the city, it's hard to meet unobserved."

"And he couldn't have come out to Meiers Corners?"

"No time." Logan navigated the heavy traffic, his hands capable and sure on the wheel, small golden hairs glinting in the evening lights. I liked looking at the strong fingers, the clean lines of hand and wrist. "Besides, I think you'll enjoy hearing the symphony. They're doing Beethoven and Vaughan Williams."

"I know Beethoven," I said. "But I haven't heard of the other guy."

"I knew them both." Logan pulled into the driveway for Grant Park South, the self-park lot under the grassy park of the same name. "I actually sang for Beethoven in the debut of the Ninth Symphony in 1824. Nearly lost my voice trying to talk to him, though. He was deaf by then."

I stared at him. "When I said I *knew* Beethoven, I didn't mean it quite that way."

Logan grinned at me as he took a ticket. "You'll enjoy the concert. Chicago's always good. You're fortunate to have world-class talent so close."

I watched him beat out two other cars for a really sweet spot without the least apparent effort. As he spun his little coupe into the space I asked, "Who's conducting?"

To my surprise, Logan grimaced. "Zajicek." He got out of

the car and locked up.

We started walking. "Zajicek—you mean *Dragan* Zajicek? *The* Dragan Zajicek?"

The grimace became a scowl. "Naturally. You've never heard of Vaughan Williams, but you've heard of Zajicek."

"Well, sure. Who hasn't? The man is so finger-licking good, he single-handedly put classical music into the top ten charts. Don't you like him? Or is it his music?"

"It's not that. He's one of *us*."

I fit my jaw back on its hinges. "I should have known. He's been around since the eighties. No normal man can be that delicious that long."

Logan prepaid the parking before we exited the structure. "That's part of the problem. He refuses to lie low. His exhibitionism endangers all of us. We've argued with him for years. Came close to blows." He snorted. "Even Elias can't make him change."

"That's headstrong." I remembered Elias's deep, sure voice and shivered, not the least because it reminded me of the explanation I owed Logan. "I can't imagine Mr. Elias ever losing an argument."

"Strictly speaking, he hasn't had it yet. Elias prefers to let people live their own lives. But he's sent a few of us to try to make Zajicek see reason. I assure you, if Elias ever decides Zajicek's an immediate deadly threat, Zajicek's dead."

"That'd be too bad. The man—er, v-guy—is a major musical talent."

Logan hooked my elbow as we crossed South Michigan. "Maybe. But he's as unpredictable in his own way as Ruthven. And that makes him a danger."

"So where's the meeting with Mr. Anonymous?"

Logan opened the door to Symphony Center, ushered me through. "Subbasement, at intermission."

Our tickets were in the third row, center. I took off my coat, settled in. "Nice seats."

"Courtesy of our anonymous friend," Logan said. "They were sold out."

"Nixie doesn't like sitting so close." I watched the musicians wander out and warm up. "She says the sound is better in the middle. But I like being able to see."

"All the seats are good, acoustically. But from here, we can see if Zajicek sweats." Logan grinned.

"Ooh, muscles glistening with man-sweat. Well, not exactly *man*-sweat but...oh, never mind."

"You're still cute when you're flustered." Logan's grin widened.

"And I can still slap you."

He lowered his mouth to my ear. "Promises, promises."

Logan's breath on my neck was hot enough to singe away thoughts of Zajicek. When the lights lowered, I nudged him. "They're starting. Behave yourself."

"Always, princess." As Logan's breath teased my neck, his fingers slipped up under my top and teased something else.

I suppressed a yelp. "Behave *well*."

Smirking, he removed his fingers.

The concertmaster came out and cued the tuning. Only string players sat onstage. I checked my program, saw the first piece was *Fantasia on a Theme by Thomas Tallis*. I'd never heard it.

Still reading the program, I was barely aware of the pregnant silence that followed the tuning until the click of heels brought my head up.

Sweeping onto the stage was a strikingly tall man, effortlessly elegant in black tails. Long ebony hair was shot with one dramatic river of silver. Jet brows slashed over brilliant dark eyes. Strong, high cheekbones were complemented by a razor-sharp jaw.

My eyes swung to him and stuck. Seriously. The guy was that magnetic. In his pictures, Zajicek was classically handsome. In person, handsome intensified into stunning. There was instant, wild applause.

Zajicek vaulted onto the podium with athletic grace, spun and bowed to the audience. If Logan hadn't been beside me I would have melted into goo. As it was I felt like royalty had acknowledged me.

Spinning back to the orchestra, Zajicek held up one hand. A slim white stick balanced lightly in three long fingers, relaxed yet full of coiled energy. It seemed that the whole orchestra's consciousness was in that white tip, because when the stick clicked down, they played.

The first chords were both rich and divine, an organ filling a great cathedral. Beautiful, restrained music stirred my ears. But even in those first few moments, I could feel something coming—something overflowing with pure emotion.

Like the music, Zajicek's movements on the podium were spare, his gestures exquisitely elegant. And like the music, you knew that beneath that elegance was a simmering volcano.

As the music progressed, it came. In waves of sound, tickling, nudging, pushing. Logan's fingers threaded through mine. Increasingly lush music crescendoed, rose higher, the current deeper and stronger. Logan's fingers tightened.

The music swelled bigger and bigger until it washed *over* me. Ocean waves of sound pushed me off my feet, unleashed me from my moorings. Threatened the very foundations of my soul. I grabbed Logan's hand harder.

The notes soared higher. The throbbing rhythm quickened. My breath quickened with it. Faster. Higher. More. The whirlwind of sound carried me along, up, up into air so rarified I could barely catch my breath.

The violins hit the peak. Held me there in a bliss of perfection. It went on and on, so beautiful that I shattered.

If the soul can climax, that was my first time.

As the notes came back down I blinked, realized I was clutching Logan's hand so hard his fingers were white. I released him with a sheepish grin.

He simply took my hand again, folded between both of his, and smiled into my eyes.

We stared at each other, knowing we had shared something exquisitely beautiful. A soul-deep moment had touched him too—how could I not love him?

On the way downstairs Logan muttered, "I may have to forgive him."

"Who?"

"Zajicek. You're right. To lose talent like that would be a crime, even if it would be safer for the rest of us."

"Steel. This way." A tall shadow waved us in just before disappearing into the dark. We circled a steel girder to meet our mysterious informant.

"You." Logan hissed.

"You have brought a human. Why?"

"Leave her alone." Logan's back tensed and the warning growl was becoming familiar.

Last time Logan had hidden the truth from me in a silk bag of skirt. I was wearing pants tonight, safe from being turned into a full moon (so to speak). "I'm back to being 'her'? I don't think so." I found my flashlight in my purse and flicked it on.

The beam carved blackness into the perfect features of Dragan Zajicek.

"I beg your pardon. I did not mean to offend." Zajicek took my hand and bowed over it, very old-world. "Who are you, lovely lady?"

A dark sensuality bubbled under Zajicek's grace. If I weren't involved with Logan, I'd have gone beyond goo to be the gum wad on his shoe. "My name is Liese Schmetterling."

"Liese." His elegant nostrils flared. "Ah. Already taken. You are very fortunate, Steel."

"And don't I know it." Logan pulled my hand away from Zajicek. "By the way, she doesn't like to be treated like a sex object. She'll slap you if you don't watch out."

"I am not a crass youngling." Zajicek drew himself up. "I am simply properly appreciative of such a lovely female."

Ooh. Now I was getting hot. Time to return to sane footing. "You had some information, Maestro Zajicek?"

"Dragan, please." He reclaimed my fingertips, actually kissed them. I think my hair turned into a beanie propeller. I know I felt dizzy.

"Information." Logan yanked my hand away and curled it protectively in his own. I sighed and burrowed in.

Zajicek was suddenly all business. "You have made a formidable enemy in Ruthven."

"He was already my enemy. If he's pissed off now, so much the better. Pissed-off people make mistakes."

"Be wary, Steel. Ruthven is not an honorable man. He knows about your household settling in the Chicago suburbs. He plans to kill or enslave your humans." Zajicek's black eyes flicked to me, and I thought I saw apology there. "There was specific mention of a butterfly."

Logan's eyes flared flame-red. Literally, lighting up his face. "That's...that's despicable."

"Yes. It's why I risked meeting publicly. There's more. Ruthven has a mole. I'm not sure if this person is inside your household or simply has access to the Meiers Corners Blood Center. But the mole is a human."

"And so can move during daylight, when I can't. Damn." Logan's face was grim.

That startled me. Someone in Logan's household or the Blood Center was an informant for the bad guy? Someone I knew? I pulled up a mental list. Nurse Battle? Johansson? Maybe one of the Steel Security busy bees, but Logan had worked with them forever. Zinnia? Who would be so horrible as to betray Logan?

"I owe you one, Zajicek."

"Do you? Well, perhaps you can get the Ancient One off my back, hmm?"

Logan's grimace twisted into an expression of wry humor. "Ask for world peace or an end to hunger. Something easier, please."

Zajicek inclined his head. "Elias does that which he wishes to do. Well, I have told you what I know. I wish it were more. Someone must stop Ruthven, Steel. This time he goes too far."

"On that we can agree."

Logan and I were staying overnight in Chicago. We could have driven back after the concert, but Logan got us a room with a whirlpool. How could I say no a whirlpool? It was a big whirlpool too, room enough for five with mirrors on three walls and the ceiling.

Logan started the tub filling then left the room to make a few phone calls. I took the opportunity to slip out of my clothes and into the water. I didn't want the vast expanse of my cushioned flesh to interfere with me maybe getting some.

The water was hot, but unfortunately quite clear. A glance at the ceiling mirror showed my rounded stomach and hips. Yuck.

So I started the jets. Tension dropped out of me like anvils releasing, not just because my extra five pounds had disappeared. Ten. All right, fifteen but I think my shoes were at least four of that. The heat, the slap of the water, even the burr of the jets were soothing. I hadn't realized I was carrying around that much stress. I guess my mom's cancer, anxiety over my job and all the other little mysteries and uncertainties of the last few days had added up. I still had some anxieties—Ruthven was gunning for me, I didn't recognize the woman Mom had become and my job was anything but assured.

But I'd stood up to Botcher and I'd stood up to Ruthven and damned if Logan wasn't right. I was starting to trust my own ability to handle things. If I couldn't believe in Botcher or even my own mother, I could at least believe in me.

Except...could I trust myself if I had to handle the worst mistake of my life? I stared at the rings on my hands, Botcher's glass on the right and Logan's unknown on the left.

What if I could? To take a chance on Logan...a shot at heaven...even the thought made my heart soar and my head spin. Loving him would be happiness beyond the galactic rim. A lifelong relationship with him would be wonderful, paradise...and impossible, if I didn't come clean about the picture.

But if I told him, could I handle the rejection that was sure to come? Not just firing, although there'd be some of that too. But the shock and horror I'd see in his beautiful golden eyes when he realized I'd betrayed him almost as badly as Ruthven?

Whether I could handle it or not, one thing was crystal clear. I had to confess. Because I couldn't enjoy sex...*handle it, Liese*...I couldn't make love without a clean heart.

The door lock clicked. "Elias confirmed it." Logan shouldered open the door, dragging through a pedestaled ice bucket. "Ruthven's on his way to Springfield. I got us some champagne to celebrate." Grinning, he held up two slim glasses.

Sweet heavens, he was such golden perfection. "Logan, wait. We have to talk."

"Damn, are you naked under that water? No talk now, sweetheart." He dropped the bucket, tossed the flutes onto the closest surface and arrowed for the tub. "Love now."

"Logan—" I held up both hands.

He was coming so fast that I thought he'd jump in fully clothed. But his form wavered for a split second and his clothes dropped like rocks. And when he hit the whirlpool platform he was utterly nude.

His muscles pumped savagely as he vaulted in. "Gorgeous."

His eyes raked over my breasts, which were barely covered by the whirling water. "Slap me all you want, you're absolutely gorgeous." He palmed my face and swooped in for a kiss.

I turned, barely avoiding him. His mouth landed on my cheek, which he nibbled with a groan. "You taste even better than before. I'll never get enough."

"Logan, stop. You don't understand. I've done something terrible. I need to tell you about it. I...I betrayed you."

"Later, Liese." His fingers threaded through my hair and I couldn't evade his next kiss. His mouth plundered mine until I was breathless.

Even so I made one last attempt. "Logan, I can't do this until I come clean about something. I was trying to ruin you— *mphf.*"

He kissed me deeply, tongue stabbing. When he had me thoroughly silenced he nipped my lower lip. "I know about the picture, princess. And I don't care. Mmm, you taste delicious."

The words hit me. *I know about the picture.* I jerked but his grip was firm. I spoke into his marauding mouth. "I tried to get you fired."

"Yes, yes." He pressed me back against the tub with his big body. Kissed me into heaven, licked me with fire.

"You don't understand," I said when he let me up for air. "I grafted your head on a smutty picture—"

"Liese, I know. One of my men saw it when we migrated the email and showed me." He kissed his way to one ear, sucked the lobe into his mouth. I nearly shot through the ceiling mirror. He nipped down my throat to the sensitive hollow at the shoulder. I saw his golden head in the mirror, buried in my neck. His breath was hot on my skin, hotter even than the water.

"Aren't you mad? I sent that picture to...to Elias. I tried to destroy you."

Logan's head turned slightly, and full-length fangs split his lips. I nearly screamed. He sank them into my neck and the world came apart and I did scream. Pleasure zapped me, excitement cascading through my body until I was trembling with need.

The tips of his orgasmic fangs firmly embedded in my flesh, Logan began to physically torment me. His hand cupped first one breast, then the other, testing its weight, teasing the nipple lightly with his thumb.

I was trying very hard not to move, impaled on his fangs. "Don't you want to...suck, or something?"

He chuckled against my throat. His fingers pinched my nipple. I jumped. It jerked his fangs against my flesh, embedding them deeper. The resultant jolt nearly made me scream again.

"Don't—" I jerked when he pinched the other nipple. My neck was singing with pleasure so sharp it was exquisite agony. "Logan, please—!"

He pinched a third time, and my vision went black around the edges.

His fingers slipped under the water's surface, caressing my belly. I was too far gone to care how my rounded flesh felt to him. Besides, he was purring. That deep rumble threaded through the rush of the jets, dark and sensual to my ears. His fingers found my vulva, probed.

I gasped. "How can you know about the picture and still want to...make love to me?"

Logan's only answer was to sink his fangs deeper and purr against my neck. And to pet my pussy, over and over.

"Logan, I betrayed you." I arched against the tub, catching sight of his bright blond head bent to my neck in the ceiling mirror, his body, huge and golden, bowed over mine. The water sloshed gently with the movements of his muscular arm. "Doesn't that make you mad?"

He thrust a finger into me.

I gasped, clutched at the smooth back of the tub. "Are you torturing me? Are you really mad and this is you getting your revenge?"

His fangs slid out of my neck and his tongue pressed, brief and hot, to my skin. "I'm torturing you, princess, but not because I'm mad." He licked down to where my breasts floated on the bubbling water. Sucking one into his mouth, he sent shocks through the soft mound by simply tonguing the nipple. When I was nearly shrieking he released it to lick toward the other. "I'm not mad. I'm flattered. You put my head on the better-looking body."

As he licked around my nipple I squirmed on his

motionless finger. Anticipation of his strong suckling made me almost crazier than feeling it. "I didn't have a choice. Nobody'd believe you were the pudgy one."

"As angry and frightened as you were, that was almost sweet." He breathed on the nipple. After all that anticipation, it tightened instantly. "You're so responsive. One of the many things I like about you." He pulled the nipple into his mouth and sucked.

I shrieked. "The pudgy one...that was Botcher."

"Then I'm especially flattered," he said between suckles. "Since you thought we were both liars."

"I didn't know it was him at the time."

"Maybe your subconscious knew." His finger began moving in and out, gently but relentlessly.

My hips rocked in time. Water slapped against the edge of the tub. "But Logan—how can you ever trust me after I tried to ruin you?" I had done to Logan what Botcher had done to me. Logan should be horrified—heck, *I* was horrified.

He stopped to raise his head and look deep into my eyes. "Liese." His gaze was warm gold. "I trust what's in your heart. You want what's best for me there, even if sometimes things like fear get in the way."

And, with a deep breath, he plunged under the water.

His hands spread my thighs. His mouth found me and he clamped on like a wetvac. I gasped. Hot water swirled all over me, but his tongue on my clit was hotter than any of it. He lapped me to climax in about three seconds flat.

I panted and waited for him to surface.

He turned under me, his chin grinding into my pubic bone, his mouth on my slit, and lapped me to a second orgasm. I shuddered as the pleasure caromed through me, longer and more powerful this time. It left me weak and breathless. Panting, I waited for him to surface again. Instead, powerful hands twisted me in the tub, putting me directly in line with one of the jets. Logan pushed me to my knees, held my hips so the gushing water hit me bang in the clit.

Then he thrust his tongue into me like a hot muscular cock.

Pulsing jets of water assaulted me from the front. Logan's agile, practiced tongue assaulted me from below. I grabbed onto the edge of the tub and came unglued.

He added fingers. I trembled as he thrust and sucked, the hard spray of water beating against the red little berry of my clit. The contrast of my nude pussy with Logan's ruby mouth, upper lip just starting to bristle with gold, made me quiver. His mouth worked between my legs, hard and insistent. His fingers thrust almost brutally now, the mirrors revealing his stomach muscles clenching with tandem effort.

I peaked...and came. Waves of climax billowed through me, pulsing like the hot jets of water. I gasped and waited for Logan to surface.

But he wasn't done yet. *Thank you, optional respiration.* He pushed my hips forward into the tub, pressing my clit directly into the whirlpool nozzle. I shrieked. He dropped his jaw until his big mouth covered my entire pussy. And then, as the geyser of water beat me from the front, Logan bit me.

His fangs went deep into my swollen labia. I cried out, hoarse from my earlier screams. My flushed face confronted me in the mirror, lips wet and glistening, eyelids heavy and almost drugged with pleasure. My breasts heaved with my panted breaths. My body gathered for another climax. Logan bit down harder, thrust with two fingers. Rhythmically, hard. I came, shuddering for what seemed like hours.

And finally he surfaced, sliding up between me and the tub. As the last shudders wracked me, he grabbed my hips and impaled me on his thick erection.

A hoarse shriek was torn from my throat. Logan rode me mercilessly, thrusting up from the water, sheets of it running off his sleek belly and muscled thighs. Waves slapped against the tub, sloshing over the edge as he thrust powerfully. His eyes were closed, his nostrils flared, and the look on his beautiful face was pure bliss. The fangs splitting his masculine lips were long as tusks. My poor exhausted pussy tightened at the sight.

Without losing a beat, he flipped me in the water, pressed me back against the tub. Now a jet pulsed against the bottom of my spine while Logan beat against the front, strong undulations of his hips grinding me relentlessly. I looked up, saw his huge broad shoulders reflected in the mirror, muscles clenching and releasing, my hands small and pale against them. How could any man be so stunningly sexual?

Then Logan sank his fangs deep into my throat, and I

thought, *Oh, yeah, he's not a man,* just before I exploded.

Exploded. No word could really describe the hard clench of muscles, the sweet rush of pleasure, the flood of well-being. Nothing could prepare me for the intense peace.

And nothing could describe, or prepare me, for love that filled me.

It was true. I loved Logan Steel. And there was nothing I could do about it.

Chapter Eighteen

The tweedle of my cell phone saved me from having to reflect on my predicament. I wrapped myself in a towel and sloshed out of the water. Digging around in my purse I managed to find the phone before it went to voicemail. "Hi, Mom."

"Honey, I have good news."

"You're done early with your radiation? You won the lottery? Oh, don't tell me you found a V-8 vibrator."

"I'm getting married."

"You're—what? When? Who?"

"How, where, why," Logan added helpfully in my ear, reminding me he was there. I nearly told him to leave the room but supervamp hearing might mean he'd have to leave the country for any conversation to be private.

"Race proposed and I accepted."

"Mother—" Loving careful words were driven out of my brain. Marrying a *vampire*? "Are you insane? He left you once already, alone with a baby, remember? How can you trust him after that?" What kind of nutcase female would marry a vam— Logan sucked my earlobe into his mouth and I shivered. Would I marry Logan, if he asked? Assuming that a) he asked and b) he actually made it to the altar.

"Race explained it to me, Liese. He didn't want to leave but he had no choice."

"He's lying. Everyone has a choice. He just couldn't shoulder the responsibility, couldn't hack being a dad, so he lammed. Now he wants back in your pants so he's telling you what you want to hear."

"Don't be crude, Liese. He's not lying. Something happened to him thirty years ago. Something life-altering. I can't tell you what, but he showed me proof."

Good grief. Lights clicked on in my head. I punched mute and turned to Logan. "How old is Razor, vampire-wise? Thirty?"

Logan shrugged (damn, he had edible shoulders). "I don't keep track of Ruthven's minions. I can find out if you want."

"Please." I clicked off mute. "Mother, to be clear—Raz...Race said he left you because that's when he died and turned vampire?"

"You know about...them?"

"Just found out recently. But he could have come back for you after he converted."

"No, Liese. He had to serve his master for a score of years, to pay him back for the gift of second life."

I hit mute again and raised a questioning eyebrow at Logan.

"A baby vamp needs tending," he confirmed. "Not long, but Ruthven tends to play to the stereotypes."

"What about you? You've served your master for hundreds of years."

"I serve Elias out of respect, and because he's a brilliant teacher and warrior. But not for survival, not anymore."

"And Razor? Does he need to serve Ruthven?"

"A fledgling's vulnerable the first weeks. In return for helping the baby vamp, most masters demand a couple years' service. But Ruthven's not most masters. Razor might be telling the truth."

"Or he might be lying to ingratiate himself with Mom. To take advantage of her."

"Liese, I hate to point this out because I don't want to get slapped, but Hattie isn't a tasty young morsel. And Razor has a good deal of sexual allure. He doesn't need to lie to attract human women."

"Sexual allure?" I hit unmute, still talking to Logan. "That fumblebutt sleazebag? The guy who's pickup line is 'I got lots of honeys'? Sorry, but I don't find Razor the least bit alluring or attractive." And, remembering, I sputtered into the phone, "Mother, Race came on to me! How can you marry someone who propositioned your own daughter?"

"He told me about that, sweetie. He feels bad about it now. But you apparently reminded him of me."

"What a glib bastard."

"Which is it, Liese? A fumblebutt sleazebag or a glib bastard?"

Apparently Logan wasn't the only one with good hearing. "Neither. Both. I don't know! He's *bad*, Mother. Abandonment aside, he was a bad boy then, and he's a bad vampire now. In fact, his real name is Razor and he leads a *gang*. And if that's not enough, he works for the guys trying to take over the Blood Center."

"Yes, I know. He told me all about getting friendly with you so he could slip his root killer—" my mother said it but I heard Race's voice and automatically supplied root kit "—into your computer. But as he got to know you, he felt bad and couldn't do it. He's going to quit, honey. He's reformed."

"Mother, that's the oldest line in the world!"

"But true. I'm forty-seven, Liese. Why would he want to marry me, if he didn't love me?"

"I don't know. Vampires lie all the time. It's second nature. They lie, they keep secrets. You can't trust them."

"I know he's lied to me, honey. I know he's kept secrets. But underneath it all, he cares about me. And that's all that matters."

"Cares about you? When he left you pregnant and alone?"

"He sent me money. After my family disowned me."

That startled me enough to shut me up.

"Trust is a bridge, Liese. And the meeting point is halfway. Sweetheart, I know you're only getting on my case because you're worried. You care about me too, don't you? I'm so lucky to have you as a daughter. I love you, sweetie."

And, having made her points of Mom-wisdom, she hung up.

"Trust is about taking a chance," I said to the empty line. "But the other person has to *earn* the chance too."

"That's interesting." Logan gently extracted the phone from my fingers, clicked it shut. "Razor's the last person I would have picked to care about anyone but himself." He set the phone on the nightstand and came to sit by me on the bed.

"I'm not convinced he does."

"Nor I, but only time will tell." He gathered me close. "He might be good for her, you know. If he really does love her. He might make her happy."

"I make her happy." I knew that was small, coming from some childish place deep inside.

"You do," Logan agreed, kissing my hair. "You're her world. And she's yours. Your love for each other is obvious in everything you do." He caressed a hand gently down my breast. "But there are different forms of love, princess."

And, as I lay back for Logan's expert manipulations, I realized there were apparently different forms of trust. Because while I didn't trust either Razor or Logan not to lie or keep secrets, I trusted Logan with my body.

Too bad my body included my heart.

We had so much fun with the champagne and the whirlpool that we slept right up until Bo's lieutenant Thorvald called, just after dawn. Logan put him on speakerphone.

"Calling to confirm Ruthven's ritual burial just outside of Oak Ridge Cemetery." Thor had a smoky baritone, a fine whiskey sort of voice. "Nice ceremony, full of ripping off medals and badges and shit. After the defrocking, Nosferatu yanked Ruthven out of the cage and chucked him into the grave. I especially liked the part where Nosferatu backhoed it in while Ruthven was still yelling. Sounded like his mouth was filling with mushy cornflakes."

"So where are you now?" Logan asked. "Sun's up, isn't it?"

"I'm holing up in a little crypt a stone's throw from Ruthven's grave. The Maybach's shielding is only full on the passenger side so I won't be able to go home until dusk. Do you want another call then?"

"Yes. I want to hear how Ruthven's settling in."

With the sun up Logan took the room for another day and announced he was taking me to brunch. We had just started dressing (for the third time, actually) when his cell phone chirped.

"Text message." He flipped it open with a negligent hand, glanced at the display.

A change swept over him. His eyes narrowed, flashed that bright gold. His lips thinned, jutting fang, and his stance widened like a bulldog.

His fingers tightened so hard the display cracked.

That seemed to snap him out of it. "Damn. Ruthven's got me nervous. It's just Zinnia. She's thanking me for the...I can't read it now. I think it said field trip."

"What field trip?"

"I assume from Iowa to Illinois. Although she has Elias to thank for that." His eyes scanned the display again. "And why call it a field trip? If I'm even remembering the text right. Damn." He chucked the phone onto the dresser. "Can I borrow your cell? It's probably nothing, but after yesterday I'm a bit paranoid."

"Add Zajicek's warning and I'd say it's justified." I dug out my cell.

Logan punched in a number so fast I barely saw his thumb move. "It's Steel. I need a phone number for Zinnia Jones, House Elias—better yet, connect me." There was a pause during which Logan drummed fingers on the dresser. By the time he spoke again the drumming had taken on a distinct tick-tick sound. "Zinnia, it's Logan Steel. What's going on?" As he listened his fangs elongated and his eyes reddened until they were glowing.

The claws stilled. "He just showed up and said I arranged it? And you didn't question that?" There was a pause, and then his voice went cold like I'd never heard it before. "Explain."

Whatever she was saying, he didn't like it. His eyes narrowed and his fangs cut into his lower lip until blood ran. He wiped the trickles away with an impatient swipe. "Listen to me, Zinnia. Gather everyone you can find and meet me at the museum entrance." He clapped the phone shut and threw on the rest of his clothes.

I had dressed while he was on the phone. "What's Zinnia gotten into now?"

"She's in Chicago. Along with the whole damn Iowa bus."

"What? Why?"

"The bus driver showed up at her motel with some cockeyed story that I'd arranged a field trip to the Museum of Science and Industry, to give them something to do." Logan jerked on his shirt, claws clicking as he buttoned. "I'll give that woman something to do. What was she thinking, coming to

Chicago now of all times?"

I started packing. "Logan, calm down. This is probably just a coincidence. Ruthven's in the ground in Springfield. Even if he planned something, he would want to see it in person."

"He's a coward. Cackling by remote's not out of the question."

"If the group came by bus, why can't they just leave?"

"Coincidentally, it broke down." Logan threw things in his overnight bag so hard I heard smacks. "Barely made it into the underground parking before dying. Fucking coincidence. Zinnia thought they might as well see the museum while the bus was repaired. All those humans, scattered about the museum with no way to contact them, not due to meet until four in the fucking afternoon. I swear I'm getting every person in that household their own damned cell phone. I don't care how much it costs me."

The news alarmed me but I also felt a glimmer of hope. Logan was talking about the busload of people as if they were his. Maybe he was finally healing. "Zinnia might be making the bus driver story up so you don't blame her. Besides, if they're inside the museum, is it really that dangerous? Humans go to the MSI all the time, and nothing happens—especially during the day." I took my bag and waited for him by the door.

"First, this is Zinnia we're talking about. Second, you're not going. Third, though rogue vampires usually stay under the radar, I'm not betting my humans on it, not so soon after Ruthven's been pwned. Fourth, you're not going. Fifth, half the museum is underground, so vampires are there even at midday. And last, you're *not* going."

"Sure I'm going. Why wouldn't I go?"

"Zajicek's warning? The butterfly comment? I know German as well as anyone, Liese, and I know Schmetterling doesn't mean arachnid."

"Not to worry. Ruthven's in Springfield. So unless he can mist a couple hundred miles underground—"

"You're conveniently forgetting the bus driver. Who may or may not be the mole. If not, we have two minions to worry about. And a minion, while he may not be a vampire, is still dangerous."

"*She* may not be a vampire, but—"

"He or she may be a teddy bear, I don't care. You're *not* going." He glared.

I glared back. "Because I'm so much safer here alone."

"Fuck." Logan hit the wall with his palm, then spun and grabbed my phone. He flipped it open, then clapped it shut a second later and practically tore his pocket jamming it home. "*Merde.* No one I could call could get here in less than half an hour. All right, you're coming. But you're staying with me, understand?"

Since I'd gotten what I wanted, I nodded meekly.

Logan insisted on driving his Porsche. Even with tinted windows and the watery gray March sun he was smoldering by the time we pulled into the shadows of the underground structure. Literally, wisps of smoke erupting from nose, mouth, and ears. He seemed to relish it.

"This is insane." It had been his refrain all down Lake Shore Drive. "This is exactly why I don't want a household. Any move I make might provoke backlash like this. For myself I don't worry, but you humans are so damned vulnerable."

I just nodded. What could I say? He wouldn't feel better until Zinnia and company were safe. But when we got home I was so getting a bazooka from Elena.

"Fucking insane," he repeated. "Zinnia couldn't have picked a worse time to fall for some uniform's line. Ruthven's always hated the Iowa Alliance but now that he's specifically got me in his sights, there's no telling what he'll do."

"At least he's nowhere near today. And Zinnia didn't do it on purpose. She didn't know you and Ruthven have a history."

"Unless she's the mole. In cahoots with the bus driver."

"Come on, Logan. Ms. Vampire Rights, the mole? There's the bus."

The Iowa bus was on Level C of the Museum of Science and Industry's underground parking. It was locked and empty.

Zinnia met us just inside the parking entrance, bopping over with an energy that seemed slightly manic. "Master Logan, I'm so relieved you're here. I've got good news and bad news. The good news is I managed to get some of the people here with an all-call. The museum paging system is really marvelous—"

"Where are your children?" Logan's jaw was clenched hard.

Her bop drooped. "Um, that's the bad news. Bud had some research he wanted to do and you know Lilly, always wanting to tag along, and you know Bud, such a wonderful big brother, and you know how children—"

"Where. Are. They." Logan's growl was ominous.

Immediate intervention was in order. I snagged Zinnia's arm and concentrated on all the centering techniques Mr. Miyagi ever taught me. "Breathe, Zinnia."

She took a couple good deep gulps. Finally she admitted, "Bud's not answering the page, Master Logan."

"I'll find him." He grabbed my elbow, steered me toward the entrance.

"Master Logan, wait." Zinnia ran after us. "Some kids tagged along with Bud."

Logan paused for a deep breath of his own. "Besides Lilly? Exactly who is still missing, Zinnia?"

Zinnia dug into her purse, pulled out the spreadsheet. "Jane Austen Smith, age eight. Four-year-old Angela, who is actually Mr. Dodds's grandniece, a cute little girl although not as cute as Lilly..." She caught Logan's pointed glare and her eyes fluttered back to her list. "Yes. Well, another eight-year-old, Billy Wilder, whose father Thugs'll make a wonderful fixit man—er, yes. And Tad, a seven-year-old redhead. Um, he had a little too much for brunch. Oh, and Frieda, Dodds's other grandniece. But she's Bud's age, so I'm not as worried." She stuffed the list back into her purse. "Master Logan, do you really think they're in danger?"

Logan proved then that he was a great CEO and would make an awesome householder. He took her by the shoulders and looked her straight in the eye. "Don't worry, Zinnia. I *will* find them, and I will bring them back safe."

Her body sagged with relief. "Thank you."

"While I'm gone make sure everyone stays together. I have backup coming, a couple Steel Security people. They'll check over the bus, make sure it's safe to travel."

"Yes, Master Logan."

The museum is huge, four levels and almost a tenth of a mile from end to end. Logan restricted himself to my slower human pace, though we both chafed. For ten fretful minutes we scoured the entry and lower levels.

Thank goodness for his super vamp hearing. The instant we hit the main level, "Itsy Bitsy Spider" floated from the balcony. It was the first time I was grateful for arachnids.

Lilly was in the balcony restroom, Jane Austen Smith standing outside her stall lecturing. "It's a bathroom, not a potty. And you don't 'go potty', you urinate. And—Mr. Steel, you oughtn't be in the girls' room."

"It's an emergency," Logan said as Lilly emerged from her stall. "We need to get back to the bus. Lilly, your mother is looking for you. Let's go."

"I hafta wash my hands first." She trotted over to the sink but couldn't quite reach it. She tried several times, then looked expectantly at Logan.

With a deep sigh, Logan lifted her. He might have resented the time it took, but the picture of ultra male strength supporting the tiny girl shouted perfect mate to me. Stupid hormones.

We emerged from the bathroom and heard a relieved cry. Bud ran up. "Thank goodness, Mr. Steel! You've found Lilly and Jane, I was looking everywhere for them."

From the sweat on his face, poor Bud must have been running around half an hour or more searching for his sister. In some ways he reminded me of Nana in Peter Pan.

"I'm really sorry, Mr. Steel. I turned my back on the kids for just an instant to take notes." He grabbed Lilly's hand. "You wouldn't believe how fast they can disappear."

"The other children," Logan said. "Billy Wilder and the rest. Where are they?"

"Billy gabbed the whole way here about the Coal Mine so he's probably gone there. I don't know about Tad. But Angela's with her sister Frieda, so we just have to find Billy and Tad."

Logan gave a brisk shake of the head. "We need to find them all and get back to the group without delay."

Bud's blue eyes narrowed, looking so much like Logan I almost expected to see them flare red. "Something's wrong?"

Logan glanced significantly at Lilly and Jane. "Of course not." He contradicted the words by nodding.

Bud's jaw firmed and he nodded in return. "The Coal Mine's entrance is down one level, on the main floor. Tad's probably with Billy. Frieda said something about taking Angela to the Idea Factory, which is on the lower level."

"Great. Let's go."

"Mr. Steel!" A man rushed toward us, one of those young-old types with smooth skin but thin wispy hair, athletic but with a bit of a potbelly. His clothes were contradictory too, crisp pleats on his dress slacks but his shirt sleeves unevenly rolled, damp under his arms and his tie askew. "Oh, Mr. Steel, thank goodness you're here. I need to talk to you about the recent emergency modifications done on our cogen. I know the general contractor said it was to bring things up to code and we didn't need an inspection but the efficiency has fallen—"

"Smilvane." Logan's sharp tone cut him off. "I'd like to help but that's really not my area. And I'm in a bit of a hurry." He started down the yellow stairs, Bud and the girls following closely.

"But Mr. Steel, it'll only take a minute of your time. We'll nip across to the green stairs, just a quick look."

Logan stopped. The kids and I piled up behind him. I freaked that we'd all take a tumble but he held firm. Good thing or the yellow stairs would have been just a bit more yellow. "Not now, Smilvane." Logan's voice echoed, not all because of the stairwell.

Smilvane's pupils dilated until his eyes were nearly black. "Yes, Mr. Steel." He let us go.

"Who was that?" I asked. "And what's the cogen?"

"One of the facility admins. We met when I did a computers and security seminar here last year. The cogen is their cogeneration installation, but I don't know about any recent modifications." He jerked a sharp shrug. "Some people think if it has blinking lights and plugs into the wall, it's my problem. Well, I have bigger problems. Let's try the Coal Mine first."

Fifteen excruciatingly long minutes later, we'd picked up Billy and Tad, and were finally on the stairs to the lower level. Not because it took that long to find the boys. No, they were in line at the Coal Mine, first place we looked. Two floors in fifteen minutes, because—

"I gotta go potty," Lilly said for the hundredth time.

I clamped the tiny hand in mine and gritted my teeth. "You went a minute ago. And a minute before that." And, like a

Chinese water torture, every facility between the balcony and the lower level, some twice. At this rate we wouldn't reach the entry hall until the Omega point.

Two levels in fifteen minutes because of Lilly's potty training. I wondered what Freud would have to say. Of course whatever he'd say, Jane Austen Smith would say more, primly and in a voice that carried like a grade-school nun. "It's a bathroom. And you urinate, or if you have solid waste, you defec—"

"Yes, yes, enough." Logan thrust a hand through his already-disheveled hair.

He had to let go of Billy Wilder to do it. Billy screamed "Coal Mine!" and took off instantly.

"Damn it." Even as a super-fast vampire, Logan needed several steps to catch Billy. Of course, that might have been because Tad, still clasped in Logan's other hand, was doing his best imitation of a rock.

"Language, Logan." Personally I felt like screaming the thesaurus of cuss, but they were children, damn...gosh darn it.

"Fine. *Merde! Ce me fait chier.*" Logan glared at me over the children like this was *my* fault.

"I don't feel so good." Tad burped, his cheeks inflated, and his skin tinged green. "I think I'm gonna throw up."

"Not here!" Logan paled. He swallowed convulsively, nostrils flared. Apparently there were disadvantages to ultra-sensitive vampire noses.

"I gotta go potty," Lilly insisted, tugging on my hand.

Bud trundled along next to us, carrying three little sparkly backpacks and a couple Gameboy bags, not to mention an industrial-sized pack of his own. "Again, I'm so sorry, Mr. Steel, Ms. Schmetterling. I really thought I could handle keeping the kids together."

Logan gave Billy Wilder a particularly black glare. "It's not your fault, Bud. Your mother should never have saddled you with all these children alone."

"That's part of the problem." Bud shifted backpacks to rub the nape of his neck. "Frieda was with me. She was, um, impressed with how I handled the kids. I guess I liked that. But when we stopped at the bathrooms we had to split up. I came out of the men's and Lilly was waiting with Jane Austen Smith but Frieda and Angela were nowhere to be found. And then I got absorbed taking notes at an exhibit and sort of lost everyone."

That alarmed me. I'd assumed from his earlier statement that everyone had dispersed at the same time. But now it sounded like Angela and her sister had disappeared without a word. Remembering how Frieda had looked at Bud, that didn't sound right.

Logan exchanged a significant glance with me. He'd caught that, too. "Well, we corralled everyone except Angela and Frieda, and we'll find them next."

Lilly tugged emphatically on my hand. "But I gotta go potty."

Out of the corner of my eye, I saw a Frankenbanker shadow slink around the corner, did a double-take. *Couldn't* be. Ruthven was safely tucked under the sod of Springfield, in spitting distance of Lincoln's last resting place. But if I didn't know better... "No potty now, sweetie," I said to Lilly. "We need to stay together."

"We can stay together," she piped. "In the potty."

"It's a *bathroom*." Jane Austen Smith shook one finger at her. "And it's a noun, not a verb. Although some people use it as a verb, but that's wrong. You should always say urinate or defeca—"

"Let's check the Idea Factory first." Logan tugged Billy and Tad into motion. I dragged my two charges after.

"What's the Idea Factory?" Lilly asked.

As a veteran of many museum field trips, I knew the answer to that. "It's a place to build things."

Billy Wilder's eyes lit up. "Like bombs?"

"I don't know about bombs, but there's a crane, mirrors and lenses for playing with light, and a water spectacle. It's for kids ten and under."

On the museum map the Idea Factory looked like a small room. In reality, it was a huge wonderland cave full of excited, engaged children. Through the rainbow arch entry the noise was practically deafening.

"I wish we could stay," Jane Austen Smith said.

Logan said, "We'll come back. I promise."

"We will?" The younger kids started dancing.

"We will?" Bud echoed, eyebrow arching. He obviously

knew what Logan's promise implied.

Logan seemed to realize it at the same moment. He shrugged. "One way or another."

We had just passed a bunch of youngsters killing innocent plastic balls with jets of water when a cell phone started ringing, gentle compared to Logan's usual surround sound experience. He shifted children, reached into his jeans. "Beer Barrel Polka" emerged. Oh yeah. He still had my phone. "Strongwell? Why are you up? *What?*" Logan's eyes burned a sudden bright predator's gold.

"What's wrong?" I asked.

"Ms. Smelling, you're holding me too tight," Lilly said.

"It's Schmetterling," Jane Austen Smith chimed in.

"I'm sorry, dear." I loosened my grip. "Logan, what is it?"

He snapped the phone shut, did a slow three-sixty, nostrils flared. "Dam—darn. I don't sense him. Too many people."

"Who?"

"Thor called Bo." Logan spoke to me but his eyes didn't stop surveying. "He heard a car start up and drive away He didn't think to look outside for a couple hours but when he did the Maybach was gone."

"The Maybach was stolen? That's too bad. That must be a fairly expensive car, being that it's specially...shielded...oh shi—" Childish laughter from behind made me catch myself just in time. "—itake mushrooms. Ruthven? But how?"

"I don't know. But I'd guess that redhead who was with the Lestat gang yesterday."

"Logan, are you saying Ruthven could be *here?*"

"The backhoe, the shielded Maybach...couldn't have made it easier for them. One minion lured Zinnia here while the other dug Ruthven up, drove him...oh, shit."

"Language, Mr. Steel," Jane said primly.

But I'd seen what Logan had and the profanity was deserved. The Ralph Kramden lookalike in bus driver's uniform held Frieda by the wrists and was manhandling her toward the Factory's exit. Angela trailed them unhappily. Good God, had he captured the girls and been parading them around the exhibits like a normal family, all the while waiting for Ruthven?

Bud followed our gaze and saw Frieda. His face was stricken.

Logan immediately glided out on a tangent that would intercept the driver—and was brought to a screeching halt.

"I wanna stay," Billy Wilder said.

"I don't. I'm gonna barf." Tad underlined his words with some chucking noises. "Get me to the bathroom."

"I gotta go potty too," Lilly said.

"It's *urinate*," Jane Austen Smith insisted. "Or—"

Frieda saw us then. With a shriek she started struggling. The bus driver slapped her and dragged her faster toward the rainbow entrance.

The entrance where a tall, thin Frankenbanker had appeared.

"*Merde*." Logan started again toward Frieda but Billy and Tad had turned into miniature black holes. "Damn it. Bud." He thrust boys' hands into Bud's, who had to juggle backpacks to catch them. And then Logan was gone, not poof but still moving faster than any human.

But that was okay because the crowd of parents and kids had started realizing something was going on at the entrance, and weren't paying any attention to Logan.

"Hey, what're you doing?" a man shouted at the bus driver. "Let that girl go!"

The adults boiled up—directly in Logan's path. Logan, in truly heroic form, pressed through the heaving, jostling mass. Ruthven caught sight of him coming, pointed at the minion and then toward the back corridor, then filtered away.

The bus driver dragged Frieda to the entrance. A museum employee on duty there reached out to stop him. He slugged her. The woman fell back, eyes wide with shock.

The adults near the entrance roared with anger. A big guy who looked like an ex-Marine sergeant with a diaper bag slung across his chest grabbed for the bus driver. The driver thrust Angela at him instead, dashed out with Frieda while the ex-Marine was catching little Angela.

Logan stopped long enough to see Angela safe with the museum official, then ran after Frieda and the driver.

A roar of pain sounded next to me. Bud, his eyes on the spot where the driver had escaped with Frieda. As if he couldn't help himself, he started for the entrance. His grip on the younger boys loosened for just one instant.

"Coal mine!" screamed Billy Wilder. He yanked away from Bud, darted through the seething adults.

"Billy! Come back here." I gripped my two charges tighter and started after him.

"I'll get him, Ms. Schmetterling." Bud tossed three little glittering backpacks over one shoulder. He looked grim, determined and ultra-competent.

"Leave Tad with me." Logan's and Bud's deranged heroics were apparently rubbing off on me. "You can move faster alone."

Naturally the instant Bud was gone Tad covered his mouth. "I'm really gonna barf." He ran toward the exit.

"Tad, wait." I started after him, only to be caught by Lilly.

"I gotta go potty now."

Jane Austen Smith yanked loose. "If everyone else is deserting, I'm going to see Colleen Moore's Fairy Castle."

"No." I managed to seize Jane's wrist, whirled her around. "We are staying together."

"Let go." She tugged. "This is child abuse."

"I don't care. We have to catch Tad." I started dragging her after the escaped boy.

She dropped like a boulder, nearly throwing me off my feet. "Child abuse," she shrieked. "Let me go!"

Nearby adults, still seething from the bus driver, gave me black looks. I winced but held on, tugged her to her feet and made it another ten yards before she went down again.

"I want to see the Fairy Castle. You'll let me go if you know what's good for you."

I tried to haul her up but she had a one ton wrecking ball in her underpants. "Jane, come on. Be a good little girl."

Jane's eyes shifted to the adults ringing us. For an eight-year-old, they were awfully calculating. "You're not my real mom," she shouted. "Let me go. I don't like the bad touches!"

"You perv," a woman hissed.

"Let her go." The ex-Marine father who'd rescued Angela took one threatening step forward.

I practically threw Jane's hand from me. "I'm not—"

The father's arm cocked to grab me.

Jane yanked away. "She *beats* me," she crowed, and took off for the archway.

"Potty!" Lilly ripped herself free and darted after Jane.

I ran after, straight into a wall of angry adults. Beyond the red faces I could see the museum attendant tapping her talk box, no doubt reporting the disturbances. Lilly and Jane slipped through the rainbow arch and I tried to follow, but was again rebuffed by a barricade of hostility.

I could have chewed my purse batteries and spit lightning. One child was kidnapped, the others were scattered to the four winds. A bloodsucking vampire was lurking in wait, and a bunch of well-intentioned parents stood in the way. And Logan had my cell phone.

That was when I saw Ruthven flit past the rainbow arch, headed after Lilly and Jane.

Chapter Nineteen

That did it. I burst the shackles of mild-mannered Liese Schmetterling and became the Raging Bulk, for once glad of my extra fifteen pounds. Using my purse like a battering ram, I pushed my way through. My determination (and the combined weight of me and the purse) made the adults stumble back, even the huge ex-Marine.

I burst through the wall of people, tore like a mad locomotive for little Angela and snared her hand from the museum employee. I flamed through the archway, Angela trotting obediently behind me.

Smack into two burly men, bulling through the crowd from Farm Tech. They wore official tags around their necks, and their demeanor said security.

"Hey you. Stop!" The ex-Marine father hadn't given up either.

Couldn't escape forward or back so I ducked down amid the general mill of people and snuck sideways across the aisle. There I found a small cubicle (by museum standards that is—it was actually the size of a church foyer) filled with strollers, like a baby buggy parking ramp. I hid until the burly security guards and well-intentioned father passed.

As I waited I planned. Lilly and Tad were both headed for the bathroom. I'd start there. Simple.

Except for one problem. Ruthven was in the museum, somewhere close.

Crowds of potential witnesses might keep him from acting right away, but I knew some parts of the museum were sparsely trafficked. With Logan and me separated, this was the perfect opportunity for Ruthven to catch a butterfly.

The guards and father were gone. I dashed out of hiding with Angela, through Farm Tech to the lower level bathrooms.

"Itsy Bitsy Spider" drifted from the ladies' room. Inside Lilly's little shoes waved below the door of one of the stalls. Two women were washing hands, checking makeup, so I couldn't just crawl under and yank her out. Not unless I wanted another lynch mob on my hands. "Lilly, honey, hurry up."

"Okay." More foot-waving.

A couple other stall doors were closed. Occupied, hopefully by humans. Did vampires have to use the facilities? I made a mental note to ask Logan. But for now, Lilly was covered. "Honey, I'm going to find Tad, okay? I'll be right back." Angela in hand, I scooted across to the men's room.

The restrooms on the lower level of the museum were set up like an airport's, no doors, only open walkways curving in. Peeking cautiously around the corner I called, "Tad? Tad, are you in there?"

Nothing. I crept into the men's bathroom, feeling vaguely criminal. One guy was at the urinals. He saw me, squeaked, zipped up midstream, and squeaked again (I think he caught something) and fled. Angela trotted patiently at my side as I checked quickly under the doors. Empty.

"Dam...ascus steel. Tad, where are you?" A quick check of the ladies' room revealed the little shoes still swinging. Another woman was washing her hands, but that still left one stall occupied. I ran out of the bathroom, but no Tad had appeared in the meantime, not in the hallway or men's room. No revealing retching noises either. I ran toward the women's room again with a half-formed idea of snatching Lilly whether she was finished or not, when I was hit by an *oh-no* moment.

The oh-no moment, for the non-technical, is that instant just after pressing the enter key on the biggest screwup of your life. Example? Type delete c:*.*. Press enter. *Oh-no*. The entire hard drive is erased.

Sometimes it's called the oh-shit second. It's a single moment of horror knowing that you have committed the most moronic act of your life and there is *nothing* you can do to call it back.

I stood in the hallway, my bowels turning to water and my heart suddenly hammering, and saw the other bathrooms.

The Museum of Science and Industry is very modern.

Besides the regular men's/ladies' restrooms, they also have family-friendly rooms, small gas-station style cubicles with a single toilet, sink, changing table and tile floor with drain. There were four on this level, two each flanking the regular men's and women's.

Tad might be in one of these. Isolated, alone. Free for the taking by the bus driver or Ruthven. Or, remembering that someone drove Ruthven here, Carrothead Jr.

Heart tripping, I flung the door open on one. Empty. I ran to the other side of the hall, reached for the next handle. Drew my hand back.

If Tad were inside, surely the door would be locked? The human minions couldn't get in and Ruthven wouldn't chance misting in a crowd, right? So Tad was safe unless Ruthven was so far gone with revenge that he had completely abandoned common sense...yeah. I grabbed the handle and wrenched the door open.

Tad stood trembling, wrapped in the arms of a skeleton.

It was far worse than I thought. Not only Ruthven and his human minions were here. I recognized this rail-thin skull-head as the Lestat vampire Shiv. Apparently Emerson's lieutenants had let him go.

His eyes burned fire, his fangs glinted in the artificial light, and there was no doubt this lieutenant of Ruthven's could kill. Tad was in the clutches of an evil Lestat. And I had to handle it on my own.

Gollum-like Shiv grinned at me. Croaked in his whiny voice, "Schmetterling. Lord Ruthven said you'd come." He shuffled closer, dragging Tad along. "I'm gonna enjoy doing you."

My hand tightened on Angela's. Weed Whacker here had been *expecting* me. Gunning for *me*. Zajicek had been right.

And there was nothing I could do about it. I was a human, vulnerable to a super-fast, super-strong bloodsucker—because of Logan.

The horror swamping me hijacked my brain, leaving only the certainty that Logan had seduced me, brought me into his world—and conveniently left me. Yes, I know he was rescuing the kids but my old emotional tapes screamed it was happening again. Pumped even bigger by adrenalin, it felt far too real. Another man seducing me, using me and dumping me. Another man—

"Not a *man.*" Bad Liese sat on one shoulder, nonchalantly polishing her nails on her killer gold lamé gown.

"A vampire." On my other shoulder, Good Liese was equally nonchalant as she stitched at a pretty little sampler.

I glared at them in turn. "What are you two doing here?"

"Well, duh," Good Liese said. "Decision time."

The vampire's hand flashed out, grabbed my wrist and yanked me in. I released Angela who showed the good sense to stay on the outside as the door swung quietly shut behind me. "Decision?" I threw at G-Liese. "The only decision I have is how fast to die."

"She could run," Bad Liese suggested around my neck.

Good Liese leaned forward. "Except she probably knows running only excites a vampire's predatory instincts."

"True." Bad Liese shrugged. "Well, she could trust Logan."

"I'm right here," I pointed out.

"Who you talking to, blood-bitch?" That from Mr. Bonehead.

"She could," Good Liese said. "Trust him to rescue her, that is."

Bad Liese nodded. "Trust him to come back to her."

"I'm not the imaginary creature here, guys. Stop talking around me, 'kay?"

"I ain't no imaginary creature." Skeletal fingers wrapped around my neck. I was too busy arguing with the Terrible Twins to pay much attention.

"He hasn't abandoned her," Good Liese said. "He's just got a job to do."

"Yeah, catching evil minions and rounding up unruly kids," I muttered. "He'll get back to me in about twenty years."

"He's a super-fast vampire. She really ought to trust him."

I don't know which twin said that because Shiv had started shaking me and I couldn't hear squat over my rattling brains. "Who you talking to, blood-bitch?"

Tad made a wet noise. "Stop shaking us. Oh, I don't feel so good."

"Shut up, kid."

"He has her best interests at heart." Good Liese tucked away her needle. "Logan, that is."

"He means well," I choked out. "But it won't stop him from lying or keeping secrets."

"Shut up." Shiv shook us harder. "Both of you."

"There's actually four of us—"

Tad groaned. "I *really* don't feel so good."

"She's going to have to trust someone sooner or later," Bad Liese said. "If she doesn't want to die a lonely old lady."

"Pardon me for pointing this out," I gasped past the skeleton's press of fingers. "But even trusting Logan, I'm going to die alone, and not so old." Spots danced before my eyes.

"Shut the fuck up!" Shiv shook us all so hard my teeth rattled.

Tad spewed brunch all over the vampire's front.

Shiv fell back, shocked. His eyes went wide, his nostrils flared—and the first of the smell hit him. He threw hands over his face, releasing us. Cheeks inflating, eyes crossing, he stumbled for the toilet.

The twins popped out of existence. I grabbed Tad's hand. Rasped, "Feel better?"

"Yeah. A lot."

"Good." I dashed out of the bathroom with him, collected Angela and ran into the ladies' room, where Lilly was trying to wash her hands. I seized her little wrist and hurried her out. "But I gotta wash my hands," she wailed. "Mommy says."

Good ol' Sergeant Mom. While hygiene was important, there was this little thing called survival. "Not now, Lilly."

She turned into a Lilly-sized anvil. "No. I gotta wash my hands."

The short restroom hallway made an H with two main corridors. As I tried to lug forty pounds of uncooperative three-year-old toward the Farm Tech side, a shadow passed the mouth of the H. Another Lestat? Ruthven himself? We'd find out if we didn't get a move on. Desperate, I dug in my purse, but I was a geek, not a mom. I didn't have instant germ-killer or even diaper wipes.

So I grabbed Lilly's hands and blew on them. "There. All clean." Hey, mother's spit is the universal solvent, right? Everyone knows that. And I'd be a mother someday. Maybe. Probably. With Logan, it wouldn't be for lack of trying.

Anyway, it worked. Lilly miraculously turned lighter than

air and bounded along at my side. My destination the Fairy Castle, I trotted into Farm Tech.

And ran into Ruthven.

"My minions have let me down again." He sighed extravagantly. "I shall simply have to kill you myself."

"Have to? Is that a moral, physical or existential necessity?" My feet froze but apparently my sarcasm was still online. "You don't actually *have* to kill me. Just sayin'."

"Oh, but I want to. After a small snack." His eyes heated to a hungry red and wandered to—the children. He licked his lips.

The sick fuck.

I fought to maintain my self-control. My imaginary shoulder buddies were right, Logan would come, finding me by the blood scent of a donor. I only had to delay Ruthven until then.

But I had to get the children away now. I put Lilly's and Angela's hands in Tad's and covered the maneuver by talking. "Why bother with minions in the first place? Or why not get smarter ones?" I released the children with a little push. "Where'd you get yours anyway? Oxface University? Mount Holy Moses?"

Ruthven's eyes bored into mine. "Do not dare insult the underlings of Lord Ruthven, Liese Schmetterling."

Tad might have a weak stomach but he had a great brain. He edged the three of them away while I kept my eyes locked with Ruthven's, a little dangerous since Ruthie was a vampire. But Logan said I was immune to mind control. I trusted him about that, at least. "Then what was on their resume? Sets low standards and fails to achieve them? Water weekly and turn toward the sun?"

"Liese Schmetterling, you flirt with a painful death."

Logan was right about the corny dialog. "Well, I suppose they grew on you. Sort of like E. coli."

Ruthven surprised me by laughing. He laughed like a cat with a hairball. "Do not think to distract me with such an absurd attempt at humor, Liese Schmetterling."

"It was worth a try." The kids were gone. Maybe they'd run into more vampires, but anything was better than creepy-sick Ruthven. "Though really, you could stick a hose in Shiv's ear and rent him out as a vacuum cleaner."

"Enough. Come to me, Liese Schmetterling. Perhaps if you

are nice to me I will let you live—as my sex thrall."

Ew. I cased my surroundings. Yellow stairs to my right, red stairs some distance to my left. Bathroom hall behind me. "Had you ever thought maybe it's you? That your minions are underachievers because you're an incompetent boss? I bet if I put my ear to your skull could I hear the ocean."

"I said *enough*." Ruthven's eyes fired like flares. "Come to me. Now." His voice echoed with dark compulsion. The people nearest us jerked toward him like iron filings caught by a magnet, some even taking a few unwilling steps.

Fortunately Logan was right. I was a perversely willful creature. I turned tail and ran.

I dodged through fifty or more people—a milling crowd on their way to exhibits, headed into the bathrooms or just waiting for friends or family. I dared a glance back.

Ruthven stalked me, human-slow but confident. I only had to make one mistake, move into one unpopulated area, and he'd hijack me. I had no illusions as to what he'd do then. Ruthven hated Logan. Logan was an important Iowa Alliance vampire. Logan was Ruthven's enemy twice over. But Ruthven would know Logan was strong, smart, and had incredible training.

And Ruthven was a coward. He'd never use a direct attack when he could psych Logan out. Which was unfortunately very easy. Just destroy the new household like the first one. Bleed one person like he'd bled Adelaide.

No, I had no delusions. Ruthven would bleed *me*.

But as long as I stayed among other people, I'd be safe. I hunkered down amid the moving throng to wait for Logan.

And was shocked when a thin, strong hand grabbed my arm. "Darling," Ruthven said in a fake syrupy tone. "There you are."

I tried to shake him off. His fingers tightened. I pulled against his thumb-forefinger and yanked free but he'd already grabbed me with the other hand.

"We'll go now," he said, grinning like a malevolent snake. "Since you don't feel well." And he punched me in the gut.

I bent over, choking air. He dragged me a couple feet before I stuck my heels in automatically. "No, I...stop." Next to me some men were watching. Maybe I could get them to intervene.

Ruthven put an arm around my bent shoulders. "Darling, I

just want to take care of you."

Just that fast the men turned away. They thought Ruthven was my boyfriend.

Ruthven tried to drag me off. "Come with me now, love."

Love. What a terrible liar. Ruthven meant it no more than Botcher had. I stubbornly refused to move, automatically twisting my glass ring. God, I was getting so *sick* of men lying.

The ring came off. My hand felt amazingly light without Botcher's empty promise. Free. In the midst of all my fear I smiled. Elena was right. I should have taken it off months ago.

Ruthven tugged at me. "Come on, *darling.*"

The ring was glass, but it looked like the real deal. An idea formed. A little theater... I had to move fast but the more I thought about it the more I liked it. Sweet progress bar of life, the rat-bastard would finally be good for something.

I held the ring up high so it caught the light, sparkles shooting everywhere. "How dare you have sex with that woman!" I yelled at Ruthven.

The milling crowd froze, turned toward me. Faces mixed with shock and avarice. I kept my eyes locked on Ruthven, shook the ring accusingly at him. "I wouldn't marry you if you were the last man on earth." People appeared in the corridor behind Ruthven, drawn by my voice. More entered the corridor behind me.

Ruthven let out a growl like an angry badger. Okay, I don't know what an angry badger sounds like, but imagine something really unattractive.

Anyway, time for me to move. "Take your damned diamond back, you lying cheat!" I twisted loose and threw the ring down between us.

Like baking soda tossed into vinegar, the ring fomented the crowd into a mob. Grabbing for the ring, diving for it, people pushed between Ruthven and me. He grabbed for me but I drew back. More people boiled out of the bathrooms, rushed in from the ends of the hall. They foamed into a big, mean, impenetrable wall between us.

Ruthven's angry face, just above the diving heads, imprinted on my brain. Oh, he wasn't happy.

I spun and hightailed it. Benches lined the wall ahead. To my right but some distance away were the blue stairs and the entrance to the Brain Food Court. To my left were the green stairs. They were cordoned off with a sign saying *Maintenance Work—No Admittance* but they were much closer. I went left.

A man-tall, elephant-wide vent in the left wall caught my attention. Just beyond it was a small set of unlabeled stairs. I wouldn't have seen the stairs if not for the vent.

I paused. I didn't know where the unlabeled stairs led, but the green stairwell in front of me was cavernous and open. Ruthven would get through the mob eventually, or head around. I had only seconds to hide. I ducked up the short flight of stairs.

They emptied into a corridor. Elevator left, bend ahead. The elevator was visible from the main hallway, so I bypassed it for the bend.

Which dead-ended in a door. I ran into it—and bounced off with a smack. Locked. Flash-fry my bios. Maybe I could just hide in the corridor?

"I am coming for you, Liese Schmetterling." Ruthven's voice rang from behind.

Maybe not.

The echo of polished hallways made it impossible to judge how far away he was. But if I could hear him at all, he was too close.

What to do, what to do? Head back out and hope that with the crowd I could dodge Ruthie until Logan came? Stay here and cower, hoping Ruthven wouldn't find me? Either seemed a vampire recipe for Liese pâté.

The door had a window. I stared through, saw a bolt lever. Beyond it was a room, a really nice janitorial station by the look of it.

If I could break the window and reach the knob, I could open the door and hide in the room. Problem solved.

Except breaking a window was noisy. And vampire hearing, as I knew from experience, was super-keen. Ruthven would come running.

I ran a finger over the glass. Unless I could break it without shattering it... A glint of light hooked my attention. Logan's supposedly-diamond ring. If it were real, I could score the glass and break it with a crack instead of a crash, maybe so quietly Ruthven wouldn't hear it over the crowd.

If it were a real diamond.

If Logan could be trusted.

Hell. I had wanted Logan to prove himself trustworthy. I just hadn't expected my life to depend on it. I pulled off the ring, put it to glass. Ran it sharply over the surface. It made a hissing, etching sound.

To my amazement a line appeared. I don't know if I was more surprised Logan had told me the truth—or that he'd given geeky, chubby old me a ring worth tens of thousands of dollars.

I slashed two more half-inch scores, used a knuckle to crack out the resultant tiny triangle. It hit the floor with a small tinkle. But now I could score a bigger piece and pull it out without a sound.

Then I simply reached through, opened the lock and ducked in. My eyes lit on a yarn mop which I used to jam the door shut. I wet the mop fibers to increase the force of the wedge.

Now I just had to wait. I sank to the floor, my back to the door. If Ruthven found me, his vampire strength might push open the jam, but maybe not if I added a hundred forty pounds of me. Well, that's what I told myself. Really, my legs were shaking too hard to hold me.

Time is funny when your heart is pounding so hard you can feel it thump your chest. It was a second, it was an hour. It was a whole bunch of seconds but each one was terror anew. My memory of sitting there, waiting for Ruthven, is totally psychedelic. I know time passed but I only remember it moment to moment.

"There you are, Liese Schmetterling. I will enjoy this more than you know." Ruthven's face appeared at the hole in the window above me like a psycho Gatekeeper in *The Wizard of Oz*. I would have peed my pants if I hadn't been potty thirty times already in the last half hour.

But Ruthven was here. I had hoped Logan would find me first, but he did have the kids to protect. I drew in a breath, gathering strength for battle, however short it might be.

Ruthven tugged at the door. It didn't budge.

Well, good news. Apparently not all vampires had super strength.

"Liese!" And more good news! Logan's voice echoed down

the hallways. "I'm coming, princess." He sounded far away but he was coming. I was saved.

I'd forgotten one tiny little detail.

Ruthven cackled. "Oh, this is too rich. The door cannot stop me, you know." His face disappeared from the window.

And to my horror a thin stream of mist ran up the window and through the hole I had so carefully cut.

Chapter Twenty

I jumped to my feet. Logan was coming but I had no idea how far away he was or how soon he'd get here. A carotid artery cut with laughable ease. Ruthven could slash my throat long before Logan got here. And what if Logan arrived but couldn't get through the door? What if he froze again and forgot how to mist?

What if this was just like Adelaide?

Mist boiled in. I had no stake, no bazooka, not so much as a nail clipper. I had pepper spray but that didn't work on mist. I'd have to wait until Ruthven formed and hope I could squirt his eyes before his superior vampire speed made me an aperitif.

Damn it, *no*. I had to trust Logan. Trust his heart and nose to lead him to me. Trust his training, which from all I understood was the best in the business. Trust his nature as a lethal protector. Logan would come in time.

The mist started to solidify. Double damn. Even if Logan came soon, Ruthven was here *now*.

And if Logan panicked and forgot how to mist, he might not get in at all. I knew a slashed throat eventually led to bleeding out.

Then I would be dead. I might no longer care, but Logan would. If he couldn't mist it would hurt his self-esteem. Hurt his self-esteem if he couldn't selfa-steam. Get it? Ha.

I covered my eyes with my hand. Damn it, I was punning under stress just like Logan, who would probably pun while fighting the whole Coterie, lithe, graceful, deadly, his brain and tongue working as fast as his sword arm...I uncovered my face. I was punning. That meant my brain was working—no, it was in overdrive. Conversely my heart was no longer pounding so loud I couldn't hear myself think and my breathing was completely under control.

Punning wasn't merely a goofy reaction to stress. It was, like everything else in Logan's arsenal, a deadly weapon.

With my brain online I remembered I wasn't an eighteenth century sheeple meekly waiting for Logan to rescue me. I was a twenty-first century gal.

And better yet, a geek. I reached into my purse. Oh, I trusted Logan to come. But first I trusted myself. *I* had to delay Ruthven.

A little surprise would do that. Or, should I say, shock.

In the sewer I'd fumbled through the entire contents of my purse to locate one item. Thanks to the centering effect of punning I reached in and laid my hand directly on the tape-mummy camera I'd made to entertain the kids and distract myself so long ago. I pulled it out and hit the picture-taking button. A whine swelled and died.

Crossing mental fingers, I stuck the wires into the gathering mist.

My home-made Taser discharged with a click and a bang. The click I expected, the electric current zapping from wire to wire, connecting through the mist.

The bright flash of light and bang I didn't. Hadn't seen that on the Internet. Apparently tasering vampire mist isn't like tasering flesh. Electric current will shock a solid human, maybe disrupt some muscle and nerve action.

Tasering mist was more like setting a spark in a grain elevator. The fuliginous gray that was Ruthven poofed into flame.

Ruthven snapped into being with his face *on fire*. He screamed and started slapping at himself to put the fire out.

Well, I had to, didn't I? I slapped his face too.

I laughed, pleased with myself. What a fitting insult to this creep who'd threatened to eat children and who'd ruined Logan's life.

Except my slap zone was also Ruthven's kill zone. He seized my wrist with a growl. Note to self. Good idea—indulge in a little slap-and-tickle with sexy good-guy vamp. Bad idea—bitch-slapping crazed, on-fire rogue.

Although it had been satisfying.

"Liese!" Logan's angry face showed through the window only a second before a mist poured through, fast and furious. Guess I didn't have to worry about him choking. His mist boiled up behind Ruthven like an enraged sea. It ran up and over the bad vamp's body, swirling around him like a blanket.

Ruthven released me with a jerk, tried to dance back. Logan's mist thinned and spread, wrapping Ruthven in mummy's bandages, tighter and tighter. Ruthie's face went from furious (and a little charred) to confused to downright terrified.

"Steel!" Ruthven struggled hard, managed to jab a hand into his coat pocket. "You cannot win. I am Lord Ruthven, Ruler of the Night."

Whew. Talk about corny. Logan's mist was streaming tighter and faster. Ruthven barely managed to jerk his hand free but when he did, he was holding—a Big Red Button. Race's BRB, if I wasn't mistaken. More corn but suddenly I wasn't laughing.

"Stop," Ruthven repeated. "I engineered this to topple Nosferatu but I will get a greater pleasure using it to destroy you."

I nearly fell off my feet. *Ruthven* was the challenger for Nosferatu's territory, the target of Project Shield. The terrorist who was going to destroy not the Willis Tower but the one-hundred-seventeen-year-old landmark Museum building.

Not if I could help it. "Hey, Lorne. Isn't it a bit extreme to blow up thousands of innocent visitors just to kill Logan?" I snatched at the button as Logan's mist rose on Ruthven's body, gathering around the vampire's neck.

It left Ruthven's hands free. He yanked the button away from me, snarling. "I hate Steel and his whole family. Nothing is too extreme to rid me of him."

Whoa. I thought I had issues. Ruthven had a whole can of festering hate-worms.

"And rid myself of you, Liese Schmetterl—*gack*."

Logan's mist whirled around Ruthven's neck, so concentrated and fast it looked like a ghostly garrote, or a noose tightening.

Ruthven's neck snapped.

I swallowed a shriek, jumped back. Good thing because an

instant later Logan condensed from the mist, his long dagger drawn. "That's for Adelaide. And this is for daring to threaten Liese." A single, powerful slash severed Ruthven's throat.

Blood spurted. Another hard cut severed the neck. The head toppled. And the body—

Ruthven's final act was to slap a hand down on the button.

"Damn it!" Logan caught it as the body collapsed. But I could see the button was depressed and it was too late. I covered my head with my hands and breathed a final *I love you* to Logan and... and...

And nothing.

No pain, no shock. Not even a long black tunnel and beckoning point of light.

I opened my eyes. Logan was rapidly dismantling the button using a claw for a screwdriver. I trotted to his side, studiously ignoring the headless body. "Why didn't we blow up? Is that a fake?"

Logan's brows knit. "No, it's hooked into a radio transmitter... Oh, of course. Ruthven's too much a coward not to give himself time to escape. He must have built in a delay."

"How long do we have?" I clutched Logan's melon-sized biceps. "Are the kids safe?"

"The kids are fine. I made sure Bud was shepherding them out before I came for you. And time? Long enough for Ruthven to escape. That should mean I have long enough to evacuate the museum. I'll call Smilvane to start that, then look for the bomb." He yanked my mop door-wedge loose with one hand while he thumbed numbers into my cell with the other.

"Don't you mean *we*?"

"No." His tone was as flat as I'd ever heard, his resolution punctuated by punching open the door. "You are leaving. Quickly, quietly, and—" He stopped so fast I ran into his back.

The museum had been struck by Noah's flood.

"What the—" Logan's head swiveled, taking in the scene around us in that fast, almost supercomputer way I'd come to know and love. Water sprayed all around. People ran past us, skidding and sliding, headed for the exit like they couldn't get out of there fast enough. As evacuations went, it was messy and unplanned, but any port in a storm.

Speaking of which...I squinted up, wondering if the Storms exhibit had gone horribly wrong, but the indoor rain was the fire sprinklers. No alarm and no fire, yet all the sprinklers were busy fizzing, as far down the corridor as I could see. "This isn't possible. Sprinklers are heat-sensitive. They go off individually in response to rising temperatures, not all at once for no reason."

Logan grabbed my hand, strode briskly after the fleeing people. "It's a setup."

My eyes snapped to his face, his ferocious frown the only indication of how hard his superb brain was working. "What do you mean?"

He led me past the blue stairs, across the center concourse. "Ruthven said he set this up to topple Nosferatu. The button triggered the sprinklers."

"What kind of terrorist act is that? Make everybody catch pneumonia?

"No, there's more to it. Scare people toward the exit, but then what? And how did Ruthven engineer this when he's as technically literate as a gnat?" He screeched to a halt and cocked his head. "Shit."

"What?" But a moment later I saw what he'd heard.

The mob of people who'd thundering down the frozen escalator and stairs were coming back. Hundreds of people, shaking and trembling, and not just with wet.

Behind them, driving them like cattle, were over fifty fanged Lestat vampires brandishing guns.

Smack in the middle of the humans was the white face of supermom Zinnia Jones.

Logan's swearing took on a distinctly French tinge. "If we live through this I will personally guillotine that woman."

"She probably just wanted to help."

"And instead she's made herself a target. Now you see why I want you out of this?" Logan picked me up and in a twinkling we were at the blue staircase. The Foucault pendulum swung a gentle rhythm behind us, trailing water.

I clung to his strong shoulders. "Haven't I been a help up to now?"

He snarled at me. Snarled. "Yes, damn you. I still want you safely out of this."

"And I want to be a size six. Since that ain't happening, why don't we try to figure out where the bomb is?"

"I've been trying. None of this makes any sense. Why start an evacuation just to herd people back into the museum?" He stared intently at nothing, mind obviously churning.

"Well, if the bomb could take out the whole building, it wouldn't matter where the people are. Ergo—"

"Ergo, it's a small bomb, small enough that they need to consolidate the humans into a confined area. So they start the sprinklers to gather people at the entrance, then herd them wherever they want. Okay, that makes sense. Now the only thing we need to figure out is where—" He stopped speaking and turned toward the green stairs. His pupils constricted to pinpricks. "No. That can't be it."

"What?"

"The stairwell—" His nostrils flared. "We've got company."

A very red Razor limped toward us from the bathroom corridor, trailing smoke. "Lord Logan! I've been looking all over for you. Pax. I got news. The boss is gonna elocution people. When it was you against us, well, that was one thing. But zapping innocent humans—that's abdominal. It could be Hattie." He stopped in front of us, panting. "But I don't know where."

I didn't even have time to translate that before Logan was moving past him. "Smilvane said there were modifications done on the cogenerator installation. Emergency changes to the 1.75 megawatts *electrical* generator. It's on the second floor above the meeting rooms. The green stairwell." Race fell in behind us.

My fingers clutched Logan's shoulders as the implications hit. "Electricity. That's why the sprinklers. Human skin has natural resistance."

"Dry," Logan agreed. "Wet, it's about four hundred times more conductive." He set me down just outside the green stairs and kicked aside the warning sign. The railings had been stripped down to bare metal and the stairs were covered with chain mats. "That's just fucking grisly."

"Mass electrocution." I tried to swallow, couldn't. "Electrical source above, ground below, metal in between. Current drawn through the path of least resistance. Wet humans wouldn't add much. The stairwell is a natural electrocution chamber. Ruthven did this?"

"The boss is crazy," Razor said. "But smart. He's been working with a bunch of genesis to fix this up."

Geniuses, my mind supplied.

"The Steel Software wannabes." Logan slapped the wall in frustration. It made a hollow clanging sound, a metal cladding. "Damn. I can't fight fifty Lestats, not all of them, not and still stop this in time." The crescendoing thunder of feet behind us underlined his words. "I'll have to cut the electricity at the source."

"Sixty Lestats, asshole, and you ain't getting by us," bellowed a voice from above. An instant later a big knife-wielding body crashed into Logan.

Logan only swayed with the impact, then used the Lestat's impetus against him and smashed him into the wall. Vampire skull shattered. The knife clattered to the floor.

"That's one of the boss's hand-picked guards." Razor nodded at the fallen Lestat. "More above. Want me to sweet-talk them? They know me."

Logan drew his blade and made short work of the fallen Lestat. "We don't have time to persuade them." I could see the decision to trust Razor flash in Logan's golden eyes. "Go talk to them, distract them. When I attack, you attack."

"Got it." Razor trotted up the stairs. A moment later Logan followed, lightning-fast.

I picked up the knife, slipped cautiously up the stairs after. Fifty Lestats behind us, and if the fallen Lestat was to be believed, ten above. Well, nine now. The sound of intense fighting heralded three headless bodies tumbling down the stairs past me. Okay, six. I pressed against the railing, heart pounding. Swallowing my fear, I gripped the knife harder and continued up.

At the top was a large landing. To my right, the stairs continued up. In front of me, a knot of Lestats guarded an unmarked metal door, probably the generator room. I counted eight vampires. Damn, the fallen Lestat had lied. Razor grappled with one, both vampires' fangs straining, their faces that hard, angled plate. A sheet of red ran down the Lestat's neck from where Razor's blade had bitten deep.

Logan fought so fast he was practically mist, zipping from one vampire to the next, pausing only long enough to slash a throat or sever a neck.

But the Lestats were big, armed to the teeth, and well-trained. It was taking too long. A shriek came from below. The first of the herded people had arrived in the stairwell. And there were still four Lestats left up here.

Slicing it down to three, Logan turned and saw me. A look of pain crossed his face. With a sudden, brutal roundhouse he kicked through the heads of all three Lestats, knocking them flat. But instead of finishing them, he flashed to me and took my face in his hands. "Liese, get out of here if you can. I couldn't stand it if something happened to you." He looked deep into my eyes, not his Svengali stare or laser eyes, but a clear golden hazel. "Liese. Sweetheart, please."

Scuffling broke out below. Good, someone was resisting. That would give us more time. But not much.

I threaded my fingers through his gorgeous wet hair. "Wherever you go I'm going. Remember, I'm safer with you. And you don't have time to disagree." To forestall argument I pressed a kiss to his luscious mouth.

"Damn," was all he said right before he whirled away for a hard slash that dropped a recovered Lestat at my feet.

Razor had taken out another. Logan, with a quick double-cut, destroyed the last.

But a roar from below cut through human cries and we knew it was only a matter of time before these twelve were replaced. I tried the door. "Locked."

"Move aside." Logan exploded in a spinning back kick worthy of Chuck Norris. The door bent. A second kick nearly took it off its frame. He pushed it fully open and we were confronted by a room dominated by a blue-green generator.

Logan stepped through the wreckage. Razor and I followed.

"Is that it?" I had to raise my voice to be heard. "Kinda loud."

"This size generator? Usually vibration and noise is much worse. They damp it." He was walking around the unit, eyes taking in everything.

The cries below became screams. Our time was running out. But I was overwhelmed by so many pipes and hoses, panels and conduits and wires. Which would shut the generator down? Or at least disconnect the stairwell electrocution chamber?

"Damn." Logan glared at the generator. "There's supposed to be a control panel here with an emergency stop. It's been removed. Anything that might help us has been immobilized with polyurethane foam. And I'll just bet all the circuit breakers and safety mechanisms have been disabled."

"We have to do something. What about this?" I pointed at a small display bolted to the side, its screen no more than 320 by 240 pixels. Digitized gauges were at fifty percent and edging toward the red end. "It's not foamed."

Logan's eyes narrowed. "The wannabes have set up a web portal. If this is the image of their remote annunciator—"

"Their what?"

"Remote monitor. And if I'm reading this right we have less than a minute until the electricity kicks to the stairs."

I swallowed my teeth. "Can we bring the people up here? Is this room electrified?"

Razor said, "The problem with that is it will also bring up fifty Lestats."

"Intruders!" A shout came from the doorway. "To arms!"

"Forty-nine." Logan sighed. "Damned villains. Handle him, Race, will you?" Logan tossed Razor his blade. "This will be a mite more efficient than your pig sticker."

"Hey, thanks." Razor flicked vampire-fast to the doorway, felled the Lestat in one blow. He flipped Logan's blade in his hand. "Nice."

I turned away before the inevitable decapitation. "Aren't you afraid Razor'll use your blade on you?"

"It's a risk," Logan said. "But that Lestat's warning will bring more. Race, properly armed, will buy us a few needed seconds."

"To do what?"

"This." Logan turned to a panel on the wall. He extended claws at least an inch long. With a sudden, sharp jab, he poked them straight into the metal and pulled. "The electricity is routed from the generator and split. I'm betting this holds the boxes that do that. One of them will power the stairs." The panel creaked, distorted. Logan's jaw firmed. The metal distressed further with a creaking whine, and finally gave. The panel door ripped off.

Dozens of boxes sprang out amid a hornet's nest of cables.

Not little cat-5 cables, either. Thicker than my wrist, each cable was wrapped in black conduit with only the coppery ends showing they were metal.

"Why wasn't that sealed?"

"It was. Glued down with superstrength epoxy. Guess Ruthven's 'genesis' weren't expecting him to cock up their plan by luring an Alliance vampire here. Damn." Logan stared in consternation. "How many fucking boxes are there? I'll never pick the right one in time."

I came to his side. The torn-open panel looked like open-heart surgery gone tragically wrong, with the help of a cherry bomb. "Just pick any one."

"Right." He smashed a fist into one of the boxes, splintering plastic. Inside, the cables were secured to a brass bar with screws the size of my finger.

"We need to disconnect those cables." I dug in my purse for a screwdriver but Logan stopped me with a quick shake of his head.

"Screw finesse." He tore off his jacket. Grabbing the cables he heaved with mighty strength. If I'd thought his muscles had bulged ripping open his shirt it was nothing compared to now. His jaw clenched, his chest expanded like a bellows. His biceps, pectorals and trapezius swelled under his wet shirt and hardened to boulders. The cable in his right hand tore loose, spitting electricity. A few seconds later the other pulled free in a shower of sparks.

I ran back to the monitor. The gauges were still rising, less than ten percent until hitting red. Maybe twenty seconds left. "Damn it, no."

Shouts sounded from below, and a scream, high-pitched with terror.

Logan smashed a fist into the wall, denting it. "This is taking too long. We have to find the box connecting the stairs, and we have to find it now."

"Master Logan!" Zinnia's shriek echoed up the metal well.

I spun wild eyes around the room. Time was running out. Too many options, only one right. The death of hundreds of people imminent.

How could we solve this insoluble problem?

Fear and desperation struck me so hard I nearly bent

double. Logan instantly gathered me in, folding me against his powerful chest. His warm body and a soft kiss on my hair comforted me. Panic receded.

Trust myself. As a programmer, system designer and sysop I was *built* to solve problems. So. Best option, find the correct connection. How? How to pick out a single box, the same as all the others in design, function, and implementation. Built the same, used the same, installed the same—

Wait.

The box that we wanted accommodated a new load, the stairs—so it was probably also new.

We were looking for a box that wasn't part of the original installation. A new box, which would stand out—

"Logan, that one!" I was drowned out by a half dozen screams. I tried again but the whole stairwell started ringing with horrified shouts.

I jabbed at a box. Logan, not even bothering to smash it open, grabbed its cables and wrenched. "Why this one?" He huffed it, laboring against the cables.

"Every other box in here is green. This one's blue."

"Brilliant." He closed his eyes and strained harder.

Me, brilliant. Know what? I actually believed him. To cover the absurd swell of my heart, I trotted back to the control monitor and pretended to study it. Was smacked into reality by what I saw. Five seconds. Four.

"They've...really...got this...tight." Logan's chest swelled and I could see the tendons stand out on his neck. "Coming...coming..."

Fingers bleeding, he gripped the cables harder and wrenched with all his strength until I could see the veins popping dark against the wet cotton of his shirt. His chest swelled and his biceps were beyond rigid, and suddenly the cables ripped so hard the box flew apart. Screws spat, plastic showered. Sparks zapped, rained like fireworks. The connecting bar sailed across the room.

In front of me, the display panel went dark.

We'd done it.

Logan grabbed me for a quick soul-searing kiss, twirling me until my feet lifted from the ground. Or maybe the kiss had me flying.

He set me down. "I have to go whip Lestat ass."

"I thought you couldn't take fifty vampires."

"Not when I had only thirty seconds to do it. And it's only forty-nine—" he glanced at the doorway, "Forty-eight vampires now."

"You do have Razor, I mean Race, to help you." I heaved a theatrical sigh.

He gave me another brief, giddy kiss. "And you, princess. Always you."

At five p.m. three dozen humans milled around the Iowa tour bus, me among them. Several hundred people streamed past us, museum visitors headed home. Two people had suffered heart attacks and another dozen a variety of defensive wounds. Amazingly, all the victims were now fine. Amazingly, nobody remembered a thing except what a good time they had. I suspected "Amazingly" had the last name Steel.

Lilly and the rest of the kids were safe. The bus driver was under lock and key. Turned out the times he'd come into the Blood Center to use the bathroom, he had really been casing out the servers for the root kit USB key.

Logan's Steel Security people had arrived just in time to help him round up the Lestats. Apparently even humans can whup young vampire ass armed with Tasers and laughing gas.

And Ruthven? Well, while everyone else was scrambling to understand just what had happened, Logan collected Ruthven's carcass and carted it outside onto the portico. He kicked it into the sun and we watched it go up in flames. It took twenty minutes but the sun was watery for March. I kinda wished for marshmallows.

So Ruthven was destroyed, his minions and lieutenants rounded up and ready to be carted away, their judgment in the surer hands of the Iowa Alliance this time. We didn't know how the wannabes had infiltrated the Museum but the Alliance was investigating. Everything was nicely wrapped up—except for two things. One of them was on that bus.

At 5:05 the bus's door whooshed open and Zinnia bounded out looking smug. Practically bursting with triumph, she started waving people into line.

Logan stumbled out behind her. He raked slim fingers

through his bright blond hair. Seeing me, he tottered over. "Damn. I could use a drink right now."

I took his arm, led him toward his car. "You okay?"

"I've fought rogues, ravening monsters and even executives bent on rape and pillage. But that woman may be the death of me. Again."

"She is energetic."

"You have a gift for understatement." He pulled keys from somewhere in his painted-on jeans and clicked open the locks.

"I thought you were going to guillotine her. What happened?"

Logan leaned over the top of the car and sighed. "What do you think? I'm starting a household. The woman is relentless."

"You know, for a deadly strong vampire, I'm beginning to think you're a bit of a softie."

"I prefer to think I'm practical. I don't want to go through my afterlife deaf. Get in the car if you're just going to snark."

"A household. Well, congratulations. You met Elias's deadline with hours to spare." I slid into the passenger side. "Householding won't be that hard, now that you know you can do it. You're not the newbie you were then."

"I know. Even if Elias hadn't taught me what to do, I've picked up some wisdom along the way. Doesn't stop me from worrying."

"Part of the job. You know, I've been thinking about how I zapped Ruthven earlier and I remembered you describing your first encounter with him. You said before he misted to enter the house to kill Adelaide, he slashed you with a knife—and something about it feeling like a bolt of lightning."

"Yes, I—" He stared at me. "Static electricity?"

"There's no way of proving it, but it makes sense. If he built up a charge and released it into your body, it would have scrambled your ability to mist."

"Damn." Logan shook his head. "Just...damn. Not stress or overconfidence, but actual sabotage."

"You know, your humans aren't the same as that first household, either. We...I mean *they* won't huddle like scared rabbits. They'll fight back."

Logan cocked his head, a wistful expression settling on his face. "I rather like *we*. In fact, I like it so much—well, I meant to do this more formally. Again." He dug into his pocket. "Liese Schmetterling. I love you and want you in my life." He brought out something in his closed hand, but instead of offering it to me, leaned over the gearshift and kissed me.

Even after the non-stop sex of the night previous, my pulse jumped. "You want me to be—your donor?"

"I want you to run my company. Be CEO of Steel Security."

"You...you what?" I stared into his gorgeous face, wondering how I'd missed the pun, because he had to be joking. "You want me to run Steel Security? But you're CEO."

"I need to concentrate on the household, focus on getting it right. I'd have to step down sooner or later anyway. Logan Steel is getting a little long in the tooth, as it were."

He really meant it. It was a startling, amazing offer, but I felt let down. Silly me, I'd been hoping for something not nearly so lucrative but a little more personal. Even though I still didn't exactly trust him, I was beginning to think I couldn't live without him. And beginning to hope he felt the same. "How would you have done it? If I weren't around?"

"Turned it over to my 'son'. The records are getting harder to falsify, but it's still possible with the right kind of expertise. Which Steel Security has."

"In abundance. But why me?"

"Because you're the best manager I know."

I got the feeling he wasn't lying. Botcher put me out of a job. Logan was actually giving me one. "I don't know what to say."

"You could try 'yes'." He smiled ruefully at me. "Liese, think about it. As CEO of Steel Security, the only way you could lose your job is if you fire yourself."

"Unless Elias doesn't want me. I don't think he tolerates anyone he doesn't want."

"I talked with him and he was already thinking along those lines. He was impressed with your cool thinking during this Museum crisis. And your ability hacking his code."

"That was *his* code?"

"Actually churned out by a dozen genius assistants. But he designed it. Nobody knows vampires better. So, will you take the job?"

"Oh. Well, I guess."

"Not terribly enthusiastic. Maybe this will help. As my last act as CEO I'm moving the corporate headquarters to suburban Chicago. So you'll need a new place to live."

"Why? Even if you move to the north side, that's only a couple hours commute. I can—what's that?"

Logan had opened his hand. Resting on his palm was another jeweler's box. "I'm not Botcher, princess. This is real. Just like my feelings for you are real." He snapped open the box. A five-carat diamond dazzled me. "Marry me, Liese."

I blinked rapidly. "Oh, Logan. I'd love to but...you're a rich, powerful CEO, and now a master vampire too. I don't belong in your world."

"Liese, Liese." He shook his head, bright blond hair swishing lightly. "Princess, you *are* my world."

Pop! "You believe him? A *male*?" Bad Liese, with perfect, horrible timing. "A *male* abandoned you at the altar. This one's no different."

I hesitated. *No, Logan. I can't trust any man.*

"I'll wait if you're not ready." Logan kissed the tip of my nose. "Nothing's too much, Liese. I'm a forever sort of guy, and you're my key to eternity. Whatever I have to do, I'll earn your trust."

I shut my eyes, squeezed against my confusion. Botcher gave me meanness, pettiness, and vindictiveness. Logan was giving me kindness, understanding, and love. How could I say no?

Pop! "You don't deserve him." Ms. Sanctimonious Good Liese. "Not after you betrayed him."

That was how. She was right too. *No, Logan. I'm not good enough.* I looked longingly at the ring. "But Logan—how can you ever trust me?"

"Liese." He set aside the box and took my hands between his. "Remember, I trust what's in your heart. Now it's time for you trust what's in *my* heart. I love you."

"You'd be insane to trust him," Good Liese said.

Bad Liese chimed in. "I have to go with Ms. Goody-Goody on this—hey!"

Logan, with that almost preternatural understanding, kissed my left shoulder. *Poof* went Bad Liese. He kissed my right shoulder. *Poof* went Good Liese.

"Now. What does *your* heart say?"

Trust was a bridge. And Logan was meeting me more than halfway.

I sighed with relief. "Yes, Logan."

Chapter Twenty-One

I stood in the organ balcony of the church, twisting my five carats, watching the chancel door with held breath. My face almost matched my blue flowers. In about two minutes, Logan would emerge from that door. If he showed up.

Most brides dressed in a back room or the basement of the church. I insisted on coming up here because this time I wanted to know before I marched down the aisle whether I had a groom or not.

Feminine gasps came from behind me. I tore my eyes from the door to see a vision of lithe male beauty gliding toward me encased in a perfectly tailored tux, long hair gleaming gold under the hanging lights. While he wasn't supposed to see me before the wedding, I was hugely relieved to see him. How thoughtful to come up and reassure me. How typically Logan.

I waited for the zing of pleasure, was shocked to feel...nothing.

Then I realized the bright hair swayed to the male's waist, and the insouciance in the gold-flecked hazel eyes covered pain instead of confidence. I said, "You're Logan's twin, Luke?"

"The Best Man, at your service." Luke's eyes touched my bridesmaids one by one, leaving no doubt who he was really talking to (not me) or what service he was talking about (wink-wink, nudge-nudge). I remembered Mr. Elias and *ménage à trois* and began to understand. With a final blown kiss to the bridesmaids he turned to me. "My apologies for missing last night's rehearsal. I unfortunately ran into a bit of trouble."

Of the Lestat variety, no doubt. "It's okay. What are you doing up here?"

"Just came to set this up." Luke slid a dead-sexy ultra-slim brushed aluminum briefcase onto a table at the edge of the balcony. Opened it. I peered inside.

It held a satphone with some awesome Klipsch speakers. And what looked like a high def vid screen which was blank.

With no warning, the awesome speakers very faithfully reproduced the canyon-deep voice of the most frightening being on the planet, my new boss, Mr. Ancient One Elias.

"Congratulations, Ms. Schmetterling, on your upcoming nuptials. I regret not being there in person. Unfortunately I am at, well, let's just say an undisclosed location, prevented from leaving by omnibus contract. However, I felt this would be an acceptable alternative, even for the government."

Good Lord. Did he mean what I thought he meant? "I'm sorry you couldn't see the wedding, but it was nice of you to call."

"Actually, I'm able to see quite well. Satellite. You have an eyelash on your cheek."

I bent over for a quick look in the organist's mirror. The bench was empty so I didn't disturb anyone. A string quartet played downstairs—it pays to have musician friends. He was right. "How could you see that? Sat video is horrendously choppy. And sound is just awful, unless you have a dedicated bandwidth the size of...well, it'd have to be a military satellite to...oh, no."

A deep chuckle emerged from the speakers, sex laced with sin. Luke just smiled.

I looked at the brushed aluminum case with new respect. "*Ooh.* Can I play with this later?"

Luke gave me a brief eyelash-singeing kiss. "I'll be back to pick this up. Welcome to the family." He strode from the balcony, waves of gold licking the small of his back. Women's sighs followed him.

I ignored them. I'd had exactly two phone conversations with Elias, the first when he'd told me he knew about the picture and the second when he'd given me my salary and benefits and I'd fainted. I had so many questions for him, about my job, about this new world I found myself in. But most important: "Are you the one who rescued Logan's household the first time? Because if you are, I owe you."

"You rescued him the second time, Ms. Schmetterling. So we're even."

I blushed. "I only rescued him after I tried to get him fired."

"I think you've paid enough for that, hmm? *Let it go.*"

His compelling voice darkened to a black so absolute it blinded me. Then my vision cleared and the world was suddenly a brighter place. "Whoa. You could make a mint in psychiatry. I guess Logan was wrong when he said I was immune."

"Merely a matter of degree. Here they come."

"What's a matter of—oh." The small chancel door opened. Men, each one incredibly gorgeous, filed out. Luke sauntered out last, impossibly boyish, mischief gleaming from gold-flecked hazel eyes that were so like the male's I knew.

The door swung shut. No one emerged behind Luke.

My heart started pounding. Oh, God. It was happening again.

"Ms. Schmetterling. What is the converse of trust?"

Only Elias's deep, powerful tones could have broken through my pounding fear. "Um, mistrust?"

"Not the opposite. The converse. Trust backing up, as it were."

"Doubt?" If he was trying to distract me from the great gaping hole in the line of men, it was working, but only barely.

"No, Ms. Schmetterling. The reverse of trust is patience."

"You're saying I should be patient?" I glanced at the shut door, started twisting my five carats so hard I practically screwed my finger off. "I don't think I can."

"Not you. Logan. You healed him. His patience will eventually heal you."

And finally, *finally* the door opened again. A long lithe body roped with lean strength glided through. Gold-flecked hazel eyes were lit with laughter and intelligence. The blond hair that rippled to broad muscular shoulders shone brighter than the sun. Perfect lips curved in a smile so sensuous my guts exploded.

It was my wedding night, and Logan had actually shown up.

I clutched the aluminum case as if it were Elias's arm. "He's here."

"So I see." Amusement silvered the dark tones.

The music changed. At the balcony door, Zinnia clapped her hands. "Ring bearers, flower girls. Downstairs. Go."

"Ah, Ms. Jones. Such boundless energy."

I didn't take my eyes from Logan. "Makes you want to just shoot her, huh? You can see out the back of this thing too?"

"The camera is three-sixty." Which omitted the location of said camera, but Webster probably invented the word cryptic to describe Elias.

With long-lived vampires, that might be more literal than I knew.

Ten boys and girls dutifully started down, among them Bud, Lilly, Angela, Billy Wilder, Tad and Jane Austen Smith. The children of Logan's—of *our* household. Though I didn't think so, Bud and Lilly might be Logan's in a more personal way. More likely playboy Luke's. I wondered if I'd ever find out.

"She'll make you a good admin, though," Elias said, then added, "Logan isn't their father."

I nearly swallowed my teeth. "Do you read minds?" Over the balcony railing I watched the children march down the center aisle, Lilly with her bright blonde hair, Bud sauntering with Luke and Logan's easy grace. "They look so amazingly like them."

"Yes. Interesting, isn't it? You're probably wondering why I picked you to run Steel Security."

Talk about a change in topics. I'd have called him on it but Zinnia clapped her hands again. "Bridesmaid four. Go."

"A little. There must be scores of better candidates. Why let Logan retire in the first place?"

"He needs to concentrate on his household. And I'm sure he told you I found your inventiveness intriguing."

"Bridesmaid three, your turn."

I flushed. "Hacking open a file isn't so inventive."

"No, Ms. Schmetterling. I meant the modifications you made to my program. A cell phone pre-alarm. Most useful."

I reddened. "Did Logan tell you...? No, never mind. I don't want to know."

"Bridesmaid two. Go."

He chuckled, a deep caress so sensual my tongue fell out and I had to stuff it back in with my fingers. "I'd like to add those modifications to our base product. With proper recompense to you, of course."

"Matron of honor. Go."

I glanced at my matron of honor, standing across from me at the railing of the balcony. My mother gazed down at the front pew, a small smile on her face. My rock, my anchor. My love for her swelled in my heart.

"Mrs. Gillette, stop drooling over your hubby and go!"

I winced. My rock, my anchor, married to a vampire who looked half her age. Not just a vampire, but a bad-boy.

Although Race, spiffy in his dove gray tux, was actually more of a reformed bad boy. He'd officially joined the Iowa Alliance in a ceremony wedged in last night between the wedding rehearsal and dinner.

And my husband-to-be had shown up for the wedding. Jack Frost was partying in Hades. "Ruthven's really dead, right?" I touched the brushed aluminum case, let the cool texture sooth me. Mr. Lethal Ancient was as unreal as the rest, but he was smart. And I had a feeling he knew way more than he passed on. "No reboot possible?"

"He's destroyed." The deep voice was certain, and I relaxed. Until he added, "But there's still Camille and Giuseppe, and Nosferatu himself."

"And the Coterie will eventually replace Ruthven, I suppose. Maybe with someone worse. Nastier."

"Perhaps with someone better. We can hope. It doesn't happen often, but it does happen. We'll just have to deal with it then."

"We? You mean Logan."

"And Strongwell, Emerson, and their allies. And their human partners."

Zinnia clapped. "Ms. Schmetterling. Your turn."

I ignored her, intent on Elias. Who knew when I'd talk to him again, with him at his "undisclosed location"? "Elena and Nixie and me? What kind of help are we? We're puny in comparison to v-guys. Nixie more than most."

"There's strength of mind as well, Ms. Schmetterling. Of will, of heart. It's time."

The music had changed again. Not "Here Comes the Bride"—Nixie would have killed me. Apparently that was from an opera where the new couple is torn apart almost as soon as they join. Not *Canon in D*, either. Julian Emerson, playing cello in the string quartet, would have killed me then. (There were disadvantages to having musician friends too.) No, Julian and Nixie had picked out the Clarke Trumpet Voluntary—but they were nice enough to provide the trumpet player free.

"Time? I suppose." I rose.

"Ms. Schmetterling. Thank you."

"For keeping Steel Security ultra-profitable?"

"For healing Logan. Now go make it permanent."

I don't remember how I got down the stairs, and I barely remember walking down the aisle. I didn't realize I was at the end until Logan took my hands, didn't know how cold they were until he engulfed them between his large warm palms.

"Liese," he murmured, taking a moment before we faced the pastor. "It's okay. I'll earn your trust, no matter how long it takes. I love you, princess."

Logan was so smart. He knew I was still scared, that the trust Botcher had so completely crushed would take time to heal. "The diamond being real helped. And your actually showing up today helped even more. You are earning my trust, Logan—by what you do. But the words 'I love you'?" I shook my head. "Easy to say, easier to break. They don't mean anything."

"No, princess. The words *are* important. Not yet, but some day. Some day they'll have meaning for you. A meaning built on a lifetime together." He took me up the stairs.

We stood before the minister and I realized it was really happening. Commitment, hell. I was tying myself to a drop-dead sexy creature of the night, opening myself to a world of hurt. I stood at the edge of the bridge of trust, and it was a swaying crumbling footbridge over a hundred-foot drop to a chasm of raging death.

Then Logan took both my hands and faced me. And when he spoke the words "I do," I saw the truth of them in his golden eyes.

And I stepped out on that rickety bridge to meet him.

About the Author

Mary Hughes is a computer consultant, professional musician and writer. At various points in her life she has taught Taekwondo, worked in the insurance industry, and studied religion. She is intensely interested in the origins of the universe. She has a wonderful husband (though happily-ever-after takes a lot of hard work) and two great kids. But she thinks that with all the advances in modern medicine, childbirth should be a lot less messy.

Please visit Mary at www.maryhughesbooks.com/.

Author's Note

The lean-burning cogenerator mentioned in this book came online at the Museum of Science and Industry in 2003. The description of its installation, including room, contents and electrical connections, are my own invention.

HOT STUFF

Discover Samhain!

THE HOTTEST NEW PUBLISHER ON THE PLANET

Romance, fantasy, mystery, thriller, mainstream and more—Samhain has more selection, hotter authors, and everything's available in ebook.

Pick your favorite, sit back, and enjoy the ride! Hot stuff indeed.

SAMHAIN
PUBLISHING

WWW.SAMHAINPUBLISHING.COM

LaVergne, TN USA
14 January 2011
212444LV00013B/7/P